1636
MISSION TO
THE MUGHALS

1636
MISSION TO THE MUGHALS

ERIC FLINT
GRIFFIN BARBER

1636: Mission to the Mughals

This is a work of fiction. All the characters and events portrayed in this book are fictional, and any resemblance to real people or incidents is purely coincidental.

A Baen Books Original

Baen Publishing Enterprises
P.O. Box 1403
Riverdale, NY 10471
www.baen.com

ISBN: 978-1-4767-8214-0

Cover art by Tom Kidd
Maps by Michael Knopp

First printing, April 2017

Distributed by Simon & Schuster
1230 Avenue of the Americas
New York, NY 10020

Library of Congress Cataloging-in-Publication Data

Names: Flint, Eric, author. | Barber, Griffin, author.
Title: 1636: mission to the Mughals / Eric Flint and Griffin Barber.
Other titles: Mission to the Mughals
Description: Riverdale, NY : Baen, [2017] | Series: Ring of fire
Identifiers: LCCN 2016054504
Subjects: | GSAFD: Alternative histories (Fiction)
Classification: LCC PS3556.L548 A618668 2017 | DDC 813/.54—dc23 LC record available at https://lccn.loc.gov/2016054504

10 9 8 7 6 5 4 3 2 1

Pages by Joy Freeman (www.pagesbyjoy.com)
Printed in the United States of America

I wish to dedicate this book
to Donna, Karen, and Isabelle.
I need not look far for fine examples
to model Princess Jahanara on.

Contents

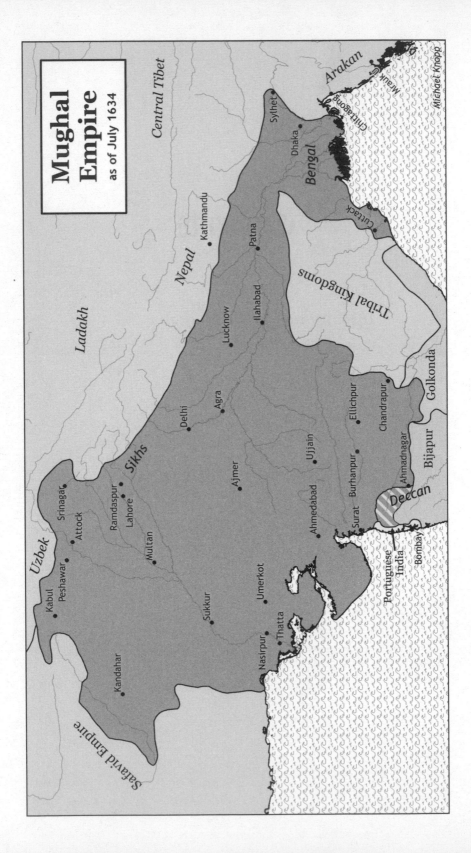

Mughal Empire as of July 1634

Michael Knopp

Central Tibet

Arakan

Mrauk

Sylhet

Chittagong

Dhaka

Bengal

Cuttack

Kathmandu

Patna

Nepal

Tribal Kingdoms

Ilahabad

Lucknow

Golkonda

Ladakh

Ellichpur

Chandrapur

Delhi

Agra

Ujjain

Ajmer

Ahmednagar

Bijapur

Sikhs

Srinagar

Burhanpur

Deccan

Attock

Ramdaspur

Surat

Uzbek

Lahore

Ahmedabad

Multan

Portuguese India

Kabul

Peshawar

Bombay

Umerkot

Sukkur

Kandahar

Thatta

Nasirpur

Safavid Empire

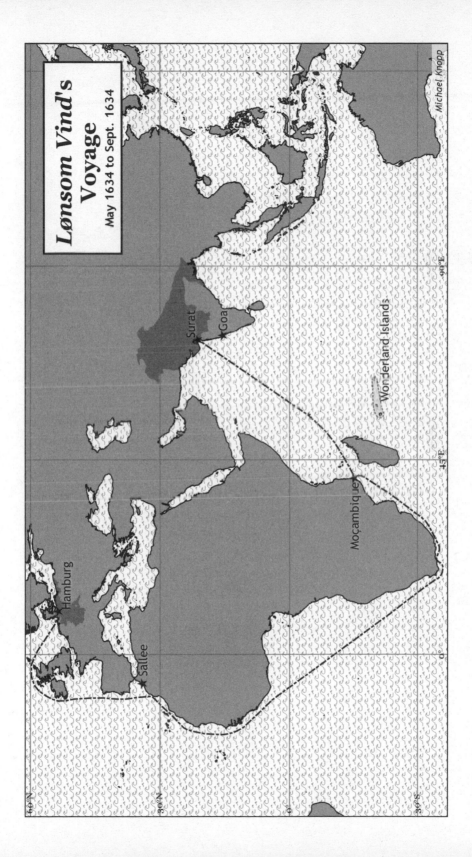

Lønsom Vind's
Voyage
May 1634 to Sept. 1634

Michael Knopp

Hamburg

Sallee

Surat

Goa

Moçambique

Wonderland Islands

90°E

45°E

0°

66°N

30°N

0°

30°S

1636
MISSION TO
THE MUGHALS

Prologue

February 1634

Lyon, France

Salim let the door to Baram Khan's sickroom close before addressing the man who walked out. "Any change?"

The physician started and wheeled to face him. "I didn't see
you there."

Salim stepped into the light of the candle the man held,
quirking an eyebrow.

The local man shook his head. "No, no change. I must be
going. A—another patient, you understand."

Salim did not blame him for being frightened. Knowing the
fate of physicians who failed to save the lives of powerful men
in his own nation, Salim could forgive the man thinking Salim
might attack him.

Waving him away, Salim turned to look at the door.

Beyond it, surrounded by a very few of his remaining loyal
servants, the emperor's envoy was dying a slow, painful death. A
week, perhaps a bit longer, and the man would breathe his last
and go to his final reward, whatever it might be.

Taking his prayer beads in hand, Salim said a prayer in the darkness to speed Baram Khan's passage to Paradise. Just because one
thought little of another man's deeds did not make them unworthy
of Paradise; it only showed the unworthy state of one's own soul.

Hearing a horse in the courtyard below, he stepped to the

window at the end of the hall in time to see the physician ride out of the torch-lit courtyard.

Good riddance. The man had proved almost worthless, failing, even, to see what was plain to Salim and anyone else with even the slightest experience of court life: Baram Khan had been poisoned.

It wasn't even entirely the pompous courtier's fault he was dying, since Baram Khan's tasters had all died in various mishaps before the envoy even entered the Germanies. Then, understandably angry at being robbed by Grantville's mercenaries—which the Mughal noble could only see as confirmation of the histories Salim was translating for him—Baram Khan departed the wonders of Grantville before new tasters could be found.

No one knew who had killed Baram Khan but, like everyone else in the man's entourage, Salim had an idea who it might be.

Salim shook his head. Regardless of the who and the how of the current situation, decisions had to be made.

Rehan Usmani, Baram's first servant, would want to return immediately to Agra and report events to Nur Jahan, Baram Khan's patroness.

Fear seized Salim's heart at the thought. Little could be worse for the empire and Mian Mir's hopes than *that* woman possessing proofs that Aurangzeb would, in his hunt for the throne, imprison his own father and murder his brothers. She would certainly seize the opportunity that any conflict in the family might offer to again attempt to place her own choice on the throne.

Baram Khan's exile on what the court had believed a fool's errand had led to this much, at least: Salim had the books from the future; he had the pictures.

He could return to Mian Mir and ask the living saint what to do, couldn't he?

Finding his answer in the question, Salim turned from the window and started for his chamber.

Grantville's mercenary company might have stripped Baram Khan of everything of value he'd carried on his person, but his servants had passed largely unmolested. Salim still had several small pouches of fine gemstones, and knew where to sell a few.

At least five hours remained before morning prayers. He would pack quickly, walk a couple of the pathetic excuses for horseflesh from the manor and, once out of hearing, be on his way.

A long, dangerous journey lay ahead.

Part One

Spring and Summer, 1634

Then, wakened by the crash and cries,
The fierce shefiends unclosed their eyes

Chapter 1

Magdeburg, capital of the United States of Europe
April 1634

The brow of the prime minister of the United States of Europe was furrowed with doubt piled atop doubtfulness—doubt with respect to the proposal being made, and doubtfulness concerning the motives of the proposer.

"Let me see if I've got this straight, Francisco," said Mike Stearns. "We're about to send a diplomatic and trade mission to China—that is to say, roughly halfway around the world."

"Oh, it's not *that* far, Michael." Francisco Nasi waggled his hand back and forth, indicating a small degree of uncertainty. "A bit over four thousand miles, I believe. Nautical miles, that is."

Mike's brow furrowed deeper, as suspicion piled onto doubt and doubtfulness. "That would be the great circle distance, you're talking about. But pray tell, which one of our Boeing 747s were you planning to use to make the flight? Oh, wait, I forgot—we don't have any Boeing 747s, do we? Or DC-3s, now that I think about it. And exactly which one of Beijing's modern—that would be modern as in twentieth century—international airports were you planning to land our nonexistent 747 on? Oh, wait, I forgot—this being the year 1634, Beijing doesn't have an airport big enough to land a Cessna on, does it?"

"I grant you—"

"What's the nautical distance from here to China, Francisco? Not 'nautical' as in country boy miles on steroids but 'nautical' as in actual distance to be traveled by sea."

"Well..."

"Look it up, when you get a chance. I believe you'll find the distance is pretty close to twelve thousand miles—that is to say, about halfway around the world. Like I said."

"Actually, I did look it up. It is 12,776 miles by sea from Hamburg to Shanghai. That would be nautical miles, of course." He cleared his throat. "I confess that presupposes using the Suez Canal which, ah, is also not in existence at the moment."

Mike grunted. "So in country boy miles it's actually way more than halfway around the world. Francisco, I agreed to that China mission—reluctantly—mostly because you had a team ready and willing to go. If you're planning to tell me that you found another half dozen or so—I'm trying to avoid terms like screwballs here— people in Grantville who've expressed a burning desire to travel to India given the crude realities of so-called Early Modern Era transport, I have to tell you that I'm going to be a mite skeptical."

"Actually, I have found a couple of people who'd like to make the trip. Well—one person, but her husband's amenable. And I'm sure I can find others."

"Who?"

"Priscilla Totman, and her husband Rodney."

Mike's suspicious gaze now swiveled to the third person in his office. "Which explains why you're here, James. I'd been wondering. You're not usually given to Francisco's type of web-weaving."

"Oh, leave off, Mike," said James Nichols. "I had nothing at all to do with the Totmans' decision."

"I find that a little hard to believe. Seeing as how—"

"What? I work in medicine—and they work in medicine? So do lots of people. And I've hardly seen them since they moved to Jena last year."

Nichols pointed a finger at Nasi. "Whatever scheming's going on is being done by him—but I have to tell you I approve of it, if it'll get us a reliable supply of opium."

Mike wiped his face. "What has the world come to," he muttered, "when a supposedly upstanding citizen—a doctor, no less—openly declares his support for drug smuggling?"

"Smuggling, my ass. Opium's not illegal in this day and age. The problem isn't legality, it's accessibility."

Mike saw his chance and pounced. "Exactly! You said it yourself. It's not illegal—in fact, you can buy it on the open market in

Amsterdam. Venice, too, I believe. So why do we need to go all the way to India to get stuff that's coming our way in any event?"

"Yes, you can. And I'd be very relaxed about the situation if we lived in—oh, let's say the Year of Our Lord 2000—back in the days—excuse me, ahead in the days—when the U.S. Navy ruled the waves and we had NATO and well-established international laws governing maritime trade. But we don't, do we? No, we live in the year 1634—just eleven years after the Amboyna massacre in the East Indies, where the Dutch East India Company tortured and murdered more than a dozen men working for the British East India Company."

He glanced at the woman sitting next to him. "Melissa told me about it. Mike, in the world we live in today, so-called 'foreign trade' looks a hell of a lot like Al Capone's Chicago. I can think of two or three ways the opium trade could get disrupted and I'm sure you can think of at least that many."

He nodded toward Nasi. "I don't even want to think about how many he could come up with."

"Let me see...," Nasi began counting off his fingers. "One, the Dutch trade is severed because Spain attacks Don Fernando. Two, the Dutch trade is severed because France attacks Don Fernando."

"Why would France—?" Mike started to protest.

"Same reason France would attack the Dutch in 1672. Imperialist rivalries." He went back to finger-counting. "Three, the Dutch trade is severed because England attacks Don Fernando."

"Why would—?"

Nasi clucked his tongue reproachfully. "Don't you read any of your own history books, Michael? England would attack the Dutch for the same reasons they attacked them in the universe you came from, in 1652, 1665 and 1672—that last one in alliance with the French. Imperialist rivalries. Which is usually just a fancy way of saying 'trade rivalries,' in the here and now."

The finger-counting resumed. "Now, as to Venice. Four, the Genoese—"

"All right, all right." Mike waved his hand, irritably. "I get the point. And I suppose you're going to claim the same applies to the saltpeter trade."

Nasi shook his head. "Oh, no. I could come up with twice as many reasons the saltpeter trade might get severed."

He leaned forward in his seat. "Michael, face facts. We are

in the middle of perhaps the greatest war to afflict Europe since the barbarian invasions that destroyed Rome. Except it's not really one war but a whole constellation of wars that interlock with each other. Wars over dynastic ambition, religion—and, yes, trade. Wars nowadays are fought with gunpowder, whose critical ingredient—certainly the hardest to come by—is saltpeter. The biggest source of saltpeter is India."

He held up a restraining hand. "Please! Don't bother to tell me that's why India's own rulers guard saltpeter so jealously. I was brought up in the Ottoman court, you may recall. Isn't there some witty West Virginia saw to that effect...?"

Mike made a face. "Don't teach your grandmother how to suck eggs."

"Indeed. That makes no sense, by the way. No one sucks eggs, so why would anyone worry about the right way to do it? But the meaning is clear enough."

Nasi sat back in his chair, planting his hands on his thighs. "You are the one who made me your chief of intelligence. Please consider the possibility that you may have made a good selection."

Mike sighed, and ran fingers through his hair. Then he looked at Nichols.

"Does opium really make that much difference, James?"

"Yes, it does. Without a reliable source of good anesthetics, surgery in this universe is effectively stillborn. So is dentistry, for that matter. And opium is our best bet. It's the source of morphine and there are other ways it can be used as an anesthetic." The doctor shrugged. "There are some alternatives. Diethyl ether's been available for almost a century in Europe. They call it 'sweet oil of vitriol.' Nitrous oxide wasn't developed up-time until late in the eighteenth century, but we ought to be able to manage it. Same with chloroform. But none of them are as good as opioids and they all have various negative side effects."

Mike rose from his desk and went over to the window in his office. He liked to look out of the window when he was trying to come to a decision.

Without turning his head, he now addressed the last person in the room. "Okay, Melissa, I figure it's your turn. You didn't come here just to provide James with moral support."

"No, I didn't. For what it's worth, I don't have an opinion one way or the other on how important it is to open our own trade relations with India. My concern is with something a lot broader—and, I'll say it right out before you do, something that's admittedly a lot more nebulous."

"Which would be what?"

There was a pause that lasted long enough for Mike to swivel his head around and look at Melissa directly. "I'll be damned," he said. "This may be the first time I've ever seen you unsure about something."

"Very funny," she said. "And I'm *not* unsure about it. I'm just unsure about how to explain it—and I'm really unsure about whether there's anything we can do about it."

Mike returned to his desk and sat back down again. "Now you've got my interest. So what is it?"

"Well... You know how you like to say the two great historical evils that emerged in this era were New World chattel slavery and the second serfdom in eastern Europe?"

"Yeah." His lips quirked a little. "I got that from you in the first place. Are you now going to tell me I got it wrong?"

Melissa looked moderately embarrassed—which was also not a common trait of the woman. As a rule, Melissa Mailey was to embarrassment what a duck is to water. Impervious.

"No. Not wrong. Just... let's say, incomplete."

"How so?"

"It's maybe too Eurocentric. Or I guess I should say, white-people-centric."

"The victims of New World slavery were Africans—Indians, too, at the beginning—not whites."

"Yes, I know." She waved her hand. "But Europeans and their descendants were the agents of it, and we had to deal with the mess we created. I'm talking about something that never affected people in Europe or America—or most of Africa—very much until just a short while ago. By 'ago,' I mean up-time 'ago.'"

"Keep talking."

But it was Francisco Nasi who spoke. "I think she's referring to the evolution of Islam, Michael. And if so, I probably agree with her."

Mike frowned. "What does India—? Oh. Yeah, I tend to forget. We're talking about Mughal India, in the here and now—and they're Muslims."

"Yes," said Melissa. She gave Nasi a quick, thankful glance. "And he's right—that is what I'm concerned about. We live in an era where there are three great Islamic powers—the Ottomans, the Safavid dynasty in Persia, and the Mughal dynasty in India. Two of them, the Sunni realms of the Ottomans and the Mughals, are both rather tolerant when it comes to religion."

Nasi nodded. "I can attest to that with respect to the Ottomans. It's true that they favor Muslims in most respects, but their rule does not weigh heavily on Jews or Christians."

"That much, I know." Mike folded his hands on his desk. "As my wife likes to say when she feels especially peeved toward bigots, after the Spanish drove out the Sephardic Jews, the Ottoman sultan welcomed them to his own land. He's reported to have said—"

Nasi finished the sentence for him: "'Ye call Ferdinand a wise king, he who makes his land poor and ours rich!' He did have a point."

"In a lot of ways, the Mughals are even more tolerant," Melissa continued. "I think that's probably because while there are a lot of Muslims in India, the majority of the population is non-Muslim. Mostly Hindus, but there are also Sikhs and other religions. The great Mughal emperor Akbar—the current emperor, Shah Jahan, is his grandson—established a policy of religious toleration and it's been kept ever since. But that's about to change."

"Change how?" Mike asked.

"Say better: change *who*," said Melissa. "In our history, the change came after Shah Jahan's youngest son Aurangzeb took the throne following his victory in a civil war with his three brothers. Aurangzeb was a Muslim diehard, and he's the one who broke the Mughal tradition of religious toleration. I think the world's history would have gone a lot better if one of the other brothers had won that civil war. I don't know if us sending a delegation to India would change that outcome, but... it might. I figure it's worth a try, at any rate."

"And this civil war happened when?"

Melissa chuckled. "Depends on which universe's calendar you want to use. By the one we came from, it all happened long ago. I forget the exact date but it was somewhere around 1660. By this universe's calendar, though—"

"For Pete's sake, Melissa!" Mike exclaimed. "You're talking about something that's not going to happen for another third of a century!"

She smiled at him coolly. "All the more reason to get an early jump on the problem, wouldn't you say? Mr. Prime Minister."

Mike glowered at her. "It's just 'Prime Minister,' thank you. 'Mr. Prime Minister' is silly."

He now transferred the glower around the room, bestowing it in turn upon each and every occupant. Then, sighing, he raised his hands in a gesture of surrender.

"Fine, Francisco. Do it. But if this scheme goes haywire, I'm blaming you. Publicly, too—don't think I won't."

Nasi nodded solemnly, as if he didn't know just as well as everyone in the room that the threat was hollow. Mike Stearns had his faults, but passing the buck was not one of them.

"I think it hardly matters, Prime Minister," he said. "By the time we find out if my schemes have come to fruition—especially Melissa's part of them!—we may all be long dead, anyway."

Chapter 2

Magdeburg, capital of the United States of Europe

Bertram's coat was still damp when the secretary ushered him into Don Francisco's office.

The light Magdeburg rain pattering at the window panes failed to darken the heavy wooden desk Nasi was bent over, a small electric lamp serving to keep the shadows at bay.

"Don Francisco," Bertram said, bowing nervously. He had not seen Nasi since being sent to Geneva, and while they were distantly related, Bertram had never had occasion to speak more than ten words to the man. They were not far apart in age, Bertram being twenty-eight and Francisco Nasi somewhere close to that. But there was a much greater social distance, as Sephardic Jews measured such things. Bertram came from a modest family; Nasi from one of the branches of the sprawling, influential and wealthy Abrabanel clan—or Abravanel, as some people spelled it.

Nasi looked up from his work, gracing Bertram with a thin smile that hardly settled nerves. "Bertram Weiman. Thank you for coming so quickly, and on such short notice."

Bertram held up his hands. "I had no other business."

"No, I suppose you had not. Sorry to keep you in the dark, but while that business in Geneva worked to our benefit, it was not without ramifications."

Bertram tried to hide a wince.

Nasi did not miss it, waving his visitor to a chair.

Bertram perched on the edge of the seat, waiting for the other shoe to drop.

Again Nasi did not miss his unease: "This is not a dressing-down, Bertram. By all accounts you did what had to be done to accomplish the job I set you. You even managed to improve our relations with Geneva and the Confederation as a whole. No, *I* have been slow to find you additional work because I wanted you out of reach of the Church, if possible."

Bertram smiled. *Please let it be Anatolia, let me practice my skills against the Ottomans...*

What about Monique? The thought made his smile die a quick death.

"I see you wonder where that might be."

Bertram nodded. "Of course."

"Ever consider India?"

"Wh-where?" Bertram stammered.

"Mughal India, to be precise."

"Ummm, no."

Another of those thin smiles. "No, you never considered it or, no, you are not interested?"

Bertram shook his head. "As in, 'No, I hadn't considered it.'"

"It is beyond the Church's grasp, at least the part we are sending you to."

"Not Goa?"

"No, Portuguese India has too many churchmen. Besides, Goa does not produce what we are after."

"And what, pray tell, is that?"

"The latest assessment has it that we will soon need significant amounts of opium for the war effort. That, and saltpeter, of course."

"But I am no merchant."

"No, but you can fake it."

"Of course, but there has to be someone trained to be a merchant—"

"There is not. At least not readily available, not needed elsewhere, and in possession of your language skills. And you will not be solely responsible for securing the trade. There is to be a trade mission made up of several up-timers, you, and your two associates, the...ah, Vieuxponts—"

"Them, too?" Bertram blurted.

Nasi patted a stack of papers on his desk. "I read your report, even did some digging on my own. I was most impressed with their résumés..." He looked at Bertram. "Assuming they can be relied upon not to abscond with property that is not theirs?"

"They can, when suitably motivated," Bertram said, wondering when he'd agreed to the assignment.

"And what will motivate them...suitably?"

An uncomfortable bark of laughter escaped Bertram's lips. "Money. Lots of it. Some security, but mostly money."

"As I thought. Everyone on this mission will be well compensated. Besides, they need protection from the Church as much, if not more, than you. And if we get full value for that protection, why, that's just good government."

"Compensated, how?"

"Any trade concessions secured will also pay a dividend to the mission...or their heirs. Make no mistake, we are aware how dangerous this will be. That's another reason you are going."

"I'm no soldier."

"No, but the hope is that our family connections will be of service along the route, if not in Mughal territory, then in Africa."

"Our Cristião-Novo cousins?"

Nasi nodded. "Exactly so. Are you up to date on who is where?"

"Not at all."

"Understandable. I have a list of our kinsmen who should at least give you the time of day. You'll have to memorize the names—writing it down risks handing the Inquisition a death list—but some of them may be of critical help."

"But aren't the Portuguese routes all owned and financed by the Spanish Crown?"

"They are, though that's changed a bit under Hapsburg rule, but you mistake me: I wasn't counting on our kinsmen providing ships or other material aid, but rather providing the mission with up-to-date information on the political landscape."

"Seems a risk for them to even speak to me."

"I will provide funds for you to use in helping overcome any such minor concerns they may have."

"How many ships are you sending?"

"One."

Bertram looked away. He thought one ship was not enough. They would have far too few resources to guarantee they could even make it to India, let alone come back safely. The Dutch went out in fleets, and rarely returned with all the hulls they shipped with.

"I know it seems too few," said Nasi, "but we will make certain the mission has every technological advantage we can provide."

Bertram mulled that over a moment before deciding to change the subject: "And what are we going to offer them?"

"We have some ideas regarding that..."

Chapter 3

Hamburg, United States of Europe
May 1634

The door slammed behind Papa, ending another pointless argument.

At least the rooms they were renting were nicer than their usual, giving him a room of his own for his childish sulk. Monique sighed. Gervais had been in a funk since they'd been forced to leave Geneva, bickering with both Bertram and her at nearly every turn of the road from there to Hamburg.

Bertram shook his head. "I'm sorry, I shouldn't have said that."

She smiled. "Please, Bertram, you needn't apologize for Papa's childish behavior."

"Still."

"If there is fault to be found, it's with Papa. He just isn't happy unless he's working on—or in the hunt for—a wealthy mark."

"I know, and I've been keeping him from pursuing his . . . natural inclinations since Geneva."

"Your payment for our travels and promise of an offer of employment are . . . unprecedented in Papa's experience. Makes him nervous, waiting for things to turn sour when he's not running a con on someone."

"But why?"

"There is a reason confidence is the name of the games Papa and I play. One must have it, or the mark will start to pick at the threads weaved to manipulate them. The mark must also have confidence in what the player presents as truth, or they don't do as the player desires.

"Papa owes you, so he can't run a game on you. His confidence suffers as a result."

"But I don't see him as in my debt."

She smiled to take the sting from her next words: "Doesn't really matter what you think about it. We might be confidence players, but we've our own set of scruples."

"What do you suggest I do?"

"What is this employment you mentioned, this work that might be—how did you put it? Oh, yes: 'suitable to our talents and skills'?"

Bertram smiled. She liked it a lot. It made his normally unremarkable face light up, his brown eyes shine.

"My relation will tell all, tomorrow."

"Teasing a woman that way is most unkind."

"I'm sorry," he said for the second time, "but I was given strict instructions."

"You don't trust me?" she asked, pouting in the manner she knew gave rise to urges he was uncomfortable with. She had, in the months since he'd rescued her from the Bishop of Geneva's dungeon in Annecy—where she'd been kept by the Bishop as surety against her father's compliance in the bishop's plot to undermine the Calvinist faith—come to realize Bertram was far more knight than knave. And this despite the gift for guile he'd shown in telling the bishop outlandish lies, even to the point of claiming service to Cardinal Richelieu. That internal knight made it difficult for him to look on her as a woman who might entertain his affections, not out of a sense of obligation to her rescuer, but out of desire for the man himself.

His serious tone surprised her. "I do, just as I trust that I will not want to feel my relation's ire, should he discover I've been speaking without leave."

"How much?" Monique heard her father ask again.

It all sounded terribly exciting to Monique. Hoping to keep her father from ruining it, she spoke up. "Papa, you heard Don Francisco very well!"

Her father ignored her, asked Nasi, "But why us?"

Don Francisco set aside his glass of wine and leaned forward. "Because you like money and we're offering a great deal of it?"

Monique had to agree with the USE spymaster on that point:

Aside from the actual payment, the offer included a tiny percentage of profits from whatever trade deal was agreed to, an incentive that could prove profoundly profitable. Yet Gervais was acting as if it were nothing special. She couldn't let him get away with it: "Even without the promised percentage of trade, it's more than we made on our best five jobs, and in just three years. It took us the better part of two years setting up for the Turin caper."

"No," Gervais hiked a thumb at Bertram, "why *us*?"

"You're smart, have useful skills, are adept with languages, and most importantly: you're eminently *available*."

"When I agreed to work with Bertram I thought we'd be in France, maybe the Papal States—not halfway round the world in heathen India."

"Muslim India, really," Nasi said. "Mughals are Muslims, somewhat like those of my former home, though they're not terribly oppressive of other religions just now..."

Gervais sniffed. "I know the Mughal *rulers* are Muslim, thank you very much. But I am also told there are lots of Hindus in positions of power and prestige."

"And rich, Papa, don't forget: fabulously rich," Monique added. Appealing to Papa's greed usually worked.

Gervais turned on her, "Oh, no, don't you try and play to my greed, that's what got us here in the first place!"

"If I may, Gervais: Bertram's bit of fast-talking was effective in freeing your lovely daughter," Nasi said. Monique's smile at the compliment died as Nasi went on, "But it also destroyed his cover. Every priest that travels through the bishopric gets an earful, and every one of them has sent letters to *their* friends to be on the lookout for you."

"So? You do know I'm a thief, right? I've always had nobles and churchmen after me."

"But you aren't *just* a thief, are you?"

"What's that supposed to mean?"

Nasi's thin smile sent a thrill of alarm down Monique's spine. "Only that I know a little about the where, the who, and the what of your studies. Not to mention how they ended and why you took to a life of crime."

Gervais sat back, face gone whiter than just about any time Monique could remember, save when he'd seen her in the tiny cell in Lyon.

Nasi wasn't done: "Frankly, your skills at alchemy will provide a useful and legitimate reason for you to gain access to the court."

"All right, I'll be useful," Gervais looked at Monique, "and I know how much I owe your man Bertram here, but there's no reason my daughter should be exposed to su—"

"Papa!" Monique snapped.

Nasi continued on the heels of her outburst. "She's an adult, Bertram speaks highly of her abilities, and there's a good chance that you'll need her to gain you access to people that men would be killed for even trying to lay eyes on. The harem-bound ladies of the court are powers unto themselves. If Monique wants to go, she'll be welcome, and just as well-compensated as you."

Papa opened his mouth to speak but Nasi held up a hand to silence him. "In the final analysis, while I think the mission might need your collective resourcefulness in an emergency, it's still a *trade* mission, not one of your criminal enterprises or," he looked significantly at Bertram, "some effort at espionage against an enemy power."

Gervais shook his head, a legitimately sad look on his face. "Do you have any idea how many of the Dutch return from trade in the East? Because I do! When in Amsterdam I watched the widows cry for lost husbands every single time a ship made port. On those occasions they actually *made* port!"

Nasi shrugged. "While your concerns are certainly valid, the Dutch did not have the advantages of medical care the up-timers brought us."

"I don't want my daughter dying on some foreign shore, some exotic illness eating her alive."

"Not when the outbreak in Milan could have killed us both with a perfectly home-grown plague," Monique drawled.

Gervais was struggling to find an answer to that when the door opened and a tall couple walked in. If their height wasn't sign enough, Monique identified them as some of Bertram's up-timers as soon as they smiled. No down-timer's smile ever displayed so many even, straight, and above all, *white* teeth.

Nasi climbed to his feet and bowed in courtly fashion over the woman's hand. "Frau Totman." The woman was extremely tall and expensively-dressed, if skinnier than Monique knew most down-time men preferred. The man with her was enormous.

Monique wondered if he was another athlete like Tom Simpson who played that bizarre American game called "football."

"Don Francisco," the man said.

"Herr Totman," Nasi returned with a smile, continuing around the circle of seats to make introductions. Both seemed at least as young as she was, though Bertram had said it was hard to tell with most up-timers.

Once everyone had taken seats and been introduced, Rodney Totman spoke. His English had an accent Monique had never encountered before: "Don Francisco, was that French I heard as we came in? Sounded heated."

Nasi nodded, "Gervais has serious reservations about Monique participating in our trade mission."

Priscilla Totman looked at Gervais and asked in heavily accented French: "Maladies?"

Gervais nodded emphatically.

Priscilla continued in that strangely accented English, "Forgive me, but I have exhausted my French."

"Pray continue," Gervais returned in that language.

"We have medicines to defeat some of the more common sickness, if we're careful about food and water we'll avoid most of the ick, and as we're not headed to Bombay or the wetter regions of India, there's less risk of mosquito-born infections like malaria."

Monique watched Gervais grasping for some argument. "Less is not—"

"Aren't you always telling me that risk is what makes life worth living?" she snapped.

Gervais threw his hands wide. "Oh, but it does!" He shot a dark glance at his daughter. "It's right up there with the joy of haggling for a good price for one's skills. A joy you killed, thank you very much."

Realizing, at last, that her father's antics had—mostly—been a tactic, she tossed her curls. "Papa!"

Don Francisco Nasi snorted. The Totmans chuckled.

Given time and a few choice words, Gervais could charm the hardest heart. It was a gift, and a curse. She saw that he'd already worked his magic on the Totmans, and likely Nasi as well, though the man was a much harder read.

Realizing the room had gone quiet, she turned to the up-timers. "And how were you two brought into this?"

Priscilla took her husband's hand in hers. "I have always wanted to travel to India. Too many movies, I suppose. I've always loved the idea of seeing it. I had thought, well, there was no chance it would happen since the Ring of Fire, but then we got the offer."

Her husband nodded. "As to why we got picked: we're both trained medics, with some advanced medical and pharmacological training. That included a fairly intensive course in obstetrics from Dr. Adams. We'll be along to keep everyone as healthy as we can, while maybe seeing if we can't improve conditions for the locals."

Nasi cleared his throat. "And they will consult on securing our wounded soldiers a steady supply of opium."

Monique noticed that something about the unfamiliar word made both up-timers uncomfortable.

"What?" Monique asked.

"Laudanum," Nasi tried to clarify.

"Oh," Monique said, still not sure what the substance was.

"What is it about the stones of immortality that makes you uncomfortable, Madame Totman?" Gervais asked, simultaneously informing his daughter what they were discussing. It was a substance used for treatment of some ailments, and as a powerful painkiller. It was good for putting careless men to bed early, too.

Priscilla shrugged and glanced at her husband, who tried to explain. "We up-timers are... conflicted about certain drugs." He grinned. "Aw, hell, we're entirely messed up about 'em. I blame Ronnie Raygun's wife, she had a very successful ad campaign aimed at making Americans think all drugs are bad."

Monique's continuing confusion must have been apparent, as Priscilla added: "A president when we were both really just kids, back up-time: his wife was a part of a propaganda campaign in what was called, 'The War On Drugs.' When Don Francisco says, 'secure a supply of opium,' we flash over to an image of a man with an egg in one hand, saying: 'This is your brain,' then the egg frying in oil and the motto, 'This is your brain on drugs.'"

"Ah," Monique said, parsing all the unfamiliar terms.

Even Nasi looked as if he'd learned something new.

Rodney Totman's laughter was loud, even in the large space: "Fancy being a drug kingpin, honey?"

She joined her husband, those white teeth flashing.

Monique liked the way Priscilla looked at her husband; it gave her hope for the institution of marriage.

"Forgive me being blunt, but I foresee some issues," Gervais said, setting his wine aside.

Nasi gestured for him to continue.

"Muslims, like many devoutly religious folk, have particular views on the body and its administration. Those views may render Monsieur and Madame Totman's undoubted medical skills a commodity without a buyer. Unless you wish to call on my talents for games of confidence, it seems that aside from their skills, we have very little to sell the Mughals in exchange for their opium and saltpeter."

Nasi nodded. "We have some specialists arriving from Magdeburg in the next few days who will provide additional technical expertise we believe the Mughals will be interested in: several young men trained in railroad construction and engineering. They've just been released from service on detached duty, and will provide additional security for the trade mission."

"Who?" Rodney asked.

"John Ennis."

"Ah, J.D. is good people. Met him while we were in basic training," Rodney said.

"Just so," Nasi said with a nod. "Along with him are three young men direct from the TacRail units: Maddox, Wiley, and Baldwin."

"Bobby Maddox?" Mrs. Totman asked.

Nasi nodded.

"Remember him from our wedding, Rodney? He's a parishioner."

Monique had the impression Rodney didn't, but the huge man nodded anyway.

"Railroads, eh? Can't say I know too much about them, but that I thought they required a great many up-time technical wonders to push cargo along."

"Pull," Rodney corrected, "in the case of trains, but yes, they do require locomotives." He looked expectantly at Nasi.

"We have that settled, short-term, as well as how we've chosen to fulfill one of the other requirements of court life..."

"The giving of bribes?" Gervais said as the other man drank.

Swallowing and lowering his glass, Nasi smiled without humor. "In my experience, the courts of eastern potentates prefer calling such, 'the giving of presents.' That said, if they choose to give the mission the full diplomatic treatment rendered to the Ottomans or English, the mission members can expect to come away from this trip with some substantial gifts from the court, merely for showing up."

Gervais yawned, looking terribly uninterested. Monique recognized the expression as the surest sign her father's greed was holding the reins of his mind.

"Landsmen's legs," Captain Strand said, watching the three young Grantville men walk up the gangplank to board *Lønsom Vind*.

The captain, Gervais, and Rodney Totman were standing on the poop deck of the Danish fluyt. Well, Gervais and Strand were standing; Rodney's nausea had him leaning at the rail.

Seasickness made distilling the Dane's words from his accent difficult, but Rodney persevered: "Yes, yes it will."

"And at the end of the voyage, more uncertainty."

"Yes, there is that."

"You talk little. This is good. Unexpected, but good." Strand pointed a thick finger at the young men, now making their way belowdecks. "Any of them going to prove useful?"

"At sea? Probably not. Why?"

Strand turned to face Rodney and shrugged. "Going to be a long time at sea. Each journey made, I have lost sailors, either to the sea upon transit of the Cape or to disease caught along the way. We might have a need for young men."

"I think you will find your losses to illness minimized."

"I thought it strange, the way you insisted on spraying every inch of the ship." The captain snorted. "But getting rid of my ratter? Sure, he was a flea-bitten mutt, but he was loyal, and well-liked by the crew."

"That's just it, Captain: fleas are the carriers of many illnesses. Besides, all the rats should have been killed by the fumigation process. You did set a watch on the mooring lines to prevent more rodents coming aboard, as instructed?"

The captain nodded, pulling a face. "Next you'll have us eating dainties."

Gervais smiled. "How did you know?"

Blond brows shot up in surprise. "An attempt at humor, only."

"Preserved fruits, Captain, are quite tasty."

"Your men will likely be in better shape, medically, once we arrive in India than they are now," Rodney added.

Rodney caught a glance Gervais sent at Captain Strand. Realizing too late how condescending that might have sounded, he opened his mouth to apologize.

But Strand just shrugged. "I would say it was hard to believe, but then I look at the size and shape of you and the other up-timer men, and I believe. Is there a bent back or malformed leg among you?"

"A few. Believe it or not, we had more health issues from being fat than from badly-healed limbs, rickets, and that sort of thing."

Strand patted his belly. "How is showing one's prosperity a problem?"

"When it leads to heart disease and diabetes."

Strand put a hand on his chest, brows drawing together, "Disease of the heart? Fleas carry this disease as well?"

"Well, no . . . they carry . . . Let me see . . . how to explain . . ."

Gervais, chuckling, broke in, "Normally I would dread the boredom of a long sea voyage, but with you up-timers every conversation will provide five more things to talk about!"

Chapter 4

Red Fort, The Gardens
May 1634

The siblings had barely greeted one another when the honeybee flew between them to land on the orchid. It crawled into the purple folds of the flower, seeking the nectar within and drawing the prince and princess to watch in appreciative silence. Long moments passed, the heavy bloom trembling. Eventually the honeybee took flight from the flower, releasing the siblings from stillness much as it scattered the flower's golden pollen.

As the interloping insect disappeared deeper into the gardens, wingbeats joining the hum of the others of its hive, Dara Shikoh and Jahanara leaned back and regarded one another, much as they had many times before and, God willing, would have opportunity to do for many years to come.

Putting away her desire to immediately transcribe the beauty of the bee's flight into poetry, Jahanara waited for her brother to speak. She noted his smooth brow was furrowed under the gorgeous yellow turban. She had not seen him so troubled since Aurangzeb's poem had embarrassed him before all the court. Jahanara suppressed a shudder, recalling the events immortalized therein: the great war elephant, mad with rage and entirely out of control, trampling slaves and scattering the Imperial household. Her younger brother Aurangzeb, still only fifteen years old, calmly sitting his horse while everyone fled. The way clear, Aurangzeb charged the great bull elephant and struck it between the eyes, stinging it so badly it ceased its rampage.

25

The later poem that shamed those that fled brought Mother's sage advice to mind: "Men, they will always feel the bite of words stronger than steel. Steel kills, but one must live on with the words of others. Remember this, and keep your words like sharp steel, with caution and care."

Keeping that advice uppermost in her mind, Jahanara folded hands in her lap, waiting. It was not often that their father's eldest son came to visit, but when he did, it was nearly always to ask the same questions.

"And what of Father, Sister mine?"

She smiled inwardly, not wanting to show how easily she had read him and therefore hurt his feelings. "He still pines for our beloved mother, of course. The only thing he looks forward to is the daily meeting with his advisors regarding Mother's tomb."

"His remaining wives?" Dara asked.

She smiled openly. She had been composing a verse this morning, a playful little thing, and used part of it now: "The harem persists in its perennial practices: showing their love of Father and whining at his inattention."

Dara nodded absently but didn't return her smile.

It was rare that he missed an opportunity to show his appreciation for her work. Resisting the urge to show her displeasure, she asked, "What troubles you, Brother?"

"I wonder what it will take to shake Father from his grief."

She strangled a sigh. "Must he be shaken?"

"Our family does not sit idle while one man mourns, Sister."

"No, but neither are they gathering armies to usurp Father's place."

"Not that we know of, at least."

"Our friend Mian Mir, in his wisdom, would have you set aside your fear, Brother."

Dara sniffed. "I know. I would argue: it is no sin to fear for one's family."

"If you only feared *for* your family, rather than fearing certain members *of* it."

Another sniff, this one companion to a bitter twist of the lips. "It has always been thus for the sons of our house."

Thinking on the unfairness of that remark, Jahanara refused to let him see how much his self-pity annoyed her. "But our father would have it otherwise, for you."

Looking through the walls of the garden, Dara whispered, voice so low it nearly drowned in the buzz of industrious insects about them: "Some days, I fear he might have chosen the wrong son..."

Red Fort, The Harem

Things were quite quiet in the harem, as they had been each evening since Mother had passed. Father had eaten his fill, and was in that state between sleep and wakefulness that a full belly and few puffs of the pipe always brought him to.

Shah Jahan had released the outer circle of the harem to find their own entertainments. The only remaining residents were Namrah and Netri, Shah Jahan's body-slaves, and they could be relied on to keep confidences.

The time appeared right, just as Ratna had predicted. The harem astrologer had made no less than six readings before recommending this night to Jahanara.

Realizing she was thinking of other things instead of facing her fear, Jahanara spoke. "Father?"

"Yes, Daughter?"

"I would ask a favor, Father."

"Oh?" he asked.

Jahanara swallowed sudden fear and rushed on. "I would ask that you allow me to oversee the finances of the harem."

Shah Jahan roused, propping himself up to look across at her in the lamplight. "Why?"

She looked down. "In all honesty, I find little to challenge me."

The emperor smiled. "You have exhausted poetry, then?"

Uncomfortable, she shrugged. "I will not marry, so what use the endless talk of love the poets engage in?"

"Daughter, look at me," he said.

She did as he bid.

He was smiling, dark eyes sad. "You are the jewel of the world, this court, and my heart. When you pine for marriage and love, remember that it was the perils of the birthing-bed that took your mother from us. I thank God that you shall not face such danger. I do not think I could bear to have you taken to Paradise before me."

Jahanara felt tears rising even as she bowed.

"Still, you did not come to me asking after a marriage, but control of the harem funds. The eunuch appointed the position of *Khan-i-Saman* has served us for some time."

She surreptitiously wiped away tears, nodded.

Father was looking at her again. "Why this sudden desire for control over your finances?"

"Not so sudden, really." She left unsaid the reason why she had delayed in telling him—neither of them had any desire to speak more of Mother's loss. "I suppose you can put it down to boredom alone, but I also believe I will do a better job of it than Diwan Garyan."

"Has the *Khan-i-Saman* somehow failed in his duty?"

Jahanara paused a moment. She did not hesitate for the sake of Diwan Garyan, but for her own plans—much relied on her father reacting just calmly *enough* to her news. "I have read the reports myself, and it appears he has failed to protect Mother's investments."

A gross understatement, but I don't want Father executing—

As if reading her fears, Shah Jahan said, "I shall have him executed."

"Father, please do not. At least, not yet."

"Why?"

"If you decide to leave these financial matters to me, I will need him as an example when I move to establish my authority over the harem."

"If I say you have the authority, then you shall have it."

She shook her head. "It is not the same thing, Father: if I am the one seen to discover his failures and find reason to ask you for permission to execute him, then those who serve in the harem will know who it is they must obey, and act promptly in response to my direction."

Father was silent for some time. So long, in fact, that Jahanara worried he'd fallen asleep. When he spoke, his voice was so clotted with emotion she flinched. "I doubt you realize how much your counsel sounds like that of your mother."

"You are too kind, Father."

The Seizer of the World cleared his throat. "No, it is true. Your mother was always wise to the ways of the harem, and always gave good counsel regarding management of it. Tell me, who do you recommend as the face of the harem in its financial affairs?"

"I had thought to recognize Firoz Khan."

"Who?"

"The eunuch you placed in charge of collecting the rents from the jagir you gave me last year, Father. It is due to his diligence that I discovered the...errors of Garyan."

"And as one away from our court, he has less chance of being under the sway of some other woman of the harem, and certainly will not be Diwan Garyan's creature."

She smiled. "No."

"Still. Is he not still in Surat?"

"No, Father. I asked him to return here in order to explain to us the discrepancies I noted in my incomes."

"Well then, it seems you have given this much thought. I grant you permission to the manage the affairs of the harem. Let me know when you wish me to announce it publicly."

She took his hand. "Thank you, Father."

Red Fort, The Harem

"What is *she* doing here?" Roshanara asked her younger brother as they watched the massive procession of their kinswoman entering the Lahore Gate. A contingent of *sowar* led the procession, helmets shining in the sun.

Aurangzeb tossed his head. "Nur Jahan asked to be here for the celebration of Father's weighing, and he did not refuse her."

"But she—"

"Is a respected member of the family, and Father wishes us to make her welcome."

She frowned, spoke the words she believed he wanted to hear: "She has too much to do with the Hindus."

Aurangzeb looked at her, keeping any expression from his face. "The same could be said of our grandfathers."

Roshanara ignored—or missed—his tone. "She should have remained in Lahore, maintaining Grandfather's tomb like a proper widow."

"You prefer her in Lahore, hatching plots with Mian Mir?"

She looked at him, eyes wide. "They conspire together?"

He grinned, shrugged young swordsman's shoulders. "No, Mian Mir is far too peace-loving to join causes with a tigress like Nur Jahan, not since she refused to heed Mian Mir's counsel during Father's rebellion."

"But you do not deny he plots."

"No, I do not." He pointed over the railing at the gilded howdah strapped to a massive bull elephant. "But there sits the true blade. She is not some old sufi waiting to die in Lahore. She is here for some purpose."

"Blade?"

He pulled his *katar* from his sash and held the double-edged punch dagger up between them. "It cuts both ways, this blade, just like our great-aunt."

"I don't understand."

Aurangzeb returned the dagger to its sheath. "Perhaps you should pray for guidance, then."

Roshanara stared at him a long moment, reaching for the meaning behind his words. He saw no light of understanding in her eyes as she turned away. "I will."

Aurangzeb concealed his satisfaction: It would not do to have her—or any of the family—be aware that Nur Jahan was here at his request.

Jahanara watched as Diwan Garyan made his approach to the open-fronted tent she'd caused to be erected in the garden. He was flabby, as many eunuchs were wont to get after reaching a certain age. Heavy perfume wafted to her on the breeze, announcing his proximity, if not his good taste in scents.

She felt the sheer mass of his presence as he bowed before her, and drew comfort in the presence of her guardians. Even if she decided to spare his life, Garyan would be ruined, and possibly seek to avenge himself upon her. While not as given to violence as full men, the eunuch's size made her glad of the presence of her warrior women guardians, chief among them Atisheh.

She glanced at the auburn-haired Turki, who nodded almost imperceptibly. If it came to that, her guardian would happily spill the fat eunuch's guts in the garden. Atisheh bore Garyan no love.

"Speak, Diwan Garyan."

"Begum Sahib, trade has been excellent this year." Garyan said, waving a hand glittering with jeweled rings toward the records a slave held in her arms.

Having read the actual reports and planned for this moment

for several months, Jahanara knew she could not trust a word the eunuch said. The trading concerns she had inherited from her mother had barely turned a profit this last year, despite having little to no competition. To add insult to her intelligence, the meager returns she'd gained were moved off the books, none too subtly, and into Garyan's personal treasury.

She would not let it continue: "How so?"

A look of surprise crossed Garyan's fleshy face. As the harem's long-established *Khan-i-Saman*, the Manager of the Household, he had gained far too much power during Father's long foray into grief. He had secured the position of the diwan responsible for her financial matters as well, and because Jahanara had taken so long to work up the courage to ask Father for leave to take responsibility for her and the harem's finances, Garyan had no experience of being questioned on matters of finance and trade.

"Do not look at me so, simply answer."

"We have made profitable trade in indigo, Begum Sahib," Garyan waved to the reports, his hand glittering with jewels, "but trade in betel has been off this last season."

"The profits from which are intended to cover the costs of underwriting Hajj passage for those less fortunate than us."

Garyan nodded, his usual control over his expression reasserting itself. "Such are the vagaries of trade, Begum Sahib."

Jahanara knew his words for a lie. Incomes from her jagir of Surat had been up this last year. Father had given her the tax incomes from the port, through which the majority of the empire's sea-born trade passed. And the tax on betel had shown the strongest return. This, when the reports Garyan prepared regarding her own personal betel farms all pled poor harvest and poorer prices.

"I am not pleased, Garyan."

"I humbly beg your forgiveness, but Mumtaz Mahal was content to—"

"My mother?" she snapped. "Do not think to bring even her name into this! Did you think I would not learn how you deceived her?"

Jahanara saw dawning fear in Garyan's eyes. "I—I—" he stammered.

She continued, the words an angry torrent, "Did you think to succeed? That I would not learn how you embezzled funds meant for her support, for my projects? Funds given us by our father, Shah Jahan, for our maintenance and pleasure?"

"But—"

Jahanara's henna-marked hand gestured at his expensive robes and ostentatious rings. "You must think me a fool, to come before me wearing wealth you have stolen from us! I will not have it. I will not."

"But, Begum Sahib, your father—"

"Has given me the right to dispose of you as I see fit."

Garyan at last realized how far he had fallen, and threw himself flat on the ground before her.

"Rise!" Jahanara hissed. "I have not given you leave to grovel."

When he refused the order, Atisheh advanced and stood over the prostrate eunuch. The warrior woman slapped the eunuch's turban from his head and drew a wickedly sharp dagger from her hip. She grabbed the erstwhile diwan by his hair, pulling him upright with a grunt of effort.

Stifling a cry, the eunuch continued his verbal retreat: "I beg your pardon, Begum Sahib, I am but a humble servant, tasked with great things. Tasks far above my abilities. If I have failed, it was—"

"Stop. Your lies no more excuse your malfeasance than your groveling."

Garyan spluttered to a stop, encouraged by Atisheh, who placed her blade along his throat.

Jahanara leaned forward, looking him in the eye. "You are removed from your posts and titles, Garyan. All *jagirs* awarded you are returned to the emperor. All authority lent to you is likewise returned. All wealth that you possess is forfeit. You are nothing and no one."

"What is to happen to me?" Garyan cried, tears flowing.

"That is for Father to decide, and the emperor is most unhappy with you."

Garyan wailed.

Jahanara waved to Atisheh, who, with the assistance of another of her tribe, dragged Garyan bodily from the garden. Atisheh would see to it he was dragged through the harem and into the custody of the eunuch guards at the gate to the harem.

Now, Jahanara thought as Garyan's cries faded, *everyone will know who they will answer to should they choose to go against my wishes.*

Chapter 5

Northwest African Coastline
June 1634

Bertram hissed in pain as his salt-stiffened shirt sawed across the raw meat of his neck. He looked heavenward. Four days almost without wind, baking in the sun. Even the crew was starting to grumble. Seeking distraction, he glanced at Rodney, who was bent over the port side rail, the dirty white line of the coast of Africa inching slowly by beyond him.

This devil's own sunburn was still better than Rodney's endless puking. The poor man hadn't been right since they boarded. Everyone was a touch miserable when they sailed right into that rough weather getting round Ireland, but Rodney had been a class apart the entire time.

A snort from the poop deck above drew him from thought. "This sun will make you look a redneck, that's for sure."

Bertram turned, craning his sizzling neck, and saw it was John Ennis speaking. The oldest of the up-timers with the mission for their technical expertise, Ennis had a set of the telescopic contrivances up-timers called "binoculars" hanging from his neck.

Bertram returned the smile. "In appearance only, I'm told. Randy and Ricky say there's more to being a proper redneck than a sunburn."

"A 'proper' redneck? Now there's a contradiction in terms." John beckoned Bertram to join him, stepping back from the ladder to make room.

Bertram scrambled up the ladder, finding Captain Strand, the first mate, and Gervais keeping company round the tiller. He gave the knot of men a nod and turned to John. "Could you explain that?"

"Yes, please do." Gervais said, stepping over to join them, leaning against the rail. He didn't seem the least bit uncomfortable in the heat, and his neck was already nut-brown.

John pursed his lips slightly. "Well, the term's much more popular among southerners in...the nation we came from, than it was among West Virginians. We generally prefer the slang term 'hillbilly.'"

"Yes, I have noticed that is a title all you up-timers seem to bear with pride."

A broad smile, full of teeth. "Not all of us, but," a slow nod, "yeah, most of us who came from Grantville do take being called hillbilly with a degree of pride. It was, my father told me, originally an attempt by some city flatlanders to describe ignorant mountain folk, just like 'rednecks' was a sneer at dumb farmers whose necks were burned red by the sun.

"Over time, things change, and the two terms had mixed meanings when I was growing up—which partly depended on where you grew up. The term 'redneck,' especially, got mixed in with attitudes during the civil rights movement."

"Which was...?"

John waved his hand. "I don't want to go into that right now. Hillbilly, though, more or less kept its original meaning. Sometimes people would try and insult me with it, but I always took it as something to be a bit proud of: Most hillbillies I knew were more willing to help their neighbors than most city-folk, were clever with their hands, and not above bending their back to work for a living." He shrugged. "So it wasn't a bad thing, for me, being called a hillbilly."

"Me neither," Rodney gasped, between retching sessions at the rail below. "Except I was born in Georgia so I'd go with 'redneck.' But for the love of God"—he managed to fight down another retch—"don't ever call my West Virginia-born wife a 'redneck' or you just restarted the civil war. 'We seceded from you damn secessionists!' is the first thing she'll say, and it'll go downhill from there."

Bertram was looking a bit confused again. John chuckled and

said: "I'm afraid that's another up-time history lesson we'll gave to postpone for the moment."

"But, with all the wonders you have brought to us, it's hard to imagine someone..." Bertram trailed off, trying to find the correct phrase.

"Looking down on us?"

"Exactly so."

"Well, there were a lot who did. Small towns had a reputation for being backward, just like today... and we Americans didn't have the best reputation overseas, either." Another shrug. "Hell, Grantville still ain't anyone's idea of a cultural center."

"Plebeians, then?" Gervais offered.

"Huh?" John asked.

Finding it endlessly interesting how these up-timers, so highly educated in matters technical, could be so ignorant of terms common to every modern down-timer's education, Bertram explained: "The Roman Republic had patricians and plebeians. The former looking down on and fearing the latter, who were the majority. The patricians would do whatever possible to keep the plebeians from capitalizing on their numbers and seizing power, including bribing them with food and putting on entertainments like gladiatorial combats and circuses."

"Oh, so that's where that bread and circuses thing comes from?"

Bertram smiled. "Exactly so."

John looked thoughtful a moment, then shrugged again. "Seems people have always been looking for ways to make themselves special, even at the expense of others."

"True..." Gervais murmured.

A sailor in the rigging shouted something that, between the accent and the nautical term, Bertram missed.

But he couldn't help but hear Strand cursing as the captain pulled out a telescope and stood to the rail along the port side next to Gervais.

There was another shout from above.

"Where away?" the captain bellowed.

"Port, three points."

Strand adjusted the telescope, muttered, then said clearly: "Damnation."

John appeared on the deck. "What is it, Captain?" he asked, bringing his binoculars up in the direction the captain was looking.

"Not good," Strand muttered, chewing one end of his mustache. Bertram squinted, but could not see anything. "What?"

"One of those ships with both sail and oars—" John said.

"Pirates," Strand said.

"How can you tell that at this distance?" John asked.

Strand snorted. "Xebec with her oars out, pulling hard for us."

"And?" John said.

"Damnation," Bertram breathed.

Strand ignored them both, stomping over to his first mate. "Open the arms locker and man the guns. We're in for a visit from the slaver scum."

"I still don't understand what he saw," John said, peering at the horizon again through his binoculars.

"Would you want to row in this heat?" Bertram asked.

John let the binoculars hang from his neck and looked at him. "Hell, no."

"Exactly so."

Bertram saw understanding dawn in the up-timer's eyes.

"Shit." John scrambled down the ladder and disappeared belowdecks.

Bertram heard a mechanical click, followed by a gentle whirring from just below. He looked over to see a blue-steel pistol had appeared in Rodney's hand, the cylinder opened to reveal shining brass.

Satisfied with the state of his loads, Rodney snapped the revolver closed with a practiced motion. "I'll make sure the boys are ready." He staggered off.

"And I'll see to the women," Gervais muttered.

First Mate Loke shouted from the rail, "Malte, Short Leif, Ulf, Lukas with me to the weapons locker! The rest of you, to your guns or stations!"

Bertram watched as the mast of the pirate slowly grew to reveal a ship as men leapt to their posts all over the *Lønsom Vind*.

"Knew we should have stood further out to sea," Strand grumbled.

"Not much choice; what with the weather, the English, the Dutch, and the Spanish," Bertram said, fear squeezing the words through a suddenly tight throat. He had no wish to be killed or, worse yet, watch Monique and the others gang-raped and sold into slavery.

✧   ✧   ✧

John kissed his wife and pulled the Winchester free of its case. There was barely enough room in their cramped quarters for the two of them, and the barrel of the gun bumped the low ceiling as he slung it over one shoulder.

"What's going on, John?" Ilsa had been lying down, suffering from seasickness nearly as bad as Rodney.

He grabbed the small ammo box his father had left lying around, the one labeled M25. "Pirates. Captain says they're all slavers, too."

Ilsa blanched. "Oh, no, John."

He kissed her again. "Got to go." Holding her at arms length, he added: "Keep your head down."

"I'll join the others."

"Sounds good." He left, squeezing past Gervais in the narrow gangway outside. The Frenchman was readying a coach-gun, sweat dripping from his round face. "On my life, they'll not pass, Monsieur Ennis."

Not sure what to say to that, John just nodded and climbed out on deck.

The sun beat on him as he considered his options. Setting up in the rigging would give him height and better viewing aspect on the targets, much like a deer stand in a tree, but the ropes and spars were swaying far more than the deck.

Ricky Wiley and the rest of the boys boiled out behind him while he thought it through, all shotguns and pent-up aggression.

He spat over the side and decided on the poop deck. "Ricky, do me a favor, get me . . . five or six of those winter blankets."

"Will do, J.D."

John climbed up, Rodney right behind him, and rejoined the captain and Bertram. Strand was still peering through his telescope.

"Captain Strand, what range do their guns have?" he asked, trying to keep his mind off of what he was preparing to do.

"Their cannon?"

"Yes."

"They'll probably give us a warning shot at about a hundred paces, reload, and if we don't just give up, they'll get to the business of trying to break us at around fifty."

The ship was swaying in the swell, not a great deal, but enough to pose a challenge at range. The fluyt was higher at the stern than the xebec was at the bow, so he'd still have a tiny bit of increased aspect on the targets.

Ricky climbed into view, blankets over his shoulders.

John thanked him and started setting up his rest.

"What are you doing?" Bertram asked.

"Helps to have a steady base to fire from."

"Oh. Do you think you can do much good?"

He shrugged, hands busy setting up the improvised shooting bench. "I ain't no Julie, but I can hold my own."

"Julie who?" Bertram asked, then answered his own question: "Oh, *that* Julie."

John handed his binoculars to Ricky. "I need you to call them as you see them, all right?"

The younger man swallowed. "Never done this for real, J.D."

"Me neither, but if you see the round, tell me where it's gone so I can adjust."

"Will do."

Using a bucket for his seat, John unslung the rifle and laid it across the improvised rest. "Rate of closure?"

"No clock, but, uh, call it a bit more'n hundred yards a minute," Rodney said. He even *sounded* sick.

John raised the Winchester, removed the covers from the cheap but functional Bushnell 3x9 scope Poppa Ennis had bequeathed him and said, "Captain Strand, you sure these men are pirates?"

"Certain and sure, Mr. Ennis. Nothing else they could be, not here, not behaving the way they are."

He shouldered the rifle and put his eye to the scope. "Okay."

Caid Youssef el Inglizi returned the wolf-smiles of his crew with his own.

And why not smile? Surely finding a fat merchant becalmed so close to Sallee is a sign that God favors our enterprise?

As there wasn't a good man among the crew, such signs were less wasteful than the usual methods he had to resort to in order to ensure his commands were followed. Always, the new men among the crew wanted to test him, wanted to see if the white Muslim was truly fit to lead the brotherhood.

Such behavior had only become more common since he'd sent his son off to Grantville to plumb their secrets. The other captains all believed he was trying to place his son beyond their reach, or worse, questioned his conversion to Islam. They campaigned, in whispers, against him. Their short-sighted bigotry would eventually prove their undoing, but for now Youssef needed every cruise he undertook to result in easy profits and many slaves.

The rowers of *Quarter Moon* were drawing them steadily closer to the foreign fluyt, as they had since sighting the vessel some hours ago. By his reckoning, less than half an hour remained until the sharks were fed the blood of unbelievers.

Youssef el Inglizi, born in London as Joseph Bingley, shaded blue eyes with one hand, staring hard at the slack banner hanging from the mast of the taller vessel. Several pale faces at the stern of the ship stood staring at their approaching doom.

"Hamburg?" he murmured.

"Would explain why they are alone—no convoys like the Spaniards or English," his first mate, Usem, said from beside him. "Though it's strange they should be this close in to shore."

Youssef shrugged. "Not after the storms of last week, the calm that's held since, and the current to drag them close."

Usem nodded, white turban sparkling with jewels.

"Raise our banner, let them know who comes for them."

"Yes, Captain." Usem gestured.

Moments later a young sailor unfurled the banner of the Sallee Rovers from the mast, a gold man-in-the-moon on a red background.

"Brothers, we will soon set upon the infidel and take his goods, his ship, and the lives of any who resist!"

A crashing, ululating cheer greeted his words.

"Man the guns and make ready, then!"

Youssef and Usem joined the crews of the three cannon in the bow. The xebec, although not to the extent of a galley, had somewhat limited broadside armament because of the oars, and so mounted three of its thirteen guns in the bow. Because it lacked the banks of rowers of a true galley, it didn't have the sheer speed of such a ship, either, allowing them to make only about four, perhaps five, knots. Still they closed the distance.

A meaty thump, like a mallet striking flesh, came from the gun-captain of the starboard bow gun.

A sharp crack reached his ears just as Youssef turned to look at his slowly slumping sailor.

"Wha—" The man gurgled, crimson staining his lips.

Something whistled through the air above Youssef. Another crack rolled across the water to him.

Youssef ducked instinctively, the men about him doing the same.

He saw it then, a tiny flash of light from one corner of the stern of the fluyt, like a gunshot, but without the cottony cloud of gun-smoke.

Shooting at us, from there? That's—another of his cannoneers reeled back, arm dangling by a thread of meat—*impossible!*

Again the sharp cracking noise rolled across the waves.

"Down!" Youssef shouted, unnecessarily. His men were already pushing tight behind the cannon, fighting for space.

Another flash.

Something rang off the cannon directly in front of him with a sound like hell's own hammer, then went whistling through the air between him and Usem.

Merciful Allah, how many guns does this man have?

That evil crack again.

The men were now leaning forward, close to the deck, as if bracing against a gale.

Youssef raised his head, gauging the distance. Almost four hundred yards still separated the ships.

"Faster!" he bellowed, "Row faster!"

Usem rose up to repeat the captain's order. He lost his life for it. The round took him in the jaw, sending teeth and bone rattling wetly across the deck behind his toppling corpse.

"Merciful Allah!" someone screamed.

"Faster!" Youssef barked, the now-expected crack punctuating his order.

The slaves responded at last, pulling harder at their oars. Slowly, the ship built speed. Several breaths passed without one of the horrible flashes, only the groan of wood on wood and the cries of the man who'd lost his arm. They were nearly three hundred yards out when the next flash appeared.

A dimly visible red-orange light appeared at the end of the flash. Barely visible, it crossed the space between the two ships and sailed by well above the deck.

This time, the crack of the gun was nearly drowned in the cheering of his crew.

"Down, you fools!"

A second dirty streak of light was sent their way, again appearing to have gone high. Another cheer from the men.

"Closer!" he shouted.

The crew shouted wordless aggression.

Glad his men were less afraid of the strange weapon than he was, Youssef looked up to offer a silent prayer of thanksgiving. It was then that he saw a tiny curl of smoke rising from the furled mainsail.

As he stared, another of the burning things struck the furled sail along the spar just port of the mast. It went in and didn't exit. Colored smoke began seeping from the hole as the noise of the shot followed the results across the water.

"Water the sail!" Youssef's shouted order held more of an edge of panic to it than he wished.

Nearly all the crew looked up and saw the reason for the order. A collective groan went through them.

Hassan, youngest of the brotherhood and the quickest climber among them, stood to his duty and grabbed the bucket line. In moments he was straddling the spar. He dragged the first of the buckets up and started to pour it over the growing smoky stretch of sail.

The next red-orange streak ended in Hassan's ribs. The boy shrieked, overbalanced, and fell. Even striking the deck from such a height did not end the pain for poor Hassan, who lay writhing, as if the thing that struck him continued to burn inside his flesh.

The crew moaned. Hassan was well liked.

Youssef stepped across the boy, who lay twitching like a wounded scorpion, broken limbs flailing.

Youssef's sword hissed from its sheath. A small mercy.

Why stop shooting? Bertram wondered, looking from the still-advancing pirate ship to John.

The up-timer looked pale, and no longer had his eye to the shooting telescope attached to his rifle, instead staring at the wooden rail inches from his face.

"Jesus, John," Ricky said. His voice cracked.

"I know. Fuck me, but I know," John breathed.

"Just a kid, John."

"I wasn't aiming at him!"

"They're turning," Captain Strand said.

"What?" Bertram heard himself ask.

"They're turning," Strand repeated, relief evident in his voice. "Heading for port."

John climbed to his feet. He left the rifle where it lay.

Strand grabbed the younger man by the shoulder and looked down at Ricky, addressing them both: "John, Ricky, regardless of the difference between whatever you meant to do and what happened, it was *them* who came after us. They would have enslaved your women and you, given half a chance."

"Don't make it right, Captain."

Strand released him. "But we live to make better choices."

"And remember," John said, climbing out of view.

Chapter 6

Surat
July 1634

The steady rain pounding the decks did nothing to cool the heated discussion the captain of the *Graça de São João* was having with one of Surat's many tax farmers as Salim climbed on deck.

Thankfully, neither man paid him any attention. A man with just a few parcels was not worthy of attention from grasping tax officials and he'd long since paid his passage to the captain.

Salim sent a wave the first mate's way and walked from the ship.

Despite the rain, the docks were active, slaves and their overseers managing the loading and unloading of several vessels. All but the *Graça de São João* were from ports on the Indian Ocean, most here to trade in horses, indigo, spices, saltpeter, and slaves. One ship, Mughal-built, was returning from Hajj, pilgrims forming a knot of the faithful as they navigated the waterfront.

Happy to be ashore, Salim took a deep breath. Even through the rain, the scent of spices from East Africa and Southern India warred with the odors of river, tar and tide. While not from Gujurat, it was still a homecoming of sorts. He had done much in Gujurat in the first years he'd come down from the Khyber. It was a walk of a few minutes to the English factory complex.

Wishing to avoid any entanglements with people who might not remember him fondly, Salim found a sheltered spot to observe the gate. It was nearly sunset when he saw the man he'd been waiting for.

"Dhanji Das!" he called, angling to intercept the painfully thin men bearing Dhanji's litter.

A flick of the fly-whisk he held indicated Dhanji had heard him, but the heavyset man did not order his bearers to stop, probably thinking Salim some kind of petitioner.

Which I suppose I am, all things considered.

He easily overtook the party, spoke from beside the lead bearer, "Dhanji Das, I am Salim Gadh Visa Yilmaz."

"Salim?"

"Salim, friend to your brother, Jadu, in Ahmedabad. He introduced us four years ago—"

Dhanji spoke over him, waving the whisk at an invisible fly. "I'm afraid I don't know—"

"—after I saved him from slavery or death," Salim finished. The Das family business took advantage of the Englishmen's disdain for learning the local languages: one cousin would range ahead of an English Company trader—whose translator was invariably another cousin—and buy up all the indigo or textiles for sale in a given market, then make a tidy profit selling it at a mark-up to the English. It was on one such trip that bandits had come across Jadu Das with a hundred fardles of indigo he planned to sell to the English. They'd come across him, beat him senseless, and staked him out to die.

At the time, Salim had been with a band hired by the governor of Gujurat to put a stop to the depredations of that very group of bandits. Setting upon them at night, the governor's men had killed the bandits to a man.

After the skirmish, most of the governor's men had thought to take Jadu's goods for themselves and leave him staked where he was. Salim had forbidden it. A blood-drenched argument had ensued.

Jadu knew what was owed. It remained to be seen whether Dhanji did.

"Oh, *that* Salim!" Dhanji said, rapping ringed fingers against the litter frame to bring his bearers to a stop. "We thought you dead on foreign shores!"

You hoped it was so, that you might be free of obligation. Stifling the urge to say the words out loud, Salim said, "And yet here I stand."

A smile. "Yes, yes indeed."

"God is merciful."

Hindu, Dhanji's response was a graceful nod. A silence settled.

Irritated that he had to remind Das exactly how much was owed, Salim tried again: "I trust trade with the English proceeds without difficulty?"

A twist of fleshy lips. "It does, but let us not talk of such things here: please, come to my home. I will feed your belly while you fill my head with news of distant goings-on."

Salim checked the angle of the sun, just peeking from beneath the clouds. Some time remained before Maghrib. "How can I refuse such generosity? It will be my pleasure."

They spoke of inconsequential things on the way to Dhanji's home, a large building, white-washed and thick-walled to keep the heat at bay. Salim complimented his host on it.

A smile shone through the Gurjurati's beard as he invited Salim to join him for fruit and refreshment.

"I thank you. I must pray first, however."

"Of course."

Dhanji provided him water to cleanse himself and privacy for the performance of Maghrib.

Refreshed, Salim rejoined his host.

"What news of the court, Dhanji Das?" Salim asked, plucking a date from the platter and biting into it.

"Word is slow to reach us here in Surat, but the emperor remains at Agra."

"Still?"

Dhanji nodded. "Jadu tells me the emperor personally oversees the building of Mumtaz Mahal's tomb. It is an astounding project."

"For an astounding love," Salim said, thinking of the "post-card" in his pack. He shook his head, "Jadu is in Agra, then?"

"Yes, he assists the English factors there."

"Good news, then. Surely he prospers."

Dhanji smiled and thumped his belly. "He grows fat, like me."

"I wonder, have you heard any word of Mian Mir?"

"In fact, I have: Mian Mir fell ill shortly after you departed for that strange place—what was it called?"

"Grantville."

"Grantville. An odd name..." Dhanji said, clearly hopeful of some intelligence that might earn out.

"Yes, it is. You were speaking of Mian Mir?"

"Sorry, yes. He fell ill, and while he is better now, he has yet to recover his full strength."

"Is he still at Lahore?"

"Yes. There is much doubt he will leave his residence again before he passes from this world."

"You seem concerned."

Dhanji shrugged. "Guru Mian Mir is a friend to all good men, regardless of faith. Few are the Hindus who do not know who it is who has stayed the hand of the conservatives at court," Dhanji said.

Salim nodded, relieved. Mian Mir's agenda of religious tolerance was not always appreciated, even among Hindus, many of whom still saw Islam as the religion of the invader. Encouraged enough to bring the subject back to his purpose, Salim asked, "And your brother, did he tell you anything regarding me?"

"He instructed me to render you any assistance you might need, whenever you might ask for it."

Salim nodded. "I do not need much: money for a mount and enough supplies to get to Agra."

"I have sufficient funds set aside for your needs."

"I will thank him upon my arrival in Agra and tell him how faithful his brother is to the promises he has made. Further, I will be sure to repay what is given."

"Repayment is not necessary," Dhanji grinned, "and be careful how much you offer a man before learning how things stand: horses cost very dear this season. We have had much of famine and disease since you were sent to accompany Baram Khan. Trade continues, but food and fodder are scarce."

"The city did seem quiet."

"The pestilence took a great many people, especially those weakened by hunger, of which there were far too many. Many of the Europeans died, unprepared for the sickness here. Nearly all of the English, in fact."

"How many?"

"Of the twenty-one who were here when you left, four remain among the living."

Salim shook his head in shocked sympathy. "Such mortality?"

"Indeed! And yet, every month sees more English, Dutch, and Portuguese arrive on our shores, each certain they will make their fortune."

"And do they?"

"While the court remains fascinated with their baubles, the Europeans make excellent profit."

"Baubles?"

"The bribes they offer are hardly worthy of the name, but it seems the residents of the emperor's harem are endlessly fascinated with seeing themselves in mirrors."

Salim snorted. "With the great beauties it is said that Shah Jahan surrounds himself with, I understand the appeal of such entertainments." He thought a moment, asked for confirmation: "Which of the Europeans are prospering most?"

"The English and Dutch do best, though the Portuguese are recently returned to the good graces of the Court."

God is Good! That is good news! I doubted anyone at court would even see me after being associated with Baram Khan's stink. Aloud, he asked, "How did they manage that?"

Shah Jahan had, as one of his first acts after ascending the throne, ordered the Portuguese punished for failing to render him aid during his earlier rebellion.

"It seems even Shah Jahan's anger has an end." Dhanji shrugged. "I do not know what was agreed to, or how, but everyone knows the Jesuits were involved."

"Interesting..." Salim said, running fingers through his beard.

"I doubt my news is as interesting as the adventures you've had, and the tales you might tell," Dhanji prompted.

Salim grinned. "I am a horrible guest, to ask so many questions without offering news, as you invited me here to do. I suppose it is best to start at the beginning..."

Route from Surat to Agra

The stream, swollen with monsoon rain, presented less of a challenge than climbing the far bank, an unstable slope of dark, wet earth. Salim stood in the stirrups as his recently purchased and exceedingly expensive Arab warmblood slipped sideways halfway up the bank.

Something pointed made a dangerous whistling as it hummed through the space he'd just left, cutting off all thought of cursing his as-yet-unnamed horse.

Salim heard the snap of more bowstrings as he heeled his mount up the bank. Powerful hindquarters bunched, released, sending mount and rider surging over the lip of the ravine and out of the path of the arrows.

Two men rushed from the tree line with spears, another emerging from the wood behind, urging them to the attack.

His horse's scrambling leap had landed them perpendicular to the charging men. He added their position to the tally of the many things he would have to thank the Almighty for when next he had opportunity to face Mecca.

For now, though, the sword. It hissed from sheath and to hand.

His horse, shying from the shouting men, curvetted. Salim leaned sideways, using the mount's momentum to bring his curved Persian steel sweeping across in a cut that connected with one of the spear-shafts. The crude iron head flew free and over Salim's shoulder, surprising Salim almost as much as the wielder, who stood staring at the cloven wood stump just above his hand. From the youth's openmouthed expression, he was clearly imagining what might have been had the sword struck below where he held it.

The other spear-bearer bored in and stabbed. The blade swept past Salim's nose by a hand's breadth.

While the first man stared at his severed spear, Salim's still-spinning horse clipped his companion with a hoof, folding him with a grunt that ended in a roll down the riverbank.

Mindful of the target he now presented to the archers on the opposite bank, Salim spurred the Arab into flight. He angled away from the track and any additional brigands who might be lying in wait.

He heard a horseman pound into pursuit behind him.

An arrow flew past from the far shore, then another. A third traced a hot red line across his forearm, making him drop the reins. Thanks be to the Almighty, the horse had drawn his own conclusions about where safety lay and ran flat out through the narrow opening among the trees.

Out of sight of the archers, Salim spared a glance for his wound. It would keep. Leaning low over the horse's neck, he retrieved the dropped rein and glanced behind.

On an inferior mount, the horseman had fallen behind in Salim's short gallop to cover. Now, however, the tight confines of the trail favored the shorter horse and the rider with more intimate knowledge of the land.

At least the other wouldn't be able to ride up alongside to strike.

There being nothing for it but to ride, Salim did just that. Long moments passed, the blowing of his horse and the pounding of hoofbeats beneath and behind his only company.

With a suddenness that hurt the eyes, the pursuit exploded from the wood and into bright sunlight. He felt his mount lengthen stride and gain speed, hoping it could see better than he could. Knowing he was gaining distance, Salim kept his face in the mane, hoping to present as small a target as possible in case his pursuer had a horse-bow.

Eyes adjusted, he looked back and saw the other rider was letting his horse slow, giving up the pursuit in a storm of curses.

Bandits, then.

Good. For a moment he'd worried that—despite all the measures he'd taken to avoid it—that someone knew of his return and sought to kill him before what he carried could be explained.

Salim let his mount slow to a walk once he was certain the chase was ended. Remaining in the saddle, he spent some time dressing his wound and eating some of the food he'd purchased at the last caravanserai.

Many *kos* remained between him and his destination. Checking the straps of his saddlebags, Amir Salim Gadh Visa Yilmaz rode on, contemplating suitable names for the horse.

Chapter 7

Agra, Home of Jadu Das
August 1634

The emperor's palace of Red Fort, hard by the Yamuna, was a welcome sight after so many kos and so much time abroad.

Welcome, but still distant in both physical and figurative terms. Jadu's roof was kos from Red Fort, and Salim didn't dare approach Red Fort until he knew more about how things stood at court. Two years, more or less, had passed since he'd departed as part of Baram Khan's entourage. Many things had changed. Even Red Fort had been modified: white marble superstructures were being added while older, plainer ones were torn down.

"Do you have a plan?" Jadu asked, following the line of his gaze.

Salim shook his head and resisted the urge to finger the fresh bandage on his arm. "Not yet, no."

"You could just walk up to the gate and ask."

Salim snorted. "I could, but Mian Mir instructed me to present my findings directly—and privately—to the imperial family, preferably to Dara Shikoh."

"You move in august circles."

"I did not, Mian Mir did." Salim gave a crooked smile. "He merely asks the impossible of me."

"Come, have something to drink while you consider how to ride the impossible to victory." Dhanji Das' elder brother offered his guest a cool glass of fruit juice and one stem of the water pipe.

Grinning, Salim turned from the roof's edge and joined Jadu.

Careful of his wound, he settled on one cushion and took the offered refreshment. "My thanks for your hospitality, Jadu Das. You and your family have more than paid your debt to me."

"Not so, Salim." Jadu waggled his head. "With respect, I will be the judge of when my debt to you is fully paid, and I say that day has yet to arrive."

"You do your family honor, Jadu Das."

Taking a pull from the pipe, Jadu exhaled, speaking through a cloud of fragrant smoke: "I do, but this talk of honor and debts does nothing to bring you closer to accomplishing your goals, my friend."

"No, it does not." Salim looked out across the city at Red Fort again.

"I know a few officials at court. I can inquire among them, see if perhaps there is a chance to see the emperor without all the world knowing of it, but I very much doubt it possible." Jadu took another thoughtful pull at the pipe. "The emperor does occasionally hear petitions tied to the begging chain let down the east wall during his morning appearance before the people..."

"But?"

"But it is only occasionally, and while you would not have to present your information to some court functionary in order to go before the emperor, you would still have to present whatever you have in full view of the public."

Salim nodded. "A route of last resort, then."

"As you say, Salim."

"What of Dara?"

"He is easier to approach than the emperor, but not by a great deal. Especially for those who have not gone through the emperor first."

"Is he still in favor?"

"Oh, yes. Very much so. In fact, it is rumored that Shah Jahan has been too lenient with his eldest son, who spends too much time reading from books other than the Koran and playing *chaugan*."

"Rumored?"

"Well, this much is true: Dara hasn't held even a notional field command. This, despite being far older than Shah Jahan himself was upon being given his first command."

"I see."

"As does the rest of the court."

Salim glanced at Jadu. "But not Shah Jahan?"

A shrug. "I do not claim to know the mind of the emperor, but it is widely known that his advisors are rarely heeded where his children are concerned."

"An understandable result of his own failed rebellion." It was well known that Shah Jahan felt that Jahangir had been turned against him by Nur Jahan and a coterie of advisors, so it was understandable that he ignored his own advisors on family matters.

Jadu shook his head and gently corrected his guest: "I believe there is more to it than the war of succession and the events surrounding the deaths of all the possible rivals to his claim."

Salim slowly nodded, considering. Shah Jahan's brothers and all of their sons—his own nephews—had been executed by Asaf Khan, another kinsman. Most everyone agreed the executions were on Shah Jahan's orders, but who would say anything about it, one way or another?

And, judging from all Salim had been able to find in Grantville's libraries, Mian Mir was right: those killings placed a shadow on the dynasty that was never successfully removed. That shadow was used to cloak fratricide in an aura of legitimacy, weakening the dynasty and ultimately leading to British rule.

"A thought occurs, Salim."

"Oh?"

"I have a kinsman who provides betel to the harem. Jahanara Begum has recently been given full responsibility for the harem's finances. Perhaps I can get you into Red Fort with his party..."

"It seems a good idea, but the requirements of purdah will still force me to speak through some intermediary, and that one no closer to Dara or the emperor."

"True..." Jadu sucked thoughtfully on the pipe.

They sat in companionable silence for some time, smoking and eating.

An elephant's trumpeting reached Salim's ears. The sound led him, through roundabout paths, to what he must do.

Agra, Red Fort, The Harem

Sighing in satisfaction, Nur Jahan slowly closed the tiny glass valve and turned the heat down under the flask of concentrate.

The new perfume would be ready soon and, if she was correct in her calculations, would out-last and linger on the body far longer than any of her previous concoctions.

Things had settled into a comfortable pattern in the months since she'd returned to court, allowing her time to pursue her hobbies and slowly, carefully extend her reach through the court.

She had reason to be satisfied on multiple levels: the perfume would improve her already-excellent reputation for such creations, and serve to further lull her adversaries into complacency. Men, and to a lesser extent, eunuchs, were rather easy to mislead into boredom when reports reach their ears of activities they considered unmanly. Boredom led to disregard for the person involved in such pursuits, which was exactly where Nur wished to remain, for the moment.

Gargi, her favorite advisor, entered.

"My lady?"

Nur turned from the apparatus, "Yes?"

"Some news, from Lahore, my lady," Gargi said, tapping a packet held in her right hand.

Important, then.

"For later. Come, let us play some chess while I wait for this," she waved at the flask, "to cool."

"Yes, my lady."

They sat, Gargi more slowly than her mistress. She didn't have the benefit of Nur's many years of training to keep the body supple.

Gargi took the first move, as was their habit. They played for some time, engaged in quiet conversation full of banalities intended to erode the patience of any listeners. Eventually, a faint snore from beyond the *jali* rewarded their patient game. The spy assigned to watch them had difficulty keeping awake in the heat of the day.

Nur smiled, held out her hand.

Gargi handed the packet over.

Nur read through the dispatches quickly, filing them between hennaed toes: the most important messages requiring responses went between the largest toe of her right foot and its delicately decorated neighbor, the rest in descending order of importance. On the left, items of news that did not require a response, in the same order of precedence. There were far more messages finding a place between her left toes than her right these last few years, something she hoped to rectify in the coming days. The last missive was in a hand she did not immediately recognize, requiring a frustrating moment to place.

She must have shown some of her discontent, because Gargi quietly asked, "Mistress?"

Nur Jahan held up the missive. "Rehan Usmani, one of my clients, writes from Surat to tell me Baram Khan is dead."

"Some disease of the Europeans?"

She shook her head. "Poison, apparently."

"Not entirely unexpected. Baram Khan was not the most circumspect of men."

"He had his uses."

"Does it say where he was? Did he find the fabled city the Jesuits spoke of?"

"Yes, Rehan claims they did, and that there are many things he needs to tell me of what was discovered there. He desires an audience as soon as he arrives from Surat." She held the message up. "As this was sent to Lahore first, we are unlikely to have an opportunity to question him for another month or so."

"And when he does arrive," Gargi waved at the jali where the spy continued to snore, "meeting in private will be nearly impossible."

"Yes." Nur reread the next few lines, parsing the message laid out between the lines of carefully adequate calligraphy. "He also warns that Amir Salim Gadh Visa Yilmaz departed the diplomatic party without leave. He suspects the amir of working against me, and expresses concern the man will return to court with inflammatory news that could do my position harm."

"I do not recognize the name of this amir. Why should one such as he work against you?"

"Another of Mian Mir's students, Salim was ever one of his favorites. And, since my fall from Mian Mir's good graces during Shah Jahan's rebellion, I'm sure he's had his head filled with poison against me."

"But what could the man carry that might be a threat to you?"

Nur cocked her head to one side. "Rehan perhaps misreads opportunity as threat."

"Better to kill this amir and forego the risk, then," Gargi said, louder than she should have.

Nur cast the hem of her sari over her feet, concealing the papers as the spy's disoriented snort warned them he was awake.

The women resumed their small talk over the chessboard.

Nur Jahan, most beloved widow of Jahangir, considered her opponent as she hounded Gargi's king across the chess board. *Poor Gargi, her advice has become so much more conservative since my forced retirement. Still, she may be correct in this. Perhaps I should tell Aurangzeb my news when next we meet. Such information, promptly delivered, should serve to increase my credibility as an ally, and costs me nothing but the breath to speak the words.*

Agra, Pulu Grounds

I simply hate *losing!*

Dara's feelings on the state of play proved unhelpful as the talented new addition to Mohammed Khan's team cracked the ball in a perfectly timed pass. The wooden ball slipped between two of Dara's teammates, rolling between the galloping horses of the two captains.

Keeping clear of the other rider's line, Dara leaned over in his saddle and tried to intercept with his mallet.

With a quick flick of his wrist, Mohammed bounced the wooden ball into the air and over the prince's mallet. Dara stretched in a desperate attempt to deflect it, but Mohammed caught the ball on his stick again, keeping it out of Dara's reach.

Mohammed put heels to horse, the ball rolling ahead.

Having slowed to accommodate Dara's lunge from the saddle, his horse lost ground on the young noble's. Dara righted himself and set out in pursuit, quickly making up ground. He was almost in reach of the nobleman when Mohammed wound up and cracked a shot between the raised uprights.

Subdued applause came from the sidelines.

No one wants to be seen applauding another of the prince's failures, Dara thought bitterly, turning his horse and slowing to a walk. His mount needed time to cool and the teams had to re-set.

The new player, the one who had made such an excellent pass, sidled up beside him and spoke. "Shehzada Dara Shikoh, it is good to see you well."

Dara looked at the horseman, who had covered the lower

half of his face to keep the dust and turf off and said, "Do I know you?"

A polite bow of the head. "We were once students together."

"Oh? Did you school me on the *pulu* grounds before?" Dara asked, still fuming over conceding the point.

The other man bowed deeper in his saddle and pulled down the end of his turban to show his face. "No, Shehzada Dara Shikoh, I was referring to our study under Mian Mir when you were an honored guest of your grandfather, Jahangir."

Dara checked his horse's reins. "Salim! How are you, old friend?"

Salim had been an older student of Mian Mir's, one of his inner circle of followers. He had proven kind, respectful, and easy to talk to during the long years Dara and his brother had been held in Jahangir's court, hostages against another rebellion from Father.

"I am well, Shehzada." Salim's grass-green eyes flicked to the courtiers lining the edge of the pitch. "I have news," he said. "News I fear to impart to any but you."

Dara, made cautious by the seriousness of Salim's tone, set his mount in motion again. Still trying to recover from the surprise, he muttered, "I never understood why you accompanied Baram Khan."

Baram had been sent from the court in disgrace; too powerful to execute, too weak to withstand Father's ire for his transgression and still remain at court. Instead he'd been sent to Europe to investigate rumors of a town said to have sprung, full of wonders, from the earth in a single night.

Salim, covering his face again, said simply, "Mian Mir asked it of me."

"I see."

Dara noticed hoofbeats approaching and turned his head to see Mohammed riding up. Quietly, he said, "I shall make arrangements for you to be brought before me privately. My chief eunuch will know to look for you." He considered a moment. "Tomorrow afternoon?"

"Thank you, Shehzada," Salim said as Mohammed, flushed with success, rode between them both.

Dara, covering for the conversation, mock-scowled and raised his voice: "Thank me by failing to make such passes as that last one! What's more, you say you haven't played at pulu in years? You make rough sport of my poor skills!"

Their horses' ears flicked as Salim chuckled.

Mohammed shot Salim a look that Dara read quite easily: *You had better not be pouring salt on the prince's wounded pride.*

To save Salim from the courtier's ire, Dara spoke to Mohammed, "Well done! I believe the wager was five horses of your choosing from my stables?"

Mohammed revealed his face and bowed in the saddle, "Shehzada, you are too kind! While that was the wager, you are perhaps a bit early in conceding defeat. The last—" The time-keeper's horn, sounding much like an elephant's angry trumpet, cut across Mohammed's words.

Over the nobleman's shoulder, Dara saw Salim give a barely perceptible nod before turning to ride from the field.

Chapter 8

Agra, Red Fort
August 1634

Her favorite garden was quiet but for the buzz of insects and the musical sounds of water over stone. Most of the court were at Mother's tomb while the emperor oversaw some detail of its construction. His absence and the oppressive heat left the Red Fort unusually quiet. Jahanara was taking full advantage of that quiet, enjoying a mango *julabmost*, idly crunching the flavored ice between her teeth while pondering the next few lines of the poem she was composing. The scroll was ready before her, as were ink and brush, but she would commit nothing to paper until the verse was ready in her mind.

One of the harem eunuchs entered the garden and approached her small pavilion. As was proper, he knelt some distance away and waited to be recognized, sweating in the afternoon sun.

Taking pity on him, she handed the remainder of the julabmost to Atisheh, tipping it to indicate the Turkic guard maiden was free to drink it if she chose, and said simply, "Speak."

"Begum Sahib, your brother's wife, Nadira Begum Sahiba, inquires whether you are available to come to her sometime this afternoon?"

Sudden concern stabbed her. Nadira was pregnant with Dara's first child. "Did she say why?" Jealousies ran deep in every harem, and poisoning a rival to end a pregnancy was far from unknown.

"It is some matter that Shehzada Dara Shikoh brought to her

attention, Begum Sahib. Something between him and an amir," a brief hesitation and licking of lips, "whose name escapes this witless servant."

"Oh?"

The eunuch bent forward over his large belly, head nearly touching the grass. "Begum Sahib, I beg forgiveness; it is a worthless slave who forgets too much of his mistress' business to ever warrant the trust placed in him."

Jahanara nodded, understanding the subtext quite well—Nadira had not told the slave the name of her husband's guest, clearly wanting to surprise her. Or the prince himself wanted to limit the ears that would hear the amir's name.

Interest piqued, she spoke: "I will attend Nadira Begum once I am finished here. Take word to her and comfort in knowing that she will not hear of your lapse in memory from my lips."

"You do me great honor, Shehzada Dara Shikoh," Salim said, bowing low over rich carpets. It was not often a lowly amir found himself invited into the inner chambers of one of the Princes of the Blood. So private was the interview that only the carved sandstone of a jali separated the men from the prince's harem. A rare honor indeed.

"It is I who is honored to have you as guest." Dara waved a hand at a cushion beside him. "Please, take your ease and tell us of your travels and the fate of Father's mission to the west and this city the Jesuits claim appeared with a snap of Shaitan's fingers."

A wordless sound of surprise escaped the jali at this announcement of Salim's most recent adventures. Careful not to look too closely at the screen and therefore see the forbidden, Salim crossed to the offered seat and bowed deeply again. While they had been students together, that had been long ago, and he wanted to show the prince every respect. He decided it was better not to ask who was watching from the harem, assuming the prince would tell him if the prince wished him to know.

So close was the rich cushion to Dara Shikoh that Salim was suddenly very glad he'd had opportunity to bathe and perfume himself before the audience. He leaned on his injured arm as he sat, wincing as the movement pulled at the wound. He ignored the pain, hoping it had not been pulled open: far easier to replace a bit of blood than the cotton tunic purchased for this interview. Or worse yet, to spill blood on a cushion or carpet worth more than his yearly income.

The prince's slaves entered and presented refreshments on trays of ornate plate of gold. "First, take refreshment before you tell us of your adventures and the fate of Baram Kahn."

Salim protested, only to have Dara direct a mischievous grin at the jali while speaking to him: "Salim, allow me to fill your belly before you fill our ears. It will serve to whet our appetite for your news."

A throaty, musical note of feminine laughter issued from beyond the jali.

Dara ate little himself, but encouraged Salim to try some of the more exotic dishes.

Too nervous to take note of what he was eating, let alone enjoy the delicacies offered, Salim managed to eat a few sweets and was sipping a deliciously cool drink when a soft voice issued from beyond the jali: "The amir is hurt, Brother."

Dara stopped packing his pipe of opium and looked at Salim, brow arching. "You were injured in our pulu match?"

Mortified, Salim glanced at his arm. Sure enough, blood stained the sleeve. "It is nothing, Shehzada, a momentary disagreement between flesh and arrow."

"Arrow?"

"Robbers on the road here, Shehzada."

"A plague. Some hillmen never learn."

Salim nodded. "They are a problem in every kingdom."

The female voice returned: "Hillmen or robbers?"

Unsure if he should respond directly, Salim did not answer.

Another wicked grin from Dara. "My sister, the Begum Sahib, would have an answer, I think."

Clearing his throat, Salim spoke. "Begum Sahib, not all robbers are hillmen, though it has been my experience that the more successful are."

Another woman giggled, but the penetrating questions continued through it. "Then you were not attacked by hillmen, were you?"

"I thought them Bhils, from their lack of horses and skill at archery. I would not be before you if they had such knowledge."

"And you are a proper hillman, are you not?"

Salim nodded. "My village is just this side of the Khyber Pass, Begum Sahib."

"Pashtun?"

He nodded again. "Yusufzai, yes." He glanced at Dara and found the young prince looking at him, eyes glittering.

"Our forebear passed through there after many great battles."

"A similar tale is told in my family, Begum Sahib," Salim answered, thoughtlessly.

The Princess of Princesses pounced on it. "Similar, only?"

"Oh, you've done it now!" Dara chortled.

"Stop it, Dara! I will not beg Father to have this man trampled by elephants simply for disagreeing with me on points of history!"

Dara laughed outright, then held his breath.

Salim prayed silently.

The moment stretched like the skin of a drum.

Softly, the Begum Sahib spoke again: "Though I might consider going to him if the amir does not answer promptly."

The prince doubled over on his cushion, laughing hard and loud.

"Yes, Begum Sahib. Our family history claims that Emperor Babur took for one of his ten wives the daughter of one of our greatest chiefs, a beauty named Bibi Mubarika. Thus, he and his army had the way opened for them through the Khyber."

"Don't let my little brother—or Father's generals—hear you say that," Dara said between fits of laughter.

A delicate sniff from beyond the jali. "Aurangzeb will not hear it from me, Dara."

Hoping to return the conversation to safer ground, Salim ventured: "It is that marriage, in a roundabout way, which brings me to serve the emperor, Begum Sahib."

Dara gestured at his guest. "The amir Salim is also a fellow student of Mian Mir's teachings, Sister."

Salim nodded. "The saint is wise, and asked me to accompany Baram Kahn on his mission."

Dara looked at the jali. When there was nothing further from Begum Sahib, he gestured for Salim to continue.

"Nur Jahan's man, Baram Kahn, is dead. Poisoned by someone in the kingdom of Thuringia. It was done so that he would not bring back word of the future and what happens to this land."

Agra, Red Fort, The Harem

"Thank you, Shehzada Dara Shikoh," Amir Salim Gadh Visa Yilmaz said with a bow. The man turned and faced the jali, bowing nearly as low as he had for Dara.

She willfully turned away from the impure thoughts that rose up as she looked into the man's pale green eyes, aided by the fact that he could not see her strong reaction.

Nadira, sitting beside her, nudged her with an elbow.

She looked at her sister-in-law. A great beauty, and cousin through their mothers, Nadira was also a friend to Jahanara. When Mother died, Jahanara had been left with the responsibility of planning Dara's marriage celebrations, during which she had come to know and appreciate the kind and gentle spirit of her sister-to-be. Such spirit was not common in the harems of powerful men.

Nadira bent close, whispering, not unkindly, in her ear: "Do not make your brother kill the honorable—and very handsome—amir for loving what he cannot have, Begum Sahib."

Jahanara winced.

Obeisance paid, Salim departed with a horseman's rolling gait.

The Princess of Princesses tried—and failed—to avert her gaze from his strong, broad back.

Nadira giggled softly, shaking her head.

Dara, meanwhile, picked up one of the books the amir had left behind and muttered, "Fascinating."

Fingers twitching with the desire to read them for herself, she cautioned him: "And dangerous, Brother."

He glanced at the jali and frowned, "Well, of course."

"If it is true, how do we present this information to Father?"

"If?"

"Well, I haven't seen the images he gave, and his story beggars belief."

Dara, more excited than she had seen him since his wedding day, picked up the books and two flat pieces of paper Salim had called "photographs" and walked toward the jali. One of his eunuchs opened the concealed portal, ensuring his master did not have to slow. A few more strides and Dara was standing over his wife and sister.

He handed Jahanara the image. It was on a piece of paper,

glossy on one side, no bigger than a large man's hand. The subject within was of a large white-marble building of enormous size and great beauty, surrounded on all four sides by matching minarets with a great giant onion of a dome in the middle. Lettering in the Latin alphabet, inked in lurid red, lined the top of the image.

Nadira, leaning to look over her shoulder, asked, "What did he say this reads?"

"Greetings from the Taj Mahal! Greatest of the Seven Wonders of the World!" Dara answered from memory, smiling fondly at his wife. "They even have the coloring of the letters the correct red, to honor the colors of the family war-tent."

"But what—"

"It is a corruption of Mother's title," Dara answered her question before it was fully voiced.

Nadira even scowled prettily, "Mumtaz Mahal becomes Taj Mahal? How does this happen?"

"I presume it happens after near four hundred years and across several languages, my love."

"But how do you know it's accurate, light of my heart?"

"Father's plans are set and construction begun." He tapped the photograph. "Mother's tomb will look like this, though you cannot see the Moonlit Garden across the river."

Tears filled Jahanara's eyes. To think her father's grief had carried across the centuries and thousands of kos to peoples so distant caused her heart to ache—not for her father, but for her own fate. She would, as a daughter of her house, never marry, never know the heat of a love that would make a man like her father grieve so terribly he would build a monument to their love that would last through the ages.

She lowered her head, shamed by the depth of self-pity she felt. It seemed extraordinarily sinful in the face of what the amir had told them the future histories contained: that two of her brothers would be executed and her father left to wither and die, while Aurangzeb expended the strength of the empire in bloody attempts to suppress the Hindu religion and conquer the remainder of the subcontinent.

Fear and concern for the future of her family rode self-pity and shame down under flashing hooves. Jahanara cleared her throat. "I am willing to believe the amir, but how do we tell Father?"

"Don't you mean what?"

"No, I mean how."

Dara shrugged. "I didn't think he needed to—"

She interrupted: "Father will not be inclined to overlook anything less than full disclosure, Dara. The amir told us that the remainder of Baram Kahn's followers should return within the month." She gestured at the books, "and that they have more of these."

"Yes, but—"

She held up a hand. "Father will find out if we withhold information—Nur Jahan will make sure of it—first Aurangzeb, and then Father, will be told what we have learned today."

Dara sighed so deeply his wife laid a hand on his arm. "I still hold hope that we might yet get Aurangzeb to abandon his religious bigotry and open his heart to Mian Mir's teachings."

"An admirable—even saintly—hope, Dara. Unfortunately, there are far fewer saints in the world than sinners."

Chapter 9

Buy of Moçambique
August 1634

"Gently, lads," Loke hissed as the crew lowered the skiff into the gentle swells.

"You sure about this, Bertram?" John asked as Bertram straddled the rail.

The down-timer looked over the side at the skiff, then back at the distant torches along the walls of Portuguese fort on the north end of the island. "No, not at all. But then again, we need information before we let the monsoon carry us across."

"Got your light?"

Bertram nodded, nervously touching the small but powerful flashlight concealed in his clothing. "Just make sure you are here to see my signal."

"Will do. You sure you don't want one of the boys with you as security?"

"Not unless they learned Arabic? Or can suddenly pass as Swahili?"

John snorted.

Strand stepped up to the rail. "We need to get sailing if we're not to be seen."

"Right." Bertram climbed the rail and down the ropes into boat. He had some limited experience of sailing small boats, but never in the dark of night, in strange waters, in any kind of swell.

Much about this could go so terribly wrong. But despite his misgivings, he set sail and course for the island.

Isla da Moçambique

The beach was a strand of pale white with a blue-green phosphorescence surging along it. Dark lozenges—silhouettes of either fishing boats or longboats drawn up on the sand—marred the strand only occasionally, flaws that framed the beauty rather than detracting from it.

Bertram put his back to that beauty and started rowing as hard as he could. Between his efforts and the better strength of the lightest of onshore breezes in his sail, he rode the gentle surf until the keel of the skiff gouging sand brought the boat to a halt.

It was supposed to be high tide, so the boat shouldn't float off, but Bertram jumped overboard to make sure. The water was cool around his ankles, the night air cooler still as he applied every ounce of his strength to drag the boat a little farther out of the water. He managed to move it barely a handspan before giving it up.

At the far end of the isle squatted the massive, torch-lit bulk of Fort St. Sebastian. An excellent example of the last century's *Trace Italienne* design, the fort had already resisted two serious attempts by the Dutch to take it.

Between his position and the fort were a number of flat-topped stone houses owned by the prosperous Portuguese merchants, mercenaries, and sailors residing on the isle.

While he had a serviceable story ready, Bertram really didn't wish to call any attention to his presence if it could be helped. To the Portuguese he'd be just one more Arab, and the Swahili would be more likely to answer polite inquiries than either the Arabs or the Portuguese. To that end he'd chosen to land at the predominantly Swahili and Arab end of the isle because he hoped to attract less notice come the morning.

As no one seemed to have noticed his arrival, and assuming that he would not be welcome so late at night, Bertram climbed back into the boat.

Wrapping himself in a blanket, he slowly drifted into a fitful doze.

Swahili Town, Isla da Moçambique

"*Simama!*"

Bertram jerked awake to find a large man standing next to his boat, looming over him in the pre-dawn gloaming.

"*Simama!*"

Entirely lacking Swahili, Bertram dusted off his Arabic. "*Asif, sadiqi?*"

A white smile creased the man's face. Using an Arabic dialect Bertram understood with a minimum of concentration, the man said, "Best get off the beach, the Portuguese have been bitten by sand fleas again."

"I do not understand?" Bertram said, collecting his bag and throwing it over his shoulder.

"They are angry."

"Regarding what?"

"Yusuf, again." A shrug accompanied the bald statement that implied he explained all.

"Sorry, friend?" Bertram repeated. Stepping out of the boat, he found himself dwarfed by the local.

They stood a moment as the light gathered, each assessing the other.

"I am Ali," Bertram said.

"And I am Zuberi," the local answered, gesturing toward the round houses of the Swahili village just coming awake with the dawn.

Bertram retrieved the rest of his baggage from the boat while the local explained: "Yusuf was made Christian and then sultan by the Portuguese. Now he fights them after returning to Islam. That is why there are no Portuguese ships in harbor: the captain-major seeks Yusuf with those ships at his disposal. With them gone, those soldiers left in the fort and the people of Stone Town look with suspicion on everyone not Portuguese, making the life of a trader difficult."

"Why am I so blessed to have met a man of such wisdom upon my arrival?"

Another flashing smile and nod toward the fort. "Only wise enough avoid the notice of tax men and soldiers. Speaking of wisdom, or a lack thereof, how did you come to be here, alone, in such a small boat?"

"Calamities, Zuberi. Calamities."

Among the round houses now, Zuberi stopped and turned to Bertram. "I suggest you have a more specific answer ready if confronted by one of the foreign churchmen or Portuguese."

"I have many reasonable lies prepared. I did not wish to employ them with you, Zuberi."

The smile returned. "I appreciate not being lied to. Why are you here?"

"I seek an old acquaintance among the Portuguese."

"Oh? May I know his name?"

"Laurenço De Melo."

Zuberi nodded. "I can show you to his home."

Bertram could not hide his relief. There had been no way of knowing if any of the list of contacts Nasi had furnished would still be alive when he got here, let alone the very first name on it, at the very first port of call. "It is good to know he lives."

"Sorry. You misunderstood: I can take you to the De Melo *family*. His son, Joao De Melo lives there now, carrying on his father's trade."

Hopes dimmed but not undone, Bertram made a few mental adjustments and said, "My question remains: the younger De Melo does not fear or suspect foreigners?"

Zuberi waved a hand. "Only when the priests or soldiers are about."

Bertram nodded. Some assumptions were safer than others, it seemed.

"Do you wish to go to the house now?"

"If you think it safe to do so?"

"Perhaps some food and drink first. Then we can discuss what tiny concessions you might give in exchange for my assistance. *Then* I will take you to the De Melo residence."

Bertram grinned. "Zuberi, I believe you and I shall get along quite well."

Stone Town, Isla da Moçambique

The door closed behind the last of Joao De Melo's servants, leaving Bertram and Joao alone for the first time that evening.

The master of the house picked up one of the silver cups

and the sweating silver pitcher they'd left behind and said, in Spanish, "Drink?"

"Please," Bertram answered in the same tongue, carefully observing his host from one of the high-backed chairs around the small, heavy table dominating the room.

Joao was in his early twenties, about Bertram's height, thin under the fine robe, and dark. Clever hands poured for them both. He handed Bertram his drink and sat across from his guest.

"Nasi sends his regards," Bertram said, placing his other hand on the table. "And his hopes that this," he pushed a small, unmarked gold bar across the table, "will help your interests prosper despite any inconvenience my presence may cause."

As De Melo did not seem moved by the appearance of the small fortune, Bertram tried another approach: "I was saddened to hear of the passing of your father. By all accounts he was a good man."

"He was. For his part, he told me of Don Nasi, who kept so many of our people safe. He had high hopes when he learned Nasi and Abravanel were now in the employ of that town from the future..."

"Grantville."

"Yes, Grantville." Joao drank from his cup again, casting a level look at Bertram before glancing away. After a moment he set his cup down and continued, "Well... despite my father's hopes for the future, I do not wish to join him any time soon."

"How so?"

"If anyone who wishes to ingratiate themselves with the captain or the Church should learn of your presence here, there will be questions. Questions I will have difficulty answering. Questions of the type that often lead to a burning of New Christians."

"The Inquisition is here?" Bertram asked, unable to keep alarm from raising his voice.

Joao nodded emphatically. "In numbers."

"We knew they were in Goa, but not—"

"At first they were only in Goa. They have spread out to the various captaincies in the last year."

"I understand. I will make my stay as brief as possible."

"You are not here hoping I will get you passage on one of His Majesty's ships, then?"

"I am not." Bertram waved a hand. "I simply seek current

information on the situation in the *Estado* in general and Mughal India in particular."

Joao relaxed, marginally. "Seems a great risk merely for information."

"We were not aware the Inquisition was active here. Such dangerous ignorance validates my reasons for coming to you, I should think."

"I see your point." Joao drank, refilled his glass, drank again.

Bertram waited for his host to continue, sipping from his own cup.

"The Jesuits generally presented no great threat to us in themselves, but the other orders followed, and with them, the Inquisition. The seat of every captaincy has had at least a visit, and Goa is uncomfortably thick with servants of the Quaestors. New Christians are wise to be circumspect and avoid notice in these times."

"What about the viceroy? Our information indicated Linhares was not inclined to support the Inquisition."

"He is not. He counts several New Christians as friends, and has openly supported them. But, even his influence can only protect so many, especially when each ship from Lisbon brings more churchmen than soldiers. Indeed, if rumor is to be believed, he is in conflict with some Jesuits over one of the *Estado's* client-kingdoms on the west coast of India."

"Armed conflict?"

Joao nodded and drank.

"The Jesuits are fighting the *Estado*?" Bertram asked, incredulous.

"Using a faction in the *Estado's* client kingdom as their proxy, yes."

Bertram shook his head. "Unbelievable."

"But not a bad thing, as Linhares has sent a small fleet south of Goa to bring the client kingdom to heel, meaning fewer ships to interfere with your journey."

Which led Bertram to ask, "What about the Mughals?"

"I have little specific information on the court. Shah Jahan isn't quite as liberal as Jahangir, but still better than the average European king when it comes to those who don't share his religion."

"Truly?"

"Yes. He only tore down a few temples, and those at the beginning of his reign."

"Anything in particular they are in need of? Trade goods?"

Joao laughed. "Shah Jahan and his senior courtiers can buy kings and their kingdoms—regardless of price—and laugh at the expense."

"I take that as a no, then?"

"You may take it as you like, I am just being realistic: Unless you have some miracle from the future to sell, I doubt you will ever be allowed to join the court."

"Are there other opportunities for trade?" Bertram asked, finishing his drink.

"You mean smuggling?" Joao asked, pouring another for his guest.

Bertram shrugged. "Or other ports, other kingdoms..."

"No other empire or kingdom is such a nexus of trade, and no other port is as free of European dominance as Surat."

"What of the English?"

"They have a factory in Surat, but never regained the influence they enjoyed under Jahangir, and that before the plague and famine of the last few years. Now they don't have many men at all, and relatively few ships."

"Pirates?"

"The most successful are Portuguese, followed by the Dutch. Both are careful not to pirate Mughal trade unless the prize just can't be passed up, however."

"No locals?"

"A fair number, but they generally steer clear of western ships unless they are certain of both victory and a port in which to sell their loot, both of which are at relatively short supply at the moment."

Bertram filled his host's cup, wishing he could take notes... "You have my thanks, Joao. Truly."

"Oh, this—" Joao set his cup down on the gold bar, "goes a long way to settling accounts. And to make us entirely even, you will tell me of Grantville and this USE I have heard so much of. Is it true the people there are free to worship as they please?"

"It is. What's more, the law applies to everyone, not just those who can purchase justice," Bertram said, settling in to answer the man's questions. Grantville provoked interest in all who heard of it, a useful thing when recruiting agents.

Chapter 10

Agra, Red Fort
August 1634

"Shehzada Aurangzeb, a moment of your time, if you please?" the mullah asked, approaching the young prince as he strode along the gallery leading to the stables.

Aurangzeb stopped but motioned for his retinue to continue without him. "Of course, Mullah Mohan."

As a relatively young man, Mullah Mohan had been given responsibility for Aurangzeb and Roshanara's education. And since leaving the harem for adulthood, Aurangzeb found the imam's strict orthodoxy aligned well with his own designs for the future. Especially as that orthodoxy carried with it a core of believers who could very well prove the deciding factor when he and his brothers began the inevitable contest for the throne.

"Peace be upon you, Shehzada," the mullah said with a nod.

"And upon you, peace." Aurangzeb noted he was, at fifteen, already taller than Mohan.

"Forgive my lack of manners, but there is a matter I want to broach with your father but I am told the Sultan Al'Azam is not available."

"That is true. He is overseeing the construction efforts."

"I see. Perhaps, as one of his councilors, you might be able to advise me..."

"This is most unlike you, Mohan. I must say I am disappointed. Never before have you come to me in an attempt to gain access to my father."

"Again, I ask forgiveness for my lack of manners. The matter is very important."

"Perhaps I can hear it, and better judge what is to be done?"

Was that a look of satisfaction? Aurangzeb wondered, watching the other man as he made his reply: "There is a man who is here, now, in Red Fort, one who has turned his back upon God's holy message and made mockery of our faith by engaging in worship before false idols."

"Surely the determination of such is the purview of the learned religious courts?" Those were entirely under Mullah Mohan's thumb.

A sharp nod. "Normally, yes. However, this man, he is . . . favored by certain parties at court and, having been absent the court for years, the case against him has languished because of a lack of complaining witnesses."

"What is it you would have of me?"

Mullah Mohan edged closer and said, voice tight with emotion, "A death, Shehzada."

"What?"

"I would see a sinner dead."

"Who is this man?"

"Amir Salim Gadh Visa Yilmaz."

"I have never heard of him."

"He was sent into exile while you were still in the care of the harem."

"He returns, despite exile? Surely that is sufficient grounds to have him executed and explain your actions later, if necessary."

"I misspoke: he, specifically, was not exiled."

Wishing for a better class of ally, Aurangzeb responded carefully: "Mis-stated details lead to unintended deaths in such matters, Mullah."

"Apologies, Shehzada, in my zeal to do God's work, I overstep."

"Yes, you do. Who is it that favors this man?"

"Your siblings, Shehzada."

"Which?"

"Jahanara and Dara Shikoh, Shehzada."

"I see. I take it, then, that this amir is also a servant of Mian Mir?"

"He was once, yes."

Therein, clearly, lay the true reason the mullah wished him dead. "But no longer?" Aurangzeb asked.

"Truthfully, I do not know."

"Yet you would have his head."

Eyes glittering with intensity, Mohan nodded. "God wills it so, yes."

God? Or his own pride? Aurangzeb had to turn his head to hide his incredulity. "Take no precipitous action. I will consider what to tell Father," Aurangzeb said, turning to leave.

Mohan laid a hand on his arm.

Aurangzeb covered the offending hand with his own, pulled it from his arm and rolled Mohan's fingers back and to the outside of the man's shoulder, twisting fingers, hand and wrist.

Mohan, eyes wide, went to his knees.

Shifting his grip and pushing down, Aurangzeb thrust his face into the older man's. "You dare lay hand upon *me*?"

Pale with pain and shock, Mohan struggled to speak. "I forget myself, such is my desire to do God's work: please, the man *must* die."

"Why?"

"Because God—" Aurangzeb cut him off with more pressure. He had to lean over, he'd bent and twisted the man's arm so far. "Your true reason. Tell me."

Beads of sweat popped from beneath the mullah's turban. "He refuses God." The words were halted behind a cage of pain-clenched teeth.

Aurangzeb wondered if he would have to break his arm to get the truth. "That may be, but there is something else. Answer."

"Mian Mir always favored him."

"And?"

"Favored him over *me*. Loved him, not me..."

Aurangzeb released the man's hand. Mohan pitched forward, cradling his arm.

"The truth will win what you desire of me, Mohan. Remember this as you take what you want."

"Then..."

Aurangzeb straightened. "Do what you will with this man, just be certain the act cannot be placed at my feet."

Agra, Red Fort
The Harem

Aurangzeb stepped away from the balustrade and collected a julab-most. He surveyed the people on the balcony as he drank deeply of the cold juice. Roshanara and Nur Jahan were present, as well as a number of the court's lesser luminaries. Father was off overseeing the construction, again. Jahanara and Dara were entertaining elsewhere in the fort. There were just a few of Father's other women present, all of them engrossed in the elephant fight taking place by the riverside.

It was, due to the many distractions, the only time he was likely to get a private word with Nur Jahan.

Roshanara stepped away to tease one of their younger siblings.

He joined his great-aunt, taking a seat among the many cushions.

"Aurangzeb," she said, handing off her empty drink to rid herself of it and the nearest ears that might overhear their conversation.

"Nur Jahan," he answered, suddenly wary. Her reputation and their shared history made her loom large in his imagination, despite her current distance from power.

"You are looking well."

"And you . . . smell like the original garden," he said, truthfully.

She smiled, teeth stained red with betel-juice. "A new perfume."

"Yours?"

"Of course."

"You must teach my wives this art."

"Wives? I had thought you only married the one time, thus far."

"I will have many more." And he would never allow any of them to rule his life as Nur Jahan had ruled his grandfather's.

"Indeed, and you will have them, and many strong sons, I am sure of it."

That might be a genuine compliment—or a barbed reminder of his own position, surrounded by inferior siblings.

Aloud, he asked a different question: "You wished to speak to me?"

"Do you recall Baram Khan?"

"The one who was banished? The last of your allies at court, wasn't he?"

"I would hope that you speak of past days, and not current state of affairs," she said, a gentle rebuke he refused to acknowledge.

"I remember him."

"He is gone to his greater reward."

"Oh?"

"Poisoned, though we do not know by whom"—she waved a hand—"but the 'who' is really not that important. Of greater interest is that word has reached me that the amir Yilmaz left Baram Khan's party without leave. I am told he is carrying information of great import to the court."

"What news?" he asked, immediately annoyed at how easily his voice betrayed his interest.

"I do not know. The message I received was conveyed in a medium which is, for reasons I am sure you'll understand, not trusted to keep secrets from parties who would read my correspondence without permission."

"I see. What did you say the man's name is?"

"Amir Salim Gadh Visa Yilmaz." That was the very man Mullah Mohan had petitioned him for permission to slay. *Interesting*.

"Does the name mean anything to you?" she asked.

"No, should it?" The lie was easy.

"He and Dara Shikoh became fast friends while you both were your grandfather's guest."

Anger flashed, made him snap: "Is that what we're calling it now?"

"I believe it a polite fiction that serves everyone involved."

"Yes, I can see how *you* would take comfort in that belief. It was not you who was taken from the arms of loved ones."

Her only response was to sit silent, expression unreadable.

Silently, he cursed himself. That had not been a useful thing to say. She needed to think that all was forgiven, that she was a partner in his plans, if he wanted her to be the lodestone for any ill-will his actions might cause.

Resolving to exert more control over such fits of temper, Aurangzeb looked her in the eye: "That was unworthy. It was not my intent to speak thus. Forgive me?"

She nodded.

"Any idea what news this amir carries?"

"None." A delicate sniff. "My astrologer claims the man carries news from the future."

He smiled. "She does, does she?"

She did not return the smile. "Yes."

Aurangzeb cautioned himself to have a care with casual

dismissals of possible truths: such was the claim of the Portuguese, as well, and all things were possible in God's Design.

Agra, The River Yamuna

As his hired boat turned in toward Agra's docks, Salim noticed a boat that had departed Red Fort just after his changing course for shore. Two armed men stood behind the boatman paddling at the bow, but there was no visible cargo for them to guard, and both looked away when Salim turned his face in their direction.

He leaned over and spoke to the boat's master. "If you can push the men hard for shore without appearing to, it will mean another rupee for you."

The boatman, likely experienced with court intrigues, simply bobbed his head and started pulling deeper and harder with his paddle. His men took their lead from him and did so as well. Salim, not wanting to give the game away, looked straight ahead and fished in his sash for the payment.

During the last hundred paces to the dock, his boat had to maneuver around an outgoing craft. Salim took the opportunity to cast a surreptitious glance at the other boat. The distance between them had grown to nearly fifty paces, but he could see one of the armed men was bending their boatman's ear about closing the distance while the other openly stared in Salim's direction.

Now certain they were following him, Salim wondered who they served: Nur Jahan, would-be chooser of emperors, or her brother, Asaf Kahn, the emperor's first minister—or perhaps Mullah Mohan, Aurangzeb's strictly orthodox teacher and advisor?

Not that it mattered if they were sent to do him harm. And, being armed and lacking in subtlety, just watching him go about his business didn't seem likely.

Their lack of skills at intrigue did seem to rule out Nur Jahan, but she might be running short of skilled servants this long after being consigned to the harem with her grandniece.

Asaf Kahn was still in favor at court, and therefore had no need of subtlety, but Salim knew of no reason the wazir would want him accosted or killed.

No, the more he thought on it, the more likely it seemed that Mullah Mohan was behind these men. The mullah had no love of Mian Mir's accepting policy toward the Hindus and other religions of the land, and had tried to get the living saint removed from his position as teacher to Shah Jahan's children on more than one occasion.

As the boat nudged the dock, Salim dropped payment in the master's lap and stepped off. The man's breathless but cheerful thanks followed the Pashtun as he turned for the crowded market at the foot of the docks. He glanced back as he neared the first of the merchant's stalls. The men had made landfall and were hurrying to catch up, shoving people out of their way.

Salim merged with the crowds of shoppers, bearers, and traders. The market had the frenetic atmosphere such places took on before the muezzin called the faithful to sunset prayers. Not that all, or even most, of the people shared faith in Allah and His Prophet; but the Hindus of the capital were cautious, not inclined to even the appearance of disrespect toward the religion of their ruler, and would slow or cease business during the hours of prayer. That could pose problems once the call to prayer began.

He lost track of the men within three steps. Hoping they would do the same, he started in the direction of his lodgings. The sun continued its dive to the hills beyond the river.

Salim saw the boy hanging by one hand from the trellis of an inn as he was leaving the market. He wouldn't have thought anything of the skinny urchin but for the fact the boy pointed straight at him and continued to do so as he moved through the crowds.

"Paid eyes," he muttered. Were he given to cursing, Salim would have. Instead he quickened his steps, hoping to get out of sight before the boy could direct the men to him.

"There!" It wasn't a shout, but the word was spoken with an air of command.

Salim turned and saw one of the men from the boat. The man was already pounding his way, naked steel in hand. The more distant man was waving an arm, most likely summoning more men.

Breaking into a run, Salim looked for places to lose his pursuers or, if he must, make a stand. Nothing looked promising in the first length of road but he hesitated to take one of the side streets for fear it would dead end. He held little hope of outrunning the pursuers. Had he a horse, even a nag, under him, things would be different. But afoot—he could already hear the first man closing the distance.

He picked a spot, deciding it was as good as any. Placing his back to a stack of great clay urns, Salim turned to face his pursuer, blade flickering to hand.

The younger man didn't slow, charging in, howling "God is great!" as he swept his blade down in an untrained and fatally stupid overhand cut.

Salim deflected the blade to his outside right and twisted his wrist, sending his own slashing across the man's torso.

Unable to stop, the man ran up the blade and opened his gut to the evening air, the battle cry becoming a wail for his mother. He tripped in his own entrails, fell to his knees. Salim hacked his head from his shoulders, counting it a mercy.

He turned and saw that the easy killing of the one had given his other pursuer pause. Knowing he was done for if the man waited for more assistance, Salim smiled.

The man didn't respond.

Salim rolled his wrist. Steel hissed as it parted air, casting a thin line of blood in the dust of the street. By happenstance instead of intent, a drop of blood just reached the other man's boot.

Eyes wide with rage, uneven teeth bared behind his thick beard, the man advanced. Despite the anger, this man was a far more capable adversary. Salim was forced to retreat, working to deflect several fast and powerful strokes.

Timing them, he found an opening and chopped a short hard strike at the other man's hand. It missed the mark but slapped the inner curve of the other's sword, sending it out of line.

Switching tactics, Salim stepped closer and forced the other man's sword farther out of line. He shot his free hand around the back of the man's neck and pulled, hard, even as he threw his own head forward.

Cartilage and bone ruptured under his forehead.

Fireworks exploded.

Still blinking, he chopped a blow at his reeling opponent that had more of savagery than art. His sword cleaved the man's collarbone and hacked through the first three bones of the upper ribcage.

"Heretic!" the man burbled, mouth quickly filling with blood.

Mullah Mohan, it is, then.

The dead man collapsed, eyes still full of hate.

The muezzin called the faithful to prayer as Salim turned and resumed his run.

Chapter 11

Agra, Red Fort, Diwan-i-Khas
August 1634

Dara joined his younger brothers, standing before Father's throne in the Diwan-i-Khas.

As befitted the hall of private audience, there were comparatively few courtiers present, and those who were held high *zat* and sowar ranks—either diwans, holders of large *Zamind*, or extensive *Mansabs*.

"Any idea what this is about?" Shah Shuja asked, as Dara came to a halt beside him.

"None."

"Possibly," Aurangzeb answered at the same time.

Both elder brothers looked at their younger brother, who punched his thin beard at the pair of generals standing to one side. "Military matters. Either the Deccan or the Sikhs."

Field command, then. Dara tried to hide his excitement.

"The Sikhs?" Shuja scoffed, "What, did they refuse to pay their taxes?"

"No. The new guru, he has caused a dais to be built. One, it is said, higher than that of our father."

Shuja made a throwing motion. "An insult, but not a threat requiring an army."

"Perhaps."

"Farmers?" Shuja sneered, "How could such as they prove a threat sufficient to warrant Father's attention?"

It was Dara's turn to disagree with Shah Shuja: "Guru Hargobind has not sat idle, Brother. It is said he took up two swords at his investiture, one denoting temporal justice and the other, spiritual. Further, he trains his followers to defend themselves."

Shuja didn't look convinced.

Aurangzeb nodded. "Still, barring some further provocation I'm not aware of, I doubt the Sikhs are the reason for this sudden summons. It almost has to be the Deccan." He looked at Dara. "Wasn't your teacher a friend to the last guru?"

Dara nodded, uncomfortable at the thought. "He was. I—I don't doubt that he still is."

"Then he will not be pleased to hear of this."

"We shall see," Dara murmured as Father entered.

The emperor strode across to his dais and seated himself on the throne, the majordomo declaring the audience open and announcing to the Diwan-i-Khas the emperor's lengthy title and honors.

For his part, Dara watched Father closely: the emperor's expression revealed little, but one of his slippered feet was gently tapping the floor, a sign he was deeply concerned by what he was about to reveal. Eventually the majordomo wound down, and Father revealed the purpose for the assembly.

"My sons, my people, there has been yet another incident with the Sikhs. A party of my nobles, Mukhlis Khan chief amongst them, were entrusted with the training of the royal hawks and were engaged in that duty to me when my white hawk went missing." A murmur went through the crowd. The white hawk was a rarity, and losing it would surely mean Mukhlis Khan would suffer the emperor's ire.

"They discovered the hawk, shining in the mews of a Sikh hunting party encamped nearby. When they went to claim the hawk from this party of Sikhs, they were not only refused and insulted, they were assaulted! The insult might have been forgiven, but this Hargobind refuses to return my hawk, given to me by my friend, the Shah of Persia!"

Angry murmurs went through the assembled nobles. There was, if Dara wasn't mistaken, a strong undertow of contentment beneath the anger. War meant plunder and glory, and a chance to rise.

"Told you," Aurangzeb muttered.

Dara caught the dirty look Shuja cast Aurangzeb's way. He didn't like having his face rubbed in it. Their younger brother just smiled.

That was neither kind nor wise. Things had been unpleasant enough since Aurangzeb published his damned poem. It was one thing to talk like that to Dara himself, but Shuja wasn't one to lie down and take it.

"Check your tongue, little Brother," Shuja grated.

"Why, does a fool wish to add something?"

Dara felt Shuja tense beside him and glanced at the throne. Sure enough, the muttering of his siblings had brought Father's gaze down on them. He did not look pleased.

Probably Aurangzeb's design, this making his brothers look bad before Father. Ah well, each must be disappointed, from time to time.

Dara stepped forward, bowing his head and waiting to be recognized.

He heard Shuja stop mid-mutter, saw Aurangzeb twitch out of the corner of his eye. *Thought you'd keep us off-balance and secure the command for yourself, did you? I'm tired of the whispers at court: those that say I am content to sit in Father's shadow, that I avoid fighting as distasteful. I long to put paid to the rumors that it is my wish that makes it so.*

The truth is, Father refuses to send me away from him, fearing I might turn against him, as he turned against his father.

Realizing the emperor was watching him, and conscious of the entire court standing silent behind, Dara spoke: "Your son stands ready to ride out and punish your enemies, Father."

"Does he?" The emperor's tone was not enthusiastic, and his expression dark.

"If it pleases you, yes."

"Your first wife is pregnant with Our first grandson, is she not?"

"She is, indeed," Dara answered, swallowing fear. It had occurred to him that Father might use his unborn child as yet another excuse not to send him.

"And you would suffer to be parted from her at this time?"

Dara, expecting the question, answered immediately: "To serve you, I will...while taking comfort in the knowledge that they will have the very best of care here."

In Father's day, Mother had gone with him on every campaign, but her death in camp guaranteed he'd never allow another pregnant member of the family on campaign.

"Will you listen to the general I will send with you? More than that: will you heed his advice?"

"I will." Though he would like to know who, exactly, the emperor would send to be his shepherd. He glanced at the gathered nobles, but none met his eye or gave indication that they knew who would command.

"Very well, I name you Amir of Amirs; you shall command five thousand, and have the Red Tent to crush this upstart, take his wealth, take his women, take his life. Bring all before me and be rewarded."

Dara bowed, glowing inside. *At last, the Red Tent, symbol of the emperor for the campaign!*

"I will personally oversee the gathering of your staff for this campaign, Dara Shikoh. Be ready in a week's time, when all is in readiness for your journey to Ramdaspur."

"I shall, Your Majesty!" The words came louder than he'd intended, such was his excitement. Not even the jealous looks his brothers cast in his direction could dim the fires of his enthusiasm.

Aurangzeb quickly smoothed his expression. It would not do to let Father see how displeased he was with Dara's good fortune.

Shuja did not bother to hide his displeasure, and Aurangzeb saw Shah Jahan's eyes tighten fractionally as the emperor watched his sons.

Wazir Asaf Khan strode before the emperor and bowed. "I would serve you, Shah Jahan. With your permission I will assist Dara Shikoh as he enacts your will." Aurangzeb thought that was typical of his grandfather: clinging to whoever held the reins of power.

"I must deny you, Asaf Khan. Mukhlis Khan will be Dara's subordinate and chief advisor for this, as it is his complaint we seek redress for. Fear not, father of my most beloved, I will be sending you to face down Ahmednagar."

Aurangzeb did not miss the surprise the emperor's order caused to flit across Asaf's face, as their eldest male kinsman bowed and said: "Certainly, Shah Jahan. I serve."

"You will command my armies there, and coordinate with

Mahabat Khan to bring the Sultan to heel. You will assist Dara ordering his troops as you gather your own."

"Yes, Shah Jahan. May I invite you and your sons to hunt with me? The sowar will need training, and there have been reports of tigers to the east."

The emperor waved a jewel-studded hand. "Affairs of state prevent me, but my sons will be happy to accompany you."

Aurangzeb hid his displeasure. A hunt would hardly prove a sufficient sop to this new injury.

"While regretting the affairs that keep you here, I am honored to host your sons to the hunt."

Dara, still riding the high of his appointment to command, nodded acceptance of the invitation.

Shuja actually looked excited by the prospect of hunting.

Aurangzeb let none of his thoughts show. They were always a disappointment to him, his elder brothers: one a heretic lover of Hindu philosophy constantly rewarded for his mediocrity, the other easily baited into dissolution by whatever new entertainment crossed his path. He did still hold out hope that Murad might prove a man worthy of respect.

Aurangzeb supposed he should be content enough at the situation, however. Dara was not likely to succeed as a general, and failing to do as ordered would surely wake his father to the fact that he'd chosen to favor the wrong son. Shuja would be dealt with, when the time came, and Murad was still young enough to be easily influenced, once he was free of the harem.

Court went on. Aurangzeb scarcely paid any attention, so caught up in thinking through his next moves that he almost missed Shah Jahan declaring the session at an end.

Released to do as they would, a pack of lesser courtiers approached Dara, hoping to ingratiate themselves with the rising star and improve their position in life.

Shuja turned to him. "Dara gifted me a new musket from the production of his *kharkhanas*. He is always bragging about the fine weapons his *Atishbaz* make. I will use it on the hunt, and prove his words true or false."

"And I am sure you will take a few prize beasts with it," Aurangzeb replied absently, watching who was pressing forward to congratulate their brother. Such sycophants would not be permitted positions of power when he ruled.

"A few! Care to wager who will take the greater portion of game?" Shuja spoke loudly enough to gather the attention of courtiers not in their immediate circle. Most of them preferred Shuja over Aurangzeb because the former was an indolent wastrel and Aurangzeb's reputation was abstemious.

"Not really."

"I insist!"

"Very well, what stakes?"

"My gun against the horse Father gifted you last week!"

"You know I do not favor guns as you do."

"All right, one of my horses, then."

"My choice?"

Shuja grinned. "Of course."

"Very well. I will take more game than you and win a horse of my choosing from your stables. If I fail, you may select one of mine."

"I shall win, and take your finest steed!" Shuja crowed, the herd of sycophantic cattle lowing in agreement as they followed him out.

Agra, Red Fort, The Harem

"What is it?" Nur asked.

"My Lady, your servant Vidya has taken ill." Gargi made a small gesture that indicated Vidya was dying, if not already dead.

"Oh?" Nur said, conscious of the eunuchs listening at each guard post. Something was seriously amiss. Gargi had identified the young woman as a spy in someone's service almost as soon as she started working for Nur, but they had still been trying to discover who, precisely, her hidden master was.

"Yes, some ailment of the digestion. I am afraid she will soon die."

Nur arched a carefully manicured brow.

Gargi gave a barely perceptible nod in response to the unspoken question. She'd ordered the girl killed, then. For Gargi to take such precipitous action indicated a greater threat.

Damn these listeners, I did not want to get the new henna wet. "Come with me, Gargi, this sad news makes me wish to see growing things and feel the grass beneath my feet. Let us walk in the gardens."

"Yes, mistress."

They stepped out of the apartments and into the gardens, making their way to one of Nur's favorite features: a man-made stream rushing down a sloping ramp of scalloped stone, causing it to ring and splash like playful music. The grounds immediately next to the fountain were damp with cast-off water, but the noise served to cover her murmured question: "Why did you kill her?"

Kneeling, Gargi extended a cupped hand to the fountain as if catching some spray. Only Nur could see the small vial nestled there. "She was going to poison you."

Nur Jahan hid a smile. Someone thought her a threat significant enough to warrant assassination. That was quite flattering.

"How was it done?"

"I fed her some of my own."

"I see. And the body?"

"It will be dumped this evening. Another dead slave."

"Did you discover her master or mistress first?"

Gargi sniffed. "There was no time."

"Make time, in future."

Gargi bowed her head, all humility.

"She will not be easily replaced. We will have to watch carefully who is selected to replace her."

Gargi stood. "Yes."

"What to do in the meantime?" Nur mused.

"I will be sure to check with our sources, see if I can uncover who is discomforted by news the girl is dead."

"Wait a bit...Perhaps I should take ill?"

Gargi nodded, thoughtful. "That might prove useful. I can observe who seems pleased at your 'illness' or takes some unprecedented action with you out of the way. What were you to do tonight?"

Nur shook her head. "Nothing special: feasting with the emperor and his harem."

A thin smile creased Gargi's lips. "And how much would we have given for you to be able to say that this time last year?"

Nur matched the smile with her own. "True."

Aurangzeb's face flashed before her eyes, killing the smile.

"What is it, mistress?"

"Aurangzeb said something that remained with me, if only because it seems to indicate he does not consider himself an ally: he said Baram Khan had been the last of my allies here at court."

"If he does not think you can aid him in his designs, why ask you here at all?"

"He plays a deep game, my brother's grandson. Deeper than I would have thought for one so young."

Gargi's lips twisted, a good indication she didn't believe the words about to come from her mouth: "Perhaps he has no other design than to have you here, under his eye?"

"He has other designs, of that I am sure..."

"Dara?"

"No, I don't see him attempting something like this, his nose pressed in Hindu texts."

"The emperor?"

That gave Nur pause. She shook her head, eventually. "I see no reason he should suddenly shift from his longstanding policy of ignoring me."

Gargi shrugged. "You have come to his court, making it harder for him to ignore the fact that you yet live."

"A point, but he could have simply denied my request and sent some favor-currying courtier to end my life in Lahore, had that been his wish. No, a slave-girl poisoner is not Shah Jahan's style, nor has it ever been. He was my adversary too long for me to fail to recognize his hand, were he involved."

"Your brother?"

"No, and for much the same reasons as the emperor. Besides, he—even more than the emperor—would not stoop to use a woman to do such things."

"Which sets me to thinking that this does smack of a woman's hand..."

"Or a eunuch..."

"Certainly the harem..."

"Yes—" she shook her head, "It's all just conjecture until we have more information. I will stay in tonight, and you will send messages to Jahanara and the emperor that I have taken ill."

"And keep watch."

Nur smiled. "Oh, yes."

Father settled himself, the unrelieved white of his robes of mourning making him stand out among the reds and golds of the cushions like a lily among orchids. Prayer beads in hand, he nodded at Jahanara.

Two slaves, selected for their pleasing manner and skill at anticipating the emperor's needs as much as their desire to serve as tasters, knelt to either side of him, ready to serve the choicest morsels. At her direction, other harem girls entered carrying tray after tray of delights for his meal.

Beyond ensuring the service was faultless, Jahanara spared no thought for the food. Instead she watched Father closely from under long lashes. There were lines on his face and white in his beard that had not been there before her mother passed. The thought of Mother, especially at this moment, brought a hollow ache to her spirit.

Instead of turning from the ache, she embraced it, armored herself in it, knowing Mother would approve of her actions today, despite what woe she might bring Father. And Jahanara had no doubt the plan would add to Father's woes, just as she had no doubt that what she was about was absolutely necessary for the survival of the family—most especially if her family were to mean more to history than a divisive, degenerate, and despotic dynasty that left the varied nations under their care open to occupation and subjugation by the English.

Jahanara glanced down the line of women to her left, those who were not his wives but lived under Father's protection in the harem. As she had arranged, Nur Jahan was not present due to an upset stomach. It had been the one point of failure of the plan: it was never certain exactly *when* her woman in Nur's service could administer some of the mild poison, and harder still to judge when it would take effect. That difficulty combined with the fact that Dara could not very well linger in the harem led her brother to grant permission for her to speak to their father on behalf of both of them.

No sooner had Dara agreed to let her speak for him than Asaf Kahn had invited Dara to a hunt a few days from Agra. He had only departed this morning, so it had been just barely possible her eunuch messenger Prasad would find Dara and return in time. Father finished the main courses, began to indulge in a few desserts.

Time was nearly up.

All the preparation and planning had led to this moment. Despite Dara's absence, she must move forward.

Mustering courage, she spoke: "Father?"

He turned his head to look upon her, eyes warming ever so slightly as they lit on her face. "Yes, Daughter?"

"I have something I wish to show you, something important."

He waved a hand, granting her leave to approach.

She rose and padded to him on henna-painted feet. The slave-girls rose gracefully and retreated to stand with their backs to the wall of the Red Fort.

Father watched her, a sad smile making his beard twitch. "You are so like your mother, Jahanara."

The princess knelt before her father and bowed deeply, smiling in return. "It is good to hear you speak of her without such pain."

He punched his bearded chin in the direction of the growing monument to his love. "The heart heals as her monument rises, Daughter. Even so, I will never be whole again until we are together in Paradise."

She bowed her head again, suddenly uncertain.

He sighed, the sound bearing more of quiet contentment than pain. He took her hand. "What is it, beloved Daughter?"

"Father, I would show you a picture."

"Oh?"

"But first—do you remember sending Baram Kahn on his errand?"

Shah Jahan's grip tightened on her hand. "To the village the Jesuits reported had sprung into being someplace in Europe?" he asked sharply.

"Yes, Father," Jahanara answered, worried that she had chosen the wrong entry to the conversation. The Jesuits and their hosts, the Portuguese, were only recently returned to, if not favor, then the tolerance of the emperor. The Portuguese and their priests had proved faithless when Father requested their aid in his rebellion against Jahangir and his stepmother, Nur Jahan. Possessed of a long memory, Shah Jahan had ordered punitive raids against the Portuguese, most notably at Hugli in Western Bengal, almost as soon as he took the throne, taking many slaves.

"What of it?" he asked, more calmly, gaze already drifting over her shoulder to the distant site of her mother's tomb.

She took a breath, dove in: "It did come from the future, as Mother's astrologers claimed."

His gaze snapped to her face, locking her eyes to his like chains of hardened steel. "And where is Baram Kahn?" he demanded.

"Where is that craven supporter of Nur Jahan? Does he think to avoid my eternal anger by telling my daughter his report in my stead? I am not the man I was when his perfidy—"

Jahanara, shaken by the heat in him, spoke quickly: "Dead, Father. Baram Kahn sickened and died in that far-off land that is host to the village from the future."

Shah Jahan looked away, sniffed.

Released from his gaze, Jahanara felt as if she had stepped from a cold darkness into warm sunlight. Remembering her purpose, she gathered her tattered calm and summoned her body-slave to bring forward the "postcard."

"Who brings his lies before us, if he is dead?"

She took the card. "I beg your indulgence, Father. Decide after you have seen the proofs before dismissing the claims."

"Who?" he asked, still insisting, but more gently.

"No one you know, Father. He is another disciple of Mian Mir, one who has proven an honest and loyal servant to the living saint and, by extension, your person. He took great risks—even feigning his own death—to bring word ahead of Baram Kahn's remaining servants."

Clearly still skeptical, the emperor opened his mouth to ask another question.

Greatly daring, Jahanara spoke over him. "This, Father, is one of the proofs." She lowered her head and presented the postcard.

His hand left hers and pulled the postcard from her fingers.

She left her hand extended, hoping he would take it again.

Long moments passed in a silence Jahanara barely dared breathe into.

A tear struck her palm. Jahanara looked up.

Shah Jahan, Sultan of Sultans, Sultan of the World, cried a river of tears in total silence, postcard in hand.

Chapter 12

Three day's ride from Agra
August 1634

Her patience growing short in the afternoon heat, Dara's favorite leopard yowled and spat at her handler, ready to hunt.

Dara grinned, ready as well, welcoming the prospect of release from the tension being around Aurangzeb always provoked in him. Now, if only they could begin. His small army of beaters had started the day before, working through the night to drive all the wild game resident in several square kos toward where the hunting party lay in wait. The camp was loud with the voices of men and animals, many of Father's more notable umara present to witness the hunt and curry favor with the wazir and princes.

Seeking distraction, Dara again took up the gun he'd had as a wedding gift from Father last year, the inlaid piece monstrously heavy yet reassuring in its solidity. He sighted down the nearly two *gaz* of barrel, arms immediately trembling from the weight of iron, ivory inlay, and mahogany. Among the many refinements, the weapon sported one of the new flintlocks rather than the traditional matchlock, and even had a trigger rather than lever.

"Here," he grunted.

Body slaves overseen by his Atishbaz gunsmith, Talawat, hurriedly set up the iron tripod needed to support the hunting piece while he struggled to hold position.

"Ready, Shehzada," Talawat said.

Trying to keep the weight under control, Dara slowly lowered

91

the gun onto the mount. Talawat slotted the pin into place that would hold the gun's weight when aimed, easing the awkward weight from Dara's arms. The prince knelt and placed the butt of the weapon on the cushion another slave hurriedly set in place.

As he rubbed the ache from his biceps, hoofbeats drew Dara's attention. He looked down the gradual slope to the pair of watering holes that formed the two sides of the killing zone for the hunt. About one hundred gaz of grassy clearing lay between the slowly drying watering holes, with about half that much distance between Grandfather's tent and the open space. The beaters were working toward that spot in a steadily shrinking circle.

One of Asaf Khan's men emerged from the wood line at a gallop, crossing the clearing and pounding up to the camp. In a fine display of horsemanship, the sowar swung down from his mount to land lightly a few paces in front of Dara's grandfather.

Standing in the shade of his tent, Asaf Khan stepped forward and listened as the young trooper made his report: "At least a hundred head of blackbuck and red antelope, a small herd of nilgai, Wazir. Tiger spoor was also found, but no one has laid eyes on it, yet. Should not be long, now, before the first of the beasts makes an appearance."

Asaf Khan dismissed his man. Gray beard dancing, the aging but still-powerfully-built wazir called out: "A tiger would make a worthy prize for one of my grandsons!"

"Perhaps for Dara, Grandfather. He has yet to take one," Aurangzeb drawled from inside the tent.

Dara watched Asaf's smile dim before he turned and answered, "One tiger could never be enough for the sons of Shah Jahan."

"I did not say it was, Asaf Khan," Aurangzeb replied, striding from the tent into the sun.

"I will kill it, Grandfather!" Shah Shuja crowed, raising his bow. Born between Aurangzeb and Dara, Shuja seemed always afire with desire to please his elders. At eighteen he was a man grown, however, and larger than Dara by a head. Of course, that head was rarely full of things other than those he might hunt, fight, or ride.

Asaf turned to face his eldest grandson. "And you, Dara?"

"I will take what it pleases God to place before me."

"Pious words," Asaf said, nodding approval.

Behind Grandfather's back, Aurangzeb shook his head and commanded his horse be brought up.

"Where are you going?" Asaf asked, edges of his beard curling down as he frowned.

"I will take the animals my brothers miss. That way I am sure to have a good day hunting."

Shah Shuja grunted as if punched in the belly, face darkening. He too had been shamed by the poem making the rounds of the court. Further, there was the wager.

Doing his best to ignore the insult, Dara gestured at his leopards. "Brother, that is why I have brought my cats, to run down escaping game."

Aurangzeb shrugged, took up a lance. "Then I will race your cats, and beat them to the kill as well."

Asaf stepped toward Aurangzeb, raising hands in a conciliatory gesture. "I would advise caution, Brave One. If there is a tiger in among them, it will easily overtake a horseman. They can only be hunted safely from elephant back."

Aurangzeb shrugged again. "Then it will be as God wills it," he said, putting spurs to his tall horse and speeding off to the left of the firing line and the sole exit to the killing ground, a trail of attendants and guards in tow.

"Here they come!" cried one of Grandfather's cronies.

As the man's cry faded, a small herd of blackbuck, no more than eight animals, spat from the line of brush and trees. Bounding with the outrageous speed of their kind, the antelope seemed to fly across the open ground.

Dara shook his head, irritation flaring. Blackbuck were perfect game for his hunting cheetahs but he couldn't risk one of the cats attacking Aurangzeb or his horse.

Dara held out a hand. Talawat filled it with one of his lighter pieces, match cord already glowing. Shouldering it, Dara picked his target: a good-sized, healthy animal just behind the leading beast.

He heard Shuja's bowstring slap bracer. A moment later Shuja muttered angrily.

Ignoring all distraction, Dara's world shrank to the chest of the beast he'd chosen. Finding it, he moved his point of aim two hands ahead along the shallow arc of its jump.

He pulled the lever and averted his eyes at the very last moment.

The gun thundered.

Dara handed it off to Talawat as the blackbuck fell, heart shot. The gunsmith handed him another piece.

Shuja shouted, his second arrow striking the lead buck in the belly.

Dara ignored the cheering of his grandfather's entourage, chose another buck, aimed, fired. Another clean hit to the chest. The antelope collapsed after a few strides.

"Well done, Talawat. Your guns speak truly," he said, passing the weapon off.

Talawat bowed, presenting another piece. "Shehzada is too kind."

Taking the third gun in hand, Dara waited a moment, allowing the smoke to clear. Behind him, Talawat's apprentices busied themselves reloading the discharged weapons.

"Your modesty is a sign of fine character, but"—Dara tapped a knuckle against the gun's hardwood stock—"in this instance, misplaced."

Talawat smiled and bowed again before gesturing at the field. "I merely prepare the weapons, Shehzada; it is not everyone that has your fine eye for shooting."

Shuja downed another of the blackbuck with an arrow that nearly passed through the animal. The first beast he'd hit finally collapsed, blood frothing from its muzzle.

The remains of the herd cleared the firing line, only to run into Aurangzeb and his mounted party. Dara's brother took an antelope with his spear as its herd mates ran past. Leaving the weapon behind and spurring his horse into a gallop, Aurangzeb switched to the horse bow. The prey were far faster than his mount, stretching their lead even as Aurangzeb drew, aimed, and loosed twice in quick succession. Each arrow struck home in a separate neck, a fine feat of archery.

Asaf's cronies cheered, as did Shuja, who had approached Dara.

Cradling his gun, Dara smiled, despite himself.

Aurangzeb cased his bow while sending his finely trained mount circling back among his followers with just the pressure of his knees, an act of understated pride in its own right.

"I should have ridden instead of standing here with you and your guns," Shuja grumbled, loud enough for Dara to hear.

Dara did not answer, even when his younger brother ordered his horse brought up and left to join Aurangzeb.

He watched his grandfather instead, pondering the old man's place in the family history as well as his possible future. Abdul Hasan Asaf Khan had turned against his own sister to support Father when Dara's paternal grandfather, Jahangir, passed and the succession came into question once again. Dara had himself been hostage and surety against his father's loyalty after that first rebellion, and was no stranger to the price of failure for princes engaged in rebellion. Shah Jahan and his allies had emerged victorious, but it had been a close-run and uncertain thing, all the way to the end. Asaf had been rewarded with position, titles, and power, though recent failings had reduced his favor at court. Father was considering removing him from the office of wazir and sending him off to govern Bengal.

As if sensing Dara's thoughts were upon him, Dara's grandfather turned from watching the slaves collect carcasses and approached Dara.

Talawat bowed and silently withdrew a few paces, giving them some privacy.

Asaf pushed his beard out toward Shuja's retreating back, "Well, first among the sons of my daughter, it seems your brothers would hunt as our ancestors preferred."

Dara nodded. "I would as well, but for this," he said, gesturing with his free hand at the new gun on its tripod.

Smiling, Asaf bowed his head and squinted at the weapon a few moments. "Big ball?"

"Large enough to down nilgai in one shot...or a tiger."

"Brave man, hunts a tiger with powder and shot rather than bow and spear."

Dara shrugged. "Surely not in the company of so many men, Asaf Khan?"

Asaf Khan waved a hand. "Abdul, or...grandfather...if it pleases."

Catching the plaintive note in his grandfather's voice, Dara smiled. "Surely, *Grandfather*, I would not be at risk among so many men."

"Jahangir once lost three favored umara to one, a great she-tiger. And they were all armed to the teeth and born to the saddle. Tigers do not feel pain as we do; most wounds merely madden them."

Dara was about to answer when another herd, or perhaps the

larger body of the one just harvested, emerged from the wood line, dashing for the open space between the watering holes. At the rate they were fleeing, the beasts would be in range in moments.

Asaf Khan stepped clear as Dara raised his gun. He felt, rather than heard, Talawat edge closer with his remaining light pieces.

He sighted along the barrel. That part of his mind not engaged with aiming noted an anomaly: the blackbuck were running straight and true rather than bouncing back and forth along a line of travel.

Just as he was ready to squeeze the lever, a thundering of hooves caused him to lower his muzzle. Aurangzeb and Shuja were riding to meet the herd, bows in hand.

Aurangzeb and Shuja had split up to either side of the herd, and were standing in the stirrups, loosing. Where their arrows fell, antelope staggered out of the herd, dead or dying. Shuja ended up on the near side of the herd, Aurangzeb disappearing into the dust kicked up by both prey and hunters.

Dara shook his head. While impressive, their antics were denying him a shot. Not that he couldn't rely on his skills and shoot anyway, it was simply not a good idea to go firing into a field occupied by two princes, whether the shooter was a brother or not.

He briefly considered taking to his own horse while summoning a drink from one of his body slaves.

"Don't want to take to your own horse?" Asaf Khan asked.

Having already decided against it, Dara punched his chin toward where his brothers were now racing back towards the firing line in a cloud of dust. "When their horses tire, there will be other game."

Asaf nodded, looking sidelong at his eldest grandson. "Married life agrees with you, Grandson."

"Oh?" Dara asked, taking the gem-encrusted goblet full of iced fruit juice from his servant.

"You are more patient than you were. I may presume too much when I think it your wife's doing," he said, shrugging, "but there are worse reasons for change in the behavior of men."

Dara hid his smile by slaking his thirst. Smacking his lips appreciatively, he answered: "Yes, many things are put in their proper places, now I have a son on the way."

"A son? You are so sure? The astrologers tell you it is so?"

"Yes," Dara half-lied. The up-timer history had it that his son rode to battle with him in his war against Aurangzeb, many years in the future.

"You must send me—" Asaf stopped in mid-sentence, peering into the dust beyond Shuja.

Dara followed the line of his gaze, saw it a heartbeat later: something gold-orange flowing along in the wake of Shuja's horse.

"Tiger!" Asaf bellowed in his general's voice, pointing at the great beast stalking his grandson.

Dara tossed his goblet aside and scrambled for his newest gun.

Shuja, hearing the shout, did the wrong thing: he reined in to look at Asaf Khan. The tiger was within twenty gaz of Shuja. When he came to a stop, it did as well. In fact, it went forequarters down, hunching its rear end.

Asaf was screaming, as were more and more of his men. He started running for his own horse and household guard.

Dara knelt and lifted the butt of his gun, surging upright.

Shuja was looking around, trying to identify the threat. His horse tossed its head, shied sideways, uneasy.

Dara pressed his shoulder into the stock, trying to cock the lock, find his target, and get his hand on the firing lever—and had a moment's panic when he couldn't find it: *Not a lever, a trigger, you fool!*

The tiger was rocking its hips, getting ready to charge.

Talawat was beside him, quietly urging: "Shehzada, please do not try to do too much at once. Slow down. Calmly."

Dara stopped. Breathed out. Found his aim point and his target. Slid his finger inside the trigger guard.

Out of the corner of his eye he saw Talawat's silhouette nod. The gunsmith cocked the hammer back for Dara. "She kicks like a mule, Shehzada. Now kill us a tiger."

Dara squeezed the trigger. The lock snapped forward, steel and flint sparking into the pan. A half-heartbeat later, the gun discharged with a thunderous roar and brutal kick to Dara's shoulder.

The tiger leapt.

Smoke obscured Dara's sight for a moment.

Shuja's horse bolted, riderless, into view.

Talawat stepped forward and turned to face Dara, hands busy as he reloaded the piece with quick, economical motions. He could hear the gunsmith praying even over the shouts of Asaf's men.

Asaf had stopped his rush to mount. It was too late.

The smoke cleared.

The tiger lay prone, part of one of Shuja's legs and a boot protruding from beneath it.

Dara's heart stopped.

It seemed years later when Shuja sat up from between its paws, face as white as bleached linen. Hands shaking, the young prince heaved the heavy corpse aside and stood, apparently unscathed.

Suddenly thirsty, Dara wished for strong drink.

The line erupted in crazed shouts of joy. Asaf came charging back toward Dara, teeth bared in a smile that split his beard.

Shuja was walking, somewhat unsteadily, back toward the line.

Placing powder in the pan and stepping back, Talawat murmured, "Fine shooting, Shehzada."

Dara pointed a trembling finger at his sibling. "I will give you its weight in silver, Talawat. Were it not for you, I would have surely rushed the shot and missed."

Talawat bowed his head, clearly aware of how badly things might have turned out. "God is merciful and loving-kind, to place one of my tools in the hands of one so gifted in their use. I will use the silver to make more fine guns for your use, Shehzada."

Aurangzeb rode into view behind his dismounted brother, stopping over the tiger for a moment. After a moment's examination, he nudged his horse into motion. Quickly catching up to Shuja, he said something the other responded to with an angry shake of the head. Shrugging, the mounted brother rode on toward the firing line.

As he came closer, Dara noticed his quiver was empty and his face had a thin smile drawn across it. For dour Aurangzeb, such an expression was a broad smile of unrestrained glee.

"I see we each took a tiger this day, Brother."

"What?" Dara asked.

Aurangzeb nodded his head in the direction he'd come from. "Another one, possibly this one's mate or nearly adult offspring, took the last blackbuck in the herd. He took some killing: all my remaining arrows are in him."

Asaf Khan arrived in time to hear the end of Aurangzeb's speech, sweating from his exertions. Pausing to catch his breath, he was still beaming when Dara remembered to be civil: "Congratulations, Brother, I'm sure it was a fine kill."

"And to you on yours, Dara, though it appears your beast had an old wound to slow it—an arrow in its flesh, turned to poison."

"Might explain why it went for Shuja with wounded game at hand," Asaf gasped.

"Anger is the poison that stirs the killer residing in the hearts of both man and beast," Dara said, trying not to look at his brother as he did so.

Part Two

Fall, 1634

Some bore the story to their king:
"A mighty creature of our race,
In monkey form, has reached the place."

Chapter 13

Surat, River Tapti
September 1634

"Right then, it'll be a while." Captain Strand sighed. "The easiest passage I've ever made, only to rot under the sun in Surat."

John spat over the rail into the river Tapti after the retreating official's boat. "Pain in the ass, this shit."

Bertram frowned. While he agreed with the up-timer's assessment of their situation, John had scarce said anything positive since foiling the pirate attack. Gervais had commented that even Ilsa, John's wife, appeared unable to lift the man's spirits.

John turned from the rail and stalked back to the gangway, leaving the sun-baked deck for the oppressive heat of his quarters. Bertram had listened while Rodney explained why John remained so upset, but it just didn't make sense to him. The youth he'd killed had been a pirate. Bertram understood the up-timers placed a higher value on life than benighted down-timers did—or, to look at it another way, they'd come from a gentler world that allowed such luxuries. But the fact remained that the boy would not have shed a tear for John and his folk as they were led into slavery.

Gervais emerged from the hold, blinking. The Frenchman had been checking one of the wonders the USE had sent along with the mission while the captain and Ennis met with Laksh Menon, the Surat tax farmer.

"Well?"

Bertram gestured at the departing small craft. "The powers that be are considering our request, apparently."

"Five months locked aboard ship getting here, and they won't let us even come ashore?" Gervais said.

"Not yet, no," said Captain Strand.

"Did you offer a bribe?"

Strand looked at him angrily. "After all this time aboard my ship, you think me a simpleton?"

Gervais held up his hands in surrender. "I apologize. I'm impatient, and let my tongue wag ahead of my manners."

Strand shook his head. "Apology accepted. I am not usually so touchy, but their translator set my teeth on edge. Damn Venetians, each thinking it was them who invented trade."

"Venetian?" Gervais asked.

"Yes."

"Did you get his name?"

Strand referred to his log. "Gradinego."

"Ha!" Gervais smiled, shook his head, "Can't be!"

"What?"

The grin disappeared as Gervais pounded a fist on the rail. "I knew I should have been up here."

"Why?" Bertram asked.

"It is just possible that I know the man. We worked together in Venice...some years back."

"Oh?"

"Yes," Gervais said, expression bland: a sure sign he was thinking very hard.

"And?"

"What?"

"Did you part on good terms or did you..." Bertram trailed off, glancing at the captain.

Gervais sniffed. "There is only one real rule we all abide by: never swindle those who choose to work a dodge with you. I have never broken that rule."

Strand was looking at both of them, scratching his beard thoughtfully.

Gervais changed the subject: "Did they say why we can't off-load?"

"They insisted that no one trades here without a firman from the emperor."

"Not quite accurate," Strand corrected. "The diwan's tax man said something about a requirement that traders hold a firman from Shehzadi Begum Sahib...That's a princess, I believe."

"But we're not here to trade in Surat, are we?"

"No, we're not. When we tried explaining that to the diwan's man, he was unmoved."

"So what do we do?" Bertram asked.

Strand shrugged. "Hope that when they come back tomorrow, Gervais' friend is the translator, and that the Venetian has some pull with the locals."

Bertram looked significantly at the ship anchored a few hundred yards upriver. "And the English?"

"They aren't likely to be a problem, and even less likely to be helpful."

"Not to contradict you, but won't they complain to the... the diwan, is it? They own sole rights to trade here, don't they?"

Strand shook his head. "The Portuguese and Dutch hold firmans as well. Firmans are not necessarily exclusive. They are more like a license to trade than a royal charter backed by the crown such as the one the Danish East India Company has. If we were flying Portuguese colors, we might have problems, but we're all of us rather far from the fights and concerns of home." The broad-shouldered captain shrugged again. "Most of the time, we all just go about our affairs," he gestured at the very busy docks, "there being plenty of trade for all."

Gervais grinned as the boat came alongside. Angelo Gradinego cut a slim figure beside the most richly dressed man on the small boat.

Passengers on the smaller craft required a bit of a climb to get to the deck of the *Lønsom Vind*. Due to the strict order of precedence, Angelo boarded well in advance of the man he was translating for.

Gervais made certain that he was standing across from Angelo when he reached the deck. Angelo looked him over, assessing his value and position in the mission automatically before it registered *who* he was actually looking at. When it did, he peered closer: "Gervais?"

"Angelo Gradinego!" Gervais beamed, holding his arms out.

"Gervais Vieuxpont! What are you doing here?" the Venetian cried, stepping into his old friend's embrace.

"Trying to make friends and influence people, of course!" Gervais said, clapping Angelo on the back.

The Venetian stepped back, smiling. "You turned me down when I asked you to come see the wonders of the Mughal court with me!"

"I did." Gervais shrugged. "Things change."

"They do, my friend, they certainly do!" Angelo's brows drew together, concerned: "Monique?"

"Well, and here with us."

Angelo gestured with one tanned hand at the ship's colors. "But, Hamburg?"

"Things became a bit uncomfortable in the south." He glanced significantly at the rail, where the dignitary was just climbing into view. "We could use your help expediting our transition inland."

"I . . . see . . ." He glanced at the tax farmer. "It really isn't up to this fellow, but . . ." Retreating to stand beside the local, he mouthed, "I'll do what I can."

Gervais stepped back and let Ennis and Strand engage with the tax farmer. Watching Angelo translate, Gervais didn't see any of the few tells Angelo had. But if he wasn't working a swindle, why do this? It was too much like actual labor for the Angelo he knew.

The meeting went on for some time. As it neared the end, Strand offered another, larger bribe. Gervais could tell the man was tempted, but Angelo looked directly at Gervais as he translated: "Begum Sahib has installed a new representative here, and the representative must be consulted before any action is taken in matters of trade."

With that, the meeting drew to a close and the boarding party departed.

Strand turned to him, expectant.

Gervais shrugged. "He'll do what he can for us."

"You hopeful?" Ennis asked.

Gervais cocked his head. "Hopeful, yes. Confident, no. I am unsure what Angelo is doing in such a lowly position."

"Lowly?"

"He's a brilliant man. Very accomplished and truly gifted."

"So he's underachieving," John said, dismissive.

Carefully controlling the urge to snap, Gervais answered: "All I'm saying is that I doubt he would be translating for some third-tier tax collector if he had other prospects."

"I... see. He did not appear to be in bondage," Strand said.

"True."

"What, like leather and shit?" John Ennis interrupted, a strange expression on his face.

"No, like slavery, though what you mean by leather and feces, I'm a afraid I don't understand..."

Blushing, John shook his head. "Never mind."

Surat, Palace of the Diwan

"Well, shiiiit..." John said, drawing out the word. The principles of the USE mission been sweating for hours in the courtyard, waiting for Diwan Kashif to see them.

"John!" Ilsa snapped.

"What?"

"Stop cursing at every turn."

He gestured dismissively at the supplicants crowding the courtyard. "Like there's anyone who understands me around here."

"Your wife can, John Dexter Ennis," Ilsa returned, an edge to her voice.

"Yes, dear." He'd meant to assure her he'd try to abstain from cursing, but something in the way he said it made her eyes tighten above the veil. She stalked away, joining Monique and Priscilla, the shapeless bag she wore failing to conceal the rigid set of shoulders.

Thankfully, none of the women had raised a fuss about having to wear those stupid modesty tents here.

"J.D.—" That came from Rodney, this time.

"I know, man, I know," he grated. "I just need folks to back the fuck up for a bit."

He was saved from finding some way of apologizing to his wife by the appearance of the translator, Angelo, at the entrance.

"The diwan will see the petitioners now."

"About damn time," Ennis muttered.

"Monsieur Ennis?" Gervais asked, as he joined John and Rodney as they left the rest of their party to enter the building.

"Nothing," John said.

"Patience, Monsieur Ennis—"

"I have been patient."

Gervais grinned. The expression seemed honest, though John

suspected from his words that it was forced: "Indeed we have *all* have been patient. Just a bit longer, I think."

They were led into another courtyard, this one lined with a covered portico. John shook his head. The place looked like someone had gone through and rubbed gold on everything that wasn't covered in jewels, bright tile-work, or silks.

A fat man in ostentatious clothing sat on a raised dais, deep in the shade of the portico, his rotundity fanned by sweating slaves. Failing to deal with the heat and discomfort, John's mind wandered as the mission was introduced: The number of honest-to-God slaves and what they had to put up with just seemed unbelievable to him. People so thin, they made the hardest-up homeless guy from back up-time look fat.

That's the fate Strand says that kid I... that kid would have sent us to, given half a chance.

Diwan Kashif Khan started speaking in an improbably high voice, interrupting John's train of thought.

After a moment Angelo translated into flawless German: "The diwan has heard your petition, and decided you may leave Surat with your goods."

John bowed and recited the words Gervais and Angelo had offered as least likely to offend: "We thank the diwan for seeing us, and for granting his permission. We hope the diwan will find a use for the gifts offered in friendship." The bribe Strand claimed to be appropriate had seemed bizarre to John: a load of sequins, most of which looked like they came straight off the disco-era clothing stored in some of the attics of Grantville.

From the tone of his high-pitched voice, the diwan seemed genuinely pleased. Angelo translated: "The diwan will certainly find a use for them."

"Diwan, may we inquire as to the location and status of the court?" The Mughal court was nomadic, and Bertram and Gervais had thought it wise to ask.

"Still in Agra, despite the season. The emperor is still in rude health, Allah be praised."

"Indeed."

Angelo picked up a scroll. "These papers grant you and all your goods safe passage from Surat."

From Surat? Wait a second, we need protection and guides to Agra, not just out of town!

He took the paper from Angelo, seals dangling. "We were hoping for passage and protection *to* Agra, perhaps even an introduction to the emperor's court."

Angelo bit his lip, turned and translated.

The diwan shook his head, high voice detracting from the firm speech he was clearly trying to deliver to his subordinate.

"The diwan clarifies his position: he has no authority to introduce you to the court nor can he give offer safe passage to Agra. Such is not his place."

John reined in his first impulse, which was to grab the fat functionary by the throat and bellow, "Then why the hell are we here?" Instead he tried to keep his voice level, asking, "Are you not a servant of the emperor?"

John could feel the rest of the mission tense behind him as Angelo worked through the translation.

"We are all servants of the emperor."

"And?"

John watched the chubby functionary's eyes narrow as the man took issue with John's curt question. Angelo's translation of the single German word into Gujarati required quite a few words. He'd have to remember to thank the man for trying to smooth that over.

"While it is not my usual habit to answer rude questions, you are foreign, so I shall educate you: I serve Diwan Firoz Khan, who is Diwan of Shah Jahan's Harem, chosen for that position by Jahanara Begum Sahib, herself."

Temper, John. "I'm grateful for your patience, Governor. I meant no offense."

Listening to Angelo's translation, the diwan's expression softened. He wagged his head, said something in a conciliatory tone.

"There is the source of your misunderstanding, John Ennis of the United States of Europe. The diwan is not what you would call a governor, he is . . . a manager of Begum Sahib's interests here in Surat."

John glanced at Rodney. "Forgive my ignorance, but could the diwan please explain?"

"The diwan collects the incomes from Shehzadi Jahanara's jagirs here, which includes an income from all trade passing through the port of Surat. He has authority over some other aspects of trade here and in the surrounding lands, but does not govern the province or command many soldiers."

"Sorry, we did not know how things work here..." John let the words trail off, looking from Rodney to Gervais for help.

Gervais stepped forward. "But, as a trade mission, his authority extends to our protection, does it not?"

The diwan nodded.

"And, given that we carry gifts for Begum Sahib, the most wise Diwan would have every right, indeed a duty, to ensure her gifts were protected on our journey to Agra, would he not? We would, of course, inform the Diwan Firoz Khan of the excellent service done us by his most wise and forward-looking subordinate."

A calculating look crossed the diwan's face.

John held his breath.

A few moments passed in sweating silence, then: "The diwan promises twenty sowar with your goods to provide for their protection." Gradinego explained further: "The men were charged with delivering the diwan safely on his journey here, and have asked leave to return to Agra, and so cost the diwan nothing."

Gervais gave a courtly bow. "The diwan is most wise. I beg forgiveness if I offer insult or difficulty in asking, but would it also be possible to employ Mr. Gradinego as our translator as we travel inland?"

John thought about telling Gervais to drop it, but thought better of it when he caught the gratitude in Gradinego's eyes before the other man turned to translate.

The diwan and Angelo exchanged a few quiet words.

"What terms do you offer?"

"I do not know what I am negotiating for."

"I am working off a debt of ten thousand rupees."

John calculated the amount in terms of the goods they carried for trade and "gifts," then shot a questioning look at Gervais.

Gervais put his hand on his heart and nodded.

Damn. He'd better be worth it. John returned the nod.

"We can make such a payment, if you will accept goods instead of specie?"

The diwan said something and waved a fat hand.

"The men will be assembled for you the day after tomorrow, including this humble translator. We have the diwan's leave to depart in health," Angelo said, a broad smile creasing his tanned face.

Chapter 14

Dara Shikoh's Camp
September 1634

Dara stepped out into the late afternoon sunlight, striding past his personal *nökör* to greet Wazir Khan. He allowed himself a moment of pride that these men were his to command.

Grandfather dismounted smoothly. A life spent in the saddle might have given the old Persian decidedly bowed legs, but he remained otherwise unbent and unbowed. "God is great, Amir of Amirs, Dara Shikoh."

"God is great, Wazir Asaf Khan." Dara smiled and gestured toward the awning spread above the entrance to his tent. He had come out merely so that his followers could see the esteem in which he held Asaf Khan, and to allow Father's wazir a chance to inspect the warriors who would accompany him into battle. Such political maneuvers were important, even here among the warrior elite.

"All the sowar are mustered?" Asaf asked, inspecting the dismounted troopers lining their path as the pair walked slowly toward the tent.

Each of the men of his personal guard wore a metal helm over padded armor, a cavalry sword and leather shield, and had a heavy composite bow ready to hand. Their mounts were sleek and well fed. While the rest of the men of his command were not so well equipped, they all bore hand weapons and bows, and had at least one remount.

"Yes, the men are ready—eager, even," Dara answered with a smile.

"All are the proper age and skilled?"

"Yes, Wazir." There were mansabdars who tried to pass false rolls on to the reporters, hoping to collect pay for mansabs greater than their actual ability to field troops would justify. When called upon to muster, they would try to make up the lack with old men, grooms—even slaves—on mounts good only for the knackers.

"Their mounts?"

"Twenty thousand and several hundred more horses, all up. Fodder for same. Eight elephants. I have no guns, but my advisor indicates such would only serve to slow our advance." Amir Mukhlis Khan was in a terrible hurry, greedy for the productive farmlands the Sikhs held.

Slaves presented refreshment as the prince and his grandfather turned, more slaves placing cushions beneath them as the pair settled in to watch the camp. It was already smaller than that of the wazir's army, as the Deccan excursion would require tens of thousands of fighting men.

"I had thought to see matchlock men," Asaf said, gesturing at the camp.

Dara wagged his head. "I thought it best to avoid any . . . possible rumors that I used some trick of technology to win against my opponent, rather than through honorable and traditional strength of arms."

Asaf Khan fixed him with a penetrating stare, taking a persimmon wedge and biting into it.

Recognizing the wazir was considering how best to say something his grandson might not wish to hear, Dara gave him permission: "Speak freely. I value your experience above all but Father's."

Asaf swallowed, spoke quietly: "You have read the biographies of your ancestors, have you not?"

"Of course."

"Traditions have their place, but your ancestors put little stock in them, most especially Babur. I would remind you how his twenty-five thousand, lined up behind carts, succeeded against Sultan Ibrahim of Delhi's hundred thousand."

"Guns."

"Yes. I can cite other battles won with the tools created by the artifice of men like your Atishbaz gunsmith, but I think you get my point."

"Yes, but Babur was a blooded general with years of experience and on the rise to power by then. I am not...do not...know...my advisor, he..."

"The advisor your father appointed?"

Dara nodded, glad for the sudden change in subject. "Amir Mukhlis Khan has been most helpful."

"I am sure he has."

"Indeed, he is most eager to come to grips with the upstart."

"Be sure not to let his eagerness lead you into folly. He is not known for his restraint. By all reports, his ambition exceeds his ability."

A twinge of annoyance bit through Dara's good humor. "Perhaps you should have told this to Father?"

Asaf Khan nodded, jeweled turban glittering, "I did. I can only caution you."

"Oh?"

"Yes. I suspect Shah Jahan wishes to see exactly how you deal with such unpredictable subordinates in uncertain circumstances."

"All the more reason to restrict myself to traditional forces, commanded in traditional fashion."

"Success breeds tradition."

"I don't think I follow."

"I do not wish to contradict you, Shehzada, but is it not more important that you take command and *win* than worry what the court might say about how you secure that victory?"

Agra, Red Fort

"He cuts a handsome figure: my husband, your brother," Nadira said, as Dara led his men in a long parade along the riverbank before the court.

"He does." Jahanara smiled, taking her sister-in-law's hand in her own. Dara was in full military kit, sparkling like a jewel among the barely-more subdued dress of his bodyguard.

"I do not see the gloves I gifted him," Roshanara grumbled from Nadira's other side. She was leaning hard against the jali, trying to get a better look.

Trust my sister to try and make this moment about her.

Aloud, Jahanara said: "Do not squint so, Sister. It will line that smooth brow of yours with wrinkles. Besides, he bade me tell you that he has set them aside to wear into battle."

Roshanara sniffed, but said nothing more. She left the balcony a moment later, whether in search of other entertainments or better company, Jahanara could not say.

Jahanara felt Nadira squeeze her hand in thanks and smiled gently at her. To be left behind—pregnant—she could not imagine the fear. Her mother always shared her father's campaigns; was always there, even when her father was losing, to support him even as he returned to the tent each night to support her in her latest pregnancy.

She turned, saw Nadira wiping tears from her face and tried to comfort her: "He will return victorious, I'm sure."

"But he has only five thousand, while the wazir is taking tens of thousands south into the Deccan."

"True, but eight elephants and five thousand troops, all of them mounted, is a significant command. Besides, Father says the Sikhs can barely field two thousand, most without horses. I do not claim to know a great deal about such things, but it seems to me Father would not have sent Dara without sufficient means to accomplish the task."

"Did the emperor... did he change his mind about giving Dara a command because of—" She glanced around, making sure no one could overhear. "Of what you showed him?"

Having failed to consider that possibility, Jahanara's brows rose. "I do not know, Nadira. It may have been that."

"Then I wish God had seen fit to stop Salim coming here."

Jahanara shook her head. "Nadira, you must not say such things. Grantville did appear, and Salim did bring back such proofs. We can argue all we wish to with Him, but in the end we must submit to God's will."

"I know, it's just so..."

"Difficult. I know. Take heart. Dara will likely return before you give birth."

Nadira nodded, tears still falling through long lashes to glisten on smooth cheeks.

Jahanara resisted the urge to shake her head. Her sister-in-law even looked pretty crying! She could never have managed that herself.

They stood in companionable silence for a while, watching the rest of Dara's troops parade past.

"You said your good-byes last night?"

"Oh, yes, at length." Nadira's grin was wicked. "I'm even a little tender."

A startled laugh escaped Jahanara's lips. "Is that safe? I mean, with the baby coming?"

"My mother always told me it was good for the baby, but then she was always after Father for more pillow time."

"Really?" Jahanara said, suddenly uncomfortable with the conversation.

Be honest—you are not uncomfortable with it, you're angry. That I'm to never know what it is that other women experience in the arms of their husbands is an idea I shall never find comfort in.

"Oh, yes," Nadira said.

"I am sure he will not stop thinking of you while he is away."

"Nor I, him," Nadira replied, laying palms across the gentle rise of her belly.

"And you can write him daily, and be sure that he will do the same to you."

Nadira nodded. "Even so, I shall miss him dearly."

"Come, we shall tell the astrologers to discern for us when Dara will return to us, victorious."

Agra, Mullah Mohan's Madrassa

"Enough. Shehzada Aurangzeb is here for private instruction. Leave us." The other students and servants of Mullah Mohan, obedient to their master's will, retreated.

Aurangzeb waited in silence, rolling prayer beads between his fingers as he considered how best to capitalize on the conflict between Father and the guru. Perhaps by stirring religious discord? Thus far, the conflict was between one ruler and another. He glanced at Mullah Mohan. If the proper people could be convinced that the Sikhs were actively opposed to Islam and, perhaps, desecrating the Quran, then many things could happen....

But, not now. Such a course would only add strength to Dara's position by giving him more soldiery to command. But perhaps it would prove useful to Aurangzeb at some later time.

"Should you have stayed at Red Fort?" Mohan asked as the doors closed.

Aurangzeb left his musing and answered: "And watch my brother depart in search of martial glory? I have better things to do with the time God has given me to walk the earth."

A solicitous smile. "Indeed, Shehzada."

"I don't know what you are smiling about. The court buzzes with rumors about a pair of deaths in Agra last month."

The smile disappeared. "Men often quarrel."

"Men known to be supporters of yours."

"I'm afraid my supporters are yet men, with all the flaws of common men."

"Do not think to put me off with such pious mutterings, Mohan. I told you to be discreet."

"And I was, Shehzada. You know of our conversation, and therefore link the deaths to me. The bystander, however interested, has no such advantage."

"Did they succeed, at least?"

"God's work was not, unfortunately, so easily accomplished."

Aurangzeb spent several breaths resisting the urge to beat the man bloody.

When he had restrained his rage, Aurangzeb spoke: "You used your own men and they *failed*?"

Mohan waggled his head. "Members of the mosque are many. I cannot be held to answer for the acts of each and every one of them; such are the laws of the land."

Aurangzeb let slip some of his anger: "I am not concerned with *laws*, you fool! You should not have revealed your hand in this petty action. Now I have no doubt that this Salim knows who it is that seeks his death."

Mullah Mohan again wagged his head, holding up a hand. "My men would never have betrayed me: they were faithful, loyal to God and to me!"

"You stupid, stupid man. There is active betrayal, and then there is the fanatic's inability to hide his true nature."

"What does that mean, b—" Mohan snapped, face darkening with throttled rage.

Aurangzeb heard the "boy" Mohan narrowly avoided uttering.

He let how close Mohan had come to uttering his own death sentence sink in for a moment before resuming: "These men, the ones you set to kill the amir, they were faithful men, likely screaming praise to God and condemning Salim as a heretic as they tried—and failed—to kill him."

A bit of the angry color drained from Mohan's face. "I had not thought of that..."

"So, when I say Salim likely knows who was behind the attempt on his life, I am speaking from a greater understanding of the situation. You are a fool to argue with me in such circumstances. Am I understood?"

Mohan nodded, shoulders slumping, "Yes, I understand. I... I fear I have not, until this moment, realized just how much you have matured."

What, my putting you on your knees with my bare hands was not sufficient sign that I am a man grown? But it would be impolitic to say that aloud, so Aurangzeb continued instead with: "I know it is difficult for you, who was my teacher, to understand the change in our circumstance, but I am no longer the child seeking an education from a learned mullah. I am a man grown, now; and one day, soon, I will rule."

It felt good to say that aloud, for the first time; made it seem real, somehow.

"I *will* rule," he repeated, savoring the words, "and I will bring all those I rule to Islam. I will conquer, and those I conquer will be brought to Islam. I will crush the divisions plaguing our sweet religion, and bring all believers to orthodoxy."

He fixed the mullah with a steady gaze. "If you would be a part of this great future I would make for our people, if you would be the spiritual leader of all people, then you must listen and be guided by me in these affairs."

He saw the fire ignite in Mohan's eyes and knew then that Mullah Mohan would do anything for the future Aurangzeb laid before him.

Chapter 15

Agra, Red Fort, The Harem
September 1634

"Where is this man you spoke of, Daughter?" The question was quietly voiced, but Jahanara recognized the ill-concealed impatience.

"I sent people into Agra to search him out, Father," she answered, careful to keep her eyes directly on Shah Jahan. He hated the appearance of dissembling in his children.

They were alone but for a few of his body slaves, as he had summoned her to his private chambers to read to him from his favorite book, the *Akbarnama*.

She had welcomed the opportunity for private time with him this morning, when it seemed they might discuss Salim's interpretation of the encyclopedia entries he'd copied and brought to Agra, but now...

"People?"

"Trusted servants, Father." *Ones I pray were not stopped by Nur Jahan's agents.*

"Yet he has not come."

"No, Father. He has not."

"Perhaps tomorrow I shall send for the Englishmen. They are always sniffing about, hoping for some scraps from our table, are they not?"

"That is so, Father, but I hardly think they will provide accurate translation of the texts."

Shah Jahan waved a hand, jeweled rings flashing. "They will, given proper incentive."

"Still, is it prudent to ask the tiger what it prefers to eat?"

The emperor snorted. "Ruler of the World is *my* title, Daughter. *I* am the tiger, not these red-faced water nomads from the west." He leaned forward, looking at her closely. "From your words, you trust this man. Why? He is no one, not even one of my commanders of horse, and not beholden to our house."

"Because he is a friend to Mian Mir, Father, and because he did not have to bring *us* news of what happened in that place."

Shah Jahan sat back on his cushions. "Who else would he have brought it to, then?"

Not yet ready to reveal all she knew and suspected, Jahanara answered: "Those who would do you mischief, Father."

"Their contents are not mischief enough?" he asked, gesturing at the foreign-looking book and slim folio he'd not let out of his sight since Jahanara had given it to him.

"We have long sought to read the future in the stars, Father. That it, or a portion of that future, may be revealed in these foreign texts should not be so great a surprise, I think."

"Perhaps." A faint smile, then: "The mullahs who will surely pull their beards and wear out their prayer beads with consternation when they learn that the future was revealed first to those not of the Faith."

"That is also a concern, Father."

"What?"

"The reaction of certain mullahs."

"Oh?"

"I am not the equal of your learned mullahs, but if all this," she gestured at the documents, "came to pass, then it was because God willed it."

Shah Jahan pulled at his beard, then pointed at the heavens. "And if it came to pass, who are we to try and shift God's will from the path He has chosen for us?"

She nodded. "I have given this quandary some thought, Father."

"Oh?" he asked, gesturing her to proceed.

"If it was God's will, then it was surely also God's will that these facts come to us in the now, so we might learn from the experiences of those others who bent to His will in that future that was?"

Father cocked his head, again tugging at his beard in thought. After some time he sighed and released his beard. "Such weighty thoughts are best picked up in the morning, after much prayer to strengthen the soul."

Disappointed, Jahanara bowed her head obediently. *Just please don't ask them of the supposed 'learned' Mullah Mohan. I don't want him getting wind of what Salim brought us. Bigot that he is, he will call for deaths of all foreigners and use it as an excuse to persecute the Hindus.*

He looked her in the eye as she raised her head. "I am very proud of you, Daughter. You are a thoughtful and brightest of the ornaments to my throne, entirely worthy of your mother."

Flushing, she bowed her head again. "Thank you, Father."

He lay back on the low bed, shoving silken cushions aside. "Read to me of our forebear's doings, Daughter."

"Yes, Father." She took up the tome recording the life of Akbar and opened it where the silken ribbon had been left when one of her stepmothers had stopped the night before. She read ahead slightly and began reciting the beautiful words of Abul Fazl.

Agra, Home of Jadu Das

Salim stopped his pacing and settled on the cushions, putting the note from Mian Mir down. He tried to put his frustration away with it, but the contradiction held in its few lines refused to let him.

Mian Mir, ever a friend to all who sought God, had assisted the guru in laying the cornerstone of the Sikh's greatest temple and was even known to receive the previous guru at his own home in Lahore. Salim himself had been present when the two had publicly proclaimed their amity and friendship. He knew Mian Mir would tell Hargobind Singh of the doom riding toward his people.

Salim had no wish to undermine the empire in any way, but duty to the living saint came first. Guilt-ridden, he had written Mian Mir of the emperor's plan to crush the Sikhs.

Written, and received word in return.

He sighed, picked up the note once more, and read it for the tenth time:

Take comfort, my student: there is no resisting God's will. All things proceed from His plan, in accordance with His wishes.

The Sikhs will not be swayed from their present course. They, too, are moved as God wills, and know it.

Some little blood will be shed, but not as much as might be were we not engaged in foiling the workings of the Dark One.

The sound of a horse in the courtyard reached Salim's ears, driving him from consideration of the almost prophetic wording of the verse and to his feet again. Jadu had said he would return around noon with word who at court the East India Company factors paid visit to.

Salim returned to the balcony and leaned elbows on the railing before realizing Jadu was not alone in the courtyard. A heavy fellow, whose smooth, rounded cheeks and rich clothing marked him as a possible eunuch, was dismounting next to his host.

Jadu looked up, waved an arm to present the beardless fellow to Salim. "Amir, this one was sent to find you."

The eunuch bowed deeply, then craned his fat neck to look up at Salim. "Amir Salim Gadh Visa Yilmaz, I am sent by Begum Sahib, who commands you to attend her."

"Oh?" Salim asked, hoping for more.

A wobbling of neck fat. "I am forbidden knowledge of my mistress' motives, Amir."

Salim thought about that a moment. He doubted Mullah Mohan would choose a eunuch to search for him; it was too subtle.

Jadu cocked his head and covered for Salim's lack of immediate response: "Then the amir will, of course, attend to her command."

"Within the hour!" the messenger insisted, still watching Salim.

"That may not be possible," Jadu said, glancing up.

"All things are possible, God willing," the eunuch snapped, leveling a nasty look at Jadu.

Jadu bobbed his head, raising hands in respectful submission. "But surely you don't want the amir—favored of both Shehzadi Jahanara and Shehzada Dara Shikoh alike—to go before them dressed as you see him?"

Mention of both royal siblings brought the fit of pique to an abrupt end. The eunuch produced a silken kerchief and mopped his brow. "Pardon, I am tired, having spent the entire night and most of yesterday searching for the amir. Proper preparation for the visit is acceptable, of course." A fatalistic shrug of round shoulders and a heavy sigh: "I'll be punished as it is, I am so late delivering him."

Jadu cast a meaningful glance at Salim.

"I will ask that you be treated gently, having found me as soon as possible," Salim offered. "It was not your fault that I was so well hid."

Jadu smiled reassuringly at the eunuch. "And surely the amir's word will count in your favor! Go, take refreshment while I help the amir prepare as quickly as can be."

Salim retreated into his chambers once again, waiting for Jadu.

It didn't take him long, though he arrived with several servants in train. Seeing Salim on the verge of talking, he held up his hands in caution and stepped close before speaking. "There were others seeking you out, hoping to prevent you appearing at the palace. It was all I could do to get that great bag of figs to come here with me. We'll make you ready and escort you to the palace."

"I hardly think a slippered eunuch any kind of protection," Salim said, as Jadu's slaves started to dress him.

Jadu smiled. "Normally, no, but he made it plain, and in public, that he is on Begum Sahib's errand."

"Are there still a great many fighting men on the streets?" Salim asked, as the slaves wrapped him in a rich, but light, over-robe.

"Yes, the wazir has yet to depart, and has not even attempted to refuse his men the chance at the entertainments to be had here. Why do you ask?"

"Accidents are easy to arrange."

"I cannot believe any would be foolish enough to interfere with someone on a mission for Begum Sahib."

Absently noting how out of place his worn and undecorated sword belt looked in conjunction with his current attire, Salim shrugged. "What God wills to pass, will pass."

Agra, Red Fort, Diwan-i-Khas

"Amir Salim Gadh Visa Yilmaz, Your Majesty, answering the summons of Begum Sahib," the majordomo announced.

Nur Jahan heard the name and immediately looked through the jali at the man being introduced. He was tall and broad-shouldered, with the straight nose and coloring of an Afghani tribesman. The amir wore his rich clothing with indifference but moved with the grace and gait of a trained warrior as he made his way forward to stand within a few gaz of the emperor's dais.

Nur resisted the urge to look at Jahanara, seated some distance away, and feigned a cough. She had to keep up appearances, after all. She was alone and seated well away from the other women observing the court, secretly welcoming the relative solitude the lingering effects of her recent "illness" granted her.

She smiled inwardly. With such tangled skeins, it was a small wonder that she did not get more headaches.

The amir arrived before the emperor and bowed.

"You are late, Amir Yilmaz."

A deeper bow followed the emperor's greetings. "I beg forgiveness, Sultan Al'Azam, and offer no excuse for it save that I came as soon as I learned of the summons." The man's voice was resonant and pleasing, his Persian lightly accented but grammatically perfect. More impressive: it held no fear, despite the rather sharp reprimand inherent in the emperor's words.

"You may secure our forgiveness by translating the texts you brought to our notice."

Another bow. "Majesty, I have already begun to write the translations—"

"No, I want you to read the words aloud to me, translating as you go. Thus, if I should have any questions, you will be available to answer them immediately."

And no one else will know what I learn, Nur added silently for the emperor, hiding her displeasure. Such personal access to the emperor was unusual, to say the least. What might have started as a subject of idle curiosity was no longer: the amir was now a clear threat to the balance of power at court.

A further, deeper bow. "Your Majesty does me a great honor I fear I am unworthy of."

He actually seemed humbled by the emperor's regard. Nur wondered if that was an artifice.

The emperor waved as if the amir's words were of no consequence. "You have been vouched for at court."

When? she wondered.

Farther up the gallery, where Jahanara sat, there was a sharp intake of breath. She did not intend to vouch for him, then—or she did not expect the emperor to reveal she had spoken for him? Nur carefully controlled a sharp breath. If Jahanara had vouched for Amir Yilmaz at court...then Jahanara was the one who moved the slave to poison Nur, if only to be sure she was not present while she laid the groundwork for this introduction.

"Furthermore," the emperor was saying, "we grant you *zat* and sowar for your upkeep and a robe you may wear in honor."

Put it away. Reflect later. You must observe the court now.

Nur slowly moved her head, trying to catch sight of Aurangzeb without alerting those who were undoubtedly taking note of who she was watching at court. The young man's expression betrayed no particular interest in the proceedings. Nur wondered, for just a moment, whether he knew of Mullah Mohan's failed attempt on Amir Salim Yilmaz's life.

He must have known. The question was: did he sanction it?

She let her gaze wander without moving her head, searching out Mullah Mohan.

For his part, the learned Mullah—*My, doesn't he look like he's eating his own beard?*

Such anger marked his desire to kill the amir as something personal—and might prove an excellent lever to move Mohan to Nur's designs. Foolish religious bigots with an army of fanatical followers could prove useful in certain circumstances, after all.

Chapter 16

Surat to Agra
September 1634

The leader of the guards the diwan had sent along with them was clearly upset, and it didn't look like a simple temper tantrum brought on by the heat of the afternoon.

John looked hopefully at the approaching weather front. It had been either oppressively hot or pouring with rain every day they'd been in India, neither of which conditions was tailored to please a West Virginian. To add insult to already-abused sensibilities, the men in charge of the caravanserai they'd rested at last night since leaving Surat all claimed this was an unusually hot and *dry* September.

"What is it, Iqtadar?" John asked, through Angelo.

"Your women, they must be covered. They must not be allowed to lead my men into unclean thoughts, or there will be consequences that this one," Angelo gestured at the Afghan, "will not be blamed for."

"Pardon?" John said, anger spiking.

Without looking, Iqtadar pointed back along the line of riders to where the ladies were. Angelo toned down the angry snarl falling from the guard captain's lips and calmly translated: "Your women must cover themselves."

John looked over. Ilsa had removed her hat and was fanning herself with it. Her blond hair shone in the sunlight like a halo. She was, in every way that mattered, his angel.

"I am sorry," John said, dragging his gaze from the love of his life and knowing he wasn't at his best: "We do not keep..."

"Purdah," Angelo supplied.

"Right, we do not 'keep' our women in purdah. We cannot...No, we *won't* even try, to force them into a life of such restriction."

Iqtadar did not look pleased, and spat something angry.

Angelo looked less sanguine this time: "Iqtadar claims he will not be responsible for what happens if you cannot control your women."

"Is that a fucking threat?"

Angelo held up his hands and spoke over John's outburst, "Please, Signor Ennis, calmly...These *armed* men who are helping us in our travels are not asking for anything exceptional or improper under the laws and customs of this place."

"Customs and laws that treat women like property!" John spat.

A sweating Rodney rode up at that moment. "What's up?"

John hiked a thumb at their guard, "Iqtadar here was just telling me how the women got to get covered up."

Rodney shrugged. "Thought that might be a problem."

"Not ours, that's for sure! It's not like they're running around in god-damn bikinis or something!"

Another maddening shrug. "Different standards, man."

John lost it: "Which standards? The ones that allow a man to fucking *own* another human being? Or the standards that allow one guy to cut the nads off a kid so they can make 'em acceptable company for the women they keep shut up and behind walls their entire lives? Tell me, please!"

Everyone within earshot was staring at him now, but the anger wouldn't be stopped: "Fuck. Their. Standards."

"Um, please don't translate that, Angelo," Rodney said into the silence that followed John's tirade.

"Oh, I think Iqtadar has the gist of it," Angelo said.

With a savage pull at the reins, Iqtadar turned his horse and galloped back toward the rear of the caravan, passing the women of the mission.

Conferring a moment, Ilsa and Priscilla rode forward to meet their husbands.

"What's wrong?" Ilsa asked.

John, feeling like a just-cracked pressure cooker, could only shake his head. He could feel Rodney's eyes on him, willing him to get a grip.

"The guards ain't happy with you ladies going uncovered," Rodney said.

"Well then," Ilsa said, looking to Priscilla for support, "we'll just have to cover up."

Priscilla nodded agreement. "Good thing Monique bought us all burqas in Surat."

"I..." John tried to speak, but the words wouldn't come out.

God, am I this fucked up? First I lose it over this bullshit, then I can't even explain it...

Ilsa looked at him fondly then reached out a hand and squeezed his forearm. "We knew when we came that things would be different here." She nodded at Priscilla. "We even talked about it coming here. We can't stop and attack this kind of thing head-on every time we're confronted with it, certainly not here, with people we don't have any hope of convincing. Maybe, when we get to court, if there's a safe opening, we can try and turn the lights on for someone in power. Someone who can effect real change. But for now we can't risk our safety or that of the entire mission just because some locals want women to conform to their idea of modesty.

"Even back in the USE some people still have foolish, *shitty* ideas about how proper women should behave."

Priscilla snorted. "Up-time, too!"

Ilsa's light laughter soothed him, even as her use of the profanity indicated just how deeply she felt about the situation; John might curse all the time, but she rarely indulged.

"I..."

"It's not a problem we're here to take on. Not directly, anyway. Seriously, it's not a problem, right, Pris?"

"You bet...Aside from the fashion," Priscilla said.

"What's that?" Rodney asked.

Priscilla put on a British accent: "Well, I very much doubt our burqas will be the height of fashion when we arrive in the capital. We colonials are so easy to look down on, what with our simple speech and provincial ways!"

"Frightfully so, daaahling," Ilsa said.

John smiled. His German-born wife had always loved the

regional accents of English speakers, and her snobbish English-woman was even better than Priscilla's. He felt himself slowly unlock, the warm banter between friends and wife easing his mind.

"Could it get any wetter?" Monique asked, shifting her entirely insufficient umbrella to her other hand and pulling at her burqa in another vain attempt at finding shelter for her dampest parts.

As if listening to her, the rain chose that moment to increase from the hours-long soaking drizzle to a heavy downpour.

She sighed. "Silly question: of course it can."

"Indeed it can," her father mumbled from his own misery, replacing the lens covers on his borrowed binoculars. He was completely enamored of the things, borrowing Rodney's pair every chance he had. Never mind that the terrain had hardly changed in the last week; forested hills to their south and west marching unending along the gently sloping plain they rode north and eastward.

Angelo spilled water from his riding hat, spoke up. "Ah, India in the monsoon, such a joy and pleasure."

Seeking distraction, Monique said, "Those soldiers, the ones who challenged us yesterday, they didn't look like our escorts."

More water spilled from Angelo's hat as he nodded. "They were Mewaris, a Rajput caste."

"Aren't Rajputs an ethnic group, like Sicilians?" she asked.

"Not...exclusively. Rajputs are the traditional ruling caste—have been for as long as anyone recalls. So the Mewari are, well, I guess the closest thing would be...a clan of Rajputs. And the Mewaris have their own dynasty of kings."

"Muslim?"

Angelo shook his head. "Most Rajputs, including the Mewari, remain Hindu. Some have converted to Islam, though."

"In exchange for the right to rule?" Monique asked. Central Europe had been savagely divided by differences between the religions of its people and that of its princes often enough in the last decades. People being people, she figured Indians were similarly motivated.

"No. Akbar and Jahangir were both very conciliatory toward the Hindus and Sikhs, treating them quite reasonably."

"Who were they?" Gervais asked.

"The present emperor's grandfather and father, respectively."

"All right ... getting back to the Rajputs: how is it they've come to rule subject kingdoms rather than their kingdoms being ruled directly from the emperor's court?"

"The Rajputs in general have long been respected for their fierce warrior practices and the Rajput kingdoms successfully resisted the Mughals for a very long time." He scratched his sodden beard, "If I recall correctly, Mewar only became part of the empire about fifteen years ago, making peace with Emperor Jahangir. As with most peace agreements hereabouts, it was sealed with marriages and tribute."

He grinned. "The Mughals have won so many kingdoms in this way, I daresay the emperor's family have as much or more Rajput blood in their veins as Persian and Mongol."

Monique shook her head. "Castes, clans, religious divisions ... It is all very complex."

"Almost as confusing as the situation in Central Europe?" Gervais asked, tongue firmly in cheek.

"Or the city states surrounding Rome?" Angelo said, smiling.

"Point!" Gervais chuckled.

Monique didn't bother to respond to their patronizing and short-sighted humor. She had other things on her mind.

"It's actually kind of pretty when the rain stops, John," Ilsa said, looking out over the grassland. The couple had ridden up the rise to get the lay of the land while the rest of their caravan rode by below.

"What?" John asked, distracted.

He panned the binoculars across the plain ahead. The wind was in their faces, making the grass rustle pleasantly. It was nearly a perfect moment, neither too hot nor too wet.

"John."

He let the binoculars hang from the strap and turned to look at her. She had angled her umbrella toward the caravan to conceal herself from the guards and pulled her veil aside.

He couldn't help but smile, seeing her golden hair spilling out. "Yes?"

"Are you all right, John?"

"I'm ..." His usual glib response froze behind the prison of his lips.

She waited for him.

"I am—" he choked on the words.

"Are you hurting, John?"

He couldn't make his mouth work, eventually managed a nod.

She reached across to him, covered his larger hand with her smaller, finer one. "I love you, John Ennis. Nothing can change that."

John just stared at her, his throat feeling as if a giant was pinching it closed.

"Now, I insist that you listen to me a moment. That boy, the one you shot, he was a pirate. He would have killed you and enslaved me had I not been able to kill myself before his crew got their hands on me. I was ready to do that, you know.

"Therefore: you did what had to be done to protect me and our friends. No one can fault you for that, including you, my rock-headed, obstinate, lovely, kind-hearted hillbilly!"

He swallowed half a dozen replies, tried to tell her she didn't *know*, that *she* hadn't seen the kid fall and die, that it didn't matter what she thought.

But it did matter! It mattered more than life itself what she thought of him.

"I know," he managed to say at last. He looked her in the eye again. "I love you, you—"

He stopped mid-sentence as her gaze flicked over his shoulder and hardened.

She pulled her hand from his as he turned to look.

A group of about a dozen men were moving out of the tall grass in a loose semi-circle around them. The nearest was only ten yards away, filthy and hefting a spear. All of them were armed with more than unpleasant expressions under hard eyes, and a few had bows.

Shit! They must have been lying in the grass, checking the caravan out when we rode right up on them...

They were poorly armed, but John didn't think he could get the rifle off his shoulder and into play in time to stop them getting to either him or, worse yet, Ilsa.

Two of them were pointing excitedly at Ilsa's uncovered head and speaking in hushed tones. Despite the language barrier, their manner managed to convey both greed and desire.

They started to close with a will, picking up speed.

"Ride, Ilsa!" he shouted, trying to swing the rifle from his shoulder and cover her retreat. The shout made his horse rear.

He tried to get over the stirrups, but the weight of the rifle dragged him out of the saddle and back in a slow tumble over his horse's ass.

He rolled with the impact as best he could. Losing his rifle and bashing his shoulder something fierce. John ignored the pain to pop up on his knees, struggling to orient himself.

He could hear the bandits shouting excitedly among themselves, but only one horse's hooves fleeing down the rise.

Shit, she didn't run!

Belatedly, John heard someone charging through the grass at him.

"Down, John!" he heard Ilsa shout from behind him.

For once John immediately did what his wife told him to, throwing himself flat.

CRACK! CRACK! The double tapping of Ilsa's 9mm Beretta was almost immediately followed by a meaty thump and patter of liquid on grass.

CRACK! Her third shot sounded before the first bandit fell just a few steps from his position.

John looked for his rifle, started crawling toward it.

CRACK! Someone else fell thrashing in the grass.

He rolled up, saw Ilsa standing in the stirrups, hair glowing golden in the sun over her deep blue burqa. She had the reins in one hand and was carefully lining up another shot.

CRACK! A third man went down. This one didn't thrash.

Her horse stands still while she's shootin' and mine spooks at a fucking shout? The world just ain't right! he thought, rising to one knee and shouldering the rifle.

Less-than-excited shouts from the remaining bandits and horrifyingly, the snap of a bowstring.

CRACK! Ilsa was still in it, regardless of where the arrow landed.

John lined up a shot on the bowman and squeezed the trigger. The stock thumping his shoulder was a surprise, just like it always was when you did it right. The target went down.

CRACK! CRACK! Ilsa firing again.

He went in search of other targets, found them all running away down the slope. He put the rifle up and looked to his wife.

She was still standing in the stirrups, shifting her point of aim back and forth between the fleeing bandits. He could see daylight though the burqa under her shooting arm. The arrow must have missed her by inches.

He tried to call out to her, found his mouth too dry for speech. Swallowing, he started moving slowly toward her.

The movement drew her attention. Like a turret, she swiveled in the saddle. She almost had him in her sights before realizing who he was. Her eyes shot wide, whites showing all around the iris as she let her gun hand fall.

She started shaking as she tried to reholster the gun inside the burqa.

"Ilsa?" he managed.

"John!" She slipped off the horse and into his arms.

They clung to one another for some time, even when Rodney and the boys rode past in pursuit of the remaining bandits.

Her horse ambled over, nuzzled her hair.

He laughed, an edge of hysteria in the sound. "What the hell did you do to make him stick around while you were shooting?"

"Nothing, he's stone deaf."

"No shit?"

She nodded, head against his chest, making no comment about his cursing other than to clutch him tighter.

Iqtadar rode by, Angelo and a few of the diwan's guards with him.

Angelo stopped a few paces from them, leading John's horse.

Iqtadar rode around the corpses, examining them and what John supposed could be called a battlefield, from horseback.

Ilsa didn't bother to cover her head, and John wasn't about to ask her to, not after what they'd just gone through, not for anyone.

Iqtadar returned, spoke to Angelo at length while gesturing at the hilltop. "Iqtadar offers his respects, John, for the excellent shooting."

"I only shot one. Ilsa shot the others."

Iqtadar's eyes went wide under his turban.

Angelo translated into politeness what John was certain was some variation on, "Bullshit!"

"He may believe what he wants, but she shot him," he pointed at each corpse in turn, "him, and him."

Iqtadar said something his men grinned at, then bowed to her from the saddle.

"What was that?" John snapped.

Iqtadar was already riding back to the caravan.

"John!" Ilsa warned.

Angelo smiled. "Actually, the khan's words are a deep compliment."

"What?" John and Ilsa chorused.

"He gave your lovely wife a title, Mr. Ennis: *Shirhan e Zarrin*."

Eyes narrowed with suspicion, Ilsa asked, "And what does that mean?"

"Golden Lioness, Signora Ennis."

John couldn't miss the pleased upward turn at the corners of his wife's lovely mouth. He laughed for the first time in months. Laughed hard and long. "Golden Lioness! HA! Damned if he didn't get you exactly right!"

Chapter 17

Red Fort, The Harem
October 1634

"Nur Jahan respectfully asks a visit, Begum Sahib."

Jahanara had been expecting such a request since arranging her great aunt's poisoning, if not so soon.

"She is recovered, then?" she asked the eunuch.

"Indeed, her brief illness has passed, thanks be to God."

"Praise Him," she answered in reflex. And because, while she had been expecting the request, Jahanara did not feel ready to grant it: "I shall consult my astrologer before agreeing to a visit. He found some peril to my health in his last reading, and advised me to caution." She waved dismissal at him. "You may take my words to her."

The eunuch bowed low, yet remained before her.

She let him grow uncomfortable before asking, "There is more?"

"I pray you will forgive me, Begum Sahib, but my mistress waits without."

Jahanara tried not to display her concern—Nur Jahan's eunuch would surely report everything observed to his mistress. Still, a bit of pique was called for: "She presumes much, my grandfather's sister."

The eunuch pressed his head into the ground. "As you say, Begum Sahib. Nur Jahan commanded that I convey her assurances that the illness is long past, and was certainly not catching, and that she has words of import for your ears."

"Very well, I will trust to her greater experience in this. She may attend me. Go and fetch her."

The eunuch said nothing further, just bowed and withdrew.

Jahanara used the time to shore up her mental defenses. Tending Father's reignited grief had proved draining, leaving her tired and out of sorts. Worse yet, the result was still uncertain. Salim had been reading to Father almost every night, but Father had yet to make any comment on what he'd learned.

And now Nur Jahan, veteran of thirty years of imperial harem politics, was coming.

She wished Dara were here. She wished Mother was here. She wished for many things, yet none of them had come to pass when Nur Jahan entered her receiving chamber.

Head high, the older woman's direct gaze immediately fixed on Jahanara. Nur Jahan approached with the supple grace of a woman much younger than her fifty-six years, a result of a life-long regimen of dance and diet. Dressed in fine silks and damasks of her own design and pattern, Nur Jahan called to mind a great cat stalking prey.

Nur Jahan came to a halt and bowed; a delicate scent teased Jahanara's senses. "Grandniece."

Wishing to keep things formal, Jahanara used the other woman's title, "Nur Jahan," as she gestured her to a seat.

A brilliant, cheerful smile answered the formality and called to mind the reason for her title as "Light of the World." So great was the charm of that smile that Jahanara could not be certain it was false, despite knowing that it had to be.

"Must we be so formal, Janni?" Nur asked as she reclined on cushions across from Jahanara. "I am fresh recovered from illness, and would celebrate another day among the living with my family. And, as all the boys are hunting and your sister is with your father, I naturally thought of you."

Jahanara, hiding her displeasure at the other woman's use of her childhood nickname, answered in even tones: "I merely pay you the respect my grandfather bestowed upon you in recognition of your beauty, especially as you appear so well and happy."

Nur Jahan blushed, actually *blushed,* at praise she had likely heard far more times than the sun had risen over Jahanara. "Jahangir was a great man, always kinder to me than I deserved."

Marveling at the woman's control over her body, Jahanara ordered refreshments for them both.

She looked back at Nur and found the older woman regarding her with a steady gaze.

Wishing for more time, Jahanara stalled: "A new perfume, Aunt?"

A nod of the head. "Yes, I have been working on it for some time. Do you like it?"

"Very much."

"I shall see some delivered to you, then."

A silence stretched. Refreshments arrived, were served.

Jahanara let the silence linger, armoring herself in it.

"I have something I wish to tell you, Janni."

"Oh?"

"Yes."

"Must I ask?"

A throaty chuckle. "No, of course not. It is a tale. A tale from my first year with your grandfather. A tale of the hunt, in fact."

Jahanara gestured for the older woman to proceed.

"I had only been married to Jahangir for a brief while when he invited me to join him on a tiger hunt. I leapt at the chance to join him in the howdah, and had the mahouts paint his favorite elephant for the occasion. A great party of us set out, camping of a night and slowly moving through the areas where your grandfather's armies were concentrating the game for his pleasure.

"But, as you may know, your grandfather Jahangir enjoyed smoking opium far more than was good for him, and he dozed through much of the hunt, the swaying of the howdah"—she gave a throaty chuckle—"and perhaps the swaying of my hips, lulling him to sleep."

Jahanara, used to Nur's earthy storytelling, still blushed. To think of sexual congress in the hot confines of a howdah of all places, jali or no!

Nur pretended not to notice. "It was during one of his naps that there was some consternation ahead of us. I put on my veils and opened the curtains of the howdah. Several slaves were running from a wadi some tens of gaz away. It was then that I saw the reason for their flight: a pair of tigers flashing through the undergrowth after them."

Jahanara noticed the older woman's gaze grown distant, breath quickening, and felt her own pulse rising.

"They were magnificent. Terrible. Bloodlust made manifest. One man had his head nearly removed with one rake of claws.

Others fell, were torn open. Blood was everywhere." Her nostrils flared, remembering.

A tiny smile. "The screams of his slaves at last woke Jahangir from his stupor. He moved to join me, took my hand in his.

"'Protect your servants,' I told him.

"He looked at me. Too late, I could tell my command had made him most angry.

"After a moment he pressed his great bow into my hands. 'One with this. Then one with the gun, if you succeed.'

"'What?' I asked, incredulous.

"'Protect them if you wish them protected, wife.'

"I do not think he knew then, that my brother had taught me the bow in our youth. I think he thought to test me, hoping I would fail. He sought to put me in my place as his twentieth wife, however favored..." Nur Jahan let her words trail off into brief silence.

Jahanara found herself leaning forward, eager to hear more.

Slowly, conscious of the other woman's skill at courtly intrigues and careful of some trap, she sat back.

Nur resumed her tale: "I resolved to show him I was no wilting flower." The older woman sat straighter even as she said the words. "While we had spoken another pair of slaves had perished, and the tigers had pursued them much closer to our elephant. Hands shaking, I drew the bow, loosed. That first arrow missed. I did not miss with the second, though it was not enough to kill the beast. Enraged, it leapt into the air and spun in a circle. I loosed again. A lucky shot, it took the cat in the throat, stilling its roar."

A shake of her head: "The other tiger left off killing a man to raise its head, then coughed strangely, almost as if asking why his brother had stopped talking mid-sentence.

"Jahangir laughed, slapped me on the back as if I were one of his sowar, and took the bow from my hands. He handed me one of his guns, igniting the match cord himself.

"I had no experience of guns, and told him so."

"'Look along the metal, point it at his great head. When the head is covered by the barrel, tell me, and I will light it. Turn your head when I do, or you might get burned.'

"I did as he bid, aiming at a point between the great ears. I remember thinking how beautiful its fur was. 'Ready,' I whispered.

"He touched the match cord to the powder and the gun belched fire, punching me in the shoulder like nothing I felt before. I swayed back, my veil singed by the fire from the pan. I had forgotten to turn my head, you see." She shook her head. "It is amazing, what I recall of that day: I remember the feel of the elephant shivering, wanting to flee the loud noise and tigers, but too well-trained to move, while I tried to see where my shot had fallen."

She smiled, looking Jahanara in the eye, "I missed my mark."

Jahanara realized she had been showing her eagerness for the tale again, and quickly leaned back. "Well, it is understandable: you were handling a gun for the first time."

Another of Nur's throaty chuckles broke Jahanara's words. "I did not miss entirely, Janni. My ball took the tiger in the heart, killing it almost instantly. I still have the fur in my quarters."

"An entertaining tale," Jahanara mused aloud. Nur had only just departed, the air still hanging with the delicate scent of her perfume.

"Shehzadi?" her body slave and administrator of her personal staff, Smidha, asked.

"Nothing of import." She lowered her voice. "Has Prasad returned?"

"No, Begum Sahib," Smidha answered. She raised her voice slightly. "Begum Sahib, you asked to be informed when your ink was delivered. It arrived just this afternoon."

"Good," Jahanara said in an equally clear voice. She raised her head and ordered the remaining slave at the entrance to her receiving chamber, "Fetch my inks."

When she had departed on the errand: "What is it, Smidha?"

Smidha edged closer and bowed her head, speaking quickly and quietly: "My sister's man says a body was pulled from the waters of the river this morning, Begum Sahib. Nothing special in itself, but my friend who was also your sister Roshanara's nurse says that her mistress was heard to claim it was a slave who betrayed Nur Jahan. Just now, whilst you entertained her, I confirmed with one of the eunuchs that have responsibility for guarding her quarters that Nur now seeks a new cook."

Jahanara closed her eyes, said a brief prayer for Vidya. She had never personally met the young woman who, outraged by the mistreatment of her lover, had offered to spy on Nur.

Now, carrying out Jahanara's will, she would become yet another of the faceless victims of courtly machinations. Victims Jahanara would carry the guilt of in her heart to the end of her days.

She shook her head, dread encroaching on her guilt. "Which eunuch?"

"Begum Sahib?"

"Which eunuch, Smidha?"

"Chetan, Begum Sahib."

"One of the Rajputs?" she asked, running through her mental portrait gallery of the servants assigned to her enemy.

"Yes, the great big, round-headed one with the crooked nose."

Jahanara nodded. "He was one of the first she turned. He is now entirely Nur's. She wanted me to know she caught my spy. Do we know how Vidya died?"

Smidha bowed her head. "Poison is suspected, mistress."

The princess bit her lip. "Then Nur was never successfully poisoned at all?"

Smidha shrugged. "That is possible, though she did request the Italian doctor come and examine her."

"To complete her falsehood...or for something else?" Jahanara shook her head. "Set someone to watch him from now on."

"Yes, Begum Sahib."

"Any word from my diwan at Surat?"

"Kashif Khan?"

Jahanara nodded.

"He reports that Rehan Usmani made landfall last—no, two months—ago. The men set to watch his movements have not reported in since Rehan left the city with an armed party suitable for extensive travel. I begin to worry your watchers may have been set upon and killed. I also had word from my sources in Agra, proper: Salim was set upon in the city, which is why he was delayed in reporting to the emperor's summons."

"Where is she getting the men to do these things for her?" Jahanara asked.

"I do not know, Begum Sahib. She has not changed her habits significantly since Vidya came to us."

"Oh, but that's just it, Smidha. We can't know how long Nur knew about Vidya's allegiance to me. Much of our information is suspect."

Smidha's half-smile showed Jahanara that her agile mind was

working at full speed. "Yes and no, Begum Sahib. I always try to verify from multiple mouths what my ears hear from one source's lips. I do not like to look foolish, misinforming my mistress."

"So, then: what do we know?"

"That Nur Jahan is dangerous even while in your father's power."

"Who, though, is providing her with influence beyond these walls?"

Smidha shook her head. "We cannot know she is responsible for your recent setbacks, just yet, Begum Sahib." Another shrug of round shoulders. "Assuming your suspicions are correct, however, I can think of a few umara who remember Jahangir's last years and Nur's regency in all but name as good ones for their ambitions, but none that your father and grandfather are not already aware of and keeping an eye on."

"What of Mullah Mohan?"

A delicate sniff. "That man, bend his stiff neck to treat with a woman? Hardly, Begum Sahib."

"I love you dearly, Smidha, and value your service above all others, but I think you might be letting your feelings color your assessment. She has the skill, he has the manpower."

Smidha flushed and bowed her head again. "It has been my pleasure to serve you, just as it was to serve your mother, Begum Sahib. Still—" She looked up. "I find that, of late, my heart is hard when it should be soft, and soft when it should be hard."

Jahanara patted Smidha on the arm. "You are my wisest advisor, Smidha. I just want to be sure we are not dismissing a potential truth."

The older woman bowed again, looked up sharply. "And now I think on it, the idea has merit: she did have occasion to speak with Mohan while arranging Jahangir's tomb and the mosque dedicated in his name." She shook her head again, concern drawing her brows together. "If she managed to draw that dried stick of a man into her web enough that he is willing to lend her his strength, what other dark miracles can she arrange?"

"And, having seen the steel of the trap the huntress has laid out for us, what bait is meant to bring us in, and how do we spring the trap without losing a limb?"

Chapter 18

Gargi sighed as she knelt behind Nur. Nur heard a click as her advisor picked up one of the ivory combs from the tray. Soon after, Gargi's fingers and comb began the process of separating Nur's mass of thick hair to expose the gray roots.

"What news of the new spy placed upon us, Gargi?" Nur asked, the scent of the dye in her nostrils.

"Already compromised, Nur Jahan."

"So quickly?"

Nur could hear the smile in Gargi's tone. "Kamadeva favored us: the spy is quite enamored of another of the harem guards, Omid. I caught them sharing embraces Diwan Firoz Khan would almost certainly find objectionable. Especially as the guard still had use of a hard member, something that would have him trampled were the emperor to learn of it."

Nur refused to be scandalized by her advisor's news or reference to a Hindu god, and calmly opened the last of the mail. "A party of traders from the city of Hamburg," she read aloud.

The dye-laden brush in Gargi's hand paused. "I am not familiar with that place."

"Part of the north of Europe. A city-state like Venice, if I recall correctly. But that is not what is of interest here," she lifted the paper, "but that they have since embarked inland, supposedly seeking Agra and an audience with the emperor."

"As all foreigners who wish to trade here must."

141

Nur nodded, checked the date. "They should be arriving within the next few weeks."

Gargi pulled her hair back into line a little ungently. "Why this interest in trade? Jahanara appears to have all the incomes from Surat well in hand."

Ignoring Gargi's less than tactful mention of powers she no longer possessed, Nur picked another note from between her toes. "I have here information that they bribed Jahanara's new diwan in Surat—Kashif Khan—with, quote, 'sequins the likes of which have never before been seen. Not even the Venetians have ornament of such quality and lightness for sale.'"

Gargi didn't bother to scrub the disdain from her reply: "Still, it seems he was bought cheaply."

"Perhaps, but a small bit of information included in the report makes me think this particular group is more important than the usual foreigners."

"Oh?"

"These foreigners had a number of women with them, and many spoke a different language from that of the crew of their ship, one that was at least related to English, but had many words my informant did not recognize."

"I do not understand the significance of that information."

"The people from the future, the ones Baram Khan was sent to investigate, they are supposed to speak an English dialect."

"I see." The combs paused with a click of ivory. "Then you think these foreigners are from the village Baram Khan was sent to?"

"I do."

"And what, exactly, does that mean for us?"

"Opportunity, perhaps."

"What kind?"

"I do not know, yet."

"Well, I foresee one difficulty already."

"And that is?" Nur asked.

"Purdah."

Nur shrugged. The traditions that kept women separate from men had been less an obstacle for her when her husband had yet lived, but even then she'd been unable to sidestep them entirely.

"Perhaps it is time to seek additional allies; ones who might be able to talk with these foreigners, find out what they plan?"

"My options are yet limited by my tenuous return to favor."

"I know."

"Yet you have someone in mind?"

"I am sorry, but no."

"None?"

"None that are worthy of the effort, no."

"Are my options really so limited?"

Again the hands working at her hair stopped. "As I told you when you went to speak to Jahanara: you should have kept silent about your knowledge of the attempt on your life, and therefore made her see you as less a threat, even a potential ally. You insisted. Here we are."

Nur cocked her head, looking at her advisor out of the corner of her eye. "I could not let such behavior pass."

"So you said."

"Careful, Gargi. You overstep."

"I know. It is only concern for you that drives me to such extremes. Please forgive me."

Nur allowed herself a tiny sigh. "No, you are correct in nearly every detail. I let my anger get the better of my judgment and your sound advice."

Gargi's hands resumed their work, oiling and combing through Nur's thick tresses. A few moments passed in silence before she spoke again. "Speaking of anger and poor judgement: perhaps it is time to contact Mullah Mohan."

"Gargi, surely you would not choose him to try and speak on my behalf to the foreigners?"

A delicate, derisive snort. "Of course not. But he will require some time to adjust to the idea of a woman ally, and you will require some time to develop exactly the right method to manage him properly. Beyond that, there has to be someone among his supporters who has the political acumen required to keep him afloat at court. Perhaps you can learn who that is, and develop them as a go-between."

"I do not think such a person exists. Since the emperor has… returned control of government to himself, Mohan has not enjoyed the same eminence he enjoyed before."

"All the more reason to approach him now."

"Hard to believe," the emperor mused.

"Your pardon, Sultan Al'Azam?" Salim asked. Placing a finger in the book.

The emperor waved a hand to encompass Red Fort and the luxuries of his quarters. "That all this will be subjugated by the English—my empire, the people of Hindustan and the peninsula, all of them conquered and cowed in such a short span of years by a people from so far away."

Salim opened his mouth to respond, but thought better of it. It wouldn't be wise to contradict the emperor. Not wise at all.

The emperor had seen him, however. "What is it, Amir? I did not order you into my presence so that you can keep your thoughts locked behind those cheap turbans of yours."

"Sultan Al'Azam, did your own dynasty not do precisely the same thing?"

The emperor gave a snort and smiled broadly. "Indeed they did, though they came riding, not sailing. And what I meant to say was that if it is God's will that this should all fall to the English, then why resist?"

"With respect, Sultan Al'Azam, I do not think that God has chosen this medium," Salim tapped the book, "to show us a future set in stone, but to warn us where we are bound, that we might mend our ways and change our course."

Salim saw the briefest of tightening around the emperor's eyes. "If this," the emperor gestured at the book, "is not certain to happen, how do you explain the construction of my wife's tomb, exactly to my specifications, in the picture from the future?"

Salim cocked his head, considering. "I suppose that some things, improper things, might be changed for the better, according to God's will. Viewed in this light, your care for the design and construction of the tomb of Mumtaz Mahal cannot be anything *but* proper in His eyes..."

"Do you ask or tell me, Amir?"

"Neither, Sultan Al'Azam. I but seek answers. I would not presume to tell you the mind of God, just as I cannot presume to do so for any man."

"A politic response."

Remembering whom he was speaking to, Salim stopped the denial that leapt to his lips. He was less successful stopping the shake of his head.

Again the emperor caught the arrested movement: "What?"

"Politic or not, it is the truth. I do not have the education, inclination, or desire to dictate what is proper in another's path to God."

Unlike Mullah Mohan and his associates.

"Merely the future of my empire, eh?" Shah Jahan asked, picking up his drink.

Salim felt his face heat. "Sultan Al-Azam..."

Letting the jeweled drinking cup dangle carelessly from between his fingers, Shah Jahan grinned. "Relax, Amir Yilmaz. I merely jest at your expense. I know who your teacher was. Mian Mir taught many of the family. How is the saint?"

Wondering if the cup contained iced wine or some other forbidden drink, Salim answered: "I have not seen him since departing for Europe, Sultan Al'Azam."

"Really?"

"Yes, Sultan Al'Azam."

"Then?" The emperor accompanied the question with another gesture that encompassed Salim and his position in the palace.

"He had not thought to live to see me again. He asked that, whatever I found, I bring it before you and your sons. Through another of his students, he affirmed that request when I arrived in Agra."

"I see." The emperor fixed Salim with a hard stare over the rim of his cup and said, "So Mian Mir is responsible for your participation in the mission to Europe. Tell me, what did you think of Baram Khan?"

Sensing something dark lurking in the emperor, Salim chose his words with care: "He was difficult and obstinate. He did not easily adjust to changing circumstances, and he spoke harshly to those he had no need to. He was not, to use the sultan's own word, politic."

"No, he was not. Tell me, how did he die?"

"Poison, Sultan Al'Azam."

"I knew that. *How* did he die?"

"While I was not present for his very last moments, the khan was in a great deal of pain and distress, Sultan Al'Azam."

"Good."

Salim did not offer comment and managed, this time, to keep his disappointment from showing: He had hoped Shah Jahan would be above such dark and petty wishes, but a man was just a man, be he in beggar's rags or a sultan's jewels.

The emperor went silent, brooding over his cup.

Salim, unsure whether to resume reading from the book, let

his mind wander further afield while he awaited direction from his overlord.

It seemed the emperor has already changed the course of this history, he thought. Certainly everyone had been surprised by his appointment of Dara to command the punitive expedition against the Sikhs.

There was a click as the emperor set his cup down. One of the hovering slaves saw it instantly filled. Salim didn't think it wise to know what the emperor was drinking, not being sufficiently practiced at hiding his disapproval should the emperor's drink prove to be wine.

Turn away from that which offends—

Turn toward... what, though? Salim's eyes fell on the books again. Shah Jahan clearly believed these contain truths, so why hadn't the emperor asked the mullahs for fatwas concerning their contents?

Interesting. *And why haven't I asked that question before?*

"Are you ready to resume, Salim?"

"I am, Sultan Al'Azam."

"Please do."

Salim opened *India Britannica* and started reading the first chapter after the lengthy introduction:

"Chapter One: A Quiet Trade, and a Profitable One.

"India was an imperial possession long before the British made it theirs, with the notable difference that it had not become a component in an international mechanism, the rulers having simply moved in from their native soil to put down roots afresh. The ancient conglomeration of Hindu states under their rajas had first known alien occupation at the end of the twelfth century, when Turkish-speaking Muslims invaded the subcontinent and settled around the thriving city of Delhi..."

The emperor listened, his thoughts his own.

"How goes the amir's reading, Father?" Jahanara asked as he was making ready for bed.

"Well enough."

"What did you learn?"

Father shrugged. "The translation slows us, so we have barely begun."

"Still, were there many revelations to be had?"

"No, not yet."

"But Amir Yilmaz is up to the task of translating?"

"Yes." Shah Jahan sighed. "Daughter, I did not order you into my presence so you can ask me half a hundred questions about Amir Yilmaz."

"I am sorry, Father."

He sighed, pinched the bridge of his nose. "It is I who should apologize. I am weary. Things move, and I worry that I cannot see them."

"Things, Father?" she asked, trying to help him get what pained him out.

"No matter."

"If it wearies you, Father, then it must be of great import."

"Roundabout flattery will no more pry my lips apart than repeated questions."

"I am sorry, Father."

"Why do you press so?"

She spread her hands, stung. "Mother used to listen to your troubles and I thought to—"

"You are not your mother."

Jahanara swallowed past the sudden lump in her throat. "I know that, Father."

If Shah Jahan noticed the pain he'd caused her, he didn't show it: "Further, you have no idea what it is to be me. No idea what it is to be surrounded by people who want something from you at every moment of your life. Even family. Even sons." He looked at her. "Even daughters."

"I don't—"

"Yes, you do. Everyone wants something from me, my children most of all! Your brothers, all of them want—or will want—position, armies, power, all so they can kill one another off and rule when I am gone! So tell me, you, who claims to be apart from all others in my empire, what do you want of me?"

"But Murad is only a chi—"

He cut her off again. "Do not attempt to sway me from the point, to deny what you want of me: you want a husband."

Bewildered by Father's anger, Jahanara shook her head. "I—"

"You will have no husband."

"Father!" Jahanara gasped, feeling tears well. It wasn't the first time he'd said such things, but his anger and her failure to see anything she might have done to give offense left her wits a tangled mess, her feelings trampled as if by elephants.

Father went on, relentless and angry beyond reason: "Never! The decree was made by Akbar the Great himself. I will not see some upstart pretender use my daughters to claim that which my sons shall have!"

"Father?" she cried.

He was shaking with rage, now. "No. Get out!"

Jahanara fled, unable to prevent tears any longer. She was openly sobbing by the time she returned to her quarters and threw herself into bed.

Salim, concerned by the timing of his summons, approached the emperor's chambers. He was normally brought into the Imperial presence after *isha* prayers and it was barely past *zuhr*. He'd been a resident of Red Fort long enough to know Shah Jahan was something of a creature of habit, retiring to the harem after noon prayers to eat and enjoy the company of his ladies.

As Salim presented himself before the guards, a eunuch fled from the emperor's quarters, the look in his eyes that of a wounded blackbuck hunted by lions. Salim's concern ticked higher. The harem slaves and servants had been behaving strangely since last night, but no one who knew would tell him why.

Taking a steadying breath, he strode into the lion's den, ready for nearly anything.

The emperor reclined among silken pillows, a minimum of attendants surrounding him.

Salim made the requisite three bows and waited to be acknowledged.

He did not have to wait long.

"Amir. This morning's reports indicate that envoys from the United States of Europe arrived in Surat some time ago, and even now make their way to us."

The emperor leaned forward. "Did you know anything of this?"

"No, Sultan Al'Azam."

"Do you know why it is that I am only now learning that such envoys exist?"

"Aside from an awareness that someone has failed you, no, Sultan Al'Azam."

"Someone has, indeed, failed me."

Knowing he could not speak to that without appearing defensive, and therefore responsible, Salim kept his silence.

After what seemed a very long time, Shah Jahan sighed and dropped his gaze. "Do you have an idea what these envoys might bring us?"

Salim spread empty hands. "Many were the wonders of that place. Perhaps one of their many books containing technical knowledge? Or some expertise in an area of endeavor that we have not had success in? Perhaps just more of the history brought back from that other time."

"No offers of alliance?"

Salim shook his head. "I fail to see what they could offer you for such an alliance, Sultan Al'Azam. They share no borders with your empire or even with powers that share a border with us. Further: unlike the Portuguese, Dutch, and English, they have few ships to contest the seas."

"Will their envoy be a noble?"

Salim smiled. "I very much doubt it, Sultan Al'Azam."

"Oh? They would insult me with a commoner, then?"

"No, inasmuch as any of the people from the future are what we would call *common*, Sultan Al'Azam, they will be of no particular bloodline, but very well educated, in their own way."

"Will any speak Persian? Be literate?"

"I doubt, Sultan Al'Azam, that one of those people from the future has already learned our language, but they will surely be assisted by those that do."

"And their religion?"

"Christian, but..." he trailed off, uncertain how to say it without offering offense. Shah Jahan had allowed Akbar and Jahangir's religious policies to continue, not out of any particular conviction that they were correct, but rather because he had been in mourning so long he had allowed many things to continue as they had been.

"But, what?"

"They are very tolerant of religions, Sultan Al'Azam. It is one of the laws of the land." He paused, took a slight tangent in the hopes they could avoid the subject of religion. "In fact, their laws are meant to apply to all people within their lands, equally."

The emperor sniffed. "And yet Baram Khan was murdered and no one executed for it."

"I would respectfully remind the Sultan Al'Azam that we had already left the territories of the United States of Europe when Baram Khan was killed."

A dismissive wave greeted that argument. "Despite my disfavor and the intent of his dispatch to Europe, Baram Khan was an envoy of this court and therefore entitled to receive the protection of whatever prince in whose territory he found himself..."

The emperor shook his head. "But your point is taken: these people are not likely to be the author of that insult, and therefore should not be punished for it."

Salim bowed before that wisdom.

"Still, my brother sultan has expressed concerns about this country and its influence on the states between his and theirs."

Salim summoned a mental map. "You speak of the Ottoman Sultan, Sultan Al'Azam?"

The emperor nodded.

"An understandable concern for the Ottomans, Sultan Al'Azam. I have witnessed for myself how the technologies from the future can change the calculus of war."

"I would not have my Sunni brothers believe I have abandoned them by entering into an alliance with these people."

"I see the problem, Sultan Al'Azam." The Sunni powers—Uzbegs, Mughals, and Ottomans—were always interested in limiting Shia expansion, especially that of the Persian Safavid dynasty that sat between them all.

"See, but do not agree with my analysis?"

"I agree that entering into an alliance would not be wise, Sultan Al'Azam, but no sensible person could fault you for having received official envoys."

"Sensible does not always fall within those terms that define a Safavid. They ever look to take Kandahar from us. I cannot disregard the potential political costs of being seen to support the enemies of either the Ottomans or Persia."

"All true, Sultan Al'Azam."

Shah Jahan snorted. "What, no argument?"

"Sultan Al'Azam, since coming to court, I have found reason to thank God that I am not the one on whom such weighty decisions must fall. I have advised the course I think most beneficial, but make no claims to expertise in such matters."

A thin, grim smile pierced Shah Jahan's beard. "Does my most honest advisor have anything to add?"

"I cannot think of anything, Sultan Al'Azam."

Another, broader smile. "I do enjoy your economy of words, Amir. So much so that I think we must find them employment."

"You are too kind, Sultan Al'Azam."

"You will have opportunity to prove my words properly weighted in your favor: I grant you command of five hundred, a robe of office and incomes necessary to act as host to the envoys from the USE and send you forth to deliver the *dastak* to the envoys."

Salim sat silent, stunned. He had thought himself come into Shah Jahan's presence ready for anything, only to have the emperor surprise him yet again.

"Did I surprise you?"

"Yes, Sultan Al'Azam."

"Good. Gather men, and quickly. The envoys are already well on their way."

"That may prove difficult, Sultan Al'Azam. Between the armies of your son and those of Asaf Khan, there are scarcely more than a hundred men not already in your direct service worthy of the name."

"You have not called upon your clansmen?"

It was Salim's turn to smile. "I have. Those are the hundred I spoke of. Most already ride with one of your hosts."

The emperor returned the grin. "Well then, you have a core of fine riders. Still, we cannot have so small a party greet our guests." He turned and spoke briefly to an attendant, who left at the run.

"I have summoned Diwan Firoz Khan, who has the care of the harem in his department. He will supply you another hundred warriors to fill your numbers while we await fresh sowar seeking employment."

Those would likely be eunuchs and Turki warrior-women. Still, each would be a blooded warrior. In any event, if things turned to fighting, then the situation would have truly gone to ruin.

He bowed. "As you wish, Sultan Al'Azam."

Chapter 19

A few kos west of Ramdaspur
October 1634

The courier came to a halt in front of the Red Tent, dismounted and spoke: "Suleiman Khan reports he will have claimed the fort in your name by nightfall, Shehzada."

Dara offered a satisfied smile. The army had invested the small fort west of the Ramdaspur just hours before. Suleiman was making excellent time, especially given Dara's own request that none of the farmland of the Sikhs be unduly damaged.

Dara nodded and gave the messenger leave to depart. He checked the angle of the sun. About two hours remained before sunset. He looked again at the small fort and said to Mukhlis Khan: "Hardly seems a battle. Suleiman Khan is far quicker than I thought he would be."

Mukhlis waved a languid hand, drank from his chalice of chilled wine. "They can hardly be called warriors, these farmers. That they were too few to resist your vanguard, and from behind walls, even, is proof of their weakness."

Dara watched as the dust rising from all around the fort cleared briefly, showing Suleiman Khan's men atop one wall.

He hated how hard he had to work to keep the plaintive note from his voice as he continued: "I can scarce see what is going on, we are so far to the rear."

"While I would not turn down a chance at the choice loot Suleiman is sure to collect, your father would have my head should you come to needless harm, Shehzada."

152

"Perhaps both desires can be satisfied. Scouts reported Hargobind's palace, the place they call the Eternal Throne, lies just beyond the fort, and was evacuated upon our arrival. Surely securing it would be a blow to Sikh morale, and give the sowar an opportunity to enrich themselves."

Appealing to Mukhlis' greed worked: "If Shehzada insists, then I can see no reason to refuse." The older man set his goblet down and called for a horse.

"Horses?" Dara asked.

"Elephants are too slow for this type of work, and would make your presence obvious to the enemy."

"Clever."

A wry grin. "My father sired no fools."

Manor of Guru Hargobind

The guru's throne complex was a substantial set of attractive buildings designed around an open plan that made it poorly suited to withstand an assault. So poor, the Sikhs had not even bothered to defend it; Mukhlis Khan, Dara, and their combined bodyguard of nearly two thousand men rode in unopposed.

Within moments Mukhlis Khan's men had dispersed and set about stripping everything of value from the opulent residence.

"Shehzada?" Mohammed, captain of his personal bodyguard, used the single word to request permission for Dara's bodyguard to join the khan's men.

Dara gave a minute shake of the head in reply, belatedly sensing the displeasure of his men as the order to stay mounted was relayed.

So be it. Mian Mir would not look upon this day with pride in his pupil: the Sikhs were favorites of the Living Saint, and he would consider making war for loot well beneath the righteous man.

The thought was punctuated by the sounds of breaking glass and shattered porcelain from across the yard.

Mohammed spoke: "Should I set a guard, Shehzada?"

Dara shook his head. If he denied his men the chance at loot, the least he could do was not give them extra duty.

A large pile was quickly growing in front of Mukhlis: ornaments of gold and silk, casks of drink and incense as the man called out to the occasional trooper, claiming a choice piece of loot for his own.

Wishing that war were otherwise, that there existed some other manner in which he might prove himself worthy of the throne, Dara raised his eyes and squinted into the setting sun just in time to catch sight of the Sikh banners being pulled down from the ramparts of the mud-walled fort to the west of the palace.

"Mukhlis Khan," he called.

"Yes, Shehzada?"

"I return to camp. See that no fires are set here. The new governor may wish to use it as his residence."

"Yes, Shehzada."

Red Tent, Camp of Dara Shikoh

Aside from the occasional disgruntled trumpet of his war elephants, the night camp was quiet on their return. Those not actively guarding the camp were at *Maghrib* prayers, facing Mecca.

Though he wished for the solace of prayer himself, Dara found a messenger waiting for him as he pulled up in front of the red tent and dismounted.

"What is it?" Dara asked, striding into the golden glow of the lanterns set about his tent. Mohammed remained with him, removing his chain-backed gloves and taking a position near the low table Dara used for correspondence.

The messenger did not wait for his prince to take a seat among the cushions. "Shehzada, Suleiman praises God and extends his compliments: the fort is taken with minimal losses."

"How many?"

"One hundred and two dead, another hundred wounded."

"So many? How many of the enemy killed?"

"Fifty-two, Shehzada."

"Any prisoners?"

"No, Shehzada. They refused to be taken alive."

Those were acceptable losses for storming fortifications. Aloud, he said, "I see. Suleiman remains in the fort?"

"Yes, Shehzada. Further, Suleiman Khan begs permission to sally forth and take the town tomorrow at dawn."

"Extend my compliments to the Khan on his rapid and

well-conducted assault. I will see him well rewarded for his suc-
cesses." Dara drank to buy time to consider what orders he should
give next. Erring on the side of caution, he said, "Suleiman Khan
may make preparations, but he must await orders from myself
or Mukhlis Khan before launching any attack."

"Yes, Shehzada."

"Go, and tell him I am most pleased."

"Yes, Shehzada." The messenger bowed and departed.

Dara turned to his correspondence. Within moments he had
finished the report begun that morning, informing Father and
the court of his daily progress. When done, he called one of
the imperial messengers into his presence and gave the report,
in addition to his private correspondence, into the man's hands.

That done, he leaned back among the cushions and finished
his julabmost, idly reflecting that this much closer to the Hima-
layas it must be easier to fetch ice for his drinks.

He heard Mohammed sniff. It had, in the last few weeks,
become the man's method of requesting Dara's attention—initially
as an accident, now as a bit of short-hand code.

Dara turned to the man. "What is it, Mohammed?"

A clink of mail as the tall Persian shrugged. "I am uneasy,
Shehzada."

"Over what?"

"It seems too easy, Shehzada."

"What?"

"The taking of the fort. So few defenders. That place could
easily be manned by nearly two thousand."

Mohammed was a veteran of Father's wars, and Dara knew
better than to dismiss his misgivings. "Tell me your thoughts."

"Why so few defenders? We know they have not fled the
town itself. Why die to a man if not to cover the flight of family and kin?"

"Perhaps because of the religious significance of the town?"

"Then why not man the fort fully?"

"Water?"

A shake of Mohammed's head. "There is a tank in the fort,
and the monsoon has just passed."

"And we know we did not surprise them with our arrival,"
Dara said. They had made no attempt to conceal their approach,
hoping the Sikhs would attempt to meet them in an open-field

battle where the vastly superior quality and numbers of Mughal cavalry would come fully into play.

A snort. "No, Shehzada, that is certain. And we were unmolested moving back and forth to the guru's palace. Perhaps they wish to draw us into a siege? They must know we brought no heavy guns."

"Aren't their walls barely sufficient to require a ladder?"

Mohammed nodded. "And, by all reports their women are still inside. They may believe in equality between the sexes, but even that foolish notion must fail before the logic of a siege: more mouths means they will run out of food that much faster. It makes no sense."

"Agreed."

Dara's stomach growled. "This talk of food has spurred my own hunger. Come, share a meal with me and we will see if we cannot divine the guru's purpose together. At the very least, we can decide tomorrow's order of battle."

Dara just finished morning prayer when one of his slaves came in, sweating despite the cool pre-dawn air. He waved the eunuch permission to speak as another slave belted on his sword baldric.

"Shehzada, someone has set fire to the palace."

"Damn him."

Mohammed entered, fully armed and armored. "Do we go teach him the error of his ways, Shehzada?" he asked, clearly already aware of Mukhlis Khan's disobedience.

Dara considered, then shook his head. "No, I will not risk a confrontation and open break with him, not while there might still be fighting to be done." He put on his helmet. *But I will see to it that he is never made governor, here or anywhere.*

"Are the men ready?"

"They are not just ready to attack the town, they are eager, Shehzada! I have ordered all the men to join their khans in the order of battle you commanded. They have but to mount up."

"Message to Suleiman Khan: prepare to attack on my command. We will move out at first light."

Dara followed his messenger from the Red Tent, stalking toward Gajendra, his armored war elephant. The massive beast knelt at the command of his mahout, allowing Dara to climb aboard.

Once the beast stood erect again, Dara looked to the east.

The red fire and under-lit pall of smoke from the palace was clearly visible.

Damn him.

He looked to his men, preparing to issue his orders. Everyone was craning their necks to see the fire. Beyond them, Dara could even see the dawn-lit points of the helms of Suleiman's men, lined up along the eastern wall of the fort, watching the palace burn.

Then the helmets disappeared in a sudden eruption of a dirty cloud of smoke and earth with a dirty red spark at its heart.

A moment passed in silence before the deep rolling boom reached out to drum his chest, pound his ears.

"Merciful God!" the mahout groaned as the cloud expanded into the descending line of dawn's light.

Utter surprise made a hash of Dara's thoughts. A third of his forces were gone in the blink of an eye.

"Mined!" Mohammed shouted to him from the ground. He had not mounted his own elephant.

Mined. Dara nodded stupidly, kicking his thoughts into motion. They had mined the fort with a massive black powder charge, which was why they'd defended it so fiercely but with so few.

He blinked. And why they left the palace intact for looting. *Which begs the question whether or not Mukhlis Khan is even alive, let alone set the fire we were all watching like idiots!*

Horses and men suddenly started screaming along the western edge of the camp, which was now the rear of Dara's army.

BAM! An easily recognized volley of massed arquebus fire from the north—his right flank. More screams from men and wounded horses followed.

But, he hadn't brought any arquebuses. The thought came slowly, like he'd spent the night on an opium-smoking bender instead of preparing to command his first battle.

"There!" one of the bodyguard shouted. The call was chased by a sound it took his inexperienced ears a moment to identify: the heavy crunch of a hard-driven arrow striking through mail to bite flesh.

Mohammed's veteran instincts set him into motion. He started shouting at the sowar, turning them to face the threat to the rear and flank as he ran for his horse, leaving Dara and the elephants.

It was then Dara heard the pounding of hooves from the south. Dara blanched at the sight of a party of at least five hundred mounted lancers charging home into the rear of what had been his left flank.

Where were they all coming from? What should he do?

Someone was screaming at him.

"What?" he shouted back.

The mahout, yelling over the rising din of the sudden battle that had surrounded them on three sides, repeated his question, "Where do I go, Shehzada?"

Dara took a deep breath and tried to take stock of the situation. The lancers were nearing the Red Tent. Having lost their spears in the corpses of Mughal warriors, most of the Sikhs were still charging forward, laying about them with swords.

There was no further gunfire from the north, only a roar from the throats of men engaged in the life or death struggle of hand-to-hand combat. One volley and they'd charged. Now they were in among the men.

Dara's eyes slid to where Mohammed had mounted up. The chief of his *nökör* had already started to get the men to face the threat, but each trooper was hampered by the tight confines created by the man and horse beside him. Mohammed needed time.

Time the charging cavalry would not allow. The left flank was already crumbling, the Sikh cavalry having penetrated nearly all the way through that element of Dara's army and to the center.

They had to be stopped.

Dara picked up the powerful recurve bow already strung for his use and shouted, "We go to face their cavalry, mahout!"

The thin little man whose name Dara hadn't bothered to learn smiled, eyes alight with a warrior's spirit. "Yes, Shehzada!" He bent over the head of Gajendra. "Lord of Elephants, it is time you earned your keep and showed our prince your worth!"

The bull elephant responded to his handler's exhortations, turning in place with surprising agility. He surged forward, armored flanks clanking. Dara looked back and was comforted to see the other elephants following.

There was no room to maneuver, no niceties, nothing but to charge headlong and hope his own men were able to get clear before Gajendra and his brood smashed into the Sikhs.

Timing each release of the bow-string with the gait of the elephant, Dara started serving targets with his arrows.

The heavy bow drove shafts through armor and flesh, tumbled riders from saddles. He had time for only three arrows before his elephant slammed into the cavalry. Horses and riders shot away from Gajendra's passing, transformed in his wake to broken, heaving mounds of tangled flesh and broken bone.

A rider came in close, hacked at the elephant's neck, catching an ear instead. The angry pachyderm lowered his head and caught the man's mount under the withers with his tusks. With a heave he sent rider and horse together into the air.

Dara nocked another arrow. In this, at least, Dara had been lucky: most of the Sikhs had already lost their spears, and had nothing to reach him with.

He drew and loosed, taking a man in the head. Drew and loosed, taking a rider's horse in the neck with his arrow. Again. This time the arrow snapped against the man's raised shield.

His shoulders were burning now, the repeated drawing of the heavy bow tiring muscles unused to such prolonged abuse. Ignoring the pain, he drew and loosed again, but the arrow found nothing more vital than the earth.

His hand was collecting another arrow when his eye caught upon morning light splashing from a spear tip. A lancer had ridden ahead of Gajendra, turned, and was riding back toward him.

Horse and elephant closed with alarming speed. Dara nocked arrow to bowstring as the man couched his spear. He drew and loosed, but his target swayed to one side and Dara missed.

He was reaching for another arrow when the Sikh disappeared from view below the mahout and Gajendra's head. There followed a crash and a loud, crunching snap.

The massive beast stumbled. Dara leaned forward in the howdah and was nearly pitched from it as the elephant fell to its knees. Then the sliding, shuddering halt of Gajendra made the howdah snap forward and strike the mahout in the back, launching him screaming over the elephant's head.

Dara didn't see where he fell, concentrating instead on preventing his own fall. He wrenched his shoulders and lost his bow, ended hanging from one of the uprights that held the roof of the howdah, but managed to keep his grip.

When it was all over, Dara hung over the still head of his dead mount and saw the cause of Gajendra's demise: the Sikh's spear-hand had struck lucky and true, entering scarcely a hand-span of unarmored space around the elephant's eye and snapping off in the heavy skull.

Dara dropped to the ground a gaz below his feet, stumbled and fell on his back in the blood-slick turf. He rolled over, hands shaking as he put them beneath his body. Knees protesting the additional weight of armor, he drew his sword and surged erect, searching for threats.

A Sikh warrior, powerfully built and well armored but lacking a horse, moved smoothly toward him with sword and shield at the ready.

Wishing for his own shield, Dara recognized the footwork. The man was using—if not the style, then certainly one very similar to—the style Dara's Hindu sword master had taught for use on uneven ground. Dara adjusted his stance accordingly, made for a patch of clear ground.

"I am Bidhi Chand," the man announced, stopping a few steps out of reach.

"Is that to mean something to me?" Dara asked, drawing *katar* and dagger both into his left hand. Without a shield, they would be both threat and protection.

A shrug of broad shoulders: "I thought you might wish to know whom to curse when you fall dead at my feet."

"How polite of you."

A broad smile and even teeth. "We serve."

"Who?"

"All of us."

"No, who do you serve?"

Bidhi Chand's smile disappeared as he hung his chain veil. "Exactly."

The tip of Bidhi's sword was a blur as they closed. They met, parted, turned.

Again Bidhi advanced. Dara tried to dictate the flow of the combat, but quickly found he was facing a master, unable to touch the other man with his blade. He felt the mail protecting his armpit part, saw the rings spin free in the morning light as they completed the exchange.

The dance was fast, too fast for Dara to sustain for long.

"Breathing hard, already?" Bidhi Chand asked when next they parted.

Dara detected no mockery, merely a mild interest he found more unsettling than any attempt to goad him would be.

Still, if he would give Dara time to draw breath, he would not complain of it. He nodded, took a deep, controlled breath, and replied on the exhalation: "Yes. Among those failures I regret most today is that I was never diligent in training my body to prolonged combat."

"An understandable regret," Bidhi said, moving forward. Dara was fascinated by how seamlessly the man switched between styles. He tried to keep his eye on the blade-tip; got slammed in the face with the shield for his trouble, swayed sideways to avoid the following crosscut he could not see but knew was coming. Tried, but still felt the hot kiss of a blade parting the tender flesh under his arm where Bidhi had opened the armor on their last pass.

Staggering, Dara tried to duck under the return cut flashing toward his head. The blade caught him a glancing blow on the skullcap, setting his ears to ringing and stars dancing to the tune.

Something hot and wet was dribbling along his suddenly-cold flank. He swayed, felt another hot kiss, this time in the belly.

The last thing Dara Shikoh saw was the dew-and-blood-damp earth rushing to embrace him.

Chapter 20

Agra, Red Fort, The Harem
November 1634

"Shehzadi, Diwan Firoz Khan humbly requests a moment of your time this morning," Smidha said, overseeing the slaves as they applied the last touches of henna to Jahanara's feet.

"Oh? Do you know why? We aren't due to go over the harem's financials for several days."

"No, Shehzadi, I do not." Smidha shooed the slaves away. "He would only say the matter was of some import."

"Very well, send for him."

Smidha nodded to one of the attendants, who went in search of the harem's diwan.

When they were reasonably alone, Smidha leaned in close. "How are you feeling, daughter of my heart?"

Jahanara shrugged. "As well as can be expected. Father maintains his distance, but has not otherwise punished me for . . . whatever it was I did to incite his anger the other night."

"You speak, yet do not answer my question."

Feeling a smile curl her lips, the first since Father's outburst, Jahanara explained: "I hurt, Smidha. I do not know why. I have known my place for many years, yet when Father was yelling, it was as if I was hearing those things for the first time . . ." She shook her head, drew a deep, cleansing breath. "I suppose I had not realized how much hope I still held that he might be swayed from his position."

162

"Perhaps he will change it of his own accord, given time, Shehzadi."

Jahanara nodded, saved from voicing her doubts by Diwan Firoz Khan's arrival.

"You wished to see me, Diwan?"

"Indeed, Shehzadi: foreign travelers we have never seen before made landfall in Surat and are now making their way inland in hopes of an audience with Shah Jahan."

"All foreigners must use Surat if they wish to trade within the empire. Why should this group rouse your interest?"

"For three reasons, Begum Sahib. One: our spies in service to the English Company report that their factors expressed some consternation at their presence."

"Wait, something about these folk displeases the English?"

"Yes, Shehzadi. I had suspicions who they might be, but wanted confirmation before reporting to you. Diwan Kashif was able to furnish such confirmation: the strangers are, at least in part, from that town from the future that furnished the papers and books, this—" He had difficulty with the odd word—"Grantville."

"I see now why they interest you! Please continue."

"Two: the diwan you assigned to oversee your interests in Surat had reason to interact with them.

"Lastly: the emperor met privately with the man he has chosen as *mihmandar* to the visiting dignitaries."

"Fascinating. When will they get here? Never mind that! Who else knows of their approach?"

"They are two, perhaps three days from Agra, Shehzadi. The latest information—merely a day old—and learned at your father's knee: they stopped at one of your caravanserai just five days slow ride from here.

"As to who may know," he waggled his head, "I do not think a great many, despite the selection of a mihmandar. As you know, the court has been focused of late on your brother's campaign to punish the Sikhs. Between that and the departure of Asaf Khan's army, there has been little attention to spare."

"He what?" Smidha blurted.

"Who?" Jahanara asked, at nearly the same time.

"The emperor has chosen and dispatched a mihmandar to see to the needs of the foreign dignitaries and return them to court. I only know of it because he called upon me to provide riders from the harem guardians."

"Who did Father choose?" Jahanara repeated, suspecting she knew the answer.

"Amir Salim Gadh Visa Yilmaz, who has also been promoted to command five hundred and given robes so that he cuts a suitable figure and the mace for presentation to the envoys."

"I see," Jahanara said, glancing excitedly at Smidha.

"Why did Diwan Kashif treat with them?" Smidha asked, caution driving her back to her original question.

"They were unclear on certain of our ways, and thought Kashif the governor."

"Kashif corrected that misapprehension, did he not?" Jahanara asked, suddenly fearful. The last thing she wanted was for Father to remove Kashif for overstepping his authority. He'd barely taken up the post and finding a replacement would be most problematic.

"Yes, Shehzadi. He also ordered the escort we provided him when you assigned him to Surat—which was to return to Agra anyway—to escort the foreigners here to Agra."

"Somewhat beyond his purview," Smidha said.

"But excusable, given the *ferenghi*'s error," Firoz Khan offered.

"He was ordered to keep his head down and simply work at improving our holdings in Surat," Smidha continued.

"And has done an excellent job, even in the short time he has been in charge."

Jahanara hid a smile. Such public statements of support for the people he'd put up for appointment was one of the reasons Jahanara had chosen Firoz Khan to manage Father's harem. He was—if not overburdened with too many scruples—at least not inclined to withdraw his support from a subordinate at the first sign of royal displeasure.

"Still, what did they offer Kashif, to encourage him to take such risks?"

"Kashif said they gave him a number of high quality sequins. He requests orders as to how to dispose of them. Both the quantity and quality reported by Kashif are confirmed by my independent sources in this letter, here." The diwan presented a letter.

She waved his proof away, trusting his word on this subject.

The diwan slid the letter back into his robes, but Jahanara did not miss his pleased smile.

Patting the letter, he went on, "Kashif explains that the people from the future did not deign to reveal what they plan to offer in trade, but that they purchased forty pack horses from your concerns there, mounts for a dozen riders, remounts for same, and hardly blinked at the costs, which were quite high."

"Only a dozen in their party?"

"Including the wives of three of them, yes."

"*Wives?*" Smidha and Jahanara chorused in surprise.

He nodded, smile dimpling smooth cheeks once more. "Indeed, Shehzadi." He waved a hand as if such information was of little import, "There were more men aboard their ship, but they remain there as of the last report."

"You tease!" Jahanara said.

He wagged his head, put a hand to his breast. "Who, me, Shehzadi?"

"Tell me of these women, you reprobate."

He pretended a swoon. "Forgive me, Shehzadi!"

Jahanara couldn't—entirely—prevent a snort of laughter, choked out: "Only if you desist immediately and tell me of these wives!"

"They were respectful of modesty, and went about covered when required, but Khashif's spies claimed that when aboard their ship one of them displayed golden hair and all of them went about on the ship dressed in clothing completely inappropriate to the climate."

"What clothing?"

"Woolen dresses, I think."

She gestured at her own silk top, one of the class of fabrics called water for its utter sheerness and translucent qualities. "Wouldn't that itch terribly?"

Firoz Khan shuddered. "I imagine so."

"Fascinating."

"Do we have translators for these women when they join us in the harem?"

"Not at the moment, Begum Sahib."

"Who was it the amir stayed with when we finally found him?"

Firoz nodded, taking her unspoken advice. "The home of Jadu Das, a merchant factor for the English. I shall start there. Thank you, Begum Sahib."

"Any idea why the women accompany this mission?"

"None."

Along the river Yamuna

"When do we arrive?" Bertram asked, trying out his Farsi. He had been practicing intensively with Angelo, but knew he was some months, at best, from fluency. Every member of the mission needed to learn or forever be at the mercy of translators, assuming someone could be found.

"Tomorrow afternoon," Iqtadar said. He gave Bertram a measuring glance and added, after a moment: "You learn quickly."

Bertram thanked the chieftain and reined in to wait for Rodney and John. Both up-timers sent a lazy wave his direction. John even smiled. Smiles had been more frequent from him since he and his wife had survived the bandit attack unscathed.

"Iqtadar says we'll make the gates of the city tomorrow."

"Nearly there, at last," John said, adjusting his seat in the saddle.

"Ever fly anywhere? You know, before?" Rodney asked.

"A few times."

"The world got a whole lot bigger after the Ring of Fire, though there's lots of folks in the USE trying to shrink it back up again."

"Sure, they're working miracles with what we've got," John said, "but we'll be in our sixties before there's enough planes to make even short passenger flights commercially viable, let alone international flights."

"No argument here."

Bertram shook his head.

"What?" John asked.

"So much change, so quickly, and yet you complain that things are proceeding too slow!"

John shrugged. "Not complaining, exactly. I always preferred riding rails to flying wherever possible, anyway. It's just the pace of things was—"

John cut off mid-sentence, looking ahead. Bertram followed the line of his gaze, saw one of Iqtadar's scouts riding back at the gallop.

"He looks in a hurry."

Bertram looked back along the line of the column, found Angelo riding with the ladies a hundred paces or so to the rear, giving them their language lessons. He whistled as loudly as he could. Everyone in earshot looked his way. He pointed at Angelo and waved the translator forward, speeding up to a canter to rejoin Iqtadar himself. He heard Rodney and John fall in and was comforted by their armed presence at his back.

The chief was speaking to his second as Bertram rode up. Neither seemed tense, but Bertram had seen how the Afghans could go from seeming indolence to violent action in a heartbeat.

The outrider pulled up and spoke too rapidly for Bertram to understand. From his tone, the man wasn't distressed, which was some slight comfort.

Iqtadar sniffed loudly through his hooked and oft-broken nose, said something Bertram translated as, "pretty smells."

Iqtadar's men laughed harshly.

Angelo trotted up a moment later and immediately asked what was afoot.

Bertram understood one in five words that followed and what he could comprehend left him confused.

Angelo asked a one-word question, got a curt reply. He shrugged and translated. "A party approaches. Iqtadar says they are armed, but says that, as the party is composed of eunuchs and women, it is of little concern."

"But, I thought they closeted all women, kept them from public view."

"The Muslims do, for the most part. This is ... different."

"How does that work?"

Angelo shrugged, "The Turki women are an exception. There are some tribes among them that are known to provide warrior women as guardians for the harems of potentates, but it is not very common and certainly unusual in the numbers the outrider claims ride toward us."

"Then the numbers indicate someone powerful enough to ignore certain ... irregularities?"

Angelo nodded. "Almost certainly. In fact, they are likely commanded by someone in the emperor's household."

A troop of cavalry appeared in the distance, riding the shaded road that led to the capital.

"Headed toward us, that's sure," Angelo said.

"Yup," John murmured. "And Angelo's right, there's some Amazons with 'em. In fact, only a few of them have what the locals consider a proper beard."

Bertram glanced back at the up-timer; the man was using the telescopic sight of his rifle to get a better look.

"No guns, though. Just bows, swords and lances."

"Perhaps you should lower the rifle, John. They may take umbrage."

Salim let out a slow breath as the man in the van of the column lowered the up-timer rifle.

He'd seen what the weapons could do one cold European afternoon. The Albernian Mercenary Company had held the bridge against formidable odds all day, using rifles much like the one the up-timer held. That skirmish had furnished plenty of evidence that a trained rifleman could easily remove any of his riders from the saddle at distances far greater than the two hundred gaz or so of road separating them. He'd even done a fair amount of shooting with one, himself. In fact, it had only been running out of ammunition that had made him toss a wounded North off the bridge and light the bomb fuse meant to bring the bridge down. The memory of the freezing waters closing over his head and the desperate swim that followed caused him to shiver despite the rising heat of the day.

"What is it, Amir?" The woman's voice drew him from the spell of memory.

Salim glanced aside, found bright eyes regarding him over a chain mail veil, and recognized Atisheh, one of the warrior-maidens of the harem. Despite her seeming inattention, she rode with ease and practiced grace.

He waved a hand, clearing away the memories. "Nothing. A memory."

She nodded at the party on the road ahead. "This is them?"

"Oh, yes. They have at least one of the weapons from the future. See the man sitting next to the giant one, the one settling something that looks like an arquebus on his back?"

Her eyes narrowed. "I see him."

"That is a rifle. A much more dangerous firearm than any to be had outside of the village from the future."

"The bearer is no rider, though. Look how he sits his horse. He'd be thrown after shooting."

"Perhaps. The up-timers are not known for their skill at horsemanship. They relied on mechanical contrivances to convey them about."

The conversation had carried them across much of the distance separating the two columns of horse. He raised a hand. His riders slowed, came to a halt a bare hundred gaz from the up-timers. "Atisheh, you and Abdul are with me."

Abdul's expression soured slightly. Clearly, his lieutenant did not care for this assignment—or perhaps, simply didn't like to be seen riding with women and eunuchs.

"Let's not make any sudden moves," Angelo said, eyeing the riders just coming to a halt about a hundred yards away.

"No, let's not," John agreed. Every one of the warriors bore bow and blades, riding with an easy grace John could never hope to match. The women and some of the men—eunuchs, he supposed—wore both silks and mail. He never would have thought someone wearing that much silk could be so intimidating.

A big fellow emerged from the center of the riders, bearded and capable-looking. One of the women rode with him, as well as another man with a full beard, this one cut from the same mold as the first guy and—John looked sideways at Iqtadar. *Looks like small West Virginia towns ain't the only places to spawn folks with a similar look.*

By prearranged plan, John, Iqtadar, and Angelo rode forward ten yards or so and came to a stop.

Iqtadar edged forward a bit more, peering at their opposites. After a moment he shouted, "Abdul?"

John flinched. The sudden noise and his rider's movement made his mount rear. John kept his seat with far greater ease than he would have just a week ago. So much so that he was able to watch as the man to the right of the leader smiled broadly and called back, "Iqtadar!"

"You know this man?" he asked, through Angelo.

Iqtadar smiled, nodding. "I do. He is my kinsman."

When the two parties drew close enough for regular conversation, the central figure spoke in accented but perfectly understandable English, "You are the envoy from the United States of Europe?"

Swallowing surprise at the man's command of English, John nodded. "I am both envoy and authorized to speak on behalf of the others with that status in our party."

"Shah Jahan, the Sultan Al'Azam..." the man launched into another series of untranslated titles and powers before returning to English, "greets you and offers you shelter in the shadow of his power for as long as you desire."

Angelo gave a barely audible sigh. John shot a look the Venetian's way. He looked a little deflated he hadn't been called on to translate.

"We accept in the name of His Majesty Gustavus Adolphus and the duly elected government of the United States of Europe."

"I am Amir Salim Gadh Visa Yilmaz, your mihmandar—your"—he searched for the proper term—"host for the duration of your stay. I am at your service. Whatever your needs, I will make every effort to see them met."

"That is most kind of both the emperor and you, Amir. I am Mr. John Dexter Ennis of Grantville." He gestured at Iqtadar. "It appears our guide and defender, Iqtadar, is known to some of you." He nodded at Angelo. "And this is Angelo Gradinego, our translator, late of Venice. There are others in the mission I'll have to introduce you to, but on behalf of all of us, and Gustavus Adolphus, Emperor of the United States of Europe, I wish to inform you how pleased we are to be to be met with such a strong party."

"As soon as he learned of your coming, Shah Jahan was overtaken with desire to see you in person."

That might not be an entirely good thing: Don Francisco had said the Mughal diplomat bought some books in Grantville that revealed the history of European dealings in India—which had often been anything but savory.

"We also look upon the chance to meet the emperor with excitement and hope for a prosperous future."

The amir relaxed fractionally and then waved a big hand at his male companion and across at Iqtadar. "With your permission, my kinsmen desperately want to talk to one another."

"Your kinsmen?" John asked as the men in question started catching up with one another in rapid-fire Persian.

A small smile, nearly lost in the man's beard. "Iqtadar does not recognize me, as I have been gone for some time, but we are cousins as well."

"Oh?"

"I am only recently returned from Europe myself. I was part of Baram Khan's diplomatic party."

"I . . . see."

Salim's expression did not betray any feeling, one way or another, on the matter of Baram Khan's fate.

"Shall we join our two parties and continue?"

"Certainly, Amir."

Angelo spoke up, translating for Iqtadar, who called a command and waved at the rest of the mission, even as the amir did the same to his warriors.

The escorts quickly formed up on either side of the mission.

Rodney, Gervais, and Bertram put heels to their horses, moving to join them at the front. Further back, John saw their wives and the warrior women among their escorts eyeing one another like two rival packs of wolves from some nature show, each pack uncertain of the other.

He turned back to Salim in time to catch the other man watching him.

"We had information that you were traveling in company with your wives."

"Yes. Will that pose a problem?"

"No, not at all. I believe an opportunity to converse with your wives will please Begum Sahib immensely."

"Begum Sahib?"

"The Princess of Princesses: Jahanara, eldest daughter of Shah Jahan."

"Right, I knew that. It was her that, indirectly, provided our escort. Please forgive my lapse. The ah... The royal family is in good health, then?"

"Entirely."

"Good to hear."

Salim chuckled.

"What is it?"

"Forgive me if I misspeak, but I think you, like me, are not made for diplomatic speeches."

John laughed, and was still laughing when Rodney, Bertram and Gervais joined them.

"What has you in stitches?" Rodney asked in English.

"We were just commiserating over our mutual lack of appreciation for the niceties of diplomatic speech," Salim explained.

Rodney's expression on hearing both Salim's excellent English and the entirely accurate assessment of John's character was so priceless it set John off again.

Chapter 21

Agra, Red Fort, The Diwan-i-Khas
November 1634

Expectations high, Jahanara and Nadira eagerly awaited their first sight of the envoys from the future as Father made short work of the day's regular business.

Jahanara glanced up as Nur entered the women's area. Her great-aunt sent a nod Jahanara's way before sitting with her typical grace.

Jahanara hid her discontent. It would have been nice to have had this bit of excitement to herself. Now she would have to conceal the depth of her interest, lest Nur use it against her.

"Bring them forth, then," Father said.

Realizing she'd missed an announcement, Jahanara put away her thoughts and looked through the jali.

Amir Salim appeared with a significant party of strangely dressed men in his wake.

Jahanara forgot Nur's presence, leaning forward to peer at the foreigners. Almost all of them stood a head taller than the courtiers lining their path. One was of such enormous size she was sure he could crack a skull with but one hand. Two of the men had beards so blond she thought them beardless at first. Craning her neck, she spied several burqas at the rear of the party.

Amir Yilmaz strode forward and bowed three times before the Peacock Throne. The ferenghi did likewise, some with a good deal less grace.

172

Father eyed them a moment, his expression inscrutable, then waved permission for Salim to speak.

"Al-Sultan Al'Azam wal Khaqan al-Mukarram, Abu'l-Muzaffar Shihab ud-din Muhammad, Sahib-i-Qiran-i-Sani, Shah Jahan I Padshah Ghazi Zillu'llah, I present to you the party of envoys representing the trade interests of Gustavus Adolphus, Emperor of the United States of Europe." He made a sweeping gesture that took in the entire party.

One man stepped forward and bowed again, then spoke in a deep voice that was immediately translated by a fellow in his party that looked somewhat familiar. "Sultan Al—"

"Sultan Al'Azam! Sultan!" The shouts coming from somewhere else took everyone completely by surprise, Father's guards included. Blades were bared and the dais between the ferenghis and Father quickly covered in armed retainers ready to cut down any threat.

Those courtiers closest to the throne edged away, their own retainers closing about them. While not permitted arms in the royal presence, still they stood to defend their rulers and chieftains. Such were the dynamics of power in Father's lands that there were many who had cause to fear assassination, even at court.

Jahanara looked from them to search for the source of the shouts, eventually spotting a man pushing through the envoys, turban and sash marking him as a post-rider.

She saw the giant foreigner put his weight on the balls of his feet as if preparing to rush the messenger.

Before he could launch his attack and push things even further into chaos, Salim had him by the wrist. He must have found the right words to calm the big fellow, because he settled back on his heels.

"What is the meaning of this interruption?" Shah Jahan shouted, standing, ringed with steel.

"Sultan Al'Azam, terrible news!" the messenger cried, waving the satchel that was as much a mark of his station as the turban and sash.

A muttering like the wind through tall grass swept the Hall of Audience.

Nadira's hand shot out, clutching hers in a painful grip.

"What news is of such import that you interrupt the court?" Father's question knifed through the muttering with such menace it stopped the messenger in his tracks.

"Sultan Al'Azam, I bear horrible news."

Too late, Jahanara saw tracks of tears in the dust coating the man's face.

Still clutching Jahanara's hand painfully, Nadira released a slow, animal groan of purest agony, tears coursing down beautiful cheeks.

Salim released Rodney's wrist as the wailing of a fresh-made widow reached his ears. None of the envoys moved, quite likely a good thing under the circumstances.

"Lost, Sultan Al'Azam! Your son and nearly all his host were lost!" The messenger threw himself on the ground before the dais, landing beside Salim's feet.

Mutters of shock and disbelief made the rounds through the hall. He dimly heard Angelo, the Venetian translator, making sure John understood.

Though Salim had trouble understanding this himself. Dara, gone? And with him, hope of religious tolerance.

Through his own stunned surprise, Salim saw Shah Jahan pale. "Lost? How?"

"Set upon from ambush and cowardly tricks as they invested Ramdaspur."

More mutters, though now there was a hot blade of anger and rage cutting between the sobs still sounding from behind the jali.

"My son?" the emperor choked.

This time the man bowed so low it was almost a complete prostration. "Struck down while leading a counter-charge that nearly saved the situation."

The court groaned as Shah Jahan, Sultan of Sultans, Ruler of the World, swayed on his feet.

"This will not stand!" That was Aurangzeb's voice, cracking across the hall.

Dragged from his fugue by the cry, Shah Jahan drew himself to his full height and raged: "And it will not! I shall have a mountain of skulls set in a tower to rival the monuments of my forebears! Gather the hosts, I ride to crush this upstart and all his people! Gather them now!"

Cries of, "Allahu Akbar!" and "Sultan Al'Azam!" crashed against the walls of the Hall of Public Audience like waves on stone, doubling back among the pillars and courtiers.

Belatedly, Salim realized that the people in his charge were not only discomfited by the shouts and anger surrounding them, but had reason to fear for their safety.

Like hungry lions, the gathered nobles were looking for something to tear into. The foreigners were not members of the pride, and therefore game to be brought down.

Rodney leaned down, said so quietly that Salim barely heard him, "Things are about to go very bad, J.D."

"Yeah, I know," John answered, hands balling into fists.

"Do nothing untoward, gentlemen," Salim hissed. He turned to the throne and the emperor.

"Sultan Al'Azam, please!" he bellowed, raising his arms above his head. "Sultan Al'Azam!" He had to get the emperor's attention or things would—"Sultan!"

The emperor turned furious eyes on Salim and barked: "*What?*"

All of the hall went silent.

Salim lowered his arms, head, and voice. "Sultan Al'Azam, the envoys were in the midst of introducing themselves. They understand what a shock this news is, and ask leave to retire, under your protection, until such time as the Sultan Al'Azam wishes to see them again."

Shah Jahan's face didn't soften, but the mad anger of a moment before was replaced by a colder, more calculating one. "Yes, by all means. Keep them close, keep them safe. I will want them with us as I travel."

Salim bowed. "Your will, Sultan Al'Azam."

"Come to me once they are lodged and you have ensured they have mounts suitable to travel."

"Your will, Sultan Al'Azam."

The emperor turned and left, taking his councilors, Shuja, and Aurangzeb with him.

Salim slowly released a breath he hadn't realized he'd been holding. Feeling as if he'd just survived a battle, he turned to his charges and gestured them out.

Angelo, a step ahead of the rest, spoke in hushed tones.

"Don't have to tell me twice," John muttered.

Salim excused himself, stepping aside with a man—or perhaps a eunuch—in rich silks, as the rest of the mission moved out into the courtyard in front of the emperor's throne room.

"Now that didn't go as planned, did it?" Rodney asked as they halted in a loose circle near the center of the courtyard.

"No shit. I didn't relish speaking in front of the emperor, but that was no fun," John said, mopping his brow. The morning sun hadn't yet climbed over the walls, but it was still considerably warmer than it had been when they'd entered the Hall of Audience.

A steady stream of men were leaving the court to mount up in the courtyard. Most were dressed like the man who'd interrupted their audience. Messengers, John supposed, dispatched with orders.

"Did anyone else get the feeling we were about to be torn limb from limb by that crowd?" Gervais asked.

"It certainly seemed likely, but for the amir's timely intervention," said Angelo.

John nodded. "Salim does have good timing." He lowered his voice and asked, "Hey, Angelo, you didn't have a chance to translate everything in there...So what, exactly, happened?"

"Shah Jahan's eldest son, Dara Shikoh, was killed in battle along with his army. The one that yelled for blood, that's another of his sons, Aurangzeb, I believe. Or Murad. I've never seen them in person. Regardless, the emperor has called on all his might, planning to crush the Sikhs and make towers of their skulls."

"You said that before. Did he really mean it? I mean, actual, real towers? I mean, we saw some on the way here, but I thought they were old."

"They don't joke about such things. The Mughal dynasty traces its line straight back to Tamerlane and Genghis Khan, don't forget. The last two emperors put up several such towers on the road between here and Lahore."

"That's some real medieval shit."

"John!" Ilsa snapped.

John sighed, spared an old-fashioned look for Rodney. "Couldn't say something? Maybe tell me she was coming?"

Rodney shrugged. "Nope. Pris is with her."

"I sure am, Rodney, and try not to put me in the middle of fights between our friends, please?"

"Will do, honey. Sorry."

John turned to face his wife, hating not being able to see all of her behind the veil. "And I'm sorry, too."

She shook her head and took his hand in hers. "Remember how Nasi told us to act at court: as if we have no friends here, which is true, and that the walls have ears that understand English. And for good measure, we just had a great example of how volatile the court can be."

"Duly noted. Trust no one."

Rodney nodded. "X-Files all the way."

"What does that mean?" Gervais asked.

"A show... oh, I'll tell you later, our host is coming back."

Salim returned with several people in tow. "The diwan of the harem has arranged quarters for everyone. The unmarried men will be staying with me, I'm afraid."

"And my daughter?" Gervais asked.

"She has been invited to stay with Begum Sahib, if that is acceptable?"

"With the princess?" Monique asked, eyes wide.

"If that is acceptable? It is considered quite an honor, but I can explain, I think, if your traditions require otherwise."

"Will I be able to reach her in an emergency?" Gervais asked.

"Only via messenger. The other ladies of your party will be free to call on her, of course."

Monique cocked her head and switched to French to rattle at her dad, *"Mais, nous ne pouvions pas demander une meilleure chance de se rapprocher de quelqu'un dans la famille royale!"*

"Oui, Bien sur." Gervais, still looking uncomfortable with the idea, switched back to English. "She gladly accepts."

Salim nodded. "And the other ladies?"

"What about us?" Pris asked, clearly resenting being cut out of the conversation.

Salim kept his eyes off her, answered as if one of the men had asked the question: "Should they wish it, they may also reside with the emperor's ladies. They will certainly be traveling with them."

"What is your thought on this, Salim?" John asked.

Salim spread his hands wide. "I have been a widower for longer than I was married, so I can hardly speak to the difficulties of being separated from a wife, but the emperor will see that lavish gifts are given them and ensure their every need is met, not to mention ensuring their absolute safety. To do otherwise would be a great blow to his pride and primacy among sultans."

He bowed his head slightly and spoke even more quietly.

"Begum Sahib is also excellent company, a great wit, and someone I know to be most interested in you up-timers."

Gervais cocked his head. "Excellent company? I thought the harem is closed to those not of royal blood?"

"Dara and I were—friends might be too strong a word—but we shared common interests and concerns."

"Our condolences," John said. Realizing, belatedly, that he hadn't offered them to the emperor. So much for being a diplomat.

Salim accepted the platitude with a graceful nod. "When I returned from Europe, it was Dara who first heard me. Begum Sahib was behind the jali for that interview, and questioned me at length. As a result of that interview, I was eventually brought before the Sultan Al'Azam."

John nodded, then looked a question at his wife.

"I think it's a good idea, John."

"Me too," Pris said. She turned to face Salim, who promptly averted his gaze. "Could you also help us with the proper way to show our respects and convey our sincere condolences to Begum Sahib?"

A bow. "Of course. Communication will remain difficult, however."

"It will?"

"There are a very few here who speak English, fewer still who are not men and therefore barred from the harem."

"French?" Gervais asked.

"I'm afraid not. Portuguese, English and Dutch are the most common European languages here, and even they are not at all common."

"I speak Dutch, and we've all been working on our Persian," Monique said.

"I will ask the diwan what servants he can assign you that may be able to interpret."

The silk-robed man Salim had been speaking to earlier emerged from the shadowed portico, calling the amir to him. After a brief consultation, Salim summoned them and said, "It appears I should not have been so concerned. Begum Sahib is, as usual, a step ahead. She has already obtained a translator for the ladies. It seems everything is prepared."

John hugged Ilsa, whispered, "Be safe."

"I will."

Agra, Red Fort, The Harem

Monique and the other ladies looked about themselves in awe as they followed the eunuch through the harem.

"Mein Gott!" Ilsa whispered.

Everything was either covered in silks, decorated in precious stones, made of gold, or a combination of all three. Thick, luxurious carpets deadened sound and gentled each step.

"A girl could get used to this," Priscilla said.

"Papa would have a fit, there's so much gold lying around..."

"It's no wonder the men are kept out, these girls are wearing next to nothing!" Ilsa said, watching a pair of women cross the gallery ahead of them.

Ilsa plucked at her burqa. "It would be nice to wear something lighter than this blanket."

Priscilla nodded. "We'll need to figure out exactly what we can get away with, first."

Trying to hide her own level of unease with the amount of skin the women—girls, really—were showing, Monique said, "Keep in mind that what is acceptable for the family or their servants may not be for us, or for me, as an unmarried woman."

"True."

The eunuch led them into a square chamber about ten yards on a side with a pair of arches set in each. A young girl of about twelve stood in the center of the room, head bowed.

Monique shook her head. *God, but they know how to show their wealth.* If the halls leading here had been richly decorated, this room showed so much wealth as to verge on the obscene.

Papa would have a stroke.

The eunuch came to a halt beside the girl and spoke with her a moment before turning to face the mission women and addressing them in Persian. The girl began translating into thickly-accented but understandable English almost immediately, "Diwan Firoz Khan would welcome you to the harem of the Sultan Al'Azam, and wishes you to know that whatever your needs, he will see them filled if it is within his power to do so."

Neither of the other women seemed to understand what the girl was saying, so Monique stepped forward, "Our thanks, Diwan Firoz Khan, we are most impressed with our...common living area?"

The diwan flushed, stepped over to one of the arches and lifted the silk hanging. Beyond was a boudoir dressed in a riot of silks and plush pillows. "Each of you will, he hopes, be comfortable in your individual sleeping quarters."

"Of course we will."

"You have but to call, and someone will answer. Now, he begs leave to depart, as there are a great many..." she paused, looking for the word, "*things* he must attend to."

"Of course. We hope to see him again under better circumstances."

The eunuch left, obviously in a hurry.

"And what is your name, young lady?"

"Sahana, mistress."

"Monique, please."

"Pardon, mistress?"

"Monique is my name, and these ladies are Priscilla Totman and Ilsa Ennis."

Both her companions nodded.

"Where we are from, we like to be on a first name basis with those whom we are closest with." A white lie, for her part, but one that did no harm. "Now, I would love to know, how is it you came to speak such excellent English?"

"My mother served Sir Thomas Roe, and taught me the rudiments of the language. Later, I was purchased by Jadu Das, a servant of the English Company, to work at their factory, where I continued to listen to that language."

Both her companions looked uncomfortable at something the girl said. She mentally reviewed the statement, then asked, "Purchased?"

"Yes, Mistress Monique."

"And were you purchased again for this duty?"

"Yes, Mistress Monique."

She wondered just how much loyalty a slave had to any master, let alone new ones. "I see. Will there be anyone else to assist you?"

The girl looked scandalized. "No, Mistress Monique! I can do the work myself."

"Of course you can. I was only worried that speaking for three garrulous women like us might be something of a trial."

Sahana bit her lip. "Forgive my ignorance, Mistress Monique, but I do not know this word: Garuliss."

"Garrulous. It means talkative."

A broad smile drove the girl's looks from merely pretty to exotic, impish beauty. "If I can manage to understand the drunken louts of the English Company, I durst think I can keep track of the words of a few women."

"Oh dear," Priscilla said, "I think we may have stumbled upon a young lady much like ourselves, Monique."

Monique grinned. "I think you are correct."

"Well then, on to the important stuff: can we take off these infernal blankets?" Priscilla asked.

Another grin. "Of course. Durst ye have clothing suitable to the harem?"

"No," the women lamented.

The girl's smile nearly split her face in half. "Well then, let me offer my first service." She clapped her hands, calling out in liquid Persian.

Young, attractive attendants came from two of the alcoves, quickly stripping all three naked, then clothing them in garments that were far less modest but also far more appropriate to the climate.

Monique overcame her body-shyness by focusing on the clothes. She had rarely seen such fine silk, let alone worn the like. The feel of the shift was a fantastic experience. She was almost ashamed to don it, sweaty as she was.

"What's the bathing situation?" she asked.

Another, wider smile and another clapping of hands was Sahana's answer.

Monique could see how one might grow to like this, despite the hateful nature of keeping free people in bondage.

The other women, while each likely had their separate reservations, appeared likewise overcome by the luxurious comfort of their clothing and surroundings, at least for now.

Tomorrow for thought, today to ease fear and fatigue.

Chapter 22

Agra, Red Fort,
November 1634

The chamber set aside for the Inner Council was well ventilated and usually comfortable regardless of the heat outside.

But not today, Aurangzeb thought. Father's anger burned like the sun in the small space, casting servants out at the run, as if their tails were afire.

The Inner Council was not for the faint of heart. Usually the domain of princes, family, and those nobles powerful enough to win a place advising Father on critical issues, it was here that such matters were discussed and contested before Shah Jahan.

Many were the courtiers who had, thinking their star on the rise, fallen from this chamber into ruin.

This was the first time Aurangzeb had been ordered present as a participant rather than as a student, only there to observe, be silent, and learn.

Dara's death had done this much for him, at least.

"Order him back."

"But Asaf Khan is weeks gone, Father. He and his army are already well into the Deccan," Shah Shuja argued.

"I know that. Order his return."

"Are you certain, Father?"

Aurangzeb covered a wince, not out of pity for his sibling, but for Asaf Khan's sowar. For once Shah Shuja was advising a reasonable course: twenty-five thousand men and all their provisions would not easily be turned around, especially once in the Deccan. The prolonged famine there was already straining supply lines. Just the cost of fodder for Asaf Khan's thousands of horses would have beggared a lesser power, and that was before transporting that fodder across hundreds of kos of drought-afflicted territory.

"Do I look as if I am of a mood to be questioned?" Father bellowed.

"No, of course not, Father." Shah Shuja turned and repeated the order to the messenger, who fled the room in haste.

"What forces do we have on hand?"

Shah Shuja turned to a subordinate, but Aurangzeb answered from memory before his elder brother could get the information: "Assuming the court decamps with you, Father, ten thousand mounted sowar can be mustered and ready in two days. If we wait another two weeks, that number rises to thirty thousand horse and ten thousand foot."

Shah Shuja's face twitched, probably with the realization that Aurangzeb had robbed him of the opportunity to shine.

He ignored the angry look that followed and concentrated instead on Father's reaction.

Shah Jahan was nodding, one hand tugging at his beard, but he showed no sign of being impressed by Aurangzeb's ready answer.

Confident in his information, if not Father's reaction, Aurangzeb pressed on: "Numbers for supply are more difficult, but the first ten thousand can be readily supplied for travel between here and Lahore. Thereafter a question arises: if you wish to destroy the farming capability for the region, then foraging will provide supplies sufficient to needs for a week, assuming the Sikhs have not already scorched the earth to deny us. After that, everything will have to be brought in. If you decide to wait for more warriors, then the supply situation will become more acute, more quickly."

"The blade's edge."

"Pardon, Father?" Shah Shuja asked, trying to regain position by being first to ask, instead of answer.

Shah Jahan released his beard and waved his hand. "The disaffected will seek out Hargobind Singh, now that he has struck this blow to our pride and emerged victorious. If I strike quickly but with the smaller force, I may find myself caught in the same trap he used to kill your brother. But if I wait I appear weak and allow time for him to gather even more jackals to his side."

He looked up, from Shah Shuja to Aurangzeb. "What would you do in my place, Shah Shuja?"

"Attack immediately, with the forces you have on hand. You have proclaimed your vengeance before your nobles, and must maintain honor."

Shah Jahan's dark gaze shifted to Aurangzeb. "And you, what would you counsel?"

"To do as my brother says, though I have more reasons than honor alone."

"Say on."

"Moving quickly and decisively denies Hargobind time to prepare for your coming, eases questions of supply, and satisfies honor. Further, and with all fairness to the dead: you are not Dara, Father. You are far more experienced and therefore less likely to be caught in any trap he might lay for you.

"In an abundance of caution, you may wish to have one of us remain behind to gather the balance of your forces and ensure your lines of supply can be relied upon. That force can then be ready to move to assist you in the unlikely event you need it."

"All this talk of supplies and such makes you sound a cook, not a prince," Shuja said.

Aurangzeb turned to face Shah Shuja, striving to respond to the provocation calmly and with reason where Shuja, and most likely, Father, expected anger and thoughtlessness: "Our forebears, when at war, were ever aware of where grazing could be found for their mounts, even at the expense of their own meals. A famine-struck army is no army."

"I know that, you jumped-up little—"

"Enough!" Shah Jahan commanded.

Shuja bridled, but didn't finish the insult.

"I will consider your advice. Return tomorrow morning after prayers."

Both brothers bowed before Father's will and made to depart, Shah Shuja with little grace, muttering under his breath.

Aurangzeb followed more sedately, barely concealing his pleasure at successfully navigating his first Inner Council meeting. Surely, Father would grant him a command for the coming battle! A way he could prove his ability to him and to the great nobles, so that when the time came, his power base would be unassailable.

I can almost feel God reaching out to me, claiming me for His purpose. Aurangzeb silently thanked God for His mercy and the opportunity to further His will.

Agra, Red Fort, The Harem

"Begum Sahib, these are Madame Priscilla Totman, Madame Ilsa Damaschke-Ennis, and Mademoiselle Monique Vieuxpont," Firoz Khan said. Each of the women bowed before the princess as her name was called.

"I extend the hospitality of my father's home to you, our honored guests. Please, take your ease and refreshment. I am told that these climes are hot for your comfort."

The women did as Jahanara bid, evidence that Sahana was worth the outlay of silver spent to purchase her from Jadu Das.

One of the blonde ones, Priscilla, spoke to Sahana, her tone one of concerned sincerity. The woman had a most direct stare Jahanara found a bit disconcerting, even as she admired the even white teeth and beautiful blonde hair that the woman wore in a braid. For that matter, to her eye all of the women were exotic in their beauty, if a tad large for refinement.

"Begum Sahib, you are kind to receive us. We, all of us, wish to extend our condolences at the loss of your brother."

Swallowing sudden tears, Jahanara bent her head and answered only when she could trust her voice. "Your condolences are well received and appreciated in these painful times."

A slight lowering of her voice, quickly translated: "We hope we are not imposing on you in your grief, Begum Sahib."

"No, no, you bring welcome distraction."

A brilliant white smile. "I suppose we are like the cirkiss"—Sahana asked for clarification, had the word repeated, shrugged, and left it untranslated—"circus come to town."

Jahanara smiled gently in recognition of Sahana's efforts and asked, "What is this circus?"

"Usually a traveling group of entertainers that entertain as much from their appearance as from their performances."

"Something like our troupes of dancing girls?"

Sahana blanched, but dutifully translated.

Madame Totman noticed her translator's change in demeanor

and paused a moment before replying. "Not quite, Begum Sahib. Some of them, called clowns"—there was another back and forth for the term, which again remained untranslated—"wore colorful, strange clothing and painted their faces for performances."

"I . . . see," Jahanara shook her head. "To what purpose, these circus?"

"Circuses were for entertainment only, Begum Sahib. My town was considered," another broad smile, "very provincial, and could not support performers year round. So the circus would visit on occasion."

Jahanara now spoke to Priscilla. "If I take your meaning correctly, your appearance is quite extraordinary, what with your giant of a husband and your own exceptional appearance. I have seen blond Englishmen, but their women do not travel with them."

A shrug of shoulders. "One small difference between up-timers and today's society."

"Today's?"

"Yes, Begum Sahib, we traveled with—and without—our men all the time, back up-time."

Fascinating. To have such freedom, to even travel under the sun and stars with one's husband . . .

"I was going to say that we travel with our men, too, but I see you mean something more. I would hear more of this 'up-time.'"

A chuckle, quickly taken up by the other women. "How much time do you have?"

Agra, Mosque

Aurangzeb finished his prayers and climbed to his feet. He waited for the other faithful to depart the mosque, enjoying the quiet. Cleansed of distraction, he was able to focus anew on the momentous events of the day before.

Dara was dead.

Not merely dead, but killed in battle! And now Aurangzeb had an opportunity to prove Dara's failings by commanding some element of the army his father was gathering to do what Dara failed to do.

But how to keep his brother Shah Shuja out of the way?

"How, indeed?" he mused.

"Shehzada?" Mullah Mohan asked.

Aurangzeb flinched, turned to see the mullah standing beside him. "You move quietly, Mullah."

"I try to avoid undue attention. Such is unseemly, here."

"Indeed it is."

"Did you have some question I could assist you with, Shehzada?" The man had the subtlety of an ox. "I do not think so, Mullah."

"Refreshment, then, Shehzada?"

Aurangzeb cocked his head. "Certainly."

They retired to more private surroundings. Once served, and the servants withdrew, Aurangzeb began a slow count in his head.

He'd barely got to five when Mohan spoke. "Your brother's passing was an unexpected blow."

"Yes, it was."

"Surely—"

"Mullah Mohan, have I not been forthright with you?"

Mohan's eyes shot wide. "Of course."

"Then do the courtesy of coming to the point without bringing my dead brother into it."

"Of course, Shehzada. I merely thought to offer—"

"I don't care what you hoped or planned to offer, Mullah Mohan, I want you to come to the point. You have offered me refreshment and keep trying to offer condolences; I have the one in hand and I do not need the other."

"I but—"

Aurangzeb cut the older man off with a shake of his head. "The refreshments were appreciated, but the condolences are not only unnecessary, they make you appear insincere. I know what little regard you had for my brother, so please don't insult my intelligence by offering false sentiments and come to the *point*."

Mohan's cheeks reddened above his beard. "Yes, Shehzada. With your permission, I will do so. I hoped to quietly call some of the more militant faithful into your service before Shah Jahan's army marches."

Merciful God! My impatient tongue will be the end of me! I dress the fool down even as he seeks to offer me service.

He covered his brow with one hand. "I fear I have wronged you, Mullah Mohan. Please accept my abject apologies. I tire of the hair-pulling and wailing at court, and wrongly thought you about to exhibit similar histrionics."

"Your apology is accepted, Shehzada Aurangzeb. Occasional youthful intemperance in dealing with subordinates is understandable, even expected, of a young prince." He held up a finger and smiled, adding, "Acceptance of responsibility for one's error is the mark of a great prince."

Aurangzeb wondered who he was quoting. Surely he hadn't come up with it himself. Aloud, he said, "My thanks, Mullah Mohan, I appreciate your understanding and forgiveness."

"You have given me no reason to believe you will not serve the faith and faithful in the coming years. If I can do this thing in support of you and your cause, then God wills it."

"An honest question, Mullah, and one for which I will not respond to with anger if answered honestly: I would have your assessment of each of my family."

"Honestly?"

Aurangzeb spread his hands in invitation. "Please."

"The Sultan Al'Azam Shah Jahan is preoccupied with other matters, and has not given proper attention to maintenance of the faith for some time. We mullahs had such high hopes when he assumed the throne and immediately instituted the *jizya*, abolished the full prostration of supplicants before the throne, and even went so far as to stop the construction of new Hindu temples, something that had not been done by his predecessors."

Mohan sighed. "But he has since allowed the collection of the tax on unbelievers to cease. And, aside from the just punishment meted out to the Portuguese—the motive for which was their failure to support him against Jahangir rather than righteous faith—he has allowed the Christians far too much free rein. Then there was the business of Dara's and Jahanara's education under Mian Mir. *That* creature's accommodating attitude toward the Hindus is nothing short of heretical."

Mohan licked his lips, suddenly aware precisely how far he'd gone in condemning the emperor in front of the prince.

Aurangzeb smiled reassurance. "Please, go on."

"As to your brothers, Shah Shuja has not shown a predilection for supporting the faith or, as your departed brother, undermining it with the teachings of that heretic in Lahore.

"Murad is too young to have left the harem, and while an indifferent student of the Quran thus far, he takes direction as well as any little prince might be expected to."

"And the women?"

"Begum Sahib has been unstinting in providing all Murad's teachers access and time with the little prince since she took responsibility for the affairs of the harem." He paused, then went on, a bit breathlessly, "That she also allows him to be taught false science and perverse philosophy I must blame on her own time as a student to Mian Mir.

"Shehzadi Roshanara was an excellent student, but I haven't had cause to interact with her since she completed her studies and as she has no responsibilities that touch upon my own, I know very little about her. Similarly, Guaharara Begum is too young for teaching."

Thinking Mullah Mohan was done, Aurangzeb opened his mouth to speak but Mohan continued, "Nur Jahan told me that she wishes to render every assistance to your cause, that we should be allies in this. I must confess I find it hard to fathom why you would make common cause with that woman."

Aurangzeb wagged his head. "My great-aunt possesses a wealth of experience, something I lack."

The best lie is not a lie.

"Is it true that you were the one to bring her back from Lahore?"

"I moved Father on her behalf, yes."

"I see. So you wish me to make common cause with her?"

"Indeed I do."

"And if she should get the bit in her teeth, and act counter to your desires?"

"Then I will direct you how best to deal with it."

"And if you are not present?"

"Where am I going that you are not?"

"With your blessing, Nur Jahan and I will move to ensure you have the very best five thousand sowar, dedicated to you, personally, when your father names you to that rank. As a commander of such a substantial force, you will likely be assigned important tasks, some of which might carry you some distance from the court, even as it travels with the Sultan Al'Azam."

"You have given considerable thought to this, then."

"Nur Jahan broached the subject shortly after your last visit to my home, Shehzada."

"She did?"

"Yes."

"Yet you do not seem convinced of her usefulness."

"If you say she is useful, Shehzada, then she must be." He raised a finger and wagged his head. "But Nur Jahan's lust for power is unseemly in a woman and dangerous to the unwary, be they ally or enemy."

All of which make her a better lodestone for blame than you, who actually has men to commit to my cause.

"I will be wary, Mullah Mohan."

Chapter 23

Agra, Red Fort
November 1634

John stepped out from their quarters into the harsh morning sunlight and found the boys standing in a knot, grousing about something. He missed a step, memories of similar warm mornings, a crew ready to lay some road, and a job of work to do momentarily overwhelming his senses.

Shaking free of the memories and a homesick desire for baseball caps, chewing tobacco, and a styrofoam cup of black coffee to start his day, John joined his team.

"What's up, boys?"

"We thought we'd made it, John. That we were done having the ground move under us, you know?" Bobby Maddox said. Both Ricky and Randy were nodding agreement.

"I don't know what to say, boys. I'd like to spend a little time letting my frank and beans drop instead of crushing them in the saddle again," he shrugged, keeping a straight face as the younger men grinned, "but these guys are traditionally nomads, and the emperor is one pissed-off chief nomad. Come to that, I would be too if it was my kid got killed."

"Salim said something about an ambush?" Randy asked.

"Yeah, a battle against the Sikhs."

"And now the high muckety-muck himself's riding out against them?"

John nodded. "With ten thousand men this time."

"Against how many Sikhs?"

"Dunno."

"Weren't the Sikhs like a big part of India's army, back up-time?" Ricky asked.

"Almost all of it, if I remember right. And under the English they were up there with the Gurkhas for hardasses," Randy agreed.

"Salim says they're a small minority just now."

"But India's enormous, so . . ."

John tossed his head. "I trust his take on it."

"And didn't they just have an army of five thousand horse wiped out?" Bobby had that look going, the one that told his friends, "Be careful, I'm about to blow."

"Good point. We'll just have to watch things and be ready to fight or run."

"We don't like it, J.D."

More nods from the rest of the boys.

"Neither do I, guys. But we can't leave now. The emperor accepted us as envoys to his court, so we're obliged to stay until he says we can go."

"We know, it's just, you know: we're here to lay some rail, and we ain't seeing when, hell, even *if*, that's gonna happen."

"A bit early to start worrying about that, Bobby."

An angry shrug. "Never too early to worry, man."

"You're right. Shouldn't have tried to blow you off. Sorry."

Ricky chimed in, trying to smooth over the uncomfortable moment, "Well, we were looking for people who had money to blow on paying for some up-time wonders, and we damn sure found 'em. I've seen more gold and silk here in the last two days than I ever imagined existed."

"Damn straight. Even the guys are dripping with gold."

"Did you see that throne?" Bobby asked.

Nods of agreement from all around, "Yeah."

"Don't look like a peacock, though."

"That's cause it's not *that* throne."

"Thought that's what their throne was called?"

"Not yet. Salim got *that look* when I asked, then said Shah Jahan ordered it built this year. It's supposed to be delivered next."

"What look?" Rodney asked, coming up behind John.

The team smiled as John explained, "You know: *that look*, the one down-timers get when you talk about something that's common knowledge to us but just happened or is about to happen here and now."

Nods and chuckles all around.

"Got any words of wisdom for us?" John asked, looking up at Rodney.

"Stay healthy. Stay away from their women."

Rodney laughed with the rest but went on more seriously, "I know which of those is going to be easier: the nobles and their servants keep their women well hid. Angelo showed the guys where to go for...paid companionship...but once we leave, there won't be any of that..."

The guys all looked uncomfortable at mention of the brothels they'd visited, so John decided to take pity on them and change the subject. "Did you see the conditions in their cities? I can only imagine how bad conditions will be in camp, with all the horses and men shitting everywhere."

"And elephants," Randy added, playing along, "can't forget them, not with the size of them pats."

John snorted. "Nope."

Salim, worrying he'd missed something, ran down the list of things he, as mihmandar, was required to provide them on the march.

He thought he'd covered everything...So why did he feel like a man about to ride into an ambush?

Merciful God! The women! I forgot to check on their needs.

He asked a passing servant Firoz Khan's whereabouts, learned the eunuch was in his quarters, and made his way there.

As mihmandar to the newest delegation, the diwan had granted him access without challenge to his chambers. Salim stumbled to a surprised halt just past the guards. The eunuch was lounging in his darkened antechamber, one arm thrown over his eyes.

"What now?"

"Respectfully, Diwan Firoz Khan, but how do you find time to nap?"

A wave of the arm covering his face. "Excellent subordinates, Amir."

"That's it?"

"Well, that...and the court is long accustomed to moving on short notice. We *are* nomads, after all."

"Still..."

The heavy little eunuch sat up with a groan. "All right, I haven't slept at all the last two days. In fact, I only stopped issuing orders because I ran out of messengers."

Salim snorted. "Really?"

"Would I lie?"

"Of course you would. We are at the sultan's court, after all."

A tired smile, barely visible in the dimness. "I would, too." He scrubbed his face. "I suspect some of the messengers are simply avoiding me because they're footsore."

"Is the harem ready, though?"

"It is." He sighed. "Merciful God, it *finally* is."

"And the ladies of the diplomatic mission?"

"Up quite late last night with Begum Sahib."

"And their discussions were...?"

"A good eunuch never delivers the secrets of his harem into the ears of another." Firoz said, waggling his head. "Of course, I am not a good one, at least not in this case."

Salim chuckled. "They went well, then?"

Firoz heaved himself erect. "Yes. Begum Sahib is deeply interested in them. I had not thought she would be drawn from mourning for some time, but your up-timers accomplished it."

"Only the one woman is from up-time. The giant, Rodney's, wife."

An expansive yawn, "Yes, Priscilla. Such odd names."

"Indeed."

"Not to be rude, but why are you here, interrupting my sleep?"

Salim bowed with a smile. "I had forgotten to check on the arrangements for the women, and was seized with sudden worry."

Firoz puffed his chest. "Never fear, this eunuch has already fought that battle and emerged victorious."

"Knowing such a warrior protects my reputation, I shall retire in confidence, then."

"Good. I will resume watching the insides of my eyelids."

"Rest well—" He was interrupted as a messenger entered at the trot and came to a sudden halt behind him.

The young boy bowed at Salim, then again to Firoz. "Diwan?"

"Speak."

"The Sultan Al'Azam has ordered the van to march."

That meant they had until about mid-day before the harem and his charges would mount up and depart.

"I have heard the message. Get something to drink and rest a short while. I will have work for you."

"Yes, Diwan." The boy fled.

"It seems there will be no rest for me until we ride."

"Indeed. I am sorry to have interrupted your nap."

"I understand what drove you, and take no umbrage."

"See you on the trail, then?"

"Perhaps. I hope to sleep most of the afternoon in the howdah."

"Then I will look for you the next day to check on my charges."

"Oh, about that: did the husbands make you aware of their plans as to when they'll wish to visit their wives?"

"Not yet, no. I will inquire."

"I would have thought to ask, but . . ." he trailed off into another yawn.

"Understandable. I leave you to your deserved rest."

Agra to Ramdaspur

"This is almost worse than being at sea," Ilsa muttered. The swaying of the howdah was making her look a bit green about the gills. "It wouldn't be so bad if we could get some air." She fingered the first of the layers of curtains that obscured the outside world and trapped any breeze before it reached them.

"Purdah," Priscilla drawled with a shrug.

That had been a common refrain the last few hours. She'd barely been able to see Papa—and the other women their husbands—before being bundled aboard the howdah at around noon, and they'd been on the move since then. Monique didn't really find being separated from Papa all that great a hardship, but found herself missing Bertram.

"I suppose that we'd be choking on the dust, were it not for them," Monique said.

"So instead we stifle."

"Then why not turn our minds from misery to something else? For instance: I think our first audience with Begum Sahib went well."

"I agree," Ilsa said.

"She sure wore me out with questions," Priscilla said, tapping her teeth with one fingernail. "Intelligent ones, too."

"You say that like you were surprised. You even sound a bit like a down-time man—surprised to find a brain behind pretty eyes," Ilsa said.

Looking at Priscilla, Monique couldn't help but nod agreement. Some of the things the up-timers thought about women of her time were just plain stupid. *I mean, why would you think a lack of equal legal power equates to powerlessness?*

"Well, I suppose she shattered more than one of my expectations. Before meeting her, I sure wouldn't have thought to meet a well-educated woman in a harem."

"Those wealthy enough make their own rules," said Monique, running a finger along the gilt woodwork of the howdah, "and these people are certainly rich."

Ilsa nodded. "True, she has resources others lack, but she also seems genuinely interested in anything that might be of benefit to her people."

"That, from just one meeting?" Monique asked.

"And why not?" Ilsa asked.

"She's been brought up amid harem politics, so I doubt she showed us any feeling or motive she did not *want* us to see."

"Now you sound like Don Francisco, Monique."

Priscilla grinned and waved down Monique's nascent protest. "You do, Monique!" Her white teeth quickly disappeared as she continued, "Even so, we do need to be cautious. It's too early to get a good grasp of either her motives or the politics that surround Begum Sahib."

"Right."

They lapsed into silence for a few sways of the howdah.

"What about the girl?"

"Sahana?"

"Yes."

"I can't imagine what her childhood was like, a slave."

"Me neither, but who do you think she's loyal to?"

"I couldn't guess."

"At the risk of sounding like Don Francisco again—there are slaves and then there are slaves. Here the eunuchs and harem slaves have opportunity to advance to high position," Monique said.

Priscilla's expression soured. "But no choice in where they begin, no control over their own bodies. Anything short of that kind of control over your own fate is just making excuses for a despicable practice, one the USE hopes to crush."

"I'm not disagreeing, Priscilla, I'm just... reminding everyone that this society, their rulers, even their very religions, condone and perpetuate slavery. We forget that at our peril. At the very least the mission may be ignored or ostracized if we get a reputation for speaking out against things as they stand. At the very least."

"Oh, I know." Priscilla shook her head. "I don't like it, but I know."

"None of us like it!" Monique immediately regretted snapping at Priscilla. "Sorry."

"No problem, Monique. I know you're trying to make sure we stay realistic."

"Now I've made us all more miserable with this topic."

"What do you think of Salim, Monique?" Ilsa asked, changing the subject.

"Handsome, under that beard."

Both women smiled at her.

She ignored their expressions—both had showed mild interest in getting her married off to someone, just as all married women of her acquaintance were wont to do—and continued. "Dangerously competent, though he didn't look nearly as comfortable in Agra as he was on the road."

"Rodney called him a man to walk the hills with," Priscilla said.

"He and John seem to get on, as well," Ilsa agreed.

"I think he'll do what he can to keep us safe and comfortable, but I wonder just how powerful he is. He certainly doesn't seem to have the hangers-on the other court functionaries surround themselves with."

"I hadn't thought about it in that light," Priscilla said, "I just thought he was making sure to appear more approachable to us."

"There were some sour looks cast his way," Monique added.

"From who?"

"No one we've been introduced to, but there was at least one fellow in the last few rows before the throne that was giving Salim the Evil Eye the entire time we were in the audience hall. Skinny man, long beard with a fair degree of salt in it."

"Really?"

Monique nodded emphatically. "One of the most murderous looks I've seen, and I've seen some good ones."

"Maybe someone should tell our host?" Priscilla said.

"I'm sure he's already aware, but I'll tell John to let him know, and to spread that information around the men."

Priscilla nodded. "Can't hurt his impression of us."

"When are you going to see your husbands again?"

"Good question. I need to ask Begum Sahib what's normal, especially on the road."

"Did she seem sad to you?" Priscilla asked.

Ilsa shrugged. "She just lost a brother."

But Monique noticed something in the woman's voice, wanted to encourage it. "Why do you ask, Priscilla?"

"I know she'd lost him, but this was...something else. When we were talking, there was a moment she just seemed...I don't know...Down."

"You remember what we were talking about when you noticed it?"

"You were talking. Something about your experiences in the court of the Duke of Florence."

Ilsa snapped her fingers. "I remember now, you were telling that funny story about the baron and said, 'and then Papa turned to me and asked me what we should do.'"

"I missed that," Monique said, "But thinking back on it... I see what you mean." She tossed her curls, "So her father's a touchy subject...Something to think about, anyway."

"I wish we'd had a chance to get to know the court better before getting underway."

"Oh, I don't know. From the looks of things, the whole damn court pulled up roots and came with us," Priscilla said.

"Yes, but we're stuck in here with one another all day instead of mingling with the local women."

"Want me to ask if we can rotate through riding with Begum Sahib or Roshanara?" Priscilla asked.

Monique weighed the idea. "If you don't think it would be presumptuous of us to ask, then certainly."

Priscilla yawned. "I think, after how long our talk went last night, we—and you in particular—have some credit with Begum Sahib."

"I did make her laugh a few times, *non*?"
"*Oui!*"

"Our mahout is the deaf one, mistress. We can speak freely," Gargi said, handing Nur the damp cloth.

"Have you learned anything of the ferenghi from the future?" Nur asked, covering her eyes with the cloth. Between the hot flashes and the need to work quickly, the last few days had been a long and difficult trial. Her depleted power-base included a fair number of men with war-bands of their own, but quietly convincing them to back Aurangzeb, especially through intermediaries, had taxed both patience and nerves.

"Aside from their placement in the harem and men in their quarters, I learned nothing more than you observed at the Diwan-i-Khas, mistress."

"You couldn't place any of your ears among their servants?"

"Unfortunately, no. Jahanara selected each of the foreigner's attendants herself. I had thought sure she would pick at least one of the Christians her father took as slaves, but she ignored all of them, even Sol."

Nur waved a hand. "My grandniece is a clever sort, and likely remembers how poorly the Portuguese women adjusted to their status after being taken from Hugli."

Gargi sniffed. "All because the Portuguese priests refused to aid Shah Jahan in his rebellion against your husband's lawful rule. As if the foreigners should have!" She shook her head. "Foolishness."

Nur swept the cloth from her face and looked her advisor in the eye. "Lock well such words behind your teeth, Gargi. The Portuguese were punished for failing to back the winner of that war, nothing more. What we attempt is only different in that the son we back does not openly rebel against his father."

Yet, she added silently.

"Indeed, mistress. I should not speak so, but worry makes me witless."

"Worry?"

"I fear you tread in danger, and I am too old and stupid to protect you."

Nur took Gargi's hand in hers, making the woman look her

in the eye. "Gargi, sweet Gargi! I trust no other, not in this. We are in this together, you and I. We shall make them bend to my will, all of them, or cause them to fail and fall, else die in the trying. There is no other outcome. I will not return to the shadowed half-life of a widow, begging for scraps from Shah Jahan's table as if I never held the reins of an empire in my hands."

Despite her assurances, or perhaps because of them, Nur could only hold Gargi as her oldest friend and ally wept slow, heavy tears.

Chapter 24

Red Tent, between Agra and Ramdaspur
November 1634

"I have left this too long, my honored guests." The emperor gestured and attendants came forth with rich robes for each of the male envoys. "Take these robes and these gifts and be welcome."

A sweating John bowed in what he hoped was the proper manner and, through Angelo, said: "We understand the reason for the delay, Sultan Al'Azam, and wish to extend, on behalf of Emperor Gustavus Adolphus, our sincere condolences for your loss."

"I accept your condolences as kindly given, even as I inform you that the pain my son felt will be nothing compared to what I shall visit upon his killer."

Uncertain what to say in the face of such icy rage, John simply bowed.

Salim had told them they should wait to talk business until after they got the robes, but John didn't think the sultan was in any mood to talk shop right now.

But the emperor, who was decked out in white, the color of mourning here, asked, point blank: "What do you bring as gifts?"

John blinked. The rapid change in demeanor from mourning father to sharp-eyed trader threw him, and nearly caused him to forget everything. He licked his lips, tried to get it together, then answered: "Sultan Al'Azam, we bring small treasures of sequins and looking-glasses for your wives and ladies. For you, we bring books and technical expertise in the fields of medicine, road-building, railroad construction, and steam locomotion for trains."

Shah Jahan did not look impressed. "These last two are unknown to us, but you have been traveling along one of our roads, and in the shade of our trees while you did. I doubt you have much of value to teach my people in this regard."

Out of the corner of his eye, John saw Salim wince, and said carefully: "The Sultan is wise. While the road is excellent and the shade most welcome, your bridges . . . do they wash away more frequently than you would like?"

"This is so, at least for some bridges."

"Road-building is the foundation upon which railroads are constructed and stout, long-lasting bridges are essential for good roads. We have the techniques and knowledge to produce bridges that will last and support tremendous weight."

"And what are these 'trains' you speak of?"

"A method of transport that, once completed, can move many tons of material from one place to another faster than a horse, without growing tired or consuming fodder."

Shah Jahan took his beard in his hand, then released it, his expression doubtful. "Such extravagant claims. And how much will constructing one of these railroads cost?"

John ventured a smile. "They do require a large workforce to create, and the rails and locomotive will likely require the output of your best iron-workers for a number of months."

"Locomotive?"

"The complex mechanism that pulls the cargo of a train."

"I begin to understand that there is a great deal more to learn about this before I decide anything."

"We have books on these subjects as well, Sultan," Angelo added what John had forgotten to say.

"In English?"

"Yes, Sultan."

Shah Jahan did not look pleased by his answer. There was some back and forth between the emperor's advisors and Shah Jahan, but nothing loud enough for Angelo to translate.

These guys don't like English . . . or is it the English they don't like?

Does he know what the future was?

Shit.

He does.

"What about these medical advances?"

John bowed again. "Sultan Al'Azam, for questions of medicine and health, my colleague, Mr. Rodney Totman, is the expert."

The emperor nodded, inviting Rodney to speak.

Rodney stepped forward, muttering, "I'm a damn EMT, man, not Dr. Nichols."

John hid a grin.

Shah Jahan's eyes widened as Rodney came to a stop next to John. He wasn't exactly small, but Rodney made almost everyone look like a child in comparison.

"I would have expected a giant like you to be a warrior, not a healer," Shah Jahan said.

Rodney smiled. "Can't I be both, Sultan Al'Azam?" he said.

The emperor's glare killed Rodney's smile.

"Perhaps," Shah Jahan answered. He looked away, eventually. Rodney's shoulders sagged when he did.

Man, this guy is seriously *touchy, and a shit-powerful personality. That look was something else.*

Smoothing his white robes, Shah Jahan spoke again. Angelo's voice had a slight quiver as he resumed translation: "So, what marvels can we expect from you, Mr. Rodney Totman?"

"Sultan Al'Azam, we can provide you with the simple formulas for quinine water that can help a person fight off malaria." There was a stir on the emperor's platform as Shah Jahan asked a question of one of his attendants, who whispered into his ear. Rodney, too nervous to notice, went on, "techniques for purifying water, and methods for keeping healthy teeth."

Rodney drew a breath to continue, but was interrupted by the emperor. "The Portuguese have already brought to our attention a drink they claim will help fight malaria."

Rodney spread his huge linebacker's arms, making a few of the emperor's guards fidget. "Sultan Al'Azam, if it is made from the chinchona tree, then it is likely the same drink and therefore a good remedy for malaria."

Shah Jahan nodded. "What else?"

"We have techniques for treating wounded and injured people that, if followed exactly, will greatly increase their chances of surviving injuries—most especially wounds—that are currently considered life-threatening."

The sultan pulled at his beard again, then released it. Was that some mark of interest? John thought it might be.

"What else?" the emperor asked.

"Sultan Al'Azam, we have other, more general knowledge of what is called best practices for public sanitation and health, all of which could greatly improve the lot of your people."

"Peoples, Mr. Rodney Totman. I am sultan of a great many peoples, hence my title: Sultan of Sultans."

Rodney answered the correction with a silent bow.

"And what does your Emperor Gustavus Adolphus desire in exchange for these wonders from another age?"

John spoke up, "Sultan Al'Azam, we desire peace between our peoples and your permission to trade in certain goods; namely saltpeter and opium, as well as some other items we cannot easily make or obtain for ourselves that are of interest to us."

"Very well, we shall speak further at some future date."

Well, there's the brush-off...

Another group of servants came at them from the side, two of them with a small chest between them.

"Until then," Shah Jahan continued, "be refreshed, and accept this gift of a one-fifth lakh of rupees for your upkeep. I will see you soon, God willing."

John bowed, as did the rest of the men. "Thank you, Sultan Al'Azam, we look forward to speaking with you on these matters."

Shah Jahan's servants handed off the chest to Bobby and Ricky, who grunted as they took the weight.

They made their collective obeisance and made to depart.

"Salim."

"Yes, Sultan Al'Azam?"

"Return to us once you have seen our visitors to their tents."

"Yes, Sultan Al'Azam."

Shah Jahan's camp

Gervais was grinning from ear to ear as they exited the Red Tent.

"What?" John asked.

"That's a lot of cash in that box."

"Twenty thousand in silver," Angelo agreed, eyes shining.

John missed a step, nearly fell. He looked at Salim in disbelief.

The big Afghan nodded. "Yes, there is."

"Why?" John asked, rejoining Bertram and Salim at the front of the group.

They passed the inner ring of guards and started toward the their tents. "Because the emperor wished you to have it."

"But why?"

"Because the representatives of kings coming to this court should not ever be able to return home and claim they were unable to purchase the things that make life comfortable."

"But he's already putting us up."

"If by 'putting us up,' you mean giving you a place to stay, he is. But he cannot know your preferences in servants, slaves, dress, and the other required accoutrements of your positions. Lacking that knowledge, he gives you this gift so that you can keep yourself in the manner you are accustomed to."

"And at the same time, shows us exactly how wealthy he is relative to our sovereign," Bertram said.

Salim smiled. "There is that, as well."

"Does everyone get this kind of treatment?"

"No."

John heard the hesitation, asked, "Who does?"

"Usually? Dignitaries representing the Safavid, Uzbeg, and Ottoman courts are the ones most commonly gifted with such quantity of treasure, but all are given something."

"Then why us?"

"I can only assume it is because you have a larger number of envoys in your party than is traditional, and because the Sultan Al'Azam wishes to recognize the importance of your arrival."

"Larger number?"

"One is the traditional number. One prince or powerful noble, and a great number of servants and subordinates."

"Much like Baram Khan," Bertram said.

"Yes . . . though . . . Baram Khan was not . . . he was not exactly expected to be successful in his travels."

"He wasn't?"

"No. He was a powerful noble. One who supported Nur Jahan, wife of Shah Jahan's father, Jahangir, when the Sultan Al'Azam rebelled."

"So he was sent into exile, chasing dragons at the far corners of the world?" Bertram grinned.

Salim returned a wry smile of his own. "Not in so many words, but that is the essence of the matter, yes."

"Forgive me any insult in asking, but how did you come to be in his party?"

"I was asked to."

"By the emperor?"

"No."

"Can you tell us who, then?"

"Mian Mir."

"And will we get a chance to meet this Mian Mir?" Bertram asked.

"Unfortunately, I doubt we will have opportunity to visit him at Lahore."

Bertram didn't miss the sad note in Salim's tone any more than John did. The younger man shot a look at John and asked, "Sorry, but I feel I must ask: who is he to ask you to go into exile?"

"A religious man, a saint of the Sufis, my friend, mentor, and teacher." The man's tone made it clear Salim missed Mian Mir deeply. Salim nodded at one of his kinsman, one of the many that had taken service with the amir, as they crossed the perimeter of the area set aside for their tents.

"The living saint was sure in his prediction that the journey was not...how did you put it? Chasing after dragons. It was he who said that things of great importance had come to pass in Europe, some months before word of your arrival reached Lahore or Agra. And when that word reached us, he was certain your arrival foretold events crucial to the welfare and future of the peoples of the India and the world."

"I see..." Bertram said. And just how did someone thousands of miles from the Ring of Fire come to that conclusion? he wondered.

Salim stopped just inside the cluster of their tents and bowed at his charges. "I must return to the Sultan Al'Azam, gentlemen."

"Of course, Amir Yilmaz. Thank you." John said at Salim's already retreating back.

Rodney waited till he was out of earshot before wheeling to face John, expression intense. "Holy Nostradamus, Batman! Did you hear that bit about Mian Mir predicting our arrival?"

"If this guy predicted—"

Gervais raised his hands. "Gentlemen, let's not get ahead of ourselves. We don't have the timing of this supposed holy man's claims about the importance of the Ring of Fire. He may have learned of it earlier than other people around here and decided it was a good thing to spout some quick prophesy, knowing it wasn't likely to come home to hurt him."

Bertram cocked his head. "It is an interesting question, though."

"What's that?" Gervais asked.

"Did you hear how much stock Salim puts in this Mian Mir?"

All of the others nodded agreement.

"And we've all seen how capable Salim seems. Why send a loyal and capable follower chasing after something you know or even *suspect* will prove worthless?"

Gervais shrugged. "A good point... while I can think of a few reasons, they tend to require outrageous ignorance on the part of the mark."

Angelo nodded emphatically. "The Petruzzi scheme."

"The what?" John asked.

Gervais waved a dismissive hand. "Just a technique for getting others to do as you wish."

"A scam?"

"Language, sir!" Gervais managed to sound so much like Ilsa that John blinked.

Rodney chuckled. "All right, one of your moves. But who would have to be 'outrageously ignorant' for it to work?"

"In this case, Salim."

"Oh."

"Man, you guys think in entirely different circles than is healthy."

"Thank you, John."

"Wasn't a compliment."

"I know. It was, however, a recognition of our skills," Gervais answered, hiking his thumbs at Angelo and Bertram, standing to either side of him.

"And?"

"I think those skills may prove useful before long."

Angelo sniffed. "Something in the wind, eh?"

John shook his head. "All I smell is horse shit."

"Oh, there's some elephant in there too, but that's not what I meant. I just have a feeling."

John smiled. "In the space of about two minutes flat, you go from calling one prophet false and then go claiming some ability at it yourself."

Gervais just grinned, but Bertram looked around in alarm. "Be careful with such words, John."

"What word? You mean, 'proph—'?"

Bertram cut him off: "Exactly. There is no other but the one around here."

"Right. Sorry."

The Red Tent

"Come forward, Salim. We have questions for you. Questions about the ferenghis you have charge of."

"I will make every effort to answer, Sultan Al'Azam."

"These railroads the envoys spoke of, did you see any in Grantville?"

"No, Sultan Al'Azam."

"But they think this technology is so valuable we should give them firmans of trade for it?"

"Sultan Al'Azam, I do not think they exaggerate the value of the technology, once built. Transporting heavy goods across great distances without the current requirement of fodder for the pack animals, that is something extraordinary. Especially in light of the strategic value of a railway from the heart of your empire to, say, Kabul? One able to run in winter?"

Shah Jahan tugged his beard, but eventually waggled his head. "Once built, they said. That it would require significant investment of time and labor as well as iron, they said."

Salim nodded. "Yes, Sultan Al'Azam, they said exactly those things."

"And yet they offer no gifts worthy of the name. Something as surety of their goodwill. All other supplicants to the throne offer up something of commensurate value to the thing they desire in order to show us exactly how serious they are."

"Sultan Al'Azam, these people are not..." He paused, choosing his next words carefully. "I do not believe they had a full understanding of how things work here at court before they departed Europe. Lacking such knowledge, they could not properly provide such sureties."

Shah Jahan waved that argument aside, retrieving a drink from his cupbearer. "I well remember who it was who sent Baram Khan to this 'Grantville,' hoping for the very end he met." He drank, then wiped his beard. "So I suppose I should not complain overmuch about their ignorance of our ways."

The emperor lapsed into brooding silence.

They were losing him to mourning again, and Salim didn't know how to stop it. India could not afford to let him lapse into melancholy again. There was so much that could be done, if he would but stay active and interested in the knowledge the up-timers offered.

Something more personal, perhaps...? "Also, Sultan Al'Azam, I believe their advanced knowledge of medicine will prove a great boon." He looked down, took a deep, steadying breath and offered a silent prayer: *God forgive me if I offend!*

"Sultan Al'Azam, they chose not to mention it—I think out of misplaced concerns over modesty issues they think we would have—but they know things that make their women the greatest of midwives, practices that lead to many fewer deaths among newborns, healthier children, and mothers who recover more quickly from the difficulties of childbirth."

The cup clattered against the tray. Salim looked up.

Shah Jahan was staring back at him. At length the emperor of India swallowed, eyes glittering, and said quietly, "Would that one of them had been here when my Mumtaz was giving birth."

Part Three

Winter and Spring, 1635

I will, before the giants' eyes,
Their city and their king chastise;

Chapter 25

Shah Jahan's camp
January 1635

She had barely settled to supper, joints aching from the unaccustomed travel, when Gargi announced Aurangzeb was without.
He must have been praying just outside to come upon her tent
so quickly, she thought, telling Gargi to admit him.

Barely pausing to let his eyes adjust, Aurangzeb crossed the
carpets to where she was sitting and plucked a fig from the tray
beside her. "You wished to speak, Nur Jahan?"

"Indeed I did, Shehzada. Will you take a seat or must I crane
my neck?"

Aurangzeb seated himself with the ease of youth, causing her
a mild pang of envy. Ignoring the momentary urge to mourn
things long gone, she asked, "Are you satisfied with the men we
arranged to place themselves at your service?"

"Yes, they will do, for now."

"Good, have you given any thought to what we discussed?"

"I have."

"And?"

Aurangzeb refused to answer her question, instead proposing
his own: "Any word from your people in Lahore? Did they find
any evidence that Mian Mir is working with the Sikhs?"

"No, they have not. As I said before, I had doubts Mian Mir
would even think to cooperate with the Sikhs in their rebellion
against your father. It is just not in his nature."

"I keep hearing from you and my siblings what a great man this Mian Mir is. I think I need to hear a little less about how wonderful he is and a little more about how I can use his relationship with Salim Yilmaz to drive a wedge between Father and the amir."

Thank you for proving yourself unready to hear the very play I have in motion. I had nearly forgotten how youth breeds impatience like nothing else.

I suppose it should come as no surprise that he almost sounds like Mullah Mohan. Ah well, that bed is made...

"I'm sure we'll find a wedge suitable to your purpose, Shehzada."

Aurangzeb surprised her then, giving a wan smile that reminded her exactly how young he was. "Forgive me, Nur. I am impatient, not with you, but with the situation. With each passing day we grow closer to Lahore, and still I have not been able to determine how Dara was killed. That, and Hargobind Singh has not moved from Ramdaspur though he must know the doom that is descending upon him."

"It is a great mystery."

"I find I do not like mysteries."

"And is it one you must solve, Shehzada?"

Aurangzeb smiled more broadly, the humor touching his eyes for the first time, "I suppose not. Especially if Hargobind Singh is merely waiting to die rather than kill us all."

"Do you think that's really possible?"

"What? That he could defeat my father and us as easily as he did Dara?"

She nodded.

"No, but his behavior remains inexplicable. And as I said, I do not like mysteries."

Deciding she had sown enough on that point, Nur moved on to more fertile ground. "Speaking of which, have you had an opportunity to speak with the ferenghi?"

"I have not. You?"

"No. Begum Sahib keeps them close and her bodyguard, Atisheh, watches me closely whenever I am near them."

"She was always my sister's favorite."

"And you cannot get Jahanara to support you?"

"She, like Dara, is far too liberal for my taste."

Nur spread her hands wide. "And what am I if not someone you made into an ally despite our differences?"

"Unlike you, she loves Father terribly and would not see my actions as planning for the future, but, rather preparing to usurp Father."

Nur smiled. "As usual, your assessment of our kin matches my own."

"And while it might be comforting to know that, it isn't exactly helpful in resolving the issue."

It required a greater degree of self-control than Nur was accustomed to using to keep the smile fixed in place as she replied, "No, I suppose not. Have you considered using the one against the other?"

"Which ones?"

"Mian Mir has proven inscrutable, correct?"

"You know it is so. Do not waste my time."

"Apologies, Shehzada. It is the way I think best." She held up a hand to forestall his incipient objection and went on quickly, "Shah Jahan has barely met with the ferenghis and suffers the same lack of intelligence regarding Mian Mir's possible connections to the Sikhs as you, does he not?"

In the habit clearly picked up from his father, Aurangzeb touched the thin beard just sprouting from his chin. "All true, though I fail to see what it is you would like me to do."

Nur smiled again. "You said the foreigners offered Shah Jahan technologies from the future. Who is to say your father is the only one to receive such an offer?"

Aurangzeb's expression snapped closed like a lantern shuttered in bronze.

Nur hid a smile. So the young prince didn't like the feeling of being last to reach the answer. That was something to be aware of, in the future, especially after some of her other, more sensitive seeds had matured and borne fruit.

Red Tent, near Lahore

The Red Tent was full of Father's advisors, the scent of horses, men, and oils combining in an odor that Aurangzeb would forever associate with war.

This is how we were meant to live—fighting the enemies of Islam and living in camp! Ready at a moment's notice, to move to His will.

The sowar completed his report: the Sikhs had made no move to depart the area around Ramdaspur. Father gave the messenger coin from his own hand and dismissed him.

Tugging his beard, Shah Jahan spoke aloud to his gathered war council: "He has to know I will crush him. Why does he not withdraw east, disappear into the hills? He has to know I will offer no mercy, no quarter, nothing at all to the killer of my son."

Aurangzeb watched Father's councilors prattle and mumble, their answers failing to satisfy reason, let alone their ruler. If Wazir Khan were here things might be different, but as it was they provided no information the common trooper did not already suspect or know.

So Aurangzeb watched, and waited, biding his time.

Casting a glance at his younger brother, Shah Shuja spoke when the others slowed in their clucking. "Sultan Al'Azam, Hargobind Singh surely knows that your wrath will pursue him unto the ends of the earth, and that he would only die tired should he attempt to run."

Aurangzeb choked back laughter. That was actually quite an excellent line, if not a thoughtful answer.

Father must have heard something because he looked at his younger son. "And what do you think, Aurangzeb?"

"Sultan Al'Azam, your understandable and righteous refusal to parley with the murderer of one of your sons has also prevented us gaining any insight into the mind of our adversary. They are, perhaps, preparing to die. I do not believe it is so, but it is one answer."

"And you have the one, true answer?" Shah Shuja asked.

"No, I do not claim God's insight into a man's mind. I but guess, like all of us here. Firstly, Hargobind Singh might have placed his faith in some trickery, some tactic of war that might see him successful against the great odds against him."

"Our spies and scouts report no efforts to fortify or mine," insisted Shah Shuja.

Aurangzeb looked at his elder brother, resisting the urge to thank him for his objection. "You are correct, they do not. Of course, Dara's scouts no doubt reported precisely the same thing to him." He returned his attention to Father. "Secondly, Hargobind Singh may believe someone is riding to his aid."

Shah Jahan waggled his head. "My spies tell me that a few of the local chieftains, more brigands than warriors, made overtures to the Sikh leadership and were rebuffed."

You mean your spies, posing as brigands, were not allowed to join the Sikh host.

Shah Shuja, voice dripping with contempt, said, "They but show their religious intolerance and hatred of Islam."

Aurangzeb nodded even as he disagreed with the details: "While the decision could have been made on religious grounds, I think it has more to do with preserving whatever secret weapon or tactic they plan to use against us. If they let in outsiders, then there exists the chance one of your spies will uncover whatever it is they plan."

Father's advisors muttered in consternation.

Judging Father's suspicion sufficiently primed, Aurangzeb held up a finger and asked quietly, "Do we know if the people from the future have had contact with Hargobind Singh or his people?"

Father tugged at his beard, musing aloud, "Those that are in our camp have not, as far as we know..."

"But others may have?"

"An excellent question. One Salim should be able to answer for me."

Knowing he trod dangerous ground, but unwilling to let the opportunity to drive a wedge between Father and one of his favorites pass, Aurangzeb said, "Sultan Al'Azam, I would call attention to certain things about Amir Yilmaz that I have learned since he has come to court."

Aurangzeb felt a chill hand run down his spine as Father's cold gaze fell on him. "Proceed."

"Like our brother Dara he was taught by Mian Mir. Yet, unlike Dara, he *chose* to study under that Mian Mir. Mian Mir is known to be a great friend of the Sikhs, so much so that he even laid the cornerstone of their temple while Jahangir's lax policies toward upholding Islam held sway. Further, I learned that Mian Mir also moved Amir Yilmaz to travel with Baram Khan to that place from the future."

Shah Jahan raised a hand and shook his head. "I will hear no more on these vague allegations until Amir Yilmaz has had an opportunity to speak to them."

"Sultan Al'Azam, I make no formal allegations, I merely bring these facts to your attention."

"And sow discord in our ranks just days before we are to fight."

"That was not my intent. I heard nothing of these issues from your other councilors, and wished to be sure you were appraised of them."

"And I have been advised. I will hear no more on this, now."

Aurangzeb bowed, seething: *Too much, too fast. God grant that I am more patient next time.*

Red Tent, near Lahore

Salim returned to the Red Tent and immediately noticed a strangled tenseness. He glanced around as he resumed his place behind the majority of men, who commanded far more than his paltry five hundred. As Salim completed his bow and sat, he caught Shah Shuja looking at him, a calculating expression on his face.

What is that about? What happened?

He didn't have time to ponder it, as Shah Jahan dismissed his remaining councilors. He stood to leave but the emperor called out to him, "Not you, Amir. Come forward."

"Yes, Sultan Al'Azam." Salim walked past Aurangzeb and Shah Shuja as the young princes departed. Aurangzeb appeared deep in thought, while Shah Shuja betrayed none of the interest of a moment before.

Salim bowed again, began to kneel.

"Closer, Amir."

Salim moved forward again, kneeling where Shah Shuja had been. He had never been closer to Shah Jahan, even in the man's sleeping quarters.

"I would ask you a question."

"Yes, Sultan Al'Azam?"

"How well do you know these ferenghis?"

"Sultan Al'Azam?" Salim asked, confused. "I'm afraid I don't understand the question."

"Simple enough: I want to know if you met any of the ferenghi before I sent you to meet them last month."

"No, Sultan Al'Azam, I did not meet any of these envoys prior to their arrival in your lands."

"And do you know if another party of the foreigners traveled with them here?"

"I cannot be certain, Sultan Al'Azam, but nothing the envoys have said or done has made me suspect that is so."

"What contact have you had with Mian Mir?"

"I sent a letter informing him that I had returned safely and was in good health, and that his instinct regarding Grantville was correct."

"And what instinct was that?"

"That events in Grantville were or would be very important."

"Such a long journey, at so much peril, and you only had that much to say?"

Salim ventured a smile, one that was not returned. "I was more detailed in the letter, Sultan Al'Azam, a copy of which I still have if you wish to see it?"

"Perhaps later. Just now I would like to know what it is he told you to do."

"Told, Sultan Al'Azam?"

"Yes, did he give you specific instruction as to what to do or tell me regarding the ferenghis?"

"No, he did not. He only repeated his request that I do what I could to ensure you and your heirs had access to everything that I brought back with me from Grantville. I have that letter as well, should you wish to read it."

Shah Jahan tugged his beard and asked: "Do you know if Mian Mir sent anyone else to Grantville?"

"No, Sultan Al'Azam, he made no mention of any others. May I ask why I am being questioned?"

"You may... though it is not you who is truly being questioned. It has come to my attention that Mian Mir may have influenced the Sikhs or be in league with Hargobind Singh against me."

Salim shook his head. "Sultan Al'Azam, that cannot be true. He has been, it is true, a friend to the Sikhs, but there is a vast difference between respect for a faith and supporting insurrection against you, the rightful Sultan Al'Azam. Mian Mir would never support a rebellion, and would certainly not have betrayed your son, one of his favored students, to anyone."

"And how is it you are so certain of his motives?"

Salim swallowed indignation, knowing it would do his argument no good. "Mian Mir does not speak falsely to anyone, let alone those he has chosen to teach. There is no misdirection in him. That is why his students are willing to undertake such dangerous tasks as my own."

Shah Jahan sniffed. "He ordered it. You, as his servant and a student in his *madrassa*, were obliged to do it."

"No, Sultan Al'Azam. He does not order anyone. He does not command anyone. He but asks, and does not punish those who refuse him. He told me of the good that might come of my journeying to Europe. I accepted the risk and undertook the journey, that is all."

Shah Jahan did not seem satisfied by this answer.

"Do I have your leave, Sultan Al'Azam, to bring you the letters I've received from Mian Mir? They will, I am sure, explain exactly what I have told you."

"Certainly, I will look at these letters. But you have to know that whatever their content, I cannot be certain they are the *only* letters Mian Mir has been sending."

"Yes, Sultan Al'Azam. I understand that it is difficult to trust in the word of your courtiers, especially those recently come into your service."

Shah Jahan snorted and waved a hand. "And, more importantly— my other courtiers may be speaking against you and Mian Mir while you are not present to defend yourselves."

So that is what Shah Shuja was looking at me about! Either he or Aurangzeb were trying to create distance between Shah Jahan and me.

"We shall soon be in Lahore. Perhaps Mian Mir can come pay a visit to you. While he is old and frail I'm sure he would like to see you, Sultan Al'Azam."

"Perhaps. For now, go fetch your letters and the English book, I would have you read more of it to me."

"Of course, Sultan Al'Azam."

Jahanara's Tent, near Lahore

"What news, mistress?"

"Nothing good, I'm afraid," Jahanara said, opening the letter. She scanned the note quickly and shook her head, eyes filling with tears.

"What is it?"

"Mian Mir has fallen gravely ill. His physicians do not think he will live." She snapped her fingers, summoning a messenger. Quickly, she wrote her orders and gave them over to the messenger. "Give this to Diwan Firoz Khan. Tell him I want no expense spared, do you hear me?"

"Yes, Shehzadi!" The messenger turned and left at the run.

"Is that wise, Shehzadi?" Smidha asked, her expressive face pinched with concern. "Shah Jahan has already publicly questioned Mian Mir's loyalty. Can an order of execution be far behind?"

"Father only questioned Mian Mir's loyalty because Aurangzeb played him false, putting the silly idea in his ear."

"Still, you have still not healed the rift between you. Is it wise to risk still more disagreement?"

"Smidha, I must help him if I can. If Father asks, I will tell him I did it in Dara Shikoh's memory. In fact, I should send for Rodney Totman. He may have some medical technique that might save—"

Smidha interrupted her mistress, "Begum Sahib! You cannot do that! Even if the ferenghi was to agree to it, Shah Jahan would surely see it as confirmation of Aurangzeb's insinuation that the foreigners are secretly in league with the Sikhs."

That gave Jahanara pause. She let out a long sigh of frustration and reached out to Smidha, taking the older woman in her arms. "You are right, Smidha. Much as I might want to, sending Mr. Totman to Lahore and Mian Mir would be foolish."

Smidha hugged Jahanara tight and sighed. "I'm sorry, Janni. I don't want to always speak from fear, but there is so much in the world that I worry over when it comes to you, daughter of my heart."

"No, it is I who should apologize. I am too willful and heedless of the dangers." She smiled. "I suppose I've enjoyed Father's favor for so long I never learned how dangerous life can be without it."

"You will be there again, Jahanara. Shah Jahan cannot refuse his favorite daughter for very long."

Chapter 26

After years of preparation, a month of travel, a night of uneasy maneuvering, and a morning of predawn prayers, Aurangzeb was finally ready to command troops in his first battle. Mounting his horse, the prince joined the main body of his personal troops. Already formed up, the men appeared ready, even eager, to do battle.

It felt . . . proper and good, this leading of men.

He accepted the greetings of his senior captains and squinted into the dawn's light, considering the disposition of forces and lay of the land.

Father had chosen Aurangzeb to lead the right wing of his army with one quarter of his troops, committing Shah Shuja to the less important left with an equal number. Shah Jahan himself commanded the center, war elephants in the van.

Wazir Asaf Khan, despite his best efforts, was still a month behind the army. There would be no assistance from that quarter.

Not that we should need any, he thought, looking across the shallow bowl of the area around Ramdaspur. The Sikhs had fielded barely five thousand men, nearly half of whom were not mounted.

The left flank of the Sikh army, across from Aurangzeb's own force, was anchored on a small fort. Dislodging the warriors inside the fort would likely prove time-consuming and difficult. Shah Jahan had ordered him to instead attack the troops nearest the fort and defeat them, thereby simultaneously isolating the garrison and turning the Sikh flank. The Sikhs had a number of guns in the fort, but it did not appear they had taken the guns from the other side to reinforce the side facing Aurangzeb.

God is merciful. It will prove hard enough to win through the forces facing us while under fire.

Feigning a calm he did not truly feel, Aurangzeb drank from his water skin and let his gaze travel back to the center and Father's command group, waiting for the signal to commence the attack.

Salim's mount did not like being this close to the elephants, champing the bit and stepping sideways. Calmly bringing it back under control, he returned to the knot of messengers, counselors, and functionaries surrounding the emperor.

Shah Jahan shot a tense grin his way, misinterpreting the horse's idiocy for high spirits. "It looks as if someone is ready to fight."

Salim bowed over his pommel. "Sultan Al'Azam, we are all ready to do your bidding."

The emperor nodded absently, eyes returning to the army across from them. "What is that?"

Everyone looked. The center of the Sikh force had opened up to reveal a palanquin decorated in gold and jewels carried on the shoulders of eight armed warriors. Four armored and richly dressed men on fine horses rode forward with the palanquin. The entire procession marched forward a few hundred gaz before coming to a halt well out of bow shot.

"What is this?" the emperor asked.

His counselors all tried answering at once, their voices becoming nothing more than an angry noise.

Salim's fool horse chose that moment to rear, drawing the emperor's eye again. "What do you think it is, Salim?"

"I do not know, Sultan Al'Azam, but if you will permit it, I will ride forth and ask."

The hubbub from the other counselors died abruptly, each calculating what was to be lost or gained should Salim succeed or die.

"You would have me go back on my oath?" Shah Jahan asked, expression unreadable.

"Words said in grief and anger are rarely our best, Sultan

Al-Azam. If the Sikhs kill me, then you will have confirmation that your first instinct was proper, and I am—or was—a fool. If they do not, I will satisfy your curiosity and discover what it is they are attempting."

Shah Jahan tugged at his beard but eventually waved a hand. "You have my leave to speak to them."

Salim gave his horse his head and shot out from between two of Shah Jahan's elephants.

He examined the group around the palanquin as he rode to meet them. The men had the hard look of veteran warriors, were well armed and armored, and one of them . . . Salim's eyes shot wide. Hargobind Singh himself! But then, who was in the palanquin?

He slowed as he came close enough to speak without shouting. "The Sultan Al'Azam would know what it is you are doing, Hargobind Singh."

The Sikh guru smiled. "I but take a walk with my friend."

Salim came to a halt, the man's powerful personality palpable even at this remove. "Between two armies?" he asked.

Hargobind Singh spread his arms wide. "I knew I had guests coming and this is the welcome party." He waggled a finger at Salim. "But my guests were less than polite in that they refused to accept my messengers, who would have informed everyone that we were prepared to welcome them and, perhaps, give them back what was lost."

"I begin to worry that our host might have stood too long in the sun . . ." Salim blurted, immediately regretting it.

The men with Hargobind Singh bristled. One, riding at his right hand, snorted laughter and asked, "Who are you, to ask the guru his business and question his sanity?"

Salim noted the ease with which the man sat his horse and the hard, dangerous look in his eyes. *A worthy opponent. I will have to seek him out during the battle, should God will that I survive that long.*

He gave a slight nod of the head, acknowledging the other warrior's point. "I have been most impolite. Forgive me, Guru. I am the amir Salim Gadh Visa Yilmaz, humble servant and commander of five hundred in the name of Shah Jahan, Sultan Al'Azam, your rightful ruler."

Eyes glittering, Hargobind Singh smiled broadly. Appearing

to have had his fun, he backed his horse and, with a flourish, gestured Salim toward the palanquin.

Salim rode forward between the Sikhs. He dismounted next to the palanquin and pulled aside the curtain.

"I'm afraid I can't get up to greet you, Salim, but it is so very good to see you," Dara Shikoh whispered.

"Shehzada!" Salim shouted, stunned. "We thought you dead!"

Dara Shikoh swallowed, "As painful as life is, I am still in it." One hand reached out, grabbed Salim by the shoulder. "Tell me: my wife, has she given birth?"

"Any day now, Shehzada. She is healthy and will be overjoyed to hear she may discard the white of mourning."

"Good. Good," Dara Shikoh murmured.

Salim shook off his surprise and examined Dara more closely. The prince had a bandage across one side of his chest and a sling supporting the opposite arm—but, more alarming, was far too pale for good health.

He finished his examination to find Dara smiling weakly. "I do not look my best."

"No, but that is to be expected, being held by your enemies."

"Guru Hargobind Singh has been a gentle captor, and has rendered me every aid that was within his power to give."

A gentle cough from behind Salim drew both their attention. Hargobind Singh sat his horse a few gaz away, looking down on them. "Amir, can I rely on you to convey my words to the Sultan Al'Azam?"

"Of course, Guru."

The guru raised one hand and pointed heavenward. "I seek no further conflict with the Sultan Al'Azam Shah Jahan, and would return his first-born son to him, provided we can come to an equitable agreement regarding the rights of my people. A people who, in their love for him, would be his again if he would but allow them freedom to practice our faith in peace, free of the jizya that is both insult and burden to all who follow God.

"Dara Shikoh has been our guest since his defeat at our hands. We have done all we can for him, but his injuries are commensurate with his bravery in battle, and therefore prove difficult to heal. Should Shah Jahan have physicians he would send, they will be received with the utmost respect and courtesy."

Hargobind Singh curled the fingers that had pointed heavenward, making a fist. "Should Shah Jahan wish to ignore my overtures of peace, then he will find us ready to die to the last man to defend our faith and home. Please bring these words to Shah Jahan with my blessing."

Salim rose to his feet and gave the guru a respectful bow. "I will do these things." He turned to Dara Shikoh. "Shehzada, do you have any additional words for your father?"

"Yes. I ask that he forgive me my failure and remember that all things happen according to God's will."

"I shall do so, Shehzada." He looked again at Hargobind Singh. "With your permission, Guru?"

"Of course."

Salim remounted and turned his horse toward the waiting army of Shah Jahan. He rode slowly, not wishing to put fear into either army and pondering what, exactly, was going to happen when he told Shah Jahan just who was in the palanquin...and then when he gave the Sultan Al'Azam the words of Hargobind Singh. Despite the warmth of the day, Salim shivered at the thought.

At least Aurangzeb and Shah Shuja would not be present when he told Shah Jahan he could get his favored son back.

A strange sort of sigh ran through the assembled army as Salim slowly rode back from the group of Sikhs.

"I'm not sure what the hell this means," John said, lowering his binoculars. The male mission members were mounted up about two hundred yards to the rear and to one side of the emperor's command group. They were not expected to fight, but had made sure to arm up anyway.

"Didn't the emperor say he wasn't gonna talk to them?"

John nodded.

"That was Salim went out there to see them, wasn't it?"

"Yup."

"But..."

John shrugged. "I got no idea. This stuff confuses the hell out of me. Everyone standing around ready to fight, then they send somebody out to talk about it? Like something out of the Crusades."

Angelo cleared his throat. "This is unusual. Shah Jahan wasn't supposed to do that."

"Do what?"

"Shah Jahan said he wasn't going to negotiate with Hargobind Singh at all. That any who even spoke to a Sikh were his enemies."

John waved a hand in the general direction of the Imperial party and said, "Salim didn't just do that on his own, though."

"No, he did not appear to. Which seems to indicate that Shah Jahan has experienced some change of heart."

"So...who was in the palanquin?"

"Your guess is as good as mine, though Salim seemed surprised and pleased by what he saw in there."

Angelo shook his head.

"I know," Gervais said, grinning.

"What?"

"It never ceases to amaze us how good those are," Gervais pointed at John's binoculars. "I have used telescopes before, but there's just no comparison with those for depth of field and being able to quickly bring something into focus."

John nodded, failing to see a need to comment, especially as Salim had finally returned to Shah Jahan's party.

He quickly raised the binoculars again and focused on Shah Jahan. He could only get the emperor's back, but could clearly see Salim's expression as he related something.

The emperor swayed like a drunkard in the saddle.

"Damn," he muttered.

"What?" nearly everyone in the party asked.

"Nothing, I just never saw someone actually reel in shock."

Harem Tents, Shah Jahan's Camp

"I *hate* men! Leaving us to face this alone!" Nadira gasped.

Jahanara smiled, mopping Nadira's brow. "You don't mean that, it is just the pain talking."

"You would hate them too, were yoooooh!" Nadira hissed, gasped, spat: "In my place. Oh!" She clamped Jahanara's hand, hard, squeezing until it felt the bones must break.

"Breathe, Nadira Begum. Breathe," Priscilla said, her thick accent odd in Jahanara's ears. The up-timer's hands were busy pulling a series of metal implements out of the heavy bag she'd brought with her and dropping them into the cauldron of boiling water she'd demanded be brought in.

"I fail to see the value this ferenghi brings to this, Begum Sahib," Smidha groused. "Breathe? As well tell the fish to swim!"

Jahanara shot a quelling glance her way even as the midwife spoke: "No, Smidha, it is sound advice. Childbirth requires as much air as the mother can take."

Priscilla looked over at Sahana, who shook her head and said something in rapid-fire English.

Still looking at Smidha, Jahanara announced in a loud, clear voice, "Sahana, please inform Priscilla that I will not allow anyone to interfere with her kind assistance to the midwife. And that the midwife also knows that Priscilla is to be consulted at all times during and after Nadira's delivery."

Sahana bowed at the waist and translated for the benefit of the two foreigners. But Jahanara kept her gaze on Smidha.

The older woman pretended not to hear.

There was a disturbance at the tent entrance. Jahanara nodded in that direction, glad to have somewhere to send the older woman. "Smidha, see if the battle has begun."

"Yes, Begum Sahib."

"Priscilla."

"Yes, Shehzadi?"

"Are we missing anything that you or my brother's wife might need?"

"No, Shehzadi."

Nadira's death grip on Jahanara's hand relaxed. She took a deep breath and another.

Priscilla said something, looking at the up-timer device on her wrist. Ilsa took note of whatever was said in the small book before her.

"Soon," the midwife said.

Priscilla nodded in apparent agreement. Speaking slowly and clearly, so that Sahana could keep up, she said: "Nadira, I'm going to take a measurement now, and find out if it is safe for you to push."

Nadira nodded her sweating head, and groaned, "Merciful God, anything to get this over with!"

Priscilla drew the tray from the cauldron and set it aside and out of Nadira's view. The shining, oddly shaped steel implements were vaguely sinister, sitting there, steaming, even in the heat.

To distract herself as much as make sure Nadira could not see them, Jahanara squeezed Nadira's smaller hand in hers.

The younger woman smiled at her, then winced as another contraction struck. Jahanara tried to hide how much Nadira's grip hurt. It was the least she could do.

A strange noise, something she had never heard in camp before, rumbled in the distance. She looked away from Nadira's sweating face, instinctively trying to identify the sound.

It wasn't a battle—those she had heard before. Nor was it defeat, something she had also had the misfortune to hear.

Almost...

Disappointment?

Smidha returned to the tent flap and hurried to her. Such was her shocked expression that Jahanara momentarily thought the worst had happened, and Father lay dead. She opened her mouth to tell Smidha it was not so, that she had heard no sounds of combat, but Smidha spoke before the words could leave her lips, "Nadira Begum, your husband yet lives!"

"What?" Nadira asked.

"Your husband, Shehzada Dara Shikoh, lives. He is prisoner of the Sikhs, but he yet lives!"

"What cruel joke is this?"

"From who do you have these words?" Jahanara asked at the same time.

"Begum Sahib, Amir Yilmaz was sent to treat with Hargobind Singh and met with Dara Shikoh himself."

Releasing a breath she hadn't been aware she'd held, Jahanara looked down at her brother's wife and smiled, tears in her eyes.

"Am I dead, to have my one wish—" Another contraction robbed Nadira of breath.

"No," Jahanara kissed the back of her hand, "sweet Nadira, you are not dead."

"Very close now, I can see the...a foot."

Jahanara glanced over, detecting a note of worry in the midwife's voice.

More rapid-fire exchanges between the Ilsa, Priscilla, and Sahana. Priscilla rattling out a series of what sounded like commands, voice calm and controlled.

Nadira's sudden scream was no less loud for issuing between clenched teeth.

Ears ringing and heart hammering, Jahanara kept smiling. "You will live to present my nephew to my brother, I am sure of it."

The Red Tent

"Out! All of you, out!"

Salim made to rise.

"Not you, Amir Yilmaz!" Shah Jahan barked. "I may have questions. Nor you, my sons. I have orders for you..."

Within moments, Salim was the only person not a family member or slave of Shah Jahan's in the Red Tent. For his own part, Salim found it hard not to look with longing at the exit.

An expectant silence hung in the air like the dust of a hundred horsemen passing.

"Recall your men to camp, my sons."

"Yes, Father," Shah Shuja said, leaving to relay the order to his troops. He showed no resentment, just did as he was bid. Salim waited for Aurangzeb to follow suit, but the younger prince did not move.

Shah Shuja proves the better son, at least in this.

Shah Jahan didn't notice, tugging at his beard and pacing the carpets of the Red Tent. "God has chosen this moment to test me, I am sure of it."

Despite his total agreement, Salim chose not to answer with Aurangzeb there. Salim was uncomfortable speaking upon God's will at any time, but with the younger prince present, it would not be safe.

Aurangzeb spoke to it, however: "Forgive me, Father, but how does the fact Hargobind Singh keeps my brother prisoner outweigh all the wrongs done to you?"

The emperor answered without turning. "It does not! Yet I cannot ignore the fact that he *does* hold your brother prisoner, and that it was my own folly and pride that led me to disregard and ignore the many messengers Hargobind Singh sent."

"After he rose up in rebellion against you!"

Shah Jahan waved a hand. "And emerged victorious." He shook his head. "And what other sign must He send that God is using this Hargobind Singh as His instrument?"

"To what purpose, this unbeliever?"

Shah Jahan at last turned to look at his son. "To teach me humility, of course. I was too prideful of the things given me by foreign princes...to start a war over a *hawk*?"

Aurangzeb opened his mouth to argue but stopped. After a

moment's reflection, the young prince sighed and surprised Salim with a quote from the Quran: "Exult not, for God loveth not those who exult in earthly things."

"Exactly. He allowed Hargobind Singh to rob me of my son, and now gives me opportunity to redress my sin and secure Dara's safety, all at once..." The emperor lapsed into silence.

"I will order the withdrawal," Aurangzeb said. He bowed, turned, and departed.

Should I call attention to the fact that Aurangzeb refused to obey until his father explained everything to his satisfaction? He turned to do so, finding Shah Jahan watching his son's retreating back.

The emperor, too, quoted from the Quran, voice quiet and leaden. "Avoid suspicion as much as possible: for suspicion in some cases is a sin: and spy not on each other, nor speak ill of each other behind their backs."

Salim took that wisdom in silence.

At length Shah Jahan turned from the opening and sat, gesturing for a drink. "What to do?"

"Sultan Al'Azam?"

"I do not know what to do. He has my son."

Salim spread his hands. "It seems that by not making a choice, you have made a choice. Simply by ordering your sons to withdraw, you have opened a dialogue with Hargobind Singh."

Shah Jahan shook his head, a wan smile on his lips. "I suppose I have." He sighed. "Tell me, did Dara look well?"

"Sultan Al'Azam, he looked as well as could be expected, having taken at least two cruel sword blows."

The emperor nodded. "We are of good stock. Men to ride the steppe with."

"No doubt, Sultan Al'Azam. He seems to have been well treated, regardless."

"Do you think the ferenghi could help him?"

"I do, Sultan Al'Azam."

Another tug of his beard, closely followed by a tiny shake of his head. "I simply do not know if I can trust them."

A young eunuch entered the tent and bowed deeply before the emperor. "I carry Begum Sahib's words."

"Say them."

"Sultan Al'Azam: Begum Sahib wishes to inform you that

Nadira Begum has given birth to a healthy baby boy. Nadira Begum rests now, and, despite minor complications, is well."

Shah Jahan smiled and clapped Salim on the back. "Congratulate me, I am a grandfather!"

"Congratulations, Sultan Al'Azam."

The emperor's good cheer was short-lived, however. "Slave," he snapped at the eunuch, "you said something of complications?"

The eunuch bowed again. "Please forgive any errors, as I do not understand the way of such things, but the midwife said the child was born in incomplete breech, and were it not for the ferenghi women's assistance they might have lost both mother and child."

Shah Jahan looked across at Salim and shook his head in wonder. "It appears God has provided answers for all of my questions this day."

Chapter 27

The Red Tent
March 1635

John came to a halt before the emperor's throne and bowed as he'd been taught.

Things seemed tense to him. He wished they could have had a moment with Salim before this, to try and get the lay of the land. His eyes flicked to the side, where their host was kneeling. At least he was here, and hasn't been executed or something

"Greetings, envoys of the Emperor of the United States of Europe," Angelo translated.

"Greetings, Sultan Al'Azam."

"You may have noted that we did not enter into battle against the Sikhs."

"That we had observed and wondered at the reason, Sultan Al'Azam."

Shah Jahan nodded, brightened considerably. "I do not know if you were made aware of it, but your wives were instrumental in delivering my grandson to me. My son's wife is recovering safely, and in good spirits. I thank you for this boon, and will reward your women with their weight in silver or whatever they desire."

Unsure he was hearing right, John looked at the translator, who nodded, then back at Shah Jahan. "Congratulations, Shah Jahan! Is this your first grandchild?"

A slightly sad smile. "Of my first wife, yes."

Stupid, John, bringing up the man's love.

The emperor went on after a moment's sad reflection. "I thank you for your congratulations, but I have a favor to ask of you: Dara Shikoh, my eldest son, yet lives."

So *that* was who had been in the palanquin!

"He was wounded in battle and taken prisoner by Hargobind Singh. He has been treated well," the emperor gestured at Salim, "but I am informed that Dara has been slow to recover. Hargobind Singh will permit physicians into Ramdaspur to see to Dara's recovery. I ask you: as a favor to me, would you apply your skills at medicine to speed his recovery?"

John shot a glance at Rodney, who did not look confident. Unsure what to say, John bowed again. "Sultan Al'Azam, we would not want to fill you with false hope, especially without having seen Dara's condition. If you will permit, Mr. Totman may be able to further explain..."

The emperor waved permission.

From the set of his shoulders Rodney knew exactly how deep the waters were. He continued in the same cautious vein John had: "Sultan Al'Azam, as John says, we wouldn't want to give you false hope, especially without having seen your son. Beyond which, my knowledge is most useful immediately after injury, and in keeping wounds clean and supporting the body's ability to fight infection. From what you're saying, it's been a month and more since he was injured."

Shah Jahan frowned; he spoke intently but in controlled fashion. Angelo translated: "I understand the qualifiers you have placed on your ability to assist and the fact that it's possible that you may not be able to heal him. My questions still stands: *Will you assist my son?*"

Rodney bowed. "Forgive me, umm... Sultan Al'Azam. Of course I'll do everything I can to help."

The emperor nodded. "I will send my own physicians as well."

Rodney opened his mouth but thought better of it.

Shah Jahan noticed. "What is it, Mr. Totman?"

"Forgive me, Sultan Al'Azam, but my wife is at least as good as I am. I think she could help a good deal more than..."

John fought not to cringe, knowing exactly what it was Rodney almost finished the sentence with: "your poor excuse for doctors," or something similar.

Shah Jahan smiled, which showed either an astute appreciation of what had been left unsaid or a patronizing attitude toward the possible usefulness of women, John wasn't sure which. "I appreciate the great differences in our cultures, but let us just say my daughter-in-law's continuing good health outweighs the possible assistance your wife might lend you while treating my son."

A little of both, then.

Rodney bowed. "The Sultan Al'Azam is wise."

The emperor's gaze shifted back to John. "I will not forget your help in delivering me my grandson, even should your attempts to save my son fail. I understand the difficult position I am putting you in. You must also understand that we are engaged in delicate negotiations with Hargobind Singh, and must therefore avoid antagonizing him. Please treat him with respect and honor, and answer any questions he has honestly."

Ilsa and Priscilla must've really saved the day, for him to change his tune so thoroughly.

"I will, of course, provide anything you need to treat my son. Salim will also assist you as interpreter." Salim glanced at the emperor, but otherwise didn't seem surprised by this command.

Rodney either ignored the byplay or didn't notice it. "Understood. When can I expect to see him?"

"I shall send you presently, if that is agreeable?"

"May I consult with John a moment, Sultan Al'Azam?"

"Of course."

Rodney and John stepped back and put their heads together. "You okay with going now?"

"No better time than the present, I suppose. I'll need my bag from the tent, of course. Tell our minders I'd like to have dinner with Priscilla…Assuming I'll be back in time to eat."

"Will do. You sure about this, Rodney?"

Rodney shrugged. "Best to get it over with. It's been a month or so. Hard to say if I'll be able to help the guy at all. If it's an infection, we might be good to go. Jesus, I hope it's an infection."

"We don't have that many antibiotics."

"I know, John. But I think if this guy needs them, we couldn't ask for a better patient to get us an in with the emperor."

John couldn't argue with that.

"And really, it's not too hard to manufacture some more. It was one of the things we're planning on giving them anyway, remember?"

"Yeah."

Rodney nodded toward the emperor. "I think we left him wait-ing long enough. The man's aged a year since we first saw him."

"All right, you want one of the boys with you?"

"No—wait. On second thought, I think Gervais might be helpful. I trust his instincts on the politics a lot more than my own. You notice how quickly he's picking up the language?"

"Sure have."

Sensing the impatience coming off the emperor—and impressed again with the man's ability to fill a space with his personality—John turned back to Shah Jahan, who was tugging his beard. "Sultan Al'Azam, Rodney and Gervais will go and see what can be done to speed your son's recovery."

Shah Jahan released his beard. "Good. God willing, you will be successful."

Ramdaspur

The man assigned to guide them—Gervais wasn't yet sure whether he was a minor court functionary or something more—told them to wait. At least, he assumed it was the command. He hadn't learned a single word of Punjabi yet. Hard enough to learn suf-ficient Persian to be of use in most situations and he hadn't yet found the time to even attempt any of the myriad other languages spoken in these lands.

"Salim?"

"Yes, Gervais?"

"The emperor's physicians have any luck?"

Salim punched his beard at the passage their guide had dis-appeared down. "They're in there now."

Deciding Salim was a bit intense for his mood, Gervais stepped around Rodney, who as much occupied the whole passage as stood in it, and over to the nearest archway.

"Nice digs for a hospital prison," Rodney said.

"If by digs, you mean quarters, I'd have to agree." By force of habit, Gervais mentally cataloged every valuable in sight. The gilt and jewels lining the ceiling of the halls and side chambers could have easily paid for a ship, perhaps two.

Rodney joined Gervais in the arch, looking about with that

simple wonder and pleasure in things that had already struck
Gervais as an odd characteristic of the up-timers: each knew
so many practical, powerful, and world-shaking things, yet they
were so often like country bumpkins; tickled to see a building
taller than their home village's windmill.

Their attendant returned. The emperor's physicians were with
him, muttering among themselves. They didn't appear all that
hopeful.

Rodney didn't hear them and continued his observations:
"This place is almost as gaudy as Red Fort."

Salim sniffed. "If you are ready, Mr. Totman?"

Startled, Rodney flushed, "Sure. Sorry, Salim. Just a bit nervous, you know."

Salim stopped and looked up at the larger man. "My apologies for being short. I am worried about Dara Shikoh. He did
not look well, and I doubt the emperor's physicians proved any
better than the one Hargobind Singh provided. If I am right,
you are the prince's best hope for recovery."

*He must really be rattled. I don't think he's been this open
about* anything *since the day we met,* Gervais thought, retrieving
Rodney's medical kit and setting out after their guide.

The sickroom they entered at the end of the hall was large
and, unlike most such sickrooms in a Europe, sun-lit and well
ventilated.

A man stood on the far side of the bed. Gervais pegged him
as a local physician from his soft hands, rich robes, and tense,
watchful expression.

The prince was dozing, dressed in a fresh silk robe and sitting up among the pillows. The pillows and silks were likewise
clean, and there was none of the smell of corruption Gervais
associated with most sickrooms. There was, strangely, a hint of
an odor of vinegar in the air...

He puzzled over it a moment, then realized: *opium.*

"Shehzada Dara Shikoh?" Salim said, holding up a hand to
halt Gervais and Rodney.

"Uh?"

"Shehzada, I have brought one of the up-timers we spoke of.
He will examine your wounds."

"Oh." Dara slowly nodded. "Hurts..." The responses were
slow and slurred.

He'd smoked opium recently, and not a little.

Salim gestured for Rodney to join him, then eased the silken robe from Dara's shoulders.

It required some work, but they managed to remove the bandages and Rodney spent some time in a thorough inspection of the prince's injuries.

The belly wound was a shallow, lengthy cut just above where a man's sword belt rode and, thankfully appeared well on its way to healing.

Both wounds were well-sewn, but the one extending from the back of the pectoral into the armpit was mottled in shades of pink, white and red that Gervais didn't associate with healthy flesh.

"Mr. Totman, can I get a better look?"

Rodney looked at him a moment, shrugged, and moved aside.

Gervais bent close and examined the problematic wound: a sharp sword had cut from a spot about a handspan above the nipple, through the pectoral and tendons back to the mid-point of the armpit, getting shallower as it went.

"May I, Shehzada?" he asked, raising his hands above the wound.

"Yes, you may."

Gervais gently touched the skin around the prince's wound. The sutured flesh at the pectoral end of the cut felt hotter than the flesh around the rest of the wound, a bad sign. He probed a little less gently, had a mild twitch of discomfort from the patient despite the opium haze, and removed his hands.

Still, it was quite an impressive display of surgery.

"Did you reconnect the tendons?" he asked.

"I did," the physician replied, Salim translating. "The wound was a clean one, and the flesh vital."

"What manner of material was used for the sutures?"

The answer was quick: "Sheep's intestine for the internal and silk for the external. He had lost quite a bit of blood, but recovered from that quickly, as the young are wont to do."

"Has it been weeping?" Rodney asked.

"Yes, but not strongly for a wound of that size."

"How long has it looked like this?"

"Two days ago, it weeped a bit more before, then stopped. The discoloration started yesterday. Dara Shikoh was in better form then, though he complained much of pain and has had a slight fever for as long as he's been in my care. Now the fever has grown more intense."

Gervais nodded, waved at the prince: "Is all of this your handiwork?"

The physician's eyes narrowed. "Yes."

"Excellent work," Gervais said, meaning it. European physicians would never stoop to such menial labor, leaving it to barber-surgeons and similarly disreputable types.

The man bowed but offered no sign whether the recognition pleased or angered him. He was not a man Gervais would care to wager against, not with that stone face.

Salim looked at Rodney, a gambler's desperate hope in his eyes. "So he'll recover?"

Gervais glanced at Rodney, who was still looking at Dara's wound, spoke for him: "That remains to be seen. Rodney and I need to talk for a moment now we've seen Dara Shikoh."

"Of course."

Rodney and Gervais stepped aside and put their heads together.

"What do you think, Rodney? It looks like they did a clean job of sewing him up."

"They did, it's just not enough. That shoulder is infected. Back up-time, they'd have put in a drain to prevent the injury forming a walled abscess. Between the drain and a course of antibiotics, they could be reasonably sure of recovery."

"So...?"

The big man shrugged. "We lucked out, that infection was slow to start and must be walled, preventing it from spreading too far, otherwise he'd be in a lot more pain and probably be beyond saving without a complete operating room and injectable antibiotics, the kind we just don't have.

"I suspect something got in along one of the sutures if it's not one of the sutures themselves. If it was closer to the surface I'd just lance it, pack it, and give him some oral antibiotics—but I think we need to cut him again to debride and drain whatever's causing it. I hate to go in if we don't have to, and there's always the chance it's fungal, in which case nothing we do will help."

"But can you get in and clean the wound?" Gervais asked, cutting off the other man's rambling.

Rodney's lips twisted. "I'm not sure...I hardly trained to cut somebody, and then it was mostly bypassing a closed airway." He held up one massive hand. "My hands are damn big for this kind of work. That's why I wanted Pris here, she's really good with a scalpel, not to mention the fact that my sutures look like football laces."

Deciding to leave the definition of that last for later, Gervais focused on answering the younger man's unspoken question. "Yes, I am sure that's so, but the emperor was quite clear: we aren't getting your wife in here."

"I know, I know, I just doubt I'll do a good job of it..."

"I see." Gervais sighed. "Well, I've wielded the surgeon's knife before. I suppose I can do it again."

Rodney looked at him, eyes wide. "You have? I thought you were...I mean...you know..." He lowered his voice, glancing from side to side so surreptitiously it was comical, "a con man?"

"Only when all other avenues were closed to me. I was once a student training to be a physician. That's what Don Francisco was talking about back in Hamburg."

"Oh. All right, then." Rodney's initial relieved expression suddenly disappeared. "Wait a second! I thought down-time physicians didn't go in for surgery before we came on the scene."

Gervais felt a bitter smile creep across his lips. "They didn't. I was kicked out of school for exploring the mysteries of the body using *De Humani Corporis Fabrica* and other texts the administration felt an 'inappropriate representation of our storied institution.' My explorations were discovered and my work put to an untimely end."

How that memory still burns, even after all these years.

"Exploring?"

Gervais cocked his head, shrugged. "I had a cadaver I was dissecting."

Rodney's eyes shot wide. "No. Really?"

"To use one of John's favorite expressions: No shit." He took a deep breath. "So, now that you know more of my...unconventional past than I'm comfortable having anyone really know, can we get back to the matter at hand?"

"Right. Think you're steady enough on the knife to get in cleanly?"

"Using the steel these people make, certainly." He gestured at the Sikh. "I think we'll use that physician to sew him back up when we're done, though. I've rarely seen such skill with needle and gut."

"This is gonna hurt like a son of a bitch."

"From the smell, he's smoked quite a bit of opium."

"Is that what that smell is?"

Gervais nodded.

"I wondered when he didn't react all that strongly when we were probing the wound."

"Right. Shall we?"

A deep sigh rumbled through the man's vast chest. "Let's get to it, then."

Gervais gestured at the local. "First I want to go over some vocabulary with our friend. Wouldn't do to have him misunderstand something at an critical moment."

Rodney nodded. "Or wipe his nose halfway through."

Gervais chuckled. "Indeed."

"Which reminds me: we need pure alcohol and sterile water, lots of it."

It was time to put on a brave face and convince these people they knew what they were doing. So he put on his best big-con smile, turned, and clapped hands together. "Right, Salim, could you please help the prince's good physician and us to develop a shared vocabulary? Words like: here, there, stop, tighter, that sort of thing? Oh, and we also need alcohol as pure as we can get...and a significant quantity of boiled water. Boiled in copper kettles, still in the copper, mind you."

"Of course."

Aurangzeb's Tent

"I am denied."

"For the moment, Shehzada. Just for the moment. Your father cannot deny your ultimate fate and glory."

"And you know this how?"

"My astrologers, your character, and..." Nur held up a set of papers, "the contents of one of Amir Yilmaz's books from the future."

"And just how did you obtain that?"

"As I informed you when you first approached me, I have my sources."

Impassive, Aurangzeb picked up the paper. "It is even in Persian, but what is this word in Latin letters?"

"Encyclopedia. I am told that they are collections from the future consisting of short treatises on periods of history, scientific advancements, and the biographies of persons of note."

Aurangzeb quickly read the few pages of script, then reread them.

Nur Jahan watched him closely, belly tight with anticipation.

At length the prince put the paper aside and regarded her with a steady gaze. "And just how reliable is this information?"

She admired his calm. The information was explosive, especially for him. "The translation is as close to the original as possible. There are some issues of vernacular, of course, but I am assured and confident in that assurance."

"And just who—"

She held up a hand to forestall the question. "I'm afraid I cannot say."

"No, you choose not to."

She smiled and waggled her head: "Choice, or the lack of it, are two sides of the same coin in this. Were I to tell you, my utility to serve your cause would be diminished."

"Oh?"

"Should my agent learn I had informed others of their character and placement, they would be most displeased and refuse to serve further. Bad enough that I have revealed," she nodded at the papers, "this."

"Is that not always the problem with secrets and spies: when to reveal what is known...?"

She smiled. "Exactly so, Shehzada."

His gaze went back to the papers: "So this is why Father acted so differently since the arrival of the amir; sending my brother out to command when at all times previous he made excuses to keep Dara close. He's been trying to season him for the inevitable clash."

Nur nodded.

"This... This changes everything."

"Indeed. Shah Jahan's desire for secrecy regarding the contents of the works is certainly explained, as is his interest in the ferenghi and his elevation of the Afghan amir, Salim."

He shook his head in wonder and picked up the papers again.

Trusting the seeds she had planted would ripen on their own in the young man's fertile mind, Nur let him read it through once more.

At length he looked at her and said, "I must pray on this."

"Of course." *Just don't speak of it to Mullah Mohan,* she thought but did not add.

He sat back.

Taking that as a sign the interview was at an end, Nur stood and bowed. "I am at your service, Shehzada."

He nodded permission for her to depart.

She made to leave, but Aurangzeb stopped her: "It makes no mention of you, Nur Jahan. I wonder why that is?"

"I do not doubt that women—even in that time that will be or would have been—lived in the shadow of their men, and therefore did not figure prominently in the histories."

Aurangzeb was scratching thoughtfully at his thin beard as she departed.

He was too clever by half, thought Nur, but still a victim of every man's desire to believe himself superior to women. She smiled. Men, so full of themselves and their place in history. Anyone sent in search of the story of India would hardly learn of the power wielded by women from the shade and comfort of the harem.

Chapter 28

Jahanara's Tent
April 1635

"How do negotiations proceed, Father?"

Shah Jahan smiled as his grandson's tiny fist grasped his finger. "They proceed slowly, Jahanara. Hargobind Singh attempts to drive a hard bargain, thinking I have not received God's message."

Jahanara resisted the urge to ask what that message was. Father had been avoiding her presence for so long, she did not want to drive him away.

"Your up-timers have proven their worth again: your brother, I am told, is recovering well. This, when my own physicians told me there was little to no hope for him—claiming the infection would kill him."

"It was your wisdom, not mine, that kept them close."

"You are too modest." He sighed. "And I have missed you, Daughter. I fear I was too hard on you. Fear and uncertainty made me suspicious of everyone. Now I know better..." He didn't quite finish the sentence, lapsing into silence.

The baby cooed, drawing him from his thoughts. "How is his mother?"

"She is well, and resting. Would you care to see her?"

"Let her rest. This one is likely a challenge."

Such a strange mood. I hope he will not take offense: "Do you think Nadira might see Dara soon?"

Shah Jahan sighed again. "Not yet. Neither myself nor Hargobind

244

Singh want to add potential hostages to the situation. I wish it were otherwise, but there it is."

Jahanara bowed her head. "Perfectly understandable, Father. You see why it is I felt I must ask, don't you?"

"Of course." He looked down at his suddenly fussy grandson, "I would not keep my son from my grandson any longer than absolutely necessary. I have even gone so far as to tell Hargobind Singh that I will, formally and completely, lift the jizya—not just for his people, but for everyone: Hindus, Jains, Sikhs, even the Christians."

"But the mullahs..."

"Let them piss and moan, I care not. They will do as they're told and be happy about it or risk having the jagirs I gave them to support their madrassas and mosques returned to the crown."

Jahanara bit her lip against the ingrained instinct to respond with her own thoughts about the wisdom of that course.

Father didn't notice, continuing to speak as his grandson's other hand rose to wrap his ring finger in a tiny fist, "It was not as if I was zealous in collecting the jizya anyway, especially to hear the mullahs tell it. But I have had enough of listening to all of their prattling. I will decide the fate of this empire. Not foreigners, not imams, not mullahs, not Sikhs, nor gurus.

"*Me*. And what I want—no, what I will *have* is my son returned to me. He shall not be made to atone for my sins. This chance at redemption, God has given me."

Jahanara bowed, overcome by the intensity of his manner.

Shah Jahan snorted. "Get up. I must sound like a hermit emerging from his cave to spit prophecy and doom. But I am not claiming any powers of prophecy, merely telling you, my sweet child, that I have had an epiphany."

He leaned over the child and tickled his belly with one finger. "I have done things... Actions I thought necessary and right. Actions that, according to the up-timer documents, pave the way for Aurangzeb to kill his brothers, imprison you and me, and seize the throne. In so doing, he expands the empire to its greatest extent, while at the same time sowing the seeds of its destruction. We cannot rule India—not for long—without the consent of our Hindu subjects. And the Sikhs."

Jahanara bit her lip, fearful of interrupting, yet still more frightened of what else Father might say.

"What, no advice?" he asked, gently mocking.

A most unflattering noise, only vaguely similar to a giggle, escaped her lips.

He chuckled and gently rescued his fingers from the wrestling match his grandson was determined to win. He stepped around the child and opened his arms to Jahanara. "I am so sorry, Jahanara. I was cruel and unfair. Please forgive me, I will do better in future."

Tears in her eyes, Jahanara clung to her father for some time.

Ilsa's Tent

Grinning like an idiot, John rolled to one side of Ilsa and tried to catch his breath.

Ilsa sat up and poured herself a drink, blonde hair falling in waves down her naked back.

For his part, John drank in the sight of her.

Up until a short while ago she'd been wearing some of the sheerest, sexiest stuff he'd ever seen. That, and the intermittent separations forced on the couple by their living arrangements had led to surprisingly intense sex each time they'd had an opportunity.

Half-fearing she might disappear, John reached out a hand and ran it down the hollow of her back, delighting in the shiver his touch elicited.

"I'll give you exactly one fortnight to stop doing that," she said, a smile in her voice.

He did it again as he sat up and kissed the nape of her neck. "How's the littlest prince?"

She looked over her shoulder at him. "He's fine. Fussy, but fine. And before you ask: Nadira is fine, too."

"Sorry, but you and Priscilla really saved our asses by helping deliver the boy. I don't think Shah Jahan was about to give us the time of day, let alone believe us capable of providing what we promised until you two came through."

"Oh, we know what we did. We're just a little bit impatient, waiting on Shah Jahan to make up his mind whether he is going to take Hargobind Singh up on his offer or not."

"I'm not sure it is the emperor that's slowing us down. Hargobind Singh seems... Well, Salim seems to think the guru doesn't believe Shah Jahan is actually willing to grant his requests."

She turned to face him, folding one knee under her. "Perhaps it has something to do with the fact that Shah Jahan imprisoned Hargobind Singh and had his predecessor executed."

"What?"

"Jahanara told us last night. Apparently, the Sikhs were not at all militant until this guru. You saw those banners, the ones with two swords?"

John nodded.

"They represent the two swords that Hargobind Singh wore at his coronation: one indicating his spiritual power, the other his power in temporal matters."

John nodded. "Makes sense. Have you seen him?"

"No. Being in the harem, I don't get out much."

"Sorry, stupid question...It makes sense. He looks at least as much a badass as Salim. Not one I'd want to tangle with at all."

"I'm sure: Being kept like this," she gestured at the walls of the tent, "is slowly driving me mad, John."

"I don't think there's anything we can do about that right now, Ilsa. Especially since you and Priscilla have shown how valuable your skills are." He shook his head. "And I don't know if it will be offensive for us to even ask if we can, as Christians, forego the requirements of purdah while still inmates."

"I understand that. I just wanted to ask you if you thought it was safe for me to broach the subject with Jahanara, especially since the emperor mentioned a reward."

"Yeah, about that: you might want to consider putting on some weight."

She shook her head. "Wait, why?"

"Because, my dear, His Jahaniness offered a reward of your weight in silver."

Her eyes went round.

"But if you want out of this decadent prison," John snorted, "We can always forego a king's ransom in silver..."

She smacked his chest with her palm. "Oh, that's cruel."

He grinned wider, leaning into her hand. "But getting back to your question about Jahanara: I wouldn't know. Hell, with the restrictions in place between men and women, I haven't even spoken to her. I have no idea how she'll take it, do you?"

Ilsa shrugged, making it exceedingly difficult for John to keep his eyes level with hers. "She really seems quite open-minded, and interested in everything Priscilla has to say. That said, something is going on between her and her father." She lay down against him, snuggling up to his side and throwing one leg over him.

"What?"

"I don't know, but the first time I actually saw them together was just a couple of days ago, and Jahanara was...I suppose relieved would be the best way to describe her, after."

"You ask any of the servants what's up?"

"Yes, but our translator was brought in after whatever happened to estrange them, so she didn't know. I didn't think it safe to ask anybody else."

John nodded. "Yeah, that was probably the smart move."

"Speaking of smart women: did you know she's in charge here?"

"Meaning?"

"She's responsible for the finances of the harem."

"I thought Diwan Firoz Khan was responsible for all that."

"He is, to a degree. But he got his position because Jahanara asked Shah Jahan for him and she manages the books with his assistance. Don't get me wrong, I'm sure he makes reports to Shah Jahan, but she manages the day-to-day affairs and finances of the harem."

"Wait, doesn't he have some other wives?"

He felt her nod against his chest. "At least four wives, and... I can't even begin to count the number of concubines."

"So shouldn't one of those wives be in charge?"

"Jahanara's mother was the man's true love, and that's why he only seems to consider her children together as possible heirs. Which also explains why he dotes on her, and gave her the position."

"But aren't princesses these days valued more for potential political marriages than anything else?"

"Normally, yes. I had not—" She sat up abruptly. "I don't think we've even asked Jahanara what her marriage prospects are. I don't even know if she *wants* to get married. Now that I think about it, that might be the cause of the tension between her and her father. I mean, if he wanted to marry her off to some old, ugly, politically powerful man and she resisted..."

"Then there would certainly be tension between the two."

She settled her warm weight against him again.

"Lucky," he sighed.

"What's that?" she asked, idly running the knuckles of her hand across his ribs.

"I was just thinking that, as an old, ugly man, I am very lucky to have fooled you into thinking I'm politically powerful. Otherwise, we'd never have mar—"

She cut him off with a painful pinch and playful growl.

Laughing, he pushed her hand away.

"You're not old, you're just older than me."

"Yep, and before the Ring, the whole town would have been talking about the years between us... not to mention my mother."

"Silly man," she blew a raspberry against his chest, making him squirm. "Cora is still talking about it."

He chuckled. "I bet she is."

She raised her head to look at him. "Do you miss your mother?"

"Not as much as I miss being with you, of course... But yeah, now and then. Especially these last couple weeks, with so little to do but ride back and forth to meet Rodney and Gervais."

"Some problems get you no sympathy," she said, laying her head on his chest again.

He winced. "Sorry. Ask Jahanara about an outing, at least. If she approves then you might find a tactful way to ask about getting out more."

"I'll talk to Priscilla first, and see what we can come up with."

"Smart idea."

"Of which I have many: what about using the emperor's reward to purchase a house in Agra?"

"What?"

"I'm sure we could get one built, call it the Mission House or some such. The English have one, don't they?"

"I think they did, yes."

"Did?"

"As far as I can tell, there are no representatives of the English government with the court, not even of the East India Company."

"But getting back to the point..."

"I think it's a very good idea, but do we know whether we'll be going back to Agra?"

"I asked Jahanara, and she is certain of it. Shah Jahan pays close attention to construction of the Taj, always returning to it, barring some catastrophe. He spends a great deal of time at the construction site, overseeing the workers."

"All right. I'll see about it."

The Red Tent

Priscilla and the other mission women stumbled to a halt on entering the tent.

Before the emperor's informal throne was what looked like the largest balance scale Priscilla had ever seen. Joined by a single massive bronze rivet at the center, an enormously heavy iron tripod supported an iron crossbeam from which hung chains and huge brass pans, each a yard across.

"Someone's a Libra!" Monique quipped.

The others were too nervous to laugh outright, but a few chuckles were heard. After an exchange of disbelieving glances, they took the places Jahanara had them rehearse.

Nadira Begum was seated with her son in front of and below the emperor. Priscilla noticed that the princess' eyes above the veil were smiling. As she was in the harem of her father-in-law, not her husband's, she must go veiled, like them.

Shah Jahan, an equally-pleased smile piercing his beard, addressed the gathered ladies of the harem: "As I commanded, so shall it be: Madame Totman, be seated upon the scales."

Never thought I would be so happy of the veils. Might spoil the gravity of the moment, everyone seeing me grin like an idiot, Pris thought as she approached the scales. She extended a tentative foot over the beaten bronze dish hanging from the balance, trying to work out how to sit without making a sound like a gong being struck.

Sahana saved her, sliding a cushion under the pan.

Mouthing a *thank you* the young girl couldn't see for the veil, Priscilla gripped the chains and eased herself into a seated position. The scale noiselessly tipped her way, leaving the other pan well off the floor.

"As reward for your service to my family, I promised your weight in silver. Here, now, I see that promise fulfilled."

Five pairs of eunuchs entered from the side, each sweating duo carrying a chest between them. The first pair opened their chest and started pulling bar after bar of shining silver out to place them neatly on the pan opposite Priscilla.

This is some story-book silly! Too bad I lost so much weight since we came through the Ring of Fire. With what I weighed back then, I could have really put a dent in the emperor's treasury!

It required a great many bars, but gradually her pan began to rise. The workers slowed, then stopped, leaving her just a few inches higher than the pan opposite.

Shah Jahan chuckled. "Take that last bar off and bring forth coin to equal out the measure..." The emperor trailed off as Nadira gracefully climbed to her feet and approached Priscilla, her son in her arms.

She extended the child to Priscilla. "Take him," she said, eyes shining. "For surely without you, he would not be the weight and treasure that he is."

The child tipped the scales in Priscilla's favor once again.

Nur Jahan's Tent

"You lie!" Mohan hissed, prayer beads rattling with rage.

Nur swallowed her first response, instead answering calmly: "I assure you, I do not."

Oblivious, Mullah Mohan continued his rant. "I do not understand why he would even consider, let alone *say* these things! Surely he knows the faithful will not be bullied into submission by threatening to remove his support! Unthinkable! To close schools and places of worship because the true faithful *might* object to his divergence from Holy Law! Unthinkable!"

Nur waited, silently urging Mohan to control his tongue before its wagging reached the ears of someone who cared to end them both.

It took far longer than Nur would have preferred, but eventually Mohan wound down.

"If we keep our calm, this is nothing but another opportunity to advance our benefactor's position."

"Another—"

Unwilling to endure another rant, she interrupted: "Pardon, but if you quietly called on your brothers in the Order and, through them, to all right-thinking Muslims, surely this can be turned into a groundswell of support. Support from so many and from all quarters will, of necessity, be heard by Shah Jahan."

Lust for power made his eyes glow in a manner the rage of a moment before hadn't. He was a foolish man; cautious when he should be bold and heedless when he should be wary.

The mullah's expression changed, naked hunger replaced by calculation. "But with Shah Jahan's favorite back in play, Aurangzeb is even more distant from power."

"True, but Dara has already proven his willingness to lie down with heretics, and will prove yet another reason for right-thinking Muslims to rally to our cause. And who knows, Dara may yet perish from the infection."

"I doubt that. Not with the foreigners who claim to be from the future treating him."

"Which can also be turned to advantage as well: they are not Muslim. In fact, they hardly seem to practice *any* religion."

"I don't know..."

Nur, forgetting for the moment who she was speaking with, mused aloud: "Perhaps if they were seen to fail after all the faith the Sultan Al'Azam has placed in them..."

He seized on the idea, however. "Yes, that would certainly silence those who have advanced the foolish idea these people's presence here is God's will. I will leave it to you to see this idea through."

Nur opened her mouth to refuse but Mohan raised a hand, "No, I should not know any of the details. That way, when it is done, I can honestly say I knew nothing."

Nur Jahan closed her mouth. Had she become so old and stupid, to be outmaneuvered by this poor excuse for a man?

As he'd make a hash of it anyway, I suppose there's nothing for it...

"I will see what can be done to see to it they fail, Mullah Mohan."

Chapter 29

Palace of Hargobind Singh
May 1635

"You don't understand. You've never been hurt like this," Dara Shikoh's petulant tone wasn't lost on Gervais, who reined in his urge to slap the patient.

"Shehzada, you cannot have another pipe now."

"But the pain—"

"Is not as bad as withdrawal," Rodney said. Salim emerged from his giant shadow in the doorway of the sick room to translate.

Dara Shikoh turned his glassy eyes on the up-timer. "How would you know?"

"Trust me, I know. Last thing you want to be is dope sick."

"Might be a bit too late for that, Rodney. The drug already has its hooks in him. Just look at his pupils."

Rodney crossed the room and took out the tiny device for casting light into small spaces called a "pen light" and directed its beam into Dara's eyes. "Dinner platter pupils, slow to respond to light stimulus. Oh, yeah, he's chasing the dragon for sure."

Salim waved a hand. "Many smoke the poppy. The prince was known to occasionally indulge even before his injury."

Rodney muttered, in English, "One of the reasons we're here, actually."

"What was that, Mr. Totman?" Salim asked, a bit sharply.

"Poppies are the source of one of the best painkillers on earth, and as war generally means pain for the participants, we were sent to secure a ready source of opium."

"I understand. But who, exactly, is your king going to go fighting?"

Rodney snorted. "Probably better to ask who *isn't* attacking us. When we arrived in this time," he waved a massive hand to encompass everything, "the status quo was severely disturbed."

Gervais opened his mouth to explain the Latin term, but promptly shut it as Salim smiled. "No," he said, voice dripping with sarcasm, "I just can't see how that's possible. It's not like you brought profound changes with you, or something."

"Right. So, in the two years before we left to come here, Gustavus Adolphus and the USE fought the French, English, Dutch, Spanish, various German states, the Danes... Help me out here, Gervais: I'm probably missing two or three different kingdoms that tried to get rid of us."

"I think Salim gets the point, Rodney."

"Oh, and that's not counting the churches that want us—"

"I. Want. My. Pipe," said Dara Shikoh, displeased at being ignored.

Gervais glanced down at the prince, and switched to Persian: "Be strong, Shehzada Dara Shikoh. What Rodney is talking about is your future health. The opium is slowing your recovery, and will prove difficult, even dangerous, to quit."

"Very well, after this pipe."

"Sorry, no."

"I'll see you—"

"Well rewarded for seeing to his health," Salim said, deliberately mistranslating Dara Shikoh's threats.

"You should rest, Shehzada. We are disturbing you."

Dara Shikoh bit his lip, swallowed. "I'm sorry, this is not me."

"We know, Shehzada. We'll slowly wean you from the opium, try and keep you from getting too sick. But it's not going to be easy or comfortable."

"So... When?"

"Tonight, when you make ready to sleep."

"And until then?"

"Would you care to get up and move around?"

"It hurts."

"A certain level of pain is to be expected, and shows you are healing. Exercise, light exercise, should be good for you. We don't want those scars," he gestured at the puckered tissue, "getting too tight."

"And the distraction should help keep your mind off the pipe," Gervais added.

Shehzada Dara Shikoh visibly took control of himself. "Very well. I will do my best."

"Thank you Shehzada. You will be better that much sooner."

No Man's Land

John reined in on the field that had become a no-man's land between the Sikh town and the Mughal camp. He dismounted and joined Rodney for the walk back to camp. He didn't have to ride out to meet Rodney, but it was a relief to get away from the camp, its smells and its spies, even if for just a short while.

Rodney's companions, the emperor's negotiators, rode on without sparing the two up-timers a glance.

"Nearly two months we've been sitting here, and still no real change. Well, aside from Wazir Khan arriving with that," he nodded in the direction of the latest addition to the encampment, "huge army."

"Yeah, never thought to see horses and men literally cover the earth for as far as the eye can see...Something almost, I don't know, Biblical about it."

"They do have some humongous armies."

"Big place, India."

"Yeah, drives it home, seeing this many people in one place."

"Not just people. All the damn livestock: elephants, camels, oxen, and so many horses."

Rodney nodded. "I haven't seen this kind of crowd since leaving football."

John hiked a thumb at the palace. "Any change in the prince's condition?"

"Not so much a change as a problem. You remember me telling you the prince was using opium for pain management?"

"Shit."

"It's not all that bad. So long as we can control how much he's getting, we should be able to get him off fairly safely. It's not like he was mainlining it."

"Rodney, I don't know all that much about that stuff, but I thought it's really hard to quit."

"About as hard as cigarettes, but with nastier withdrawal symptoms."

"But what if he loses his mind and orders your execution or something?"

Rodney gestured at the massive camp of the emperor. "Weren't you just saying we've been sitting here for months with no change? We only need a week or so to safely drop off his intake. And if he orders it, the Sikhs ain't likely to follow their hostage's orders, now are they?"

"I suppose not. You sure you can get him off the stuff without too much trouble?"

"Now that he's healed, more or less, he should be strong enough to kick it."

"Should be, Rodney?"

"John, I can't offer sure bets—I just don't know. I ain't a doctor."

"Sorry, Rodney. We're up shit creek if this goes wrong, you know?"

"Sure do."

"So what about just leaving him on it?"

The look Rodney gave him was far more threatening than any physical display.

He held up his hands in surrender. "Sorry, stupid idea."

"Damn straight it's stupid, John. Not to mention just flat out wrong. Talking with Salim, it looks like Shah Jahan's father, Jahangir, was a total opium addict. His wife, Nur Jahan, who's with the court somewhere, seized power while her husband smoked and drank himself to death. It was her that Shah Jahan seized the throne from, not Jahangir."

"Wait, she's still with the emperor's entourage?"

Rodney shrugged. "So they tell me."

"How does that happen?"

"Don't ask me, John, I don't know. But getting back to my original point: anyone with that much power"—he pointed at the army to the west—"struggling with addiction, is going to be a complete disaster for everyone in reach of his armies."

"I get it, really. It was a stupid, thoughtless thing to say."

Rodney blinked, looked away, and sighed. "Sorry for the sermon, John, but some of the guys I played ball with got hooked on painkillers the coaches and sports medicine staff pushed on them so they could play one more day instead of get healthy. One ended up dead, and all three of 'em shot their lives to hell, and that was just at *my* school."

"I get it, man. I really do."

Point made, Rodney changed the subject. "What's this I hear from Priscilla about a Mission House?"

"Yeah, I wanted to run that by you. Salim says it's exactly what's expected of us, so the funds given to us by the emperor will have some use. He even says he knows some people in Agra that can start work on it now so we might be able to occupy it once we return."

"Sure will make Priscilla happy, not having to deal with purdah."

"Well, to an extent. It'll be more of a change of scenery than a real change."

"And we'll lose our back channel to court."

"Yep."

"If Priscilla knew I even thought about denying her this chance at even limited freedom, she'd have my balls."

"Yep."

"Guess we're buying a house in Agra."

Dara's Quarters, Palace of Hurgobind Singh

A lifetime's instinct of living in war camps spurred Salim to wakefulness, senses searching for the threat that drove him from slumber.

Nothing in here with me. The Sikhs had provided him a room attached to Dara's quarters, with Gervais and Rodney occupying another directly across a common chamber from his.

Rodney had gone to camp to see his wife. Aside from Gervais and the servants, who had been relieved for the night, there were the guards on the entrance and in the gardens below.

Nothing unusual there, either.

Trusting his instincts, he steadied his breathing and listened carefully for a repeat of whatever had roused him. A faint noise came, from the chamber around which all the sleeping areas were arranged.

Perhaps...slippers on carpet? He got up as quietly as possible and retrieved his knife. Easing it from the scabbard, he padded to the exit on bare feet.

Reaching the curtained archway, Salim moved the curtains aside to look out into the common room.

Nothing moved in the silence.

A shadow dimmed the moonlight coming through the windows set high on the walls. He glanced up, saw movement along the wall.

A serpent?

No! He realized, too late, what he'd seen was the quickly disappearing end of a rope being retrieved from outside. He opened his mouth to shout an alarm, thought better of it, and charged toward Dara's room.

He burst through the curtains in an low crouch, knife ready.

Dara struggled to his feet. "What is this?"

Thinking the assassins might have come in through the wrong window, and were even now readying themselves to strike, Salim rushed past Dara to the closest window.

"Salim?" Dara asked, then answered his own question: "Salim. What is going on?"

He heard scrabbling, realized Dara was trying to arm himself. He looked out without answering, saw no one but the guards.

Light flared behind him, Dara turning up the bedside lantern. "Down, Shehzada!" he hissed.

"What—"

"Turn the lantern down and stay away from the balcony."

The light dimmed, then was snuffed out as Dara hurried to comply.

Several tense breaths later, Salim quietly answered Dara's earlier question. "I don't know. Someone was on the roof with a rope, and may have been inside. Not knowing who or how many, I thought it best not to raise the alarm."

"What do we do now?" Dara whispered.

"I don't know, wait?"

"Till dawn?"

Salim shifted his grip on the knife. "Unless you have a better idea?"

"Perhaps I should wake the palace and get Hargobind to double my guard."

"Think on that, Shehzada."

"You think he is behind this?"

"I just don't know." He looked across at Dara's dim shadow, recalling how quickly the prince had responded to his entry. "You were awake when I came in?"

"The cravings woke me."

"I see, Shehzada."

A tense silence settled, Salim straining to hear some sign.

"Can I tell you something, Salim?" Dara asked, making the Afghan twitch.

"Of course."

"I want the pipe even more, now."

"Fight it, Shehzada."

"What's that?"

"We had visitors. You slept through it."

Gervais blinked, yawned, and gave himself a good scratch.

"And I thought it was Rodney snoring loud enough to shake the pillars of heaven."

"Oh, he snores loud enough, but he possesses an amateur's instrument compared to this magnificent piece of art," he pointed at his prominent, and very Gallic, nose.

Salim laughed. "I'm sure."

"You said something about visitors?"

"Yes, most...I would say alarming, but I didn't raise the alarm, so I suppose the word should be...intriguing."

"What?"

"They came in the night, didn't take anything as far as Dara and I can tell, and didn't make an attempt on our lives."

"Then what makes you think these 'visitors' are anyone but our hosts?"

"They entered from the roof."

"Oh?" Gervais climbed to his feet.

"Yes." Salim handed the older man his robe.

"Nothing was taken?"

"No."

"Did you interrupt them, cause them to flee before they'd accomplished their design?"

"No. At least, I don't think so."

"How is the prince?"

"Fine, I just left him. He's even up and around."

Nothing taken, nothing changed, nothing... Gervais swallowed sudden fear, hurrying past Salim and into the central chamber. Dara Shikoh roused from the cushions. "Dr. Vieuxpont."

"Shehzada. Pardon me." He walked past Dara without correcting him and went to the small table that held the herbs and medications he and Rodney were treating the prince with. He studied it a moment.

"Is it that time, already?" Dara asked, eager.

"No, Shehzada. I am merely making sure of something."

"Oh?"

"Nothing appears tampered with."

"You think they were trying to poison me?"

Gervais examined each of the containers, starting with the cabinet of herbs. "Well, it stands to reason that anyone going to all the trouble of scaling the walls, climbing the roof, and avoiding all the guards must have wanted to do more than simply lower a rope into your quarters, Shehzada."

"Yes, I can see that. I but wonder who it might be. And why so late?"

"Late, Shehzada?"

Dara Shikoh nodded. "I was far more vulnerable when you first came here. Why wait until now?"

"Unless they are new arrivals?" Salim asked. "Perhaps in Wazir Khan's entourage?"

"My grandfather would not do such a thing to me."

"No, but he marches with a substantial army made up of many men from all parts."

Gervais, finished with the cabinet, examined the urn holding Dara's opium.

"What cause have they to try and kill me?"

He held the urn up in the light. *Something's off . . .*

"I don't know, Shehzada."

Gervais bent close and drew a deep breath through his nose.

What was that smell? Something different . . . He ran a finger into the urn, dragged it across the contents, examining the residue in the light.

Clever, clever bastards. It was lettuce opium.

"I am sorry, Shehzada, but it seems you are going to need to quit the opium a bit faster than we intended."

"Why?"

Gervais wiped his finger. "I'm not absolutely certain of the method, but our nocturnal visitor appears to have added something to your opium. I suspect it is lettuce opium."

The prince and Salim's equally blank looks showed Gervais he wasn't explaining himself well. "Sorry, an extract from a particular breed of lettuce, known for its effects on cramp, sleeplessness, and mild anesthetic qualities."

"And how is that a problem?" Dara Shikoh asked.

"Alone, it isn't. But combining it with real opium might slow breathing so much that the patient—in this case, you—expires."

Salim shook his head. "Fiendishly clever."

"I must agree. Someone has, at the very least, an advanced understanding of herbalism and a complete lack of morals."

"Gervais, this isn't just about poisoning the prince. They wanted him dead in a way sure to discredit Rodney and you—all of the up-timers."

Gervais pulled at his lip. "Would have worked, as well, but for your light sleeping habits."

Using his left hand, Dara snatched the urn out of Gervais' hand, reared back awkwardly and hurled it at the wall. Shards of pottery exploded from the impact to patter against the carpets, the drug leaving a brown smear on the wall.

"Shehzada?" Salim asked, alarmed.

Eyes burning, Dara Shikoh pointed a finger at the mess. "They thought to use my own weakness against me! Planned for me to die in my sleep, victim of my own inability to bear the slightest pain. I will not be so weak again."

"Shehzada," Salim said, bowing.

Gervais followed suit and said, "We will do what we can to support you, Shehzada, but you will feel far worse before you are free of your need for the pipe. You will have to be very strong in the coming days."

"So be it. God as my witness, I shall not touch the pipe again."

"Good, Shehzada. You will need every bit of that resolve."

A pair of their guards entered, drawn by the raised voice and breaking crockery.

One looked at the wall and back at the prince. With an expression Gervais translated as, *Glad I'm not picking that up*, the man turned and led his companion from the room.

"The question remains: who stands to gain?" Salim asked as the guards disappeared through the door.

"I can think of at least three people, all of them princes," Gervais quipped.

"I think we can rule out Murad. Unless he is assigning assassins from the harem," Dara Shikoh said with a wan smile.

"Of course, but you see my point?"

"Indeed I do." His jaw working, Dara lowered himself onto a convenient cushion. "My death would also serve to enrage Father so much he would surely destroy the Sikhs, as he originally planned." He looked at Salim, "I imagine some of the more hardline orthodox among Father's subjects are not pleased with the current détente?"

Salim nodded. "To put it mildly, Shehzada."

"And there are some others who fear and mistrust the uptimers?"

Another nod.

"And what have my brothers said?"

"As far as I know, since I first revealed you were alive, Aurangzeb has had no public disagreements with Shah Jahan. Shah Shuja seemed genuinely happy that you lived, and has made no comment on Shah Jahan's negotiations with Hargobind Singh."

"Do either of your brothers have an apothecary in their entourages?" Gervais asked.

Dara looked at Salim, received a tiny shake of the head and said, "Each prince that has his own household does, but there's no one of particular note I am aware of."

"Who does?"

"Father has many physicians and apothecaries serving him and the harem."

"The harem?" Gervais mused.

Dara nodded. "And poisoning is, while not common, certainly not unheard of in harem politics." Dara winced. "It is a favored method of removing rivals or their pregnant—Oh." Dara swallowed, sweat beading his brow. He put a hand to his belly. "Uhh..."

It was coming faster than Rodney had thought it would, the onset of withdrawal. Rodney said it would likely take twelve hours, that it was safe for him to go see his wife. The opium must have been purer than they thought.

"Salim, I think our friend might need the use of his chamber pot," Gervais said, helping the unresisting prince to his feet. "As the opium loosens its grip on him, so too will he lose his grip on his bowels."

"Yet another indignity," Dara panted.

Gervais smiled, "Ah, but are you familiar with the up-timer's colorful vernacular regarding thrones?"

Dara, looking truly pale now, shook his head and spoke through gritted teeth. "No, Dr. Vieuxpont, I haven't had the pleasure."

"Well then, allow me to tell you how you're going to ascend the throne early."

Part Four

Summer and Fall, 1635

He stood and grasped his mighty bow,
Terrific as the fire of doom
Whose quenchless flames the world consume.

Chapter 30

"Atisheh, make a circuit. Assure there are no listeners who might overhear our words with the up-time woman."

The big Turkic warrior-woman bowed and departed, mail ringing.

"Is this wise, Shehzadi?"

"I do not know, but I must hear them first before making any decision."

"But—"

"I know, Smidha. I would rather not go to Father with some new request so soon after our reconciliation. Let us hope the up-timers are not going to ask a favor of me." She smoothed her robes and settled herself. "Now, let them in."

Smidha did as she was told, returning shortly with the up-timer and her two friends as well as Sahana. The women bowed and sat among the cushions before Jahanara. Sahana off to one side, ready to translate.

"Smidha informs me you have an important request to make of me?"

Priscilla nodded, the other women deferring to her. "We actually have a few things to tell you first."

Atisheh pushed into the tent and signaled the all clear.

"Please," Jahanara said, gesturing for her guest to continue.

"First," her eyes traveled to Sahana and Smidha, "are you reasonably sure what we say will not be repeated?"

Jahanara looked first to Sahana, then arched a brow at Smidha. "Sahana will not betray us, Shehzadi."

Jahanara returned her gaze to Priscilla, "Then, aside from what I must tell Father as a dutiful daughter, you need not fear any wagging tongues."

Priscilla nodded again. "Good enough for me, Shehzadi. Someone tried to poison your brother's opium two nights ago. Actually, they succeeded, but Monique's father found the drug they added before it could be administered. In fact, it was Salim who woke in the middle of the night and saw the poisoner leaving. Fearing Dara had been assassinated, he was surprised to find him both alive and unharmed. The next morning he told Monique's father of the odd event, which caused Gervais to look through their medicines, suspicious—"

"Pardon, but you used two different terms: drug and poison." She looked at Sahana. "Or was that some error of translation?"

Priscilla shook her head. "I'm sorry, I'm probably not telling this well. Whoever planned this was quite clever. They added another drug to your brother's opium, one that would likely cause him to stop breathing during the middle of the night. It's not uncommon for people who overdose on opiates to have this happen, so it would likely have gone unnoticed had Salim not seen the intruder's rope."

"So if I understand you correctly, the addition of this other drug would have had the effect of a poison?"

"Exactly, Shehzadi."

Jahanara looked at Monique, the quickest of the mission women to learn Persian and said slowly but with feeling: "Then it appears I owe your father a great deal."

Monique smiled and answered without Sahana. "While I would like to say it's nothing, I'm sure my father would disagree. He certainly does like his rewards."

"Did the poisoner escape?"

"Yes, unfortunately."

I shall have to tease Salim about that, when next we meet. She had a vision, sudden and intense, of the man's hawkish, fascinating face and broad shoulders. Blinking it away, she asked, "And what has my brother said about all this?"

"He wanted to reassure you that he does not believe the Sikhs were behind the attack. He suspects someone in the Sultan

Al'Azam's harem, as the attempt required significant knowledge of the interactions between the two drugs. Since there are few physicians without close links to their respective masters, he believes it to be either a woman or a eunuch, one who is advised by or themselves have significant knowledge of the reactions between these substances and the human body."

Jahanara looked at Smidha. "Subtle, this move against my brother."

Her servant did not respond immediately, cocking her head and considering her reply. "This is not some inexperienced concubine or eunuch trying to advance their position, but someone with patience, talent, and nerve."

"I can think of but one person who fits those criteria, but we won't speak her name just yet."

Smidha's eyes narrowed as she gave a barely perceptible nod.

"Did Dara Shikoh leave instruction as to how he wishes to deal with this matter?"

"No. He asked us to tell you he is not healthy, nor fully in his right mind. He hopes to be, soon, but his efforts to quit the opium will make him sick and unable to make"—a pause as Sahana sought clarification on a term—"trustworthy judgments for some time."

"I see." Jahanara closed her eyes in frustration.

No instruction whatsoever. Should she tell her father? And what of Nadira? The poor woman would be most upset to hear this... and likely more upset if she learned Jahanara hadn't told her.

She opened her eyes to see Monique was leaning forward, a concerned look on her face. "Shehzadi, we're sorry to put this on you. My father, your brother, and Priscilla's husband were all in agreement: you were the only one we could trust with this information." She smiled, gestured at the other women. "And, of course, we agreed."

Jahanara Begum closed her eyes again. *I prayed for power over my own fate and here I am asked to navigate this intrigue with my brother's life in the balance.*

God does surely answer in his own time and fashion.

God wills it, then so be it!

She opened her eyes. "Smidha said you had a request to make of me. I trust it was not just a pretext to give me this information?"

Priscilla glanced uncomfortably at Ilsa. "I think, given the information we just passed to you, it can wait, Shehzadi."

"I would prefer it if you told me now. We may not have another moment such as this to discuss sensitive issues openly."

"Well . . . Shehzadi, we had hoped to talk to you about purdah . . ." she trailed off.

Jahanara motioned for her to continue.

"Well, as you no doubt know, we are not Muslim and unaccustomed to the rules and restrictions placed on us as guests attached to your father's harem. We were wondering if it would be possible for us to be relieved of these restrictions. Not entirely, of course. But to be allowed out wearing veils and modest clothing rather than being escorted everywhere, having our contact with friends severely restricted."

Jahanara struggled to understand what the women were asking for. "But, you are all able to speak with one another, and with me and with all the women of the harem."

Monique smiled, answered for the others: "All true. But we . . . We often have friends of the opposite sex. Priscilla and the uptimers even more so."

"I see." She shook her head, felt a sad smile spread across her lips. "Here I was worried my brother overestimated my ability to affect Father's policies. That concern is but a teardrop in relation to the river of worry this subject causes. Father and I had a falling out just before you came to court. He accused me of trying to maneuver him into granting me permission to marry, and implied I was betraying him."

Out of the corner of her eye she saw Smidha tense, give a tiny shake of the head.

She looked directly at her servant but spoke for the benefit of all: "He ordered me from him and refused to see me until Nadira gave birth. You see, while he encourages me to manage the affairs of the harem and my holdings, Father fears that if he allows me or Roshanara to wed, it will imperil his sons' claims to the throne.

"Father believed me to be his opponent in this. I am not, but I am uncertain whether or not he truly knows this. Should I come to him on your behalf, I believe he will take it as a sign I mean to resume trying to move him to allow me to marry."

"Shehzadi—" Priscilla looked at Ilsa and Monique, who both nodded encouragement. "We didn't know. We'll bide our time and wait for you to tell us when you think it's safe to ask your father. We certainly do not want there to be any bad blood between you and him, not on our behalf."

Moved by Priscilla's understanding, Jahanara looked at her guests and spoke from the heart. "I will do my very best to seize the first opportunity to ask him about this. I'm sorry that you, who have given us our brother back, must wait for this small favor. I will make it up to you, I swear."

Red Tent, Emperor's Camp

"Peace! The Sultan Al'Azam has concluded a peace with Hargobind Singh!" The news writer's announcement went through the camp like a grass fire, a crackling heat in the air that forever changed the lay of the land for all in its path.

Concealing some trepidation, Aurangzeb turned and entered the Red Tent for the Diwan-i-Khas with Father.

Inside, he found Shah Shuja already seated, waiting. Wazir Khan was standing below the throne, giving orders to a rider.

Aurangzeb approached and bowed.

Father waved him to his proper place. "Aurangzeb, be seated."

Wazir Khan smiled at his grandsons.

Aurangzeb returned a nod. He wished that he could tell what his grandfather was thinking. He'd spent the better part of a life around him, and yet Aurangzeb still could never tell what he was thinking. Then again, he imagined that was what Nur Jahan had said right up to the moment Wazir Khan had betrayed her to the emperor.

Shah Jahan interrupted Aurangzeb's thoughts: "Now that peace is concluded with the Sikhs, I have new orders for you." He gestured at his father-in-law. "Wazir Asaf Khan will not be returning to the Deccan. I have decided that he will, instead, move from here into Bengal to better enforce our will there against Ahom and the Old King."

He looked at Shah Shuja and Aurangzeb. "While he does this on my behalf, you will both take command of armies and march them into the Deccan to attack Ahmednagar. You will reduce their capital to rubble and see to the dismantling of that troubling sultanate for good and all. I do not set you an easy task, my sons: Ahmednagar and its Nizams have repeatedly proven their willingness to contribute to strife in the Deccan, their latest offense against peace being an alliance with Bijapur against our supposed 'aggression.'"

"Wazir Asaf Khan has the freshest information from the Deccan." Shah Jahan gestured his father-in-law to speak.

"This latest conflict comes about solely because the Sultan Al'Azam insisted on his rights; that the terms of the agreement reached between himself and these Deccani Sultans be kept."

The petty border sultans were always falling behind in their payments of tribute. Which provided his father with ready excuses to invade, raid, and pillage just about any one of them at any given time.

Asaf Khan was still speaking: "They even went so far as to install a child on their so-called throne and, as the Sultan Al'Azam says, have already announced an alliance with Bijapur. Between the two sultanates, they can field an army of about fifteen thousand horse. Most of it inferior to ours, of course, but still proficient. They have few elephants—"

"Aside from those they refused to send me in tribute," Shah Jahan added.

"As the Sultan Al'Azam says. They have few elephants, but their infantry is...motivated against us. They believe us responsible for their many pains these last years. I will provide you both with more detailed information before you depart. But for now, know that you will be facing what will likely be two separate armies. This is the reason your father has decided to split the command. If any of the other so-called sultanates take the field against you with their allies, then you may take whatever action you deem appropriate against them."

Shah Jahan nodded. "Yes, they must be taught it is unwise to side with our enemies against us."

The emperor's eyes traveled from Shah Shuja to Aurangzeb. "I leave it to you to decide how best to cooperate and achieve my ends. You will be given ample resources to accomplish this task, including jagirs in the Deccan to entice your followers to good service and perhaps suborn a few Deccani fence-sitters to your side. There will also be sizable sums to offer as bribes for those who hesitate to engage with our bureaucracy. I expect success."

Shah Shuja bowed from the waist. "We will not disappoint, Father."

Aurangzeb bowed as well but asked: "And once we have successfully defeated them? What then, Father?"

"Then I will decide which of you is to remain in the Deccan as governor. Perform well and it may be you. If you both disappoint, it will be some umara of the court."

"Our forces will be equal?" Shah Shuja asked.

Shah Jahan nodded. "You are free to raise further sowar out of your personal establishment, of course."

Aurangzeb did not miss the sly look Shah Shuja sent his way. *He believes he can recruit more men than I.*

I'll even encourage that belief to allow Mullah Mohan opportunity to introduce more men loyal to me, or at least Mohan, into Shuja's army.

"That said, the purpose of this is not to see who can raise the largest army, but, through your combined efforts, bring to heel all of the Deccani Sultans so that we may avoid future conflicts with our coreligionists.

"I want the sultans to remember what it is you do when next they think to defy me. Am I understood?"

The brothers bowed, chorused, "Yes, Father."

It wasn't until after, when the meeting was over and he was leaving, that Aurangzeb began to process the actual meaning of what was said. Process, and question: Having read what he'd read, why was Father giving him an army? The obvious answer: to get Aurangzeb out of the way while Dara Shikoh recovered, did not satisfy. Dara might recover, but he'd still be far less experienced than Aurangzeb when the time came.

Realization struck as Aurangzeb stepped into the afternoon sunlight outside the Red Tent. He nearly bit his tongue fighting the urge to curse as the simple yet brilliant strategy behind Father's gambit unfolded before his mind's eye.

He wants me fighting fellow Muslims, especially Shia Muslims, *to divide and undercut my power-base. Then, even if I win—no, especially* if I win—and he gives me the Deccan to rule as governor, I will be too busy ruling fractious nobles who hate me for either religious differences or the actions I will be forced to take in order to assure the quick victory I need.*

And, to be certain it must *be a quick victory, he places me in competition with my brother.*

Shaking his head in admiration, Aurangzeb resumed walking.

But he only made it a few more steps toward his own tent when another troublesome thought surfaced: *This new plan, so soon after Wazir Khan's return? No, this was not Father's idea alone. Grandfather had a hand in this.*

He needed to speak with Nur Jahan.

Wait, tread carefully. He slowed. *Think it through. She failed to foresee her brother's hand before it was too late last time, why should it be any different now?*

"You are very thin, my son," Shah Jahan said, holding Dara at arm's length.

Though he tried to hide it, Jahanara saw the relief in Father's eyes reflected in her brother's as Dara answered, "It is only recently that I have begun to eat normally again, Father. I had no appetite. But now," he looked at his wife and child, "I find I hunger for a great many things life has to offer."

"Good. Good." Shah Jahan released Dara and sat down, gesturing for the rest of the royal party to do the same.

The baby squealed as his mother eased herself onto the cushions.

Shah Jahan smiled to hear it. "Have you considered what to name him?"

"Nadira and I have both prayed over that very question. I think tonight we shall decide upon a name for him. I'm sure you and my brothers all have thoughts on the matter." He looked around, "Where are my brothers?"

"Already departed, I'm afraid. They left this morning for the Deccan. They are to undertake the task I originally assigned Wazir Asaf Khan while he moves on to Bengal."

"I see."

Jahanara could see Dara's disappointment, though she was uncertain whether it was a result of their being picked for such an important task or the apparent lack of interest both displayed by failing to stay long enough to see him.

"Will we soon be on the move as well?"

"Not so very far. I plan to hunt in the hills here, making sure my presence is noted by the rest of the Punjabi even as I make sure my subordinates do not attempt to subvert my will to accommodate the Sikhs. There will be a great many officials upset that their source of graft and sinecure has suddenly dried up. I must make sure they do not commit some fresh offense against Hargobind Singh."

"Most wise, Father."

Mustering her courage, Jahanara leaned forward and addressed Father, "Pardon, but the up-timer physicians, Rodney and Priscilla both, suggest that Dara not be moved a great deal for the next few weeks."

Shah Jahan cocked his head. "I will not offer Hargobind Singh offense by encamping much longer in the vicinity of Ramdaspur."

"Perhaps we could go to Lahore while you complete your tour?"

"Which would also allow you both to pay your respects to Mian Mir..." Shah Jahan nodded after a moment's consideration. "He offered encouragement to both sides in reaching this peaceful conclusion."

The emperor chuckled to see the matching expressions of surprise on his children. "I give a great deal of thought to events that occurred when you were both children. Jahangir did a vicious, cruel thing when he decided your education would be different from that of your siblings, Dara and Jahanara." He looked at his hands. "I thought at the time he was continuing Akbar's search for understanding between religions of the land we live in, but I know now he was merely driving a wedge between my children to match that which he saw his father drive between me and him."

Jahanara blinked back tears.

"I would not have it so, Father," Dara said.

"Nor I, but God has already laid these things out for us and we must make do." Shah Jahan fixed his eyes on Dara. "You must get well and grow strong. None of my other sons possess the spirit of tolerance you carry in your heart. If they ascend the throne, what follows will be hundreds of years of religious strife, sectarian violence, and the defilement of our peoples and heritage by the Europeans. This cannot be my—no, *our*—legacy. To this end, I will continue to train you as my heir and do everything I can to reestablish your court as second only to mine."

Dara, white with shock, did not speak.

Hardly less surprised, Jahanara found her tongue first: "But Father, surely Shah Shuja and Aurangzeb are not beyond redemption?"

Shah Jahan shook his head. "I cannot bring myself to believe they are, but Aurangzeb in particular has chosen allies I know harbor hatred toward non-Muslims and, more directly, my rule."

Nur Jahan? Was it Aurangzeb who brought her back to court?

"He has done nothing so far to act against me. In fact, he has acted in near-perfect accordance with my wishes at every turn. While that continues, I will not move against him."

Shah Jahan sighed. The look he gave his eldest children was haunted. "Even should he rise up in rebellion, I do not know I could act against him; such is the love I bore your mother, such is the love I bear each of you."

Chapter 31

Between the emperor's camp and Ramdaspur
July 1635

"Man, it's hot," Rodney complained, wiping his neck with a handkerchief—no, that wasn't what they called it, it was a . . . *bandana*.

"That it is," Gervais said, looking to the mass of mounted men moving south just a few yards from their position. As soon as he heard they might be moving, Gervais had asked Rodney to come with him into town to restock their dwindling supply of salves and medicinal herbs. They'd left before dawn, only to be caught in the tide of riders heading south.

Gervais nodded at the passing soldiers. "I imagine it's even hotter where they're going. From what I've heard, the Deccan is no earthly paradise, not by a good margin, and the various sultanates are supposed to be quite capable at defending themselves."

"Speaking of which, aren't Muslims barred from fighting one another?"

Gervais looked at the up-timer, drawled, "Oh yes, and no Christian ever killed another Christian. Not ever. No. Not once."

Rodney raised his hands in surrender. "All right. I guess I deserved that."

"Did you?"

"Don't make me wring my bandana out in your face, Gervais."

"But getting to the gist of your question: I'm not really clear on the divisions myself, but as far as I can tell, Shah Jahan's conflict with the Deccan states isn't about religion at all." He shook his head. "Indeed, it's a lot like Central Europe before you people showed up, only with different religions for spice."

"That may be so, but just about every one of those guys"— Rodney gestured at the mounted soldiers riding by—"looks like a true believer to me."

"Perhaps," Gervais said, looking closely at the men for the first time. Some of them spared a look for the two horsemen sitting on the slight rise, expressions souring when they identified them.

A sudden chill ran down his back despite the heat. Rodney was right. Many of them did seem to have that special look in their eyes, the one that tells a sensible thief he's dealing with unreasonable men.

He tried to shake the feeling, said: "Well, I suppose it's a good thing they're all riding south while we head to Lahore."

"I suppose so . . ." Rodney had that look that said he didn't really believe what he was saying either. Expression brightening, he hiked a thumb over his shoulder at the camp. "Probably a good thing we're on the move again. The boys are getting really antsy. Having nothing to do has them ready to break everything."

Gervais looked a question at Rodney, who shrugged massive shoulders and explained, "It was hard enough while we were in Agra, but at least there Angelo was able to point them toward the knocking shops and wine sinks that are ignored by the emperor's lawmen. Here," he gestured at the camp surrounding them, "there's nothing. At least, nothing for young men with more balls than sense."

"They haven't been—"

Rodney interrupted, "No, no real trouble yet."

"But you suspect?"

"Of course. I remember being a guy just out of his teens as well as the next thirtysomething. Randy is especially living up to his namesake. There's only so much training, riding, and carrying on some guys can do before they really need a . . . a different outlet."

Gervais snorted, glad for once of purdah's restrictions on the interactions between men and women. While Monique was a sensible young lady in most things, she was inexperienced in love, and certain woes they simply couldn't afford here.

"What do you know about this Mian Mir guy?" Rodney asked, drawing Gervais from his thoughts.

"Not much. Angelo doesn't know anything we didn't get from Salim. I managed to ask a few people, but they don't seem to know anything more. I asked Monique to look into it, but she hasn't yet had an opportunity."

"Yeah, Salim said something about Jahanara being taught by Mian Mir, so the ladies might know something more—or be able to ask."

"I'll ask next time I see her, but when last we spoke she left me the impression Jahanara was already expending a lot of personal political capital on behalf of the ladies, clarifying their position with regard to the harem and purdah. Which reminds me, that Das fellow Salim engaged to build us the mission?"

"Yes?"

"He says they have a site picked out and bribed the correct people to allow construction to go forward."

"Good news, I suppose."

"Why suppose?"

"Makes me nervous, buying something sight-unseen."

John's Tent, Emperor's Camp

"And just where is *this* army going?"

Salim smiled, looking out past the shade of the awning and into the harsh afternoon light and the horsemen riding away. "To Bengal. The Assamese have proven themselves a greater threat than Islam Khan Mashhadi foresaw."

"Who?" John asked, biting into a mango.

"The present governor of Mughal-controlled Bengal. He's held the office a short time."

"Pardon, I meant to ask about the Assamese, not the governor."

"Oh. I'm not all that familiar with them myself." He shrugged. "Foreigners from beyond the eastern borders of the empire."

"But not ferenghi?" John asked, smiling broadly.

Puzzled, Salim answered the question seriously. "No. That term is used for Europeans."

"Oh, and here I thought I'd have a chance to go full Klingon."

"Sorry, but what?"

John chuckled. "It's from a show on TV, back up-time before the Ring of Fire. It had a race of aliens called Ferengi, merchants and hustlers to a man, bound only by their own set of rules, rules that often clashed with what all the other races thought of as correct behavior."

Salim tried to hide his surprise at how accurate that translation was. The ferenghi had a deplorable reputation among the peoples of India. They broke agreements, interfered with the pilgrims on Hajj, and generally disrupted everything.

John caught the look of discomfort. "Wait, that's what you guys actually think of us?" he asked, eyes wide.

Salim tried to make amends: "The merchants, they haven't been the best representatives of Europeans in general, and with what..." He trailed off. Shah Jahan would not like to hear that he'd spoken of what they knew of the history.

"With what?"

"With what has been going on with Dara Shikoh, I meant to say."

"Huh. I thought you were going to mention what the English did to India in our...that other history."

Caught out again, Salim shook his head and decided to give up dissembling. "I was, but I don't think it my place to bring it up just now."

"If not now, when? Rodney isn't here, but we, all of us, are prepared to talk openly about what happened in our history. We did some studying before we left Grantville, see."

"You would speak openly about it?"

"Of course." John's brows drew together over his eyes. "It's not like *we* did anything wrong."

"I see the distinction, but it is a fine one to draw. Perhaps too fine for the angry."

John nodded. "True, though we still believe that the more you know about what went down in our timeline, the better for everyone."

"Still, we should not speak too much on this, at least not now. I will see if I can secure a private audience with the Sultan Al'Azam."

John smiled again. "You know where to reach me."

Lahore Fort, Jahanara's Quarters

"We could have been staying here the whole time?" Monique asked, looking about in awe.

"Well, technically, yes," Jahanara said, pleased at the uniform expressions of wonder on her visitors' faces. Father had completed his renovations of Lahore Fort the same year Mother died, the project serving as the model for the later work on Red Fort. White marble was everywhere, pietra dura and inlays striking the eye from almost every surface. "And yet, at the same time: no. The emperor is the court, and the court is the emperor. Staying here while he marched to punish those he thought had harmed my brother Dara would have been disrespectful to both my brother and Father."

"I see, it's just that... knowing this is here when we were sweating it out in tents outside Ramdaspur is just... painful."

Jahanara smiled. "Then I suppose it's best we did not tell you."

She joined Monique and the other mission women in a brief chuckle.

The up-time woman, Priscilla, looked Jahanara in the eye. "You seem at ease, Begum Sahib."

"I suppose I am. I have always loved Lahore. My favorite teacher resides here still, and I have many fond memories of this place."

"We are glad to see you happier."

Jahanara smiled more broadly. "Also, I have news from my father that he will be summoning your husband and Rodney to speak with him. I made mention of your request, so I have every hope that Father will address your concerns with your husbands."

"And my father?" Monique asked.

Jahanara nodded, "Yes, of course."

Ilsa snorted in most unladylike fashion.

"What is it, Ilsa?"

"Just something my mother used to say."

"Oh?" Jahanara invited.

The ferenghi woman spoke at length, Sahana translating, "When men gather to discuss marriages and other things involving women, they think they are the ones determining our fate, when really, they're just parroting what their wives and mothers told them to say."

Smidha laughed aloud from behind Jahanara, the sound surprisingly loud.

Jahanara turned to face her advisor, finding the older woman had covered her mouth with one hand, eyes round with shock at her own outburst. "I'm sorry, Begum Sahib, but those words could have been taken from my mother's own mouth!"

"Be that as it may, Smidha, I hardly think Father would approve of this wisdom."

Her guests went still, but Smidha would not be so easily silenced: "True, Shehzadhi Begum Sahib, but your mother would have thoroughly enjoyed it. I daresay she would have also made Shah Jahan laugh in the retelling of it."

That made Jahanara smile with bittersweet memory. Mother had always been able to get Father to laugh, even when things were at their worst.

"That said, I overstep and beg your forgiveness."

Jahanara waved the matter away. "It is good to be reminded of such things, especially here amongst friends. Father's concubines and other wives do not offer him the same solace from care that Mother did."

"To the detriment of the management of his empire," Smidha added.

Surprised by her adviser's sudden openness in front of the others, Jahanara again looked at Smidha.

The older woman wagged her head. "What? I merely speak of the purpose of the harem: to provide men with time free from care and those entertainments necessary to distract the mind and relax the body."

"Father enjoys his wives and concubines every night."

Smidha nodded most emphatically. "Indeed he does. But as you said, the pleasures of the flesh do not always soothe a troubled heart. Were it otherwise, your father would have long ago recovered from the wound the loss of your mother left him with."

Lahore Fort, Harem of Dara Shikoh

"Why are we meeting here?" Rodney asked.

Bertram looked at the up-timer. "Because the emperor has every reason to see his son privately, and if those who were responsible for his care are also present, it raises few questions."

"I understand that, I just don't really understand why the

emperor should be concerned about questions. We've been here for months and he never asked us a thing."

John spoke up, "I think I said something to Salim that led him to believe now is the time. We were talking about trade and what the English might have done or did—or whatever—in our timeline, and he seemed surprised by my answers."

Bertram and Gervais shared a look.

Acting on the older man's tiny nod, Bertram said, "Don Francisco told us something like this might happen. He said one of the things that was most difficult for him to adjust to was how open and trusting you up-timers are with one another. Shah Jahan's court is nothing like that. There is little to no trust, even among siblings. When you did not mention the history, the court's natural instinct was to believe you were intentionally withholding information to your benefit."

"But, Salim—"

"Is neither European nor an up-timer. As much as he's been a good student of you and us, he does not intrinsically understand this difference of trust."

Gervais cocked his head and gave a Gallic shrug, "And even if he did, we have no way of knowing whether he could explain the difference to Shah Jahan."

"True," Bertram agreed.

Slippered feet sounded from the corridor leading to the balcony overlooking the fort where Dara had slept. One of the palace eunuchs appeared, motioning for them to follow.

The four men were led out onto a wide balcony lavishly furnished with carpets, cushions, and pillows. Shah Jahan, dressed in rich silks and a fine turban, sat next to his son.

Sitting to one side, and looking far less relaxed than the royals, was Salim.

All four guests made the proper obeisances and were given leave to sit in the emperor's presence, arrayed in a half-circle before and below him.

"The amir tells me you men have things to say regarding the English and the histories brought to us by him," the emperor said through Salim.

John nodded, spoke for the mission: "Sultan Al'Azam, rather than try and direct your thoughts, we wish to make ourselves available to you to answer any questions you might have about the English and the Europeans. We will answer with what we know."

"Very good. How is it you were not a part of the British Empire, up-time?"

"The United States—of America, not Europe; the one we had up-time—fought a war for independence some hundred and fifty years or so from now. And we won the war. Later, though, the British pretty much handed power back to the native peoples in just about all their possessions, India and Pakistan included."

"It only took a couple of world wars and the spawning of revolutionary movements advocating self-rule almost everywhere to finally make them see the light," Rodney added, his tone tinged with sarcasm.

"When was this?"

"Around two hundred years after the United States gained its independence."

Shah Jahan's eyes narrowed as he calculated. "That's three hundred years of occupation by the English."

"Not quite, Sultan Al'Azam. In our timeline, Aurangzeb ruled into the dawn of the eighteenth century of our calendar, adding to the empire considerably. His successors were not able to keep the empire together, however. So the English came in and played one sultanate against the other until they ruled it all."

"I see." Shah Jahan took very little time to digest that information before asking his next question: "What do you know of the Indian mutiny?"

John looked across at Rodney, who shrugged and said, "Not much. The English, or rather . . . The East India Company used local men as indigenous troops, drawing them from both Hindu and Muslim society. Some rumor got started about greased cartridges—"

"The muskets had the powder and shot in a paper container. Oiled paper, torn open with the mouth," John clarified.

"Anyway, the troops were concerned, as Muslims, that the grease was from pork fat, while the Hindus worried that it was beef. The English, making a huge mistake, disciplined the troopers harshly for daring to question. The East India Company's response made a bad situation far worse."

Shah Jahan nodded. "And where were the Dutch in all this?"

John shrugged. "I couldn't really say, Sultan Al'Azam. Until this mission became a reality, we didn't know much about India. See, we grew up about as far away from India as it was possible to get."

"Yet you claim to know the details of this moment in Indian history."

"Our teacher in what we call high school felt it was infamous enough we should know about it. She pointed it out as one of the clearest-cut moments in the history of racist colonialism."

"She?"

"Ms. Mailey, Sultan Al'Azam, our most formidable history teacher."

Rodney muttered something Bertram didn't quite hear. Shah Jahan asked Salim to translate it.

"Ain't that the truth," Rodney repeated.

The emperor's eyes narrowed. "How so?"

"I didn't attend her school but my wife did. Priscilla said Ms. Mailey cut her students no slack at all. She had them reading things they considered pure torture."

"But they weren't?"

Rodney shrugged his huge shoulders. "Later, Priscilla said she came to appreciate a lot of it. But at the time—"

John interrupted. "What did we know? We were just kids, all we wanted to do was chase girls and play ball."

Shah Jahan's Persian was liquid and fast, too fast for Bertram to understand. The tone he understood quite well, however.

Salim smiled a bit uncomfortably. "Sultan Al'Azam understands this desire to chase women perfectly, having enjoyed more than a few himself. He does, however, wonder what this 'playing of ball' is."

"Sports, of different kinds—but they almost all involve playing with a ball." John shook his head. "But the Sultan Al'Azam moves far afield from his original question. We are happy to discuss up-time sports, but understand the Sultan Al'Azam probably does not have all night to listen to us."

"Quite right." Almost without pause, the emperor shifted subjects: "How is it that you speak English, after so long apart from the British Empire? Did you not revert to your mother tongues?"

Bertram glanced at Gervais, saw the older man hadn't missed the way the emperor was testing John and Rodney. Rapidly shifting from one subject matter to another was an excellent method for finding liars and hucksters. Or, in this case, differentiating between practiced courtiers wishing to advance themselves and these strange people from the future.

"Neither of us are Native North Americans. My people came over from England, near as we can tell, in the eighteenth century. Rodney's sometime in the nineteenth."

Rodney nodded. "Late nineteenth, on my father's side anyway. Came from Germany."

More liquid Persian, including a gesture meant to encompass both the up-timers. "So your people conquered America?"

"In a sense, yes. The English had settled colonies all along one coast. For a couple reasons; disease, wars, and a whole series of bad faith agreements, the indigenous people—the Native Americans, they were called"—Bertram noted how careful John was in selecting his terms—"were either killed, moved off the desirable land, or died from European diseases they had no immunity to."

"These Native Americans, did they have religion?"

"Yes, many. I couldn't tell you much about those religions though." Another shrug. "There weren't that many Native Americans around to ask, where I grew up, at least not intact cultures. And those that were around, well ... It just never occurred to me to ask."

"But they were not Muslim? Not Christian or Hindu?"

"No, Sultan Al'Azam, although many of them—probably most of them—eventually became Christians. While some people did say they were bringing religion to the poor benighted savages, I think their motives were far simpler and cruder. Some folks wanted land and had the power to take it from those already on it."

"Is this what you think happened in India?"

John nodded. "Although the English didn't settle very many colonists here in India, because the climate and diseases were hard on them since they weren't accustomed to it. They—the English, I mean—were helped along by some native Indians—as they were in North America. Some people will always turn on others for the right incentives."

The look that accompanied Shah Jahan's nod quickly disappeared, like a stone dropped into deep waters. Bertram saw it anyway. Saw it, and feared for those who entertained thoughts of betraying the emperor.

Chapter 32

Nur Jahan's Manor, Lahore
August 1635

Nur Jahan carefully set Mullah Mohan's letter down. Trying to extinguish the flames of anger its contents had sparked was not as easy, however.

True to her Sufi education, she used several measured breaths to quell the flames enough to clear her head and focus on the underlying issue that fueled the fires of her anger: Leaving such instructions with her as if she were his servant! *Watch and report!* As if she had no value beyond her eyes and ears—here, in this place she ruled from.

Foolish bigot, of course the up-timers bore watching! Of course they needed to learn what Mian Mir tells Dara! And Shah Jahan: he always must be watched.

Gargi entered with the evening meal, servants in her wake. Nur Jahan made sure to conceal her correspondence as the servants went about the business of setting out her dinner, then lay back amongst the cushions, giving every outward appearance of the indolent widow.

It was foolish of him to even send her such notes, but he was so caught up in trying to show his superiority that she doubted he even realized the risks he was running.

She sighed as Gargi ushered the servants out. The failed plot against Dara had made Mohan think himself the leader of their little cabal.

"What is it makes you sigh as if for a lover, Nur Jahan?"

Nur smiled. "If my sighs sound thus, it is because power is the vilest of lovers: to raise one to such heights of ecstasy only to drop you at the first indication of a younger, livelier plaything is surely the hallmark of the most hateful of lovers."

"Are you cast aside, then?"

"I have been so since the day my husband passed to his reward. Everything since has been the struggle to maintain some place in the world."

Gargi gestured at the archway the servants had retreated through, "No matter how low, there is always further to fall. A servant is easily made a slave. I urge caution."

Angry that even Gargi had been influenced by the failure of her plot, Nur sniffed. "As I said: I will not submit silently, I will not fade like the aged blossom, curled into colorless ignominy."

Her most trusted servant bowed her head. "Your will?"

Nur smiled. "You needn't reprove me with your perfect submission, Gargi. In fact, I think you will approve of my latest plans. I think it past time I rid myself of certain problematic persons."

Gargi met her eyes, edging closer before folding her legs beneath her. "Oh?"

"Yes," she whispered, handing the older woman the correspondence.

Nur selected a morsel, ate it daintily while Gargi read the first lines. "You see where he presumes to instruct me even as he denies knowledge of what it is Aurangzeb plans?"

"Such is the way of men," Gargi answered with a shrug, reading on.

"Perhaps. For my part, I have decided I will no longer silently endure such slights."

"Oh, you plan to shout about it instead?"

Nur felt her eyes narrow in anger. She carefully smoothed the irritation from her expression and said coolly, "No, I plan vengeance. But first I must determine what it is Aurangzeb has directed him to do."

"And then?"

"And then I will decide whether to encourage Mohan to blunder far beyond his orders or discourage him entirely from acting on them."

"A delicate process. One fraught with peril."

"Your cautions are noted. Now advise."

"If Aurangzeb has left firm instruction, your aims will be difficult to accomplish. If he has left those instructions vague, then you will find fertile ground."

"One can safely assume Aurangzeb is not so confident in the security of his communications that he left such precise directions for someone else to discover."

"Correct, but barring your presence at their final audience before they parted, it is difficult to know what was agreed to in advance."

"Truth. It seems I must wait for a suitable opportunity."

"From what you said of his reaction to Shah Jahan's lifting of the jizya, he seems likely to walk into grievous error on his own anyway."

"Perhaps," Nur agreed, grudgingly.

"Forgive me for saying it, but I beg you to consider allowing Mullah Mohan to blunder into self-destruction. It might prove both satisfactory to your desire for vengeance and will certainly limit your exposure. He was, after all, merely a means to an end."

"You speak sensibly, and I will consider carefully before taking any action."

"But you will take action."

Nur let an exasperated sigh escape her lips. "I may."

But Gargi wasn't ready to let it go. "Do not be like a man in this."

"As you said, he was a means to an end. That end is not yet met, and therefore I do not consider my dealings with him concluded."

"Yet you consider betraying him."

"His betrayal, *dear servant*, is one of those ends that has yet to be met."

Gargi bowed her head and said nothing more, her silence a reproval all its own.

Camp outside Lahore

"So, Salim, your teacher . . . Just who is he?"

Salim smiled at Gervais. "He is a living saint. Mian Mir has renounced the pleasures of this world, has schooled his mind and body to mirror his sweet soul. So much so, he only breathes but four times a night."

Not wishing to give offense, Gervais picked his next words carefully: "Forgive me if I misunderstand, but if he renounced the world, why send you to Europe?"

Salim nodded. "A good question. The living saint renounced the pleasures and *distractions* of this world," the Afghan gestured at the up-timers seated across the courtyard from them, "not the events of momentous import which shake the world."

"I see. Will we have an opportunity to speak with him?"

"I do not know. He is quite frail, and has only recently recovered from illness. He's nearly one hundred years of age as it is. I know he will be seeing Dara Shikoh to bestow blessings upon him, but I do not know if he will have time for private audiences with you. I sent a messenger, but have yet to hear back."

Gervais heard the plaintive note in Salim's voice. "Surely he will make time to see you."

"I pray it is so. I had resigned myself to the possibility I would not see him again before Paradise, so it will be reward enough just to see him once more."

"Both Dara and Jahanara were his students?"

"Yes, though Dara started as a youngster with Mian Mir and then, when returned to his father, continued to study with one of Mian Mir's more accomplished disciples."

"But, on the subject of Jahanara Begum, I thought purdah would prevent—"

"Oh, purdah was observed, I assure you."

"Understood. You said something about Dara being *returned* to his father?"

"Indeed. He and Aurangzeb were both held hostage by Jahangir after Shah Jahan's failed attempt to rebel against him."

"Both of them?"

"Yes."

"Why then, and correct me if I'm wrong, was Dara a student of Mian Mir while Aurangzeb was not?"

Gervais' lifetime among liars served him well in that moment, allowing them to see Salim's lie for what it was: "I do not know, Gervais."

"I see. Thank you kindly for answering my questions, Salim. You have been a most gracious and good host."

Salim looked away, tugging at his beard. After a moment he looked back at Gervais and lowered his voice. "I suspect Jahangir was attempting to punish Shah Jahan by ensuring that a divide existed between his sons like that which existed between himself and Shah Jahan."

It was Gervais' turn to look away in an attempt to cover the twinge of guilt he felt at manipulating the Afghan. "I had not meant to..."

"And it is not my place to make such comments on the royal family. Please forget that I did so."

"Already forgotten," Gervais, unlike his host, lied with the ease of a lifetime's practice.

Lahore

The howdah's sway usually calmed Jahanara's restless mind, but not today. Today she would see Mian Mir, and receive his blessings, and her excitement would not be restrained.

Seeking distraction, she spoke to Nadira Begum, seated across from her: "Suleiman eats well?"

Nadira Begum smiled over the crown of her son's head. "He does indeed. His milk mothers complain of how quickly he drains them."

"Good, good. Mian Mir will, no doubt, offer blessings for our youngest prince."

"Truly?"

"I will ask Mian Mir if he or my brother fails to offer it." Dara had gone ahead this morning with Salim and several of his favorites, planning to spend the morning in prayer and contemplation in company with the saint.

"We have been truly blessed to see Dara come back to us. It seems presumptuous to ask for more."

Jahanara ran a finger across the soft cheek of her nephew. "For a child, anything and everything."

"I'm told the gardens your brother established in Mian Mir's name are quite exceptional."

Jahanara nodded, smiling. "My brother, your husband, certainly has excellent taste."

"It's true that he designed it himself?"

"He did. Father's chief canal builder laid out the water forms for the garden, but did so entirely to Dara's specifications."

Nadira's eyes shone. "I am so happy he lived, Jahanara. That I might have had to go on without him was so painful I could barely draw breath."

Jahanara looked away, uncomfortable with the depth of feeling in Nadira's eyes. Always, such words sparked that twinge of jealousy, her heart asking again: *Will I ever have such a love?*

As always, there was no answer to be found in the hollow desolation of her loneliness.

Loud cries from up ahead roused Begum Sahib from her self-pity. Such disruptions were not the norm; eunuchs traveled ahead of the harem ladies to drive from the route any who were not fit to lay eyes on the procession. Such noise heralded some mishap on the road, and Jahanara did not want to have to intercede with some poor family that had their son beaten by her overzealous guardians, not today.

She looked through the ornate slats of the howdah, attempting to catch of glimpse of the cause of the ruckus but there was little to see but early-morning sunlight on billowing dust.

"Atisheh!" she called.

"Shehzadhi?"

"What is that noise?"

"It appears a large mob outside the home of Mian Mir, Shehzadi."

Nadira tensed beside her, setting Suleiman to fussing again. "What manner of mob?"

"I know not. Shall I find out, Shehzadi?"

"Gopal, stop." Jahanara ordered, considering.

By the time the mahout brought the massive elephant to a halt, Jahanara decided: "Yes, take some other swords with you, but be gentle. I do not wish to offer offense to the saint by injuring those at his doorstep."

"Your will." Atisheh rode off, five of her sisters following.

Expecting she'd have to wait some time, she asked Nadira, "Have you heard Priscilla and Ilsa speak of the home they plan to build?"

"I have. Strange that they should live under the same roof and not be wed to the same man or otherwise related."

"Strange indeed, but perhaps some of the least strange things about them." She shrugged silk-shrouded shoulders. "I suppose the place will be less a home and more a caravanserai for their trade interests, but still."

"Have you seen the young men with them?"

"I have. One has blond hair, the other, red, and all of them are well-formed."

Nadira snorted, whispered: "Well-formed, indeed. The slaves prattle endlessly about them, asking one another questions."

"Oh, and what do they ask?"

"They ask if the carpets match the hangings."

"If the carpets match—" She stopped, shocked to her very bones.

Nadira's throaty laugh was infectious, and made it harder still for Jahanara to pretend she didn't find the joke both provocative and funny.

They were drawn from their merriment by the hoof beats of Atisheh's party.

The howdah swayed again as Atisheh gestured imperiously at Jahanara's mahout and the elephant knelt. With the strength and grace of her people, Atisheh left the saddle and, without touching the ground, scaled the elephant. Armor chiming softly as she crouched beside the howdah, she said, "Shehzadi, the men outside his house mourn the passing of Mian Mir. They say he has passed to Paradise."

"What?" Jahanara whispered, wind sucked from her lungs.

Atisheh, unable to hear her mistress' distress, continued to relate the details. "Shehzada Dara Shikoh's new sowar were on the gate, and told me he and Amir Salim were with Mian Mir when he breathed his last."

Jahanara swallowed and tried to regain her wits.

"Did you see my husband?" Nadira asked, anxiety making Suleiman fuss yet again.

"Yes, Begum. He was in the courtyard, weeping openly, as were all the men."

"Understandable, given the great loss the Order has suffered," Jahanara said, mind lurching along in the wake of the sudden change in circumstance.

A shrug of armored shoulders. "Nadira Begum wept less, and there was far more blood, during the birth of the babe."

The contempt in the other woman's voice snapped Jahanara

out of her funk and put a blade in her voice. "That may be so, but you will not repeat it where any man might hear."

"Yes, Shehzadi, I will not speak of it again." While the response and her demeanor were appropriate in every detail, Jahanara knew the warrior-woman's opinion remained unchanged.

"Gopal, you did not hear a thing, understood?"

The mahout turned sideways, keeping his eyes down, and loudly inquired, "What was that, Shehzadi? Did this poor servant fail to hear orders again? I am most sorry, Shehzadi."

"Do better, Gopal," Jahanara said, silently resolving to see the thin fellow rewarded for his impeccable manners.

"I shall try, Shehzadi."

"What do we do, Jahanara?" Nadira asked.

"Mian Mir outlived both wives and daughters, so I can but think we would be a burden on the household should we continue on," Jahanara mused aloud. "I'm afraid we must turn back. Atisheh, send a messenger to inform Dara of my decision, I doubt he will be back soon..."

"Yes, Shehzadi." With a strange noise that wasn't quite whistle nor raspberry, Atisheh called her horse to the elephant's side. She dropped from her perch into the saddle with a show of unconscious athleticism that reminded Jahanara that her confidence in the woman's prowess as a fighter was fully justified.

Nadira was nodding. "Funeral preparations..."

"Yes, there will be a great deal to do. I doubt Dara will have much time for anything, even family."

Nadira waggled her head, "I meant that, surely, as one of his students, you would be included in his funeral rites?"

"Men rarely think to ask," Jahanara rasped.

"But, as one of his most accomplished students, your loss is surely as great as my husband's! You should be allowed to take part in the funeral preparations."

Jahanara found she could not answer aloud, so tight had her throat become.

Chapter 33

Lahore Fort, Diwan-i-Am
August 1635

"He what?" Dara said, unsure he'd heard his advisor correctly. He was, as yet, unused to the new personnel Father had assigned to him in order to reconstitute his household court. So much so he could not even recall this one's name, especially with all the funeral preparations to see to.

"Hargobind Singh rides to Lahore, wishing to be present for the internment of Mian Mir, Shehzada," the eunuch clarified.

"He does, does he?" he said, noncommittal. *I don't have time for this. I must begin writing the eulogy.*

"Yes, Shehzada."

"Very well. Make sure he is accorded every respect, then."

"Is that wise, Shehzada?" The eunuch persisted.

Kwaja Magul, Dara finally dredged the name from memory. He sniffed, irritated at the eunuch's manner but powerless to dismiss the fellow. As an imperial appointee to his household, there was little Dara could do without offending Father and adding to the perception he could not manage his own court.

Besides, it was not this one's fault that Dara lost so many loyal men and advisors at Ramdaspur. That was his alone.

"He will be accorded every respect as he attends the funeral of my teacher, understood?"

A respectful bow of the head accompanied the eunuch's next words but did not stop them: "Of course, Shehzada. I only ask

295

as some of the other Orders will be present, and may resent his presence . . . aggressively."

"So be it!" Dara snapped.

"I merely—"

"And I heard your concerns. Now do as I command."

"Are you certain, Shehzada?"

Restraining, just barely, the urge to cuff the eunuch about the ears, Dara felt his cheeks flush. "Is there some other concern you have yet to voice? Something so critical that you decide to question orders twice given?" he asked through clenched teeth.

"Forgive me the effrontery, Shehzada, but Shah Jahan himself commanded me to be certain you were making the best decisions possible, and ordered us"—he gestured at the other advisors—"to confirm you gave careful consideration to every decision before making them public, purely because of your recent . . . illness."

Dara looked at the rest of the advisors, each of whom silently nodded agreement. He pinched the bridge of his nose between thumb and forefinger, asked: "And what is it that I am failing to consider, *my* advisors?"

Kwaja waggled his head and answered as if Dara had not laced his question with bitter sarcasm: "Certain powerful groups, among them the Naqshbandi Order, are, how shall I say it? *Content* to see Mian Mir and his conciliatory rhetoric gone from this world, and will take it amiss if Hargobind Singh is present at what they view as a properly Islamic rite."

"View? They would co-opt it, given half a chance!" Dara surged to his feet and began pacing.

"Correct, Shehzada. Shah Jahan's orders that the tax on non-believers be rescinded has already caused a great deal of unrest among the nobles and orders most affected by it . . ." The eunuch trailed off, looking sidelong at Dara's military advisor, Vidur Khan.

The Rajput nodded, taking up the thread. "It is as Kwaja Magul says, Shehzada. I would add that the entire Muslim population of the region, not just the nobility, are uneasy. They are like the grass in the dry season, waiting for the least spark that brings the wildfire. And the presence of Hargobind may just prove the match that lights a conflagration that will not be contained."

"Yet he and Mian Mir held one another in mutual admiration and respect," Dara mused. "With the recent peace concluded between the emperor and Hargobind, it may be that denying him the opportunity to pay his respects would lead to outright war, not just unrest."

"A difficult quandary, Shehzada."

A quandary that would, should Dara defer it to his father for a decision, not only fail to meet the religious requirements of their faith, but cause whatever esteem he might have with these men to evaporate, never to return.

Dara stopped pacing, feeling their eyes on him. "Hargobind will come to the funeral, as he wishes. I will write to make him aware of the delicate situation. Let the news-writers inform everyone that he comes under my protection and with my full friendship and regard."

"Yes, Shehzada," his advisors chorused.

Did his solution please them? he wondered. Or were they merely humoring him, having followed his father's instruction? It was impossible to know.

"Are there any other matters of import before I begin writing the eulogy? How goes recruitment?"

"Slowly, Shehzada. With his recent deployment of such large armies into the Deccan and Bengal, Shah Jahan depleted much of the readily available manpower."

"I see. I would prefer quality over great numbers regardless. Perhaps some of your kin would take up arms in my name? Rajput arms are respected the world over."

The Rajput smiled so broadly his teeth were visible as his large mustache curled up. "Of course, Shehzada. I have already posted to my holdings and among the families of my home, asking for sons to join your household."

"Excellent. I will ask the same of Salim."

The mustache drooped, teeth disappearing.

"What is it?"

"Few are the people who trust the Afghans, Shehzada, and rightly so."

"The Afghani rulers of the petty kingdoms in Bengal have been a problem, I'll admit, but those from the North are a different breed. Besides, the Afghans may be fractious and unruly, but they are excellent fighters, as their possession of so much of Bengal proves."

"And rather more intolerant of nonbelievers than those that have lived here long, Shehzada," the eunuch added.

"True. Who would you have me recruit, then? From among the Maratha? The Mewari?"

Vidur Khan waggled his head. "If you wish it, Shehzada. Recruiting from among those who do not share in power now has proven an effective path to power in the past."

Father had done exactly that. And yet. And yet...

"You would have me avoid recruiting Afghans and in the next breath advise me to recruit from among those who have no share of power under my father. How do you reconcile these two?"

Vidur Khan bowed his head, "Shehzada commands, we obey."

In other words: we're giving you options, and we will not only carry out those orders, we'll report exactly what you tell us to your father.

"Very well. Recruit from among the Afghans to the north and continue your drive to collect more of your kinsmen."

"As you command. There are also a great number of Atishbaz who would gladly serve," Vidur continued. "Speaking of which, Talawat the gunsmith, the fellow you employed before, he wishes to meet with you."

"Oh?" Dara asked, interested. Most of the craftsmen employed by his establishment survived his failure in battle but had found employment elsewhere while he was believed dead. That the gunsmith wished to meet with Dara might indicate a desire to return to his service. He would certainly be welcome.

"Yes, Shehzada. Something about wishing to explore the ferenghis' firearms."

"Ah, yes. Have him come to me and I will arrange it personally."

Lahore Fort, Dara's Quarters

"Amir Salim Yilmaz," Dara said, looking up from *qalam* and paper before him.

"Shehzada."

Dara waved a hand. "Please, be seated and at your ease. I yet have some writing to do."

Sitting, Salim waved away a slave's offer of refreshment and sat silent while the prince continued to work on the document.

The prince's brow was furrowed, but not with pain or frustrated desire for the pipe, as it had so often in the recent past.

No, using qalam, the reed pen of calligraphers, was no easy task, and the prince had a reputation to uphold.

He really was good. One misplaced stroke and the entire sheet of paper would be wasted, yet he worked with the surety of a scribe decades at his craft.

It occurred to Salim then, watching Dara write, how *young* the prince was.

After a long wait, Dara pursed his lips, muttered, "I think I have struck the proper tone..."

"Pardon, Shehzada?"

"What? Oh, yes...Apologies...Writing the eulogy for Mian Mir proves a challenge. A man whose spirit and teachings changed the lives of so many defies easy description..."

"I would imagine so," Salim said, feeling the loss all over again. It was one thing to know a loved one has ascended to Paradise, quite another to avoid selfish feelings of loss and pain as you marked the days of their passing.

Cleaning it carefully, Dara set the qalam in its cradle. "I asked you to attend me because I have requests to make of you."

"Where your father's demands on my time and service permit, I am at your service, Shehzada."

"These requests should not impinge on your Imperial service beyond your post as mihmandar to the ferenghi."

Salim simply bowed.

"My servant, Talawat, wishes to talk to Rodney and John about their gunpowder weapons. He is most interested in their mechanisms."

How had he learned...? Oh, of course—Salim's kinsmen talked too much. They must have spoken of the attack where others could hear.

"I will ask them. I doubt they will refuse you, but I must beg your pardon, Shehzada: does the emperor know of this request?"

The prince frowned momentarily. "I do not think so. I will inform him of the request, as I expect you to report it."

Salim bowed his head, "I am sorry to question you so, Shehzada, but—"

Dara spoke over him, waving him down: "But you must, and I understand completely. Father may wish to keep such a resource to himself, and that is his prerogative as emperor. You do him good service as one of his amirs by asking."

"Thank you for your understanding, Shehzada."

"Think nothing of it. Now, I would have your opinion on Hargobind Singh."

"Shehzada?"

"Sorry, I am not being clear: I would have your opinion on how his presence at Mian Mir's funeral will be received."

"By whom, Shehzada?"

"Father and the . . . wider court."

"Surely your advisors have given you their learned opi—"

"The advisors Father provided me have rendered their opinions. I ask yours."

"The emperor will surely see, and approve of, the reasoning behind your decision to include the Sikh."

"And?"

"Difficulty with the more conservative and orthodox Muslims will likely follow Hargobind Singh's attendance, but it is not such an outrage they will be moved to rebel, given our teacher's tolerance for the Sikhs."

"Meaning Mian Mir had already driven away those who would be offended."

"Yes, Shehzada."

"And the rest, the non-Muslims?"

"I am not experienced enough with courtly politics to know, Shehzada."

"Your best guess, then."

"Most Hindus are reasonably friendly with the Sikhs, and will likely see the guru's attendance as a sign of improving relations between all non-Muslims and Muslims."

"So, you do not think it a bad idea to invite the guru?"

"No, Shehzada, though I do worry that someone may attempt an assassination of him while he is here."

Dara smiled and rubbed his shoulder pointedly. "You have not seen Bhidi Chand and the rest of the guru's bodyguard fight. I assure you that anyone wishing to slay Hargobind Singh will have a hard time of it."

"I bow to your greater experience there, but even if unsuccessful, such an attempt will certainly cause the solemn occasion to erupt in riots and violence, potentially spreading such discord throughout the Punjab."

Dara nodded. Seeming to come to some conclusion, he looked

up at Salim. "Would you agree to the move if I were to petition Father to have you assigned to me as an advisor?"

Salim didn't bother to conceal his surprise at the offer. "Of course, Shehzada, though the emperor may not grant the move purely because of my duties as mihmandar to the foreigners."

"True. I shall make the request anyway. I will have need of men of experience I can trust."

"Surely you can trust those men the emperor has assigned you already?"

"I can trust them insofar as they will assist me in making decisions Father approves of. On matters they may have a personal interest in, they may seek advantage at my expense, reporting falsely or omitting information in their reports to sow distrust between myself and Father. Nur Jahan did exactly that when she infected Jahangir with poisoned words against my father by controlling the information my grandfather received on the goings on in my father's princely court."

"Surely the bond between you and the emperor is stronger than that?"

"Now, yes. But who can say what will happen in a year, or ten? Especially if I am given a governorship someplace distant. Beyond that, the law, as you know, is not something even emperors can ignore: every true-born son shall inherit the same share as his brothers, being twice that of his sisters.

"Father allots me a much larger stipend than my brothers. But since my failure at Ramdaspur claimed the lives of so many that I had come to rely on, I possess a great deal of ready cash but lack trustworthy men I can swear into service, not to mention men I can trust to command them on my behalf."

Unsure what to say, Salim ventured: "You face many difficulties, Shehzada."

Dara shook his head. "I complain too much."

"Given time, I know I can gather trustworthy men willing to serve you, Shehzada."

"But first we must persuade Father to place you with me."

"I will write to him tonight, Shehzada."

"Good. I will be sure to do the same." He picked up the thick, spotless paper, "once I am done with this. Will you listen to what I have written thus far?"

"Certainly, Shehzada."

Lahore

"I don't think we should get any closer," Angelo said.

"No, probably not," Gervais agreed, lifting his borrowed binoculars to watch the funeral procession come to a staggering, bunching halt at the burial site. The mausoleum Dara had decreed would be a shrine to Mian Mir was a simple, attractive building cited at the center of the quadrangle of gardens. The mob began to overflow the gardens, surrounding the grave site in row after row of mourners. One group, far smaller than the main body and separated from the rest by a mutually agreed-on space, formed a thin wedge point on to the tomb. Gervais blinked, then focused at the point of the wedge. Their turbans were tied differently, and their leader was...

Hargobind Singh had come. He must have been waiting for the procession at the tomb. A brave and possibly provocative move.

After a moment he could hear Dara Shikoh's voice rising and falling from the heart of the crowd. Gervais, unable to distinguish individual words at this remove, instead observed the audience. Based on the strong emotion evident on every face, the eulogy was a powerful one.

He'd decided to try to observe the funeral from a safe distance, in case something untoward happened. Not that he could stop it, but even a few minutes warning could prove the difference between capture and an easy escape.

Bored, Angelo dismounted and sidled into the lengthening late-afternoon shade of the upright wheel of a Persian well that had been abandoned to a slow desiccation in the dry, relentless heat.

Following suit, Gervais squatted next to his old friend and asked, "You happy?"

Angelo snorted. "What kind of question is that?"

Gervais shrugged. "I know it's not a question we commonly ask one another, but these Americans, they chase after happiness like you and I chase wealth, setting great store by it. When I bought your contract from the diwan in Surat, I knew you were in a bad way and needed help, but I never asked if you wanted in on this. Later, I never really asked if you had other plans, just set you to work."

"I hardly call translating hard labor. And translating for these people is far less dangerous than trying to skim enough from transactions in the port to pay down my debt."

Gervais shrugged again. "I just don't want to have made things worse for you." He gestured at the crowd of mourners. "There are risks, big risks, in dealing with the up-timers. Without even meaning to, they can spark sweeping, violent change."

"Of course there are risks, but I am happy to get a chance to return to the centers of power and the rewards such proximity provides. I had thought such opportunities beyond me." Angelo smiled. "And they were, until you bought my debt."

"Opportunities?"

Angelo winked. "Don't worry, nothing that puts us at risk."

Gervais looked a stern question at him.

"Your friends have generated quite the stir at court, and I've had a number of invitations to serve with nobles who would not receive me before, simply because of my association with the up-timer physicians who saved Dara Shikoh. When the mission's work is done, I will have no lack of places to make my fortune."

"I see."

"Any idea when that will be?"

"What, when we'll leave?"

Angelo nodded.

"Not sure. At least another two years."

"Careful, India may claim your soul, as it has mine."

Gervais waved a fly away. "I thank you for the warning, but while it has its charms, I will take what I can from it and return..." he trailed off, unsure where—and what—he would return to.

Angelo, watching him, chuckled quietly. "You don't know where you'd go, do you?"

"No, I don't. I suppose I'll leave it up to Monique."

"She'll likely say the same thing."

"I don't know. She's got an eye for Bertram."

"I thought I saw something there, but it's difficult to pierce the veils."

"Well, he doesn't seem prepared to act on it, even if he knows she's interested."

"He isn't an easy read."

"No, he isn't." .

"What about him?" Angelo punched his bearded chin in the direction of the funeral.

"Dara?"

"He's doing better. The wounds are almost entirely healed and he hasn't smoked in some time. I was worried he might be driven back to the pipe by this loss, but my daughter says Nadira Begum and Jahanara have joined forces to forbid the use of opium in Dara's harem."

"His sister has that kind of influence?"

Gervais shrugged. "Some oddity of Jahanara's position in her father's household, and the fact that Dara's household and court have so recently been reconstituted using personnel from Shah Jahan's establishment."

"Ah." Angelo lowered his voice. "You are aware of the rumors?"

"Which ones?"

"Those that indicate that Jahanara and Shah Jahan have an improper relationship, and that those relations are the true reason Shah Jahan refuses to let her marry."

Gervais opened his mouth to rebuke Angelo for spreading such a vile rumor, but stopped himself. Angelo was just letting him know what was being said, not gossiping. "Do you place any credence in these rumors?"

"No, and I don't think any of the rest of the royal family do, either. I just thought you should know."

"Any idea who is spreading that story around?"

Angelo shook his head. "I first heard it while we were in camp."

"From whom?"

"A minor noble, a commander of one hundred, in service to Shah Shuja. We were drinking." He smiled. "Or rather, I was drinking, and he was drunk."

"And did others confirm or contest this rumor?"

"Most treated the words as the ramblings of a drunk."

"But not all."

"No, not all."

"How many were present?"

"Ten men of the same rank as the speaker, all in service to Shah Shuja."

Filing that datum away for future thought, Gervais eyed the lowering sun. "Do they bury him by nightfall?"

"Usually, but you know as well as I that things are different for important people."

Chapter 34

Shah Jahan's column, midway between Lahore and Agra
September 1635

"Some privacy for my son and me," the emperor commanded. Instantly, his personal guard angled their mounts away, sped up or slowed, taking up station in a wide circle just out of easy earshot. Once assured he would not be overheard, Shah Jahan spoke: "You acted wisely, my son."

Dara nodded. "I am relieved to hear you say so, Father. I was most concerned that I not create discord between you and Hargobind Singh so soon after you reached accord."

"Indeed, his letter was most complimentary toward your hospitality and regarding the eulogy you gave Mian Mir. It seems he has a great deal of respect for you."

"Despite the manner of our meeting, I have found him a wise and thoughtful man, worthy of respect and honor."

Father looked at him approvingly. "To make an enemy into a friend is the single greatest distinction of good leadership."

Surprised at how emotional Father's praise made him, Dara looked away in an attempt to hide his response. When he trusted his voice would be level, Dara said, "I will pray and hope that is what I have done, then."

"Are you satisfied with the advisors I appointed to assist you?"

Deciding to answer Father's question with another, Dara said, "Did you receive the letter I sent regarding Amir Salim?"

"I did," Shah Jahan said simply.

Unsatisfied, Dara pushed: "Do you wish me to ask in person, now?"

Shah Jahan looked at his son sidelong. "I want you to answer the question put to you."

"I am satisfied with their service, but have need of more men experienced at command."

"Amir Salim has no experience at commanding armies. He's barely been made an umara."

"No, but he does have experience of war, is well-known and respected among the Afghans, and has proven himself loyal to our house. And that leaves aside his familiarity with the ferenghi and their ways."

"The ferenghi, yes . . . Salim has nearly finished reading me the last and biggest work he secured for us in Grantville."

Something about his tone sent a chill racing along Dara's spine. "And?" he asked, cautious.

"That book—and they themselves—are the reason we ride for Agra just now."

"Pardon, but *they*?"

"The English. I plan to revoke their firman and permanently bar them from trade in those lands under my control."

Dara felt his brow rise. "Just the English?"

"For now. I do not think I could bear the wailing of the Hindu merchant caste if I were to curtail all trade with Europe, especially since that wailing would join with that of the Muslim umaras I've already offended with my recent actions, and result in denial of any restful sleep."

Not to mention the devastation such a policy would wreak on their treasury. Jahanara said they were already far too reliant on imported bullion for specie.

"May I ask why?"

"Salim has not told you what the books contain?"

"Not in any detail, no."

"Really?"

"When he first came to court, Salim presented us with the postcard and read me and Jahanara some portions of what he had, but that was naturally limited by the need for quick, quiet action. I concluded that he needed to present his evidence to you without all of the court learning exactly what he had in his possession."

"And then I sent you off to fight the Sikhs."

"Yes."

"And then you were recovering from your wounds."

"Yes."

Shah Jahan scratched his beard, letting the silence stretch a while before speaking. "According to the books Salim has translated, the English will, after Aurangzeb dies, take control of all of India."

"Salim told us as much, though nothing of the particulars."

"The book had maddeningly few details on the process, focusing on the time the English were already in control. I will not make it easy for them, regardless."

"Playing the Europeans one against the other is the only way we've kept the sea lanes to Mecca open. If we lose the English, then the Portuguese and Dutch will be that much stronger, and the predations of the 'pirates' operating under their flags will, at best, continue unabated."

The emperor shrugged. "Despite their reassurances and claims to the contrary, the representatives of the East India Companies of both the Dutch and English, as well as the viceroy of the Portuguese and Spanish in Goa, have repeatedly proven they are either incapable or unwilling to prevent acts of piracy against pilgrims."

"But, Father, we're also incapable of defending our shipping."

"For now, yes. I plan to build a strong navy."

"And in the meantime?" Dara asked, leaving aside the question of how, exactly, that would be accomplished.

Shah Jahan didn't answer immediately. Looking off into the distance he eventually sighed. "In the meantime, the struggles and sacrifices of a pilgrim on Hajj only serve to make that pilgrimage all the more holy for each respective pilgrim."

It was Dara's turn to ride in silence for a time. Eventually, he broke it. "A hard decision."

"Such are the decisions, the brutal calculations, of rule. Costs must be weighed, and accepted, and outcomes—even the unexpected ones—dealt with."

"Like me at Ramdaspur."

Shah Jahan nodded. "Like you at Ramdaspur." He waggled his head after a moment's quiet reflection. "Unlike Ramdaspur, you will often have more time to decide even more complex problems. Take that time, consider your options. Even then you will frequently need to examine precisely *who* is presenting you with those options in order to make the best decision. Regardless, weigh your choices fully. Pray upon them. When that is done, or when time truly presses, you must then decide, and stick to that decision, trusting in God to see you through."

The Englishmen appeared uncomfortable, thought Nur Jahan—and, notwithstanding the rising heat of the day, understandably so. Not since her husband's rule and Sir Thomas Roe's time as the English king's envoy to the court had the English Company representatives been summoned en masse, and never without warning from—or at the instigation of—the English East India Company's Surat-based president. Her eyes picked the man out among his fidgeting underlings. The red-faced William Methwold was finely dressed, by the odd and uncomfortable standards of his people, and gave the least impression of anxiety of all his party. The man even had one of the absurd hats she supposed the ferenghi found fashionable, complete with plumage, in one hand.

Nur summoned to mind the report she'd just had on him. William Methwold had risen to the presidency some four years ago. The great mortality that had been killing off so many of the residents of Surat, both ferenghi and domestic, had also claimed the previous two presidents. That had left Methwold, an accomplished linguist and trader in his own right, in charge of the Surat Factory for the Company. By all accounts, he had done well, navigating Portuguese hostility, Dutch encroachment, and Mughal indifference with equal aplomb, turning a profit even under adverse conditions.

Methwold and the English East India Company had, for those uninitiated into the secret histories of the up-timers, an inoffensive record as far as the emperor was concerned. That is, until he'd incurred the emperor's displeasure by being slow to respond to the summons that brought him to court. *Two weeks.* The court had been made to wait for a full two weeks longer than anticipated before receiving the apologies and immediate compliance of the Company president and all traders currently in Surat.

She glanced along the rows of courtiers to Mullah Mohan, and found the man bright-eyed and eager for the emperor's announcement. Nur hid a smile. She had received reports Mohan had been excited by the carefully worded letters she'd sent, but she found visual confirmation far more reassuring than reports from even the most reliable of sources.

And if Shah Jahan does something other than you think, what then? The thought, somehow delivered in Gargi's voice, intruded on her self-congratulation. Then she would have been mistaken, and Mohan would think less of her—a loss of reputation she would scarcely notice.

She was drawn from her internal argument as the emperor had the English called before him. Nur noted the sudden increase in interest of the other women behind the jali, including her niece. That was another partial confirmation, at least, of her intelligence. Jahanara's interests in Surat would be sorely afflicted by the loss of trade with the English.

"You answer my summons late," Shah Jahan said even as the English were making their proper respects.

Methwold's bow was perfectly executed despite the emperor's angry tone. "My abject apologies, Sultan Al'Azam. I was called away on delicate negotiations, and was not present when your unexpected and unprecedented summons reached my offices."

"Oh?"

A silence stretched for some moments after the question.

"Company matters, Sultan Al'Azam."

"And?"

"They were concluded successfully, Sultan Al'Azam."

"I do not enjoy repeating requests."

"We were in negotiations with the viceroy of Goa, Sultan Al'Azam."

"Oh? And how is Count Linares?"

"Ah—well...that is, the Viceroy Count Linares is well, Sultan Al'Azam," Methwold answered, recovering with admirable smoothness.

"And what was the subject of these negotiations?"

The blunt and decidedly undiplomatic question cracked the Englishman's calm. "Sultan Al'Azam, I fear I would be breaking faith with His Majesty King Charles, if I were to reveal even the barest details of our negotiations."

"Fear?" Shah Jahan asked, voice gone dangerously flat. "When it comes to whom you should fear, you seem to have forgotten with whom you are dealing, and where you are."

Methwold's nervous swallow was audible, such was the quality of the silence that followed the emperor's statement.

It took the man a moment to find his voice, and it was admirably even when he did: "Sultan Al'Azam, you may rest assured those negotiations were not, in any way, detrimental to your interests."

Shah Jahan's cold, humorless laughter brushed aside the tatters of the Englishman's calm. "You will forgive me if I find such assurances lacking."

"Sultan Al'Azam, it appears I have offended you in some fashion. Would it please you to inform me how, exactly, I have offended, so that I might make amends?"

Shah Jahan leaned forward on his throne, "Are you, perhaps, familiar with the place from the future called Grantville?"

The Englishman nodded, color slowly draining from his red face. "I have heard of it, Sultan Al'Azam."

"Are you aware they brought with them certain histories and facts about the world we live in?"

"I am, Sultan Al'Azam." The plumed hat he'd swept off on bowing displayed a slight quiver, now.

"Then you are aware of the depredations of your East India Company?"

"Sultan Al'Azam, I can only think that what you have been told are lies. His Majesty's Honorable East India Company has only ever sought to trade in friendship with your generous permission."

"You speak of the firman I affirmed on taking the throne."

Methwold bowed again, his voice regaining confidence now it seemed the emperor had changed subjects. "And for which we have thanked you with gifts of silver and other goods not easily obtained within your mighty empire, Sultan Al'Azam. As we have always fulfilled every requirement of your generous firman of trade."

"Except when asked to defend Our pilgrims."

"Sultan Al'Azam, we have made every effort to protect Muslim shipping, but we are but one nation among the many sailing these waters."

"Not for long."

"Sultan?"

"Have you had an opportunity to read any of the works from the future, President Methwold?"

"I have not, Sultan Al'Azam. As I said, I believe much of what has been said about them to be exaggerations if not outright lies."

"I see. Please, take a look at this." the emperor said, gesturing. A eunuch walked forward with a relatively small, red book with white Latin characters on the front. "Please read the cover, President Methwold."

"India Britannica, Sultan Al'Azam."

"India Britannica," the emperor repeated, words rolling from his lips.

"Sultan—"

The emperor rolled over him. "That second word caused me some consternation, Methwold, as the only other time I had heard it was when I was present for Sir Thomas Roe's visit to my father's court. You see, when introducing himself, or rather, the sovereign he was representing, I distinctly remembered a similar word. One of King James the VI's titles was, and I do believe I recall correctly: His Britannic Majesty."

Nur glanced around; she found the entirety of the Audience Hall silent, the gathered umara watching the Englishmen in precisely the same way a pride of lions watches a wounded antelope.

"Sultan—"

Again Shah Jahan spoke over the Englishman's attempt to respond: "And within that book? A litany of things done by the English to the peoples of India, of rights taken, of wealth stolen and never returned, of a future dominated by a religion and culture not our own."

The emperor slowly shook his head. "No, I will not allow it. I will not allow you nor your 'Company' to do anything that is in that book. I withdraw the firman of trade issued your people. I withdraw it and all other rights.

"Because I am merciful, I give you and your people one month to depart Surat with all your goods and chattel. After that date, if an uninvited Englishman sets foot on these shores, he will be hunted down and made an example of. Do I make myself clear, Methwold?"

The Englishman knew better than to attempt argument, and bowed again. "Though I believe you to have been misled by liars, I understand the reasons for your anger with us as I understand your command and injunction. I will abide by them, just as I and every other president of the Company before me have always abided them."

Nur was impressed by Methwold's ability to think and speak eloquently under pressure.

Looking at her old nemesis, she could tell Shah Jahan was not immune to the man's quality, either.

"Leave us now, and depart our shores forever."

"As you command, Sultan Al'Azam." The Englishman performed the necessary obeisances and retreated from the hall with his countrymen in tow.

Nur hoped she was not the only one who noticed the greedy hunger in Mullah Mohan's eyes as he watched the ferenghi depart.

Agra, Red Fort, The Harem

"*What?*" Shah Jahan's shout shattered the peace of the harem. Jahanara flinched, and two of the dancing girls stumbled in their routine.

The music grated to a halt, allowing her to hear Firoz Khan repeat the message: "The Englishmen, Methwold and his men, were attacked on their way to Surat."

"Who dares?"

The eunuch bowed. "It is not known, yet."

"His party was too well armed and large to fall victim to a common band of bandits. Who is investigating?"

"A local zamindar posted along the Gujurat border, at the moment."

Well done, Firoz, thought Jahanara. It was safer that her father did not know the name of this poor zamindar, not while he'd been drinking.

The diwan had gone on while Jahanara extended the mental compliment. "It was he who advised us of the attack. His clansmen reported fighting on his lands. He summoned his fighting men and rode out to the scene. The bodies of several Englishmen were recovered there. Methwold's body was not among those recovered, but the report also indicates that a pursuit followed the skirmish."

All the court had been present for Father's command, and all of them had been disappointed—*no, wait*. A glance and sudden, satisfied smile caught fire in her mind's eye. She followed the memory, checked what she had seen against what she might have chosen to perceive out of her bias against the man.

No, it was as I saw it.

Jahanara felt Father's anger even from a distance. She waved the dancing girls away and returned her attention to the diwan and Father in time to hear him say, "Find out who perpetrated this violence in direct contravention of my commands. What fool would act so precipitously?"

"Your will, Sultan Al'Azam." Diwan Firoz Khan, unable to answer the question, wisely chose to follow orders, fleeing the garden in search of messengers to carry out Shah Jahan's inquiries.

Knowing Roshanara had already gone to bed, complaining of some stomach ailment, Jahanara looked around, assuring herself that only Father's closest servants remained to overhear. "Father?"

"Yes?"

"May I offer an observation?"

Shah Jahan waved permission as he drank from his golden chalice.

"All of your nobles were hopeful that you would not restrain them when you stripped the English of their right to trade. Many appeared crestfallen when you gave them a month to depart."

Father made the wine in his goblet slosh as he gestured with that hand. "I noticed it as well. Always, the court is predatory. When one umara rises, the pride is unsettled. When one falls, everyone looks to see what it is they can gain from that fall."

"True, Father. All of your umara appeared crestfallen save one: Mullah Mohan. I saw him look from the Englishman to you to the jali behind which I sat with the other women of your court, and back to the Englishman. The smile on his face grew at each stop, as if he was made happy, or satisfied that things were going according to some design of his."

Father set down his goblet and leaned forward. "I see. I have had reports he was most dissatisfied with my decision to lift the tax on nonbelievers, but why should he be at once satisfied with my actions against the English and still attack them?"

"That, I cannot say with certainty. Nur Jahan was, however, behind the jali with me and the other ladies of your harem. Given the order in which he looked at each party, it may be that he believes your actions confirmed some intelligence Nur provided him with."

"To what purpose?"

Jahanara frowned. "Nur Jahan plays a deep game. One I fear I cannot penetrate."

"Were she not so popular, I would reduce her stipend to a trifle and prevent her ever meddling in court politics again. Still, it is better to have her here where we can watch her than in Lahore left to her own devices."

Jahanara nodded agreement.

Shah Jahan sighed and retrieved his goblet. "My Daughter, it is a fine thing to have you again lending your talents and wit to my harem."

"It is good to be heard again, Father."

"You have your mother's talent and taste for politics."

Jahanara smiled. "I do?"

The emperor snorted. "She, too, was good at asking questions that led to the answers she wished me to find."

Her smile disappeared. "I hope you do not think that I am simply trying to get rid of Mullah Mohan."

"No," he said, waggling his head. "I made reference solely to that last question you asked: that you do actually take after your mother with regard to your talent and taste for politics."

Relief flooding her, Jahanara accepted the explanation with a nod.

"Now... What to do to discover Mullah Mohan's actual hand in the killing of these Englishmen I had extended my protection to?"

"Ask?"

Shah Jahan's laughter came to a sudden, choking halt.

Jahanara, alarmed, half rose from her cushions before Shah Jahan waved her back to her seat, eyes watering.

"I'm all right, I just hadn't given any thought to actually asking. Such are the machinations of the court, I am always thinking in terms of exposing the lies and deceits of my umara. I do believe I will do as you suggest. Mullah Mohan is so entirely certain of his own sanctity and rectitude, I'm sure he will respond openly. And if he does not, then he will know I suspect him of acting improperly and perhaps cease his search for those disaffected with my rule."

"You do not wish to have him continue?"

"Better the devil I know than the devil I don't, is that it?" he asked, cocking one eyebrow.

Jahanara nodded.

"He is so lacking in subtlety that most umara are cautious

of openly allying themselves with him for fear he will reveal the relationship before it is safe to do so." He drank again. "That is one of the reasons I am so well aware of his actions: many umara seek to curry favor by presenting his name to my informants."

"Forgive me, Father, but not all the world's killers are numbered among your umara. There are plenty of common folk willing to draw blood in the name of Islam, and Mullah Mohan is made *more* popular among them because of his lack of courtly refinement and simple, blunt manner, rather than less."

Shah Jahan tugged thoughtfully at his beard. "My informers are far more commonly focused upon the doings of the umara and my sons than those with less advantageous positions..."

That was understandable. Which umara wished to rise in service, and which ones sought service with what princely court, was the perennial question of import for the emperor.

Chapter 35

Diwan-i-Khas
October 1635

"Do you know why I have summoned you, Mullah Mohan?"

"No, Sultan Al'Azam." The man fairly oozed confidence.

Nur could not help but smile.

"Did you have anything to do with an attack on the English?"

"I did, Sultan Al'Azam."

Shah Jahan blinked. Twice. "You did?"

Pride made Mohan's chest swell. "I did, Sultan Al'Azam."

"Were you not here when I specifically granted them safe passage for one month?"

"I..." Mohan's expression closed into something not unlike a fist as he realized he'd been misled, and by whom. He took hold of his dignity and said, "You do not seem pleased by this outcome, Sultan Al'Azam."

The emperor snorted, shaking his head. "That is because I am not pleased by it, Mullah Mohan. I am, in fact, most incensed. That you, or anyone who claims allegiance to me, would act against my express wishes...well, I find it infuriating, and doubly so because you were physically present when I made those wishes clear."

Another deep bow. "I beg your forgiveness, Sultan Al'Azam."

"Were you asleep when I gave the order?"

"No, Sultan Al'Azam."

"Were you, perhaps, ill?"

316

"No, Sultan Al'Azam."

"In need of a toilet?"

"No, Sultan Al'Azam."

"Then how is it you failed to hear my express command?"

"I heard it, Sultan Al'Azam. But I believed that you were speaking for the benefit of those who did not know that you planned to call for a jihad against the infidel ferenghi."

Again Shah Jahan's brows shot away from wide eyes. "Whatever gave you the idea I even contemplated such a call?"

Nur held her breath, the gambler's toss before her.

Mullah Mohan stared at the beautiful carpets at his feet, then bent the knee. "Forgive me, Shah Jahan, I but sought to do justice in God's name. I thought that you planned to make the Christians suffer for their heinous acts against the pilgrims on Hajj."

"By killing ferenghi I had given safe conduct to? What idiocy is this? Further, how could you think that killing the English will help pilgrims who must now brave waters crossed by the ships of a government that will shortly become our enemy *solely because of your actions?*"

Nur swallowed sudden fear quite unlike what she'd felt before. Risk in search of vengeance was one thing, but she should have thought about the ramifications for the Hajj. *God forgive me.*

Mohan bent low, flushing dark, hands clenched into fists.

"You have nothing to say?"

"Nothing but another abject apology," he prostrated himself fully, "Sultan Al'Azam."

"Oh, you will have to do better than that! Not only did you act counter to my wishes, you also proved yourself inept. Methwold survived your attack. He and the other Englishmen will now have just cause to speak of Our empire as barbaric and uncivilized, and say that I, as Sultan Al'Azam, cannot—or will not—control my people."

He has to die, now. Anything less and he may return to avenge himself upon me. Nur realized she was leaning forward, eager for the emperor's sentence. Glancing at the other women behind the jali, she slowly leaned back.

"Sultan Al'Azam, I beg you: forgive me."

"Who was it drove you to this stupidity?"

"It was my error, Sultan Al'Azam."

"Very well, as you merely repent and offer no others to share in your shame, I will but punish you: I strip you of title. I strip you of land. I strip you of all favors bestowed upon you. Further, you will no longer be allowed on the grounds of any state-funded madrassa. If someone should decide to go against my wishes and offers you comfort at any such school, I will revoke my support from them."

The court shuffled and murmured. The punishment was unusual.

Showing greater self-control than Nur gave him credit for, Mullah Mohan made no protest.

Nur hid her disappointment. Without friends among the umara he would suffer, but his base had always been among the masses. Mullah Mohan remained a threat, not only to her now, but to the emperor as well. Shah Jahan's decision had been unwise; he should have had the mullah executed.

"Leave us."

Mohan climbed to his feet and began backing away from the emperor, head bowed.

"Oh, and lest you think to seek comfort with our enemies, know that I will use your presence as cause for war with any foreign power that should shelter your worthless carcass."

Mohan flinched. He opened his mouth to protest, but was caught on the horns of Shah Jahan's angry, expectant glare.

And there was the reason Mohan did not protest his sentence too loudly. He must have thought to find shelter with one of the Deccani Sultanates. It was actually quite an elegant solution, in some ways. Now Mohan must remain within the circle of Shah Jahan's power, an ongoing reminder to the other umara of the consequences of overstepping one's authority. But Nur still thought the emperor would have done better to simply have the mullah put to death.

Mohan finished his retreat, the lesser umara on the outskirts of the court closing ranks to cut him off from view, if not from thought.

Along the Yamuna outside Red Fort

"All of it is in there?" Talawat eyed the small brass shell with the lead tip. "Shot, powder, and wadding?"

"Not really any wadding, but yes, it's all in there," John said.

"And the powder is smokeless," Salim added.

The Atishbaz gunsmith looked at John, disbelief writ large on his face. "Really?"

"Yes."

"May I see it in action?" he asked, handing the round back to John.

John looked a question at Salim, who shrugged.

"Yes, of course, Talawat."

Salim watched as John shoved the 9mm round into the magazine, seated the black metal box into the well of the pistol and worked the action. He checked down range for anyone who might get hit if he threw a round and, seeing none, raised the pistol.

Salim, plugging the ear closest to John, shifted his gaze to watch the row of cantaloupe a slave had placed about fifty gaz away.

The back of the leftmost cantaloupe exploded even as the vicious crack of the round leaving the barrel made the short gunsmith start.

"Merciful Allah!" Talawat gasped.

"What?" John asked, lowering the pistol and, Salim noticed approvingly, keeping it pointed down-range.

"Such a sharp sound! I have only heard the like twice before, when a barrel breached under the pressure of too much explosive and a poorly fitted round."

"Oh." John shrugged. "These nine-millimeters are pretty zippy, so they tend to crack like a horse whip, but the barrel is sound."

Talawat looked at the cantaloupe. "And you hit it at this distance, even with such a tiny barrel?"

"Well, yeah. Want me to peg the others?"

"What?"

John grinned. "Might want to plug your ears."

"Oh?" Talawat asked.

But John had already raised the pistol, taking aim.

He fired five more times in quick succession, pulping the cantaloupes into a sodden mess.

As the echoes of the shots faded, one of the emperor's elephants trumpeted challenge in the distance, offended by the loud noise.

John lowered the weapon and smiled at Talawat, who was nearly bouncing with excitement.

"Such a rate of fire! May I examine it?"

With practiced motions Salim recognized as the result of long practice, John stripped the metal box holding the ammunition and worked the action across the top, exposing a greater length of the barrel for an instant which, by some mechanism, flipped one of the brass rounds into the air, where he caught it in the same hand that held the "magazine."

Pocketing the magazine, John handed the pistol to Talawat, who marveled at the light weight and precision craftsmanship of the up-time device.

John leaned close, pointing out the different features of the weapon, "This is the slide—"

Feeling someone's eyes on him, Salim turned and looked up the walls of Red Fort. He picked out a group of darker shadows in the shade of the jali-screened enclosure that allowed the ladies of the court to observe the elephant fights without the need to clear every man from the vicinity.

"I still say I shoot better than you, John!" Salim needed a moment to translate the shouted Amideutch, but when he did he turned and cocked an eyebrow at the American.

John turned, smiling, and called, "We're both here because of your better shooting!"

A hint of laughter carried to them across the intervening distance.

Salim found himself wondering which shade was Jahanara, which laugh, hers.

"Is that my pistol you're shooting?"

"Sure is."

"Don't break it. It's so hard to find nice accessories these days."

The up-timer grinned. "We won't, dear."

"Good. Shoot straight now."

"Yes, dear."

More laughter from the women.

John, still smiling, turned back to Talawat, who was inspecting the pistol with a look of avid concentration, even adoration, not unlike that of those freshly converted to Islam.

"Want to take it apart?"

"May I?" the gunsmith asked, breathless.

"Here, I'll show you." A clink and the upper part of the pistol, the "slide," including the barrel, came free of the grip. John turned the slide over to reveal a steel spring wrapped around a shaft below abutting the barrel. He covered the spring and shaft assembly with one hand and popped it free, allowing the whole assembly to part ways. He handed the barrel, which appeared to have been forged with a metal flange to house the end of the spring and shaft arrangement, to Talawat.

The gunsmith looked straight down the steel tube. "I see that the barrel has grooves inside it. To what purpose?"

"They make the bullet spin in the air, stabilizing it."

"And the spring, it makes the 'slide' travel back into place?"

John nodded. "Into battery, yes."

Talawat beamed at the familiar term.

John didn't notice. "When it slides back into place, it drags another round up into the chamber from the magazine on this ramp here, see."

"Your artisans must be geniuses, to craft such fine works out of such hard materials."

"Nearly four hundred years of advancements make us look a lot smarter than we actually are as individuals, friend. The tolerances used to build automatics are tight, I admit, but this Italian piece is pretty simple in relation to some of the crazy-complex stuff being manufactured up-time."

"And did I hear your wife correctly, that this is her weapon?"

Another broad smile, this one full of pride. "You sure as shit did. She used it to drop a few bandits on our way here."

"I heard." Talawat looked down at the disassembled weapon, biting his lip. "Can I copy this?"

John snorted. "What?"

"I mean no offense. Could I possibly try and copy this marvel?"

John gestured at all the steel parts, including the springs and odd-shaped barrel-piece. "I don't think you could even if you wanted to."

Talawat grinned. "Oh, but I beg to differ."

"Well...I like a challenge as much as the next guy, but the real problem is the rounds."

"And why is that?"

John held up the round he'd fished out of the air, showed the dimple at the bottom. "The primer at the base—where the hammer strikes and initiates the explosion—it's like the pans of your guns."

"And what is the problem?"

John shrugged. "The primers are a different formula from the rest of the powder, and I don't have that formula."

"I see," Talawat said, looking crestfallen.

"Sorry."

"Perhaps one of your less complex pieces?"

"Well, the boys have an extra Remington 870 and a lot of twelve-gauge. Primers are less of a problem with them, but still an issue."

"And what is this Remington 870?"

"A shotgun...A fowling piece, I suppose, that can also be used for war, though its range isn't a lot better than the Beretta."

Talawat looked around, clearly hopeful.

John read the expression, smiled apologetically. "Sorry, didn't think to bring one down."

"Perhaps some other time?"

"Of course."

"Thank you for showing me these things, Mr. Ennis."

"You really want to try and copy this, don't you?"

"Merciful Allah, yes!"

"Look, since it's my wife's I can't very well just give it to you, but I'll ask her if it's all right..."

"Perhaps, in the meantime, Talawat could draft plans from your piece there?"

"Um, that quick?"

Talawat nodded. "If you're not in a great hurry?"

"I'm sure Salim can find something to entertain me."

The Atishbaz's grateful smile was something to behold. They left him shouting for quill and paper.

Salim led John a few hundred gaz along the river, then stopped where they could watch the hive of activity on the construction site of what would be one of the Seven Wonders of the World. They stood in silence for some time, watching the carefully choreographed movements of the hundreds of elephants and thousands of workers completing the mausoleum's construction.

Salim thought it a scene worthy of recording in verse: the men's working-chants, the sounds of the small creatures of the riverbank, the sounds and sights of the river itself, all of it combining to form a perfect backdrop for another of man's attempts to construct something strong enough to thwart the ravages of time itself.

It was a subject for a poet more worthy than him, however.

"They're finishing up the mausoleum?" John asked.

Salim nodded. "The principal construction, yes. Putting the white marble in place. The calligraphers and carvers will be working for some time, especially on the interior, before it looks like what you saw in your 'postcards.'"

"I always wondered how, with the Taj so close to the river, they kept all that weight of stone from settling unevenly."

"There are twenty-two wells preventing the water from saturating the ground beneath."

John shook his head and stood silent a long time.

Eventually Salim noticed tears coursing down the up-timer's cheeks.

Moved, but uncertain what the cause could possibly be, Salim asked gently, "Forgive me, John, but do you care to share your troubles?"

John wiped his face, as if ashamed of manly tears.

Salim put away his puzzlement over that reaction to listen to John's answer: "Not troubles, exactly. I just..." He cleared his throat. "You know, I wonder sometimes what my life would have been like had we not come here—to this time, I mean. I don't think I would have even left the state of West Virginia, let alone the country. And now me and all of us from Grantville, we've changed—and continue to change—the whole damn world."

"I see. It has been a hardship?"

John looked at him. "God, yes... And yet: hell, no." He shook his head. "I have done things, seen things," he hiked a thumb at the palace behind them, "met people, I would never, *ever* had the opportunity to if the Ring of Fire hadn't happened."

"A mixed blessing, then."

"Damn straight."

Aurangzeb's Camp, The Deccan

The intermittent rattle of musket fire sounded from across the plain, punctuated by the slower, deeper thudding of the imperial cannon ringing the hilltop fort.

Standing alone on the slight rise to the east, Aurangzeb resisted the urge to grind his teeth. *Too slow.* Nothing one could call a proper battle, just skirmishes followed by an assault on some minor holdfast. But each of these pockets of resistance, and there are a lot of them, slowed his advance and allowed Golkonda and Bijapur time to consolidate their defenses, even arrange to cooperate against him.

The occupants of the tiny fort located in the northwest of what used to be the Ahmednagar Sultanate had decided to declare for Shahaji, a Maratha general who hoped to carve a kingdom from the ruins of Ahmednagar. Recently disintegrated by a combination of internal and external difficulties, the lands of the Ahmednagar Sultanate were being snapped up by greedy neighbors and petty rulers like Shahaji. Decades of Mughal and rival Deccani Sultanate pressures, not to mention internal strife rising from a series of weak rulers had finally disintegrated the once-mighty Ahmednagar Sultanate. That greatest of generals and statesmen, the Abyssinian slave-cum Wazir, Malik Ambar, had, by force of personality and skilled diplomacy, kept destruction at bay for more than forty years. Upon Ambar's death, the collapse had begun to gather speed as the sultanate's siblings and weaker offspring readied to feast on the corpse.

Disinclined to enter lengthy negotiations and lacking the resources necessary to feed the populace even if he did, Aurangzeb had decided that reducing such places as this was the best option, even if it slowed his advance. And while it was a race, Shah Shuja had shown no sense of urgency, and advanced at an even slower pace, complaining in his letters that "harsh conditions make advancing difficult."

A rider of his messenger corps approached and dismounted.

But Aurangzeb knew better. Shuja hunted, he lay with his slaves, he bided his time in the hope that his younger brother would spend his strength—or, even better, suffer a defeat at the hands of one of the sultanates.

The messenger strode through Aurangzeb's guards and made his obeisance.

Aurangzeb waved, indicating the man should report.

"Shehzada, Captain of Artillery Carvalho claims the eastern and northern walls of the fort will be reduced by mid-afternoon."

"I hear you. My compliments to the captain, and relay my commands to him and Samarjit. The Rajputs are to coordinate with Carvalho and his gunners to put in the assault the moment the walls are breached." Aurangzeb looked to the messenger. "You have it?"

"Yes, Shehzada."

"Repeat it for me." Trained, skilled messengers were the backbone of any army, especially when he expected to have to lead them against exquisitely skilled Maratha light cavalry that were a constant threat in the region. Defending against their hit and run tactics would make the delivery of accurate and timely commands to his subordinates essential.

"Your compliments to Carvalho and Samarjit, and their two forces are to coordinate an assault as soon as the walls are breached."

Aurangzeb nodded. "Close enough. Go now."

"Yes, Shehzada."

The messenger left. Watching him ride off prompted Aurangzeb to consider the news from court: Mullah Mohan's letter regarding the incident, if one existed, had yet to arrive. He did have the accounts of the court news writer, Nur Jahan, and Roshanara to consider.

The news writer's account was bland and only related bald facts.

Being ignorant of the ties between him and Mullah Mohan, Roshanara had barely mentioned the event in her letter.

Nur had expressed her regret at the man's actions and dismissal from court, but made no effort to explain or investigate Mohan's possible motives. And that was reasonable, given that their correspondence might be read by any of a number of his father's people.

I just don't like it. Reasonable or not, I know she was offended by Mohan's condescension after the failed attempt on Dara, but enough to strike at him so?

It seemed too dangerous a ploy, even for her.

Realizing he needed more information, and was unlikely to get it in the near term, Aurangzeb focused on what he did know of the man. Mohan was volatile and uncouth, certainly, but he knew of no personal animus he might have against the English. And with the man's inability to conceal what he was thinking, surely Aurangzeb would know if he harbored hate sufficient to drive him to ignore the emperor's order...

No, Mohan must have been manipulated into acting so rashly, but by whom?

Dara?

Aurangzeb almost smiled. Certainly not.

He would suspect Wazir Khan, but he was in Bengal.

Father?

Possibly. It would be a bit circuitous, but he might see it as a way to attack Aurangzeb's base and pry a potential ally from his grasp. Indeed, the more he thought on it, the more it fit his desires.

A whisper of suspicion: *Or Nur.*

He pondered the possibilities until the call to Asr prayer. Obeying that call, Aurangzeb returned to his tent and took his time performing the ritual cleansing.

Prayer, as always, steadied him and cleared his mind.

By the time he was rolling his prayer rug up, the Rajputs and Catholics under his command were rapidly reducing the tiny hilltop fortress to a corpse-strewn ruin.

Chapter 36

Gargi bent close to the eldest of the washer-women at work along the Yamuna. "I seek word of Mullah Mohan."

The woman, squatting on her haunches and pausing at her laundry, looked Gargi up and down. "You are not welcome here."

"I know. I have coin."

"Not enough to make you welcome, infidel."

Gargi bit off an angry retort and climbed from the step-sided riverbank where the women gathered to wash. She paused in the shade of a building to catch her breath, contemplating her next move. Nur had come to Agra to pray at the mosque, giving Gargi opportunity to inquire about town. As no other could be trusted with the task, Gargi had spent the better part of the day attempting to fulfill the need for direct intelligence on the whereabouts of Mullah Mohan.

The washer-woman's response had been typical, if more polite than some of those she'd had from Agra's Muslim population. Because she was Hindu, none of them would talk to her, though their resentment confirmed an awareness of Mohan's sentence, at least.

No doubt the man had hidden himself well enough that Gargi, with her limited resources and incorrect religion, would not likely find him. At least not today.

Sighing, Gargi left the riverside and turned her footsteps in the direction of the mosque Nur Jahan patronized.

A few minutes later she rounded a corner and ran into a man

327

who smelled of camels. Preoccupied, she opened her mouth to apologize but he punched her, hard, in the side.

Gargi grunted and, outraged, looked the man in the eye. She saw the hate there, the mad anger, and wondered at it even as she felt him punch her again, harder, in the belly.

She tried to shout but he hit her once again, knocking the breath from her lungs.

She folded her hands across her belly protectively, felt a hot, sticky wetness. He struck her again, this time on the left side, just below the rib cage.

Raising her hands, she was surprised to find them bloody. *What?* She thought, stupidly. *Stabbed? He stabbed me!*

She turned to run, wobbled on suddenly weak legs.

Another dagger-blow sent her bouncing off a basket and into the arms of another man.

Nur, oh, Nur, I cannot fail you...

Gargi tried to stand, but her knees wouldn't carry her weight.

Things came in flashes, then: the man who caught her slowing her fall, his eyes widening with concern, his mouth gone wider still as he shouted for help. And, finally, darkness as the earth reached up and pulled her close.

Agra

"What the hell is that?" Ricky asked, getting up from the table and sauntering over to the wine-sink's arched doorway.

Bertram held his breath and listened. Lots of people were shouting. And... was that the sound of steel on steel?

"Whatever it is, it doesn't sound good."

Bobby put his cup down. "No, it doesn't."

Ricky returned, his expression grave. "Lots of angry shouting, some dust, and what might be smoke from a fire on the north side of town."

"Horses," Bertram said, climbing to his feet and tossing a rupee down on the counter.

"Will do. Get Randy."

Bertram cursed. He hadn't seen where Randy went. "Where—"

Bobby pointed at one of the upper floor rooms. "With that girl he keeps dragging us here to see."

"Christ."

"No, not really."

"I didn't even want to come here, damn it," Bertram muttered, mounting the stair. He wouldn't have, either, if the other men hadn't insisted. He only ended up drinking too much of what passed for wine here while the rest of them consorted with the prostitutes.

He was behaving foolishly, perhaps. Monique had never once said she was interested in him, so why should Bertram imagine her face tighten with disapproval? And now every time he even thought about hiring a woman to share his bed, it was Monique he saw, looking angry.

The guard who normally kept nonpaying customers off the second floor just nodded at Bertram as he headed downstairs to see for himself what the growing noise outside was about.

Bertram knocked, loud and long, on the door.

"What?"

"Trouble. Get your things. We're leaving."

"What?"

"Get your things. We are leaving."

Some muffled talk from the other side of the door, then footsteps. It swung wide to reveal a disheveled and shirtless Randy. "What's so damned important?"

"A riot in the streets that sounds like it's coming this way. The others sent me to get you while they ready the horses." Bertram avoided looking at the naked woman sitting up in bed.

Randy stepped past Bertram, looked over the rail and saw the empty common room. Bertram's report thus confirmed, he retreated into the bedroom and started stomping into his boots.

Once he had them on, Randy bent over the woman and, using remarkably passable Persian, said, "Trishna, I'll be back to see you soon."

She smiled, pulling him close to kiss him.

"Come on!" Bobby shouted from outside.

"Coming!" Randy and Bertram shouted in unison.

"Bertram, Catch."

Bertram turned back to face the younger man, barely getting his hands up in time to catch the pistol the up-timer tossed his direction. Catching it, Bertram led the way downstairs and out into the mid-afternoon sun.

Randy still hadn't got his shirt all the way on by the time their respective horses' reins were being slapped in their hands.

Ricky pointed at the brothel-owner, who was ordering his men to stand by the gate to his establishment and handing them big bamboo sticks. "He says some woman was murdered down by the river. Some of the Hindus are already tearing shit up, either looking for the killer or just getting their mad out."

"Which way do we go?" Bobby half-shouted. He had to, the noise was getting a lot closer.

"Away from the river, I think, and then to the nearest gate."

"Khan's Gate?"

"Yes!" Bertram said, struggling to control his horse. He smelled the smoke that spooked it a moment later.

Bobby let out a strange yip and yelled, "Let's ride, boys!"

Together they fled, Bobby and Ricky leading off. Randy—shirt tails flapping in the breeze—and Bertram brought up the rear. For the first time in Bertram's experience the streets of Agra were nearly empty. Bazaar vendors were the only people abroad, and even they were hurriedly putting up their wares.

"What was that weird noise Bobby made?"

"I think he was trying for a rebel yell."

"Are we rebelling?"

"Nope, just something out of westerns."

"Oh."

"You know, six guns and Indians."

"No, I don't know. Sounded to me like a choking hyena."

"Yeah, needs a lot of work before he embarrasses us all with it again."

"You know I can hear you, right?" Bobby said over his shoulder, face red.

They had to slow as they negotiated a turn, silencing them momentarily. The wall was much closer now.

"Yup, just like we were all forced to hear your strangled cat impression," Ricky quipped as they cleared the corner and picked up the pace again.

"C'mon, guys, how often do we get to shout famous lines from movies?"

Randy snorted. "You mean ruin 'em?"

"Aww, C'mon! Like you could do better, Randy!"

"Wouldn't even try, not if I had a voice like yours."

Bobby went an alarming shade of red while the others laughed.

"Right turn ahead, I think."

"Yeah, Khan Gate is just a few blocks over from there," Bertram agreed.

They again slowed to make a turn, but couldn't speed up once clear of it. Traffic had increased here, farther from the incident and closer to the choke point of the gate, forcing them to keep the horses at a walk.

Bertram looked over his shoulder and watched as word of the riot spread through the crowd in their wake like an angry wave.

"Heads up," Ricky said.

Bertram looked ahead, marked the distance they had to cover before reaching the gate, and cursed silently. Getting through the narrow gateway would quickly become problematic if the crowd panicked or, more likely, turned into an angry mob.

Looking above the crowd before the gate, he saw the guards watching.

One of them—a commander, from his fine robe—started giving orders.

"We need to *move*, gentlemen, things are about to get ugly."

"Can't go any faster, Bert, not without causing a panic."

He hated it when they called him that! As if everyone liked having their name truncated to some overly familiar diminutive. Bad enough they had all these short names that end in "Y." It made Bertram feel like he was reading lists in Spanish: Gordo y flaco, arroz y pollo, Bob y Rand y Rick y . . .

Focus, Bertram!

More guardsmen were forming up on the ramparts, bows in hand. They didn't look inclined to pick their targets, either.

"Shit," Randy said.

"Yeah."

"Got yours?" Ricky asked Bobby.

"I do."

Bertram opened his mouth to ask what they were on about and caught sight of the revolver in Bobby's hand.

"All right. Don't shoot unless—"

"Don't shoot at all!" Bertram hissed, "Even if it gets us out of here, it'll trigger a massacre!"

Ricky turned to look at him. "What do you want to do?"

"Keep pressing forward at the walk. I think we can make—"

Shouts, then screams came from the avenue they'd entered on.

Bertram looked over his shoulder, saw the crowd behind them shift from milling clumps of individuals into angry, opposing mobs, and saw the first weapons appear, the first stones cast.

"Fuck it! Ride!" Bobby shouted.

More sensitive to the rising atmosphere of violence than any human, his horse was already moving away from the threat when Bertram touched heels to its flanks.

The people between the gate and the mob started running in every direction. Some right into the path of the riders, only to be tossed aside.

Bertram glanced back in time to be hit, hard, in the shoulder. Bouncing from his shoulder, the rock clipped his lip. Surprised more than hurt, he swayed a bit in the saddle, making his mount swerve into Randy's path.

Though a relatively inexperienced rider, Randy was an excellent athlete in his prime. The young up-timer pulled his boot from the stirrup before Bertram and his horse collided with his own.

Bertram screamed as his leg absorbed the majority of the impact. He managed to keep his seat, barely, as they pounded through the gateway and free of the city.

They rode a few hundred yards free of the gate, Bertram grunting in pain with each jarring step.

"Guys, Bert's hurt."

"Stop calling me that!" Bertram yelled, cold sweat popping from every pore.

Randy's brows shot up. "What, Bert?"

"Yes! I am not some love interest of yours! Don't shorten my name like you want to whisper it in my ear!"

"Okay, Bertram. Just relax."

"I will not! Anger is the only thing keeping me in the saddle just now. God, this hurts!"

Randy glanced down.

"Don't even look at it!" Bertram snapped, worried the leg had been ripped free.

The up-timer held up his hands. "All right, Jesus! Just so you know, it doesn't look broken."

"Oh, so I'm being a—what is it you call it, a '*wimpie*'?"

All three of his companions laughed.

"What?" he barked.

Randy eventually wiped his eyes and said, between chuckles. "Wimp, not wimpie. And, no, no one's calling you a wimp, not after getting the mother of all charley horses."

"Would you please, *please*, speak like a normal person for once!"

More laughter.

Randy tried again after a while. "The injury you just took, when the meat of a thigh is pulled or hit by something heavy, we call it a charley horse. No one is going to say shit about how tough you are, not when they see the monster bruise you'll be sporting tomorrow."

"Oh."

"And you were right. Shooting our way out would have been stupid."

"Oh?"

"The guard commander, he held fire till we were out of the way, then had his men fire."

"Loose," Bertram corrected the up-timer without thinking. "You loose a bow, not fire—"

The mocking laughter of his friends didn't exactly make him feel any better, but joining it did take his mind off the throbbing of his leg.

Aurangzeb's camp, the Deccan

"Shahaji himself? Are you sure?"

"Yes, Shehzada. He was recognized by three men who served with him before," Mahabat Khan said.

"And was he taken captive or killed by these sowar who were so close they recognized him?"

"Sadly, no, Shehzada. The Marathas escaped into the hills by ways we did not know."

"And made off with a healthy quantity of our supplies in the process, I presume?" Aurangzeb asked, hiding his displeasure. The local frontier governor, Mahabat, had been asking his father for an army to expand the empire into the lands but lightly claimed since the death of Malik Ambar. When two armies were delivered, though under the command of royal princes, he had promptly decided to attach himself to Aurangzeb's force. He had proven an able subordinate, providing useful intelligence on the various factions at play, but his forces had yet to prove their worth.

To his credit, Mahabat did not flinch from the truth. "They destroyed more than they made off with, but essentially correct, Shehzada."

Aurangzeb struggled to keep his calm mask in place. The last month had proven difficult. It seemed as if a party of Maratha horsemen was hidden every few kos, avoiding contact with his main force and emerging only to harry and carve bleeding chunks out of his lines of communication and supply.

"The guns are safe?"

"Yes, Shehzada. This attack was directed against our food supplies."

"Something we can ill-afford. Already the men suffer."

"Yes, Shehzada. Willingly, Shehzada, for they know the rightness of your cause, and would punish these Shi'a and their Hindu lap-dogs."

Aurangzeb was glad Samarjit Khan was not there. His Rajput pride would surely be stung by this one's contempt.

The thought was stopped by the glimmer of an idea, smoldering in one corner of his mind. He let it be, fearful he would smother it by seizing on it too swiftly, and was rewarded with an even better idea.

He considered the gambit from several angles, decided it was worth trying, and said: "These men, the ones who know Shahaji on sight: I would to speak to them."

"Your will, Shehzada."

Aurangzeb spent the next little while stretching his idea, found it could encircle a great many useful things and possibly turn them to advantage.

"And send me my swiftest messenger, pen and ink."

"Your will, Shehzada."

Agra, Red Fort, Nur's Quarters

At first Nur Jahan wept for loss, then for pain, and finally she wept with a rage that burned so hot it dried all tears.

I will make him pay for this.

Overcoming joints grown stiff from too long spent kneeling

beside her oldest and best companion, Nur stood. Unsteadily, she turned and, for the last time, left Gargi's side.

She took two steps and stopped. Shockingly, the other ladies of the harem were arrayed in a half circle about her, ready to offer what solace they could.

Jahanara, sitting slightly forward of the rest, rose and joined her. "Nur, I am sorry for your loss. She was true to her salt, and served you well."

Nur, struggling to find her voice, hated having to look away before she could master it. "My thanks. You need not have stayed with me."

"And ignore your grief at the murder of one of our own harem servants? I could not do so."

Nur was too raw and exhausted to keep the suspicion off her face.

Jahanara tactfully ignored the look. "Father wished me to ask: do you know of anyone who would do this?"

"No," Nur lied. Her vengeance would be personal, and accomplished at her instigation, not the emperor's.

Jahanara nodded. It had to be the answer she had expected, after all. "Now the rioting has been put down, Father has launched a full investigation."

Nur nodded. "Good." She gestured at her ruined silks. "I must bathe and rest." And because she appreciated the form, if not the motive, of Jahanara's respectful presence: "I thank you for remaining with me while I was lost to grief."

Jahanara waved a dismissive hand. "I know you would do the same, had I lost Smidha."

Nur, unable to detect any irony in Jahanara's tone, marveled at how proficient her grandniece had become at concealing her true thoughts.

"Can Father's household offer you any assistance?"

"Again, my thanks, but no. I will bathe and rest now, and let the attendants..." she swallowed against the knot that formed in her throat, "see to Gargi."

"As you wish, Nur Jahan. We are," she gestured at the other ladies of the harem, "all of us, at your service should you desire it."

Nur nodded, which Roshanara must have taken for a desire for the offered help. The young princess rushed forward, murmuring condolences and taking her by the arm.

Nur allowed herself to be led to her bath, her thoughts grinding slow and hateful.

I told Gargi it was too soon to investigate Mohan, but she said we had to know. Oh, how I wish I had not relented! Just as I told her to be careful and take a guardian, but I let her refuse me.

Why, God, could you not have extended her your protection?

Roshanara kept up a constant stream of patter even as the slaves removed Nur's clothes and settled her into the bath. She lay back, concentrating on her breathing and nothing else.

Nur had almost succeeded when Roshanara said something that snagged at consciousness.

She opened her eyes, looked at the younger woman. "What was that?"

"What was what?" Roshanara asked.

"What did you just say?"

"Oh...I'm sorry, I didn't mean to upset you by bringing it up again, but I was just wondering aloud whether I should ask Mullah Mohan to help us find poor Gargi's murderer."

It took every ounce of the self control Nur had learned in three decades of harem politics to just settle back into the bath instead of clutching Roshanara in her hands, dragging her face to face and shaking the information out of her. When she was certain her voice would not betray her, she said, "Oh, I think you should."

"I don't know..." Roshanara gave a dismissive wave that was such a such close copy of her mother's and, more recently, Jahanara's manner, it sent chills running down Nur's spine. "Father won't be happy if he learns I am in communication with Mohan."

"Perhaps, but then your father may also be disposed to think more kindly of Mullah Mohan if presented with the information needed to capture the murderer. When he asks you the source, you can reveal Mohan's role, improving both your reputation and his."

"I hadn't thought of that." Nur let Roshanara ruminate, carefully reining in her desire to push, and was rewarded after a few minutes: "If you think it will help?"

"I think it might help both parties come to understanding, even if Mohan does not reveal the murderer."

"Then I shall write him this afternoon."

"I am sure he will be a great help. How soon do you think he can respond?"

"Tomorrow, though I doubt he will discover anything so quickly."

Still in Agra, then, just as Gargi thought. A fresh pang of loss stabbed her. She would need to set someone to follow her messengers.

She let Roshanara prattle for a while, the warm waters easing sore joints, if not her wounded heart.

Eventually, concerned she would nod off, Nur climbed from the bathing pool. "I am ready to retire, Roshanara. I thank you for your company. We should spend more time together."

"I would like that. I know Aurangzeb would, too." She leaned in close, whispered, "He told me to give you his regards."

Nur forced a smile through her surprise. "I see. Return mine to him, if you will."

"I will. Rest well, Nur Jahan."

Nur nodded as the princess left her quarters. So Aurangzeb had enlisted Roshanara to his side. She was not as able, perhaps, as her elder sister, but he was wise to make certain of as many ears at court as possible.

"Tara," she called.

Gargi's lieutenant appeared, bowed. "Yes, mistress?"

"You now have charge of my household. Your first act is to tell Vimal I require his presence."

"Yes, mistress." Tara bowed but lingered.

"What is it?"

"Permission to approach, mistress?"

Impatiently, Nur waved the woman forward.

Tara leaned close, the scent of Nur's own attar of roses strong on her person. She spoke quietly into Nur's ear, voice husky with suppressed rage: "Are we to avenge my mother, mistress?"

Nur, turning her head to meet Tara's gaze, angry eye to angry eye, said simply: "You may rely on it, Tara."

Chapter 37

Red Fort, Agra
December 1635

"*Ah, ici t'est, ma fille!*" Papa's use of their native French was planned, no doubt, to throw any listeners off.

"I have been here all year, Papa," Monique answered in the same language, marveling at how she missed using it.

He cast a reproving look her way. "No need for a piquant tongue so early in the morning."

"Really, Papa? Are you the one who's locked up?"

"No, but that's why I wanted to visit."

"Should I even hope for good news?"

He shook his head regretfully.

"You should know, I'm contemplating getting married just for a change of scenery."

He looked at her, eyes wild.

"A joke, Papa," she said, surprised at the intensity of his reaction.

"Not funny." He shook his head. "As to the news I have: I fear it could be better."

"Tell me, Papa. I'm a big girl."

"We were lucky that our construction site for Mission House survived the rioting relatively intact, but we're having trouble finding people to continue the work."

"Really? You don't have to lie, you can just tell me if you don't think it safe for us to live there..."

"There is that, as well, and it's a real issue I'll want to see addressed before we depart the emperor's direct protection. But the thing about the workers is true, and while the site survived intact, there was some damage and theft. Besides which, between the riots and the emperor's projects like the Taj, there's a dearth of labor for any project. Add to that the fear they might get beaten or harassed for having worked for Christians, and the labor market is even smaller."

"Beaten?"

"Things are very unstable. Religious animosity and intolerance is running high just now."

"That hasn't been my experience at court."

"That's just it: it's not the powerful at court instigating this, it's the common people settling scores across religious lines."

"I'm not questioning your conclusions, Papa, I'm merely saying the court isn't reflecting what's going on out there."

"Nobles are always inclined to their own self-interest."

Meaning they suppressed their religious bias in order to keep their position in the pecking order. Aloud, she said, "I'm not sure there isn't some real blindness going on as well."

"Blindness?"

"They're all so caught up in their own politicking," she waved at the limits of the enclosure, "they can't see what's going on just outside their walls."

"That may be so, but the court is still in control of the military and the treasury, and it doesn't look like Shah Jahan's grip is going to slip from either of those."

"I agree, but I think someone must be pulling strings among the commoners."

Gervais nodded, considering. "Mullah Mohan, the one who was stripped of his titles and booted from the court seems a likely suspect to me. Salim said he was a bit of a darling among the common Muslims."

"Anyone ask Salim what Mohan's up to now?"

"I haven't, no."

"Might be a good idea to ask, no?"

"Of course."

"And I'll ask Sahana and, if I get a private moment, Jahanara."

Papa cocked an eyebrow. "You talk a great deal of Jahanara and Nadira, but I rarely hear mention of Roshanara or Nur Jahan."

"Nur keeps to herself, mostly, though she's been around a lot more since her servant was killed."

"The one that touched off the riots, right?"

"Yes. As to Roshanara... To be honest, she's been rude and unpleasant to each of us."

Gervais glanced around.

She sighed again. "I know better than to say that where someone could overhear us, Papa."

"Still, it's always good to be careful."

"And I am."

"Any idea what motivates her attitudes toward you?"

"You mean beyond being a spoiled child in a woman's body?"

"My, I hadn't realized she'd made such an impression."

Monique ran fingers through her hair, considering her reactions. Was Roshanara really that bad?

No, not really...

Then what is it that irks me so about her?

She sighed. "Harem life, it infects me, too. I'm becoming petty and spiteful."

"You sure?"

"Well, to a degree. She *is* rude to everyone."

"And her motive?"

"Spoiled bitch too easy for your suspicious sensibilities, then?"

Papa just looked at her.

"All right. She seems as devout as the rest, but not in any way that makes her stand out, so I doubt she harbors some severe religious bias against us."

"And how is she around Nadira Begum?"

"Come to think of it, I haven't seen them together at all, except on formal occasions."

"And with Jahanara?"

"The... same, more or less. I don't think she can avoid Jahanara as easily, since she runs the show in the harem. Every time they are together, Roshanara seems eager to upstage Jahanara."

"Interesting."

"Yes."

"Keep talking, Papa. Actually saying things out loud is helping me work out exactly what my thoughts are, if you take my meaning?"

"Of course. It's like our old skull sessions while we planned a swindle..." He paused to take her hand. "*Ma chèrie*, I really am sorry about the living arrangements."

"Well, there's no cure for it but to put one foot before the other, so to speak."

The Deccan

Aurangzeb sat his horse and watched the clash between his mounted archers and those of the child-sultan of Ahmednagar.

Arrows flew, dust and blood spurted, men and horses fell, the screams taking a heartbeat to reach his position on the hill opposite.

Screaming must be the one universal of battle, he decided, whether the battle be between beasts of the field or men. The dull thud of one of the Ahmednagari cannons on the ridge overlooking the field punctuated the thought.

The cannonball bounced from the hard earth and caromed through a knot of Aurangzeb's horse, spraying blood and flesh over their compatriots, who, despite their losses, continued loosing arrows into the opposing cavalry.

"Shehzada, their guns have the superior position," Carvalho cautioned as another of the foe's guns belched dirty smoke and deadly round shot. "Unless your cavalry can clear that ridge, they will take any thrust up the valley under fire, breaking it."

Another cannon spoke.

Taking his eyes from the rising smoke and dust in front of the opposing guns, Aurangzeb glanced at the Portuguese mercenary. "I know."

"But—"

"I am aware, Carvalho." More men died under the guns. "Go to your men and prepare the oxen. You will be expected to occupy that ridge with your guns in one hour."

Returning his attention to the smoke and dust clouds blowing back across the ridge-line, Aurangzeb judged the time had come. He turned and nodded to one of the messengers held against this moment. The man rode off as if shot from one of the cannon, dirt spurting from beneath his horse's hooves.

He looked again at Carvalho, who had yet to leave.

The artillerist, clearly inclined to argue, snapped his mouth closed on meeting Aurangzeb's eye. He nodded, said, "Yes, Shehzada," and turned his horse back the way they'd come, down the hill and to his heavy guns.

Aurangzeb watched the man ride away. No horseman by Mughal standards, Carvalho was an accomplished artillerist and was able to tell, quite accurately, what cannon could do—both his and those of Ahmednagar. Of course, Ahmednagar had hired its own mercenary gunners. Probably men known to Carvalho himself.

When he was emperor, Aurangzeb meant to ensure they were not dependent on Europeans for such expertise. In fact, today he hoped to take the first steps to prove they could handle their own gunnery.

A bawling ruckus erupted from the left as Aurangzeb's camel corps moved forward behind the screen of horse archers. Most of the time, camels were disagreeable animals of limited use in the line of battle. While they could carry significantly greater loads and didn't require a fraction of the water horses did, they were also slower, harder to train properly, and tended to extreme obstinacy even when not panicked.

All of which Aurangzeb hoped he'd allowed for in his battle plan.

After a few minutes, some hundred of the camel riders on the flanks of the corps slowed and came to a stop. Dismounting, they made their camels kneel side-on to the Ahmednagari lines and aimed very long muskets across the backs of their mounts. They started firing at the enemy cavalry even as the central riders continued another twenty or thirty gaz closer, almost into the rear of Aurangzeb's mounted archers. Once there, they too dismounted and turned their camels side on, before making them kneel and hobbling them. Rather than muskets, they instead pulled back the leather covers on gaz-length, heavy brass pieces, pintle-mounted on the backs of their mounts.

Zamburak were by no means new, but Aurangzeb hoped deploying them as close as possible and under the covering fire of the marksmen on either flank, combined with the poor visibility caused by the dust of the earlier engagement would keep them alive long enough to fire en masse, maximizing the impact of the forty-eight small pieces against the dozen heavy guns the Bijapuri had on the ridge.

Aurangzeb nodded to his signaler, who passed the order. After a long, bloody time, the horsemen began to withdraw, many loosing a last arrow before galloping headlong toward Aurangzeb's lines.

In the dust and confusion left behind, the Ahmednagari could not see the zamburak. While they no doubt heard the gunfire when Aurangzeb's long-musket men started shooting, their fire only occasionally emptied a saddle.

Indeed, from their ululating cries, the Ahmednagari were beginning to celebrate their victory.

As soon as the majority of Aurangzeb's riders had cleared the lines of the zamburaks, the small field pieces fired in a long, rippling crash, each brass gun throwing one pound shot up the slope and into the dusty heart of the Ahmednagari lines.

Horses and men screamed as bodies and parts of bodies flew. Dust clouds rose and concealed the carnage. A lone horse galloped out of the dust, trailing the arm of its rider by the reins.

The thick, dirty-wool smoke of their firing blew uphill into their target's faces as the camel gunners leapt up and began reloading.

Aurangzeb stood in the saddle but couldn't see whether the Ahmednagari guns were out of action.

The dust and smoke slowly settled, revealing a low mound of ruined flesh, horses and men, in a shallow crescent just below the enemy guns.

Their screening cavalry was gone as an effective force.

He scanned the gun line, saw movement: a gun captain lowering the match to his piece. An instant later the cannon bellowed. The ball struck the ground ten paces before the camel corps and bounced once, twice, three times without striking a single one of Aurangzeb's sowar.

God is with us.

He gestured for two messengers, telling the first: "After the next volley, Mahabat Khan is to strike up the ridge and overrun the guns. Once he has made certain they are out of action, he is to assist Samarjit Khan's main assault, forming up on his left flank."

He turned to the other: "Samarjit Khan is to lead his Rajputs straight up the valley floor and at the enemy. I will take the right."

The faces of both messengers were stretched in feral grins as they salaamed, turned and put heels to horses.

Aurangzeb returned his attention to the field as the camel corps' musket men resumed firing. The zamburakchi were ramming shot home atop fresh-laid gunpowder charges.

Another enemy cannon belched fire and smoke, the large ball harmlessly burying itself in the ground a few gaz in front of the closest camel.

The fastest of the zamburakchi swiveled their pieces to bear on the enemy but waited at their guns. That was good. Aurangzeb had not known if they would manage to keep to this new discipline of massed shooting while under fire. It was much more devastating to the spirit of the enemy and better for accuracy, what with the breeze at their backs.

The last of the zamburakchi had his piece ready to fire just as the third of the Ahmednagari guns spoke. This time, Aurangzeb's forces were not so lucky; the ball crashed through two teams of men and camels before rolling the rest of the way down the slope.

The remaining massed zamburak fired in answer, devastating the enemy gunners. Starting with just one or two men, they quickly became a mob as they broke and fled their position.

"Praise God," Aurangzeb said, carefully concealing the unseemly satisfaction that flooded through him.

Now, God willing, Bijapur and Shah Shuja.

Red Fort, Agra

It required some planning, but Monique managed to arrange some time in which to be alone with Sahana. The girl was returning from her daily report to Diwan Firoz Khan, walking across the balcony when Monique called out to her in English. "Sahana, do you have a moment?"

"Of course, Monique." Sahana seemed to enjoy being on a first-name basis with the women of the mission, and Monique's name seemed to roll off her tongue with special relish.

Monique gestured at the cushion opposite her. "I have a question for you."

The young girl lowered herself onto the offered seat and looked at Monique with her lovely, bright eyes. "Yes, Monique?"

Lowering her voice, Monique asked, "What do you think of Roshanara Begum?"

"I do not know what you mean..." Sahana said, looking away.

And there is an answer in and of itself.

"Please, Sahana, I would have your thoughts. I will guard them like my own," she added, lowering her voice even further.

The young slave girl looked at the chess board for a long while. So long, in fact, that Monique opened her mouth to ask once more when Sahana cut her off: "It is very dangerous for me to speak so, but... Roshanara is not my mistress, and therefore I do her no disservice, only do as you ask by informing you of her reputation: Roshanara is not liked by her servants. Most especially those of us who are not Muslim."

"Why is that?"

"She looks for things to punish us for, sometimes even breaking things intentionally so that she can later blame servants... And, it is rumored among the slaves and servants that once, when Shah Jahan found her drunk, Roshanara blamed her body-slave for giving her the drink, claiming the girl had lied to her, that it was not wine Roshanara Begum drank, but some other elixir."

"With typical results for the slave, I presume?"

"Exactly so, Monique."

"Do you know of anyone she keeps in her confidence?"

"Not really, though she has been closest to Nur Jahan since Nur lost her servant, Gargi. They have taken to speaking regularly."

"Oh? Do you think they enjoy one another's company?"

"Well, I had it from Roshanara's chief of staff's servant that she believes Nur is just currying favor."

"And do you think that's the case?"

"Well, I do know one of Nur's eunuchs was made to follow one of Roshanara's."

"My, you seem well informed."

A shy smile transformed the pretty girl into a beauty. "I try. There is a boy," the girl's lovely dark skin turned even darker, "a stable hand, and I had the tale from him."

"I see... this stable hand is handsome, I hope?"

"Navin is of different caste than I, so it is impossible."

"But, are you not both slaves?"

"Of course, but our condition does not release us of our dharma, our caste."

God in heaven! Monique shook her head. To be that inured to caste and lot in life at such a young age! Every time she began to think she understood these people, someone said something that proved how little she truly did.

A tiny smile. "But regardless of how impossible it is, he is quite...comely."

Putting aside her misgivings, Monique returned the smile. Later, there might be time to understand some portion of the vast cultural variety that was India. For now...

"I'm sure he thinks the same of you."

"You do?" Sahana asked.

Monique looked at the girl, just on the cusp of becoming a young woman, and nodded quite seriously. "If he has any eyes to see, I'm certain of it!"

"You are too kind, Monique. Still, I hope you're right." She sighed, "Even though it is impossible."

"I don't know enough about caste to be able to advise you with wisdom, but surely the presence of the up-timers here, in this time, is a sign that change is universal."

"Perhaps," Sahana said, clearly giving the notion some thought. After a moment she shrugged and resumed speaking. "But you don't want to talk about my, what was it Priscilla said she had for Rodney when they were growing up?"

"A 'crush,' I think it was?"

"That's it! It does make the chest feel a bit like I imagine an elephant pressing one foot on it might."

Monique laughed, then laughed all the harder when Bertram's face, unbidden, appeared in her mind's eye, squeezing her own chest with a sudden rush of feeling. "Too true, Sahana."

"What, the bit about the elephant or my affection for Navin?"

"All of it..." Monique wiped a laughter-born tear from her eye, then said more seriously, "Do you know whether Nur's servant was successful in his mission?"

"I think so. Once he returned, Nur sent several messengers out."

"Oh? It seems you have had some lengthy talks with this stable hand."

Sahana smiled again. "Since your party has less and less need for my translation, I have had more free time...and since none of you will allow me to clean up after you or serve you in some other fashion, I *have* had time on my hands."

Monique, suitably chastened, bowed before that logic.

"So: Navin didn't know where they were headed, though he said two of the three were prepared for long rides. And, before you ask: one returned that very evening, but the others remain outstanding."

"A useful friend, this . . . Narvin?"

"Navin," Sahana corrected.

Monique grinned. "Got you."

The pillow Sahana threw at her did nothing to silence Monique's laughter.

Part Five

1636

The foamy billows rose and sank,
And dashed upon the trembling bank
Sea monsters of tremendous form

Chapter 38

Garden of the Taj
January 1636

Father and his entourage remained in the construction site, leaving Jahanara and the ladies of the harem to continue on into the nearly complete garden that stretched from the base of the tall plinth of Mother's mausoleum southward.

Jahanara could see the work crews at their tasks well above the temporary jali set up to preserve decorum. The Taj itself was nearly complete, with only the details of calligraphy and inlay to provide the fine finish. Soon the outer scaffolds would be removed, revealing the pearl white of Mother's final resting place.

Father wanted the principal construction completed in time for the fifth anniversary of Mother's death and the prayers that custom required be said over her on that day. To her eye, it looked as if he would have his wish.

Turning from the view, Jahanara took a deep breath, enjoying the smell of the fresh-turned earth and green growing things. The mixed orchards of young trees and plants that perfumed the air would eventually help provide for the upkeep of Mother's mausoleum, but for now the fresh plantings required great care and monitoring. As that was so, Jahanara had decided the women and servants of the harem would see to that care while Father visited the construction site.

The harem had spread out in the large expanse of garden, breaking into small groups to tend to one grove or another.

A smiling Monique joined her friends in the shade of one of the largest trees, basket in hand. Even the mission ladies seemed to be enjoying themselves. And who would not enjoy a cool, sun-filled day such as this? She smiled. In fact, aside from Roshanara's stubborn refusal to come, Jahanara didn't think she could be happier with the results of this day's outing.

Jahanara decided to join the mission women and started walking that way when a child's shrill scream sucked all pleasure from the moment, stopping her cold.

She turned and saw Roshanrai with one five-year-old fist full of her slightly younger half-sister's hair. Mother's youngest daughter, Guaharara, stepped in between her half-sisters, slapping at Roshanrai, who responded with an attempt to bury her free hand in Guaharara's belly.

Jahanara waved a hand. Smidha repeated the gesture, sending a squadron of royal nannies sweeping in to separate the princesses. One of the women yelped and staggered back, cradling her hand.

Smidha tutted. "Biting, again."

Jahanara suppressed a sigh. "Indeed." While all of his children shared Father's temper to some degree, Roshanrai had a mean streak. "Have her returned to Red Fort. She is not to have any sweets or allowed her entertainments for as long as it takes the nanny to heal—or next Friday, whichever happens last."

"Your will, Begum Sahib."

"Problems?" Priscilla asked, having approached while Jahanara was distracted.

Jahanara glanced at the up-timer to see the nod Priscilla directed at the nannies ushering Roshanrai away.

"Problems years in the making can rarely be fixed with a single afternoon, even one as pleasant as this." She sighed, watching a group of harem guards form up to escort the young royal back to Red Fort.

"That's for sure."

Jahanara returned her attention to her guest: "Do I detect a plaintive note?"

"I used to enjoy the occasional hunting trip back home, but that"—she gestured at the jali separating them from the rest of the world—"isn't going to happen here."

"They didn't invite you?"

"Why bother?"

"Because you want to go, of course!"

"But—"

Jahanara shook her head. "You seem confused: Nur hunts. I hunt. Many of the residents of the harem hunt. In fact, I have some quality trophies."

"What?"

"Purdah has its requirements, certainly; but we hunt, just as we ride."

"Well, that will teach me to think solely in terms of my own assumptions."

Jahanara sniffed. "Everyone of us falls victim to such errors on occasion. Shall I send a messenger? Have them come and collect you?"

Priscilla shrugged. "They said they were leaving this morning."

"That was the plan, but I happen to know that Dara wanted to finish relating the story of his recent adventure among the Sikhs first. He has engaged the services of an historian, and I can tell you from personal experience that Dara *always* wants to get his words just right before committing them to posterity."

"I, uh, see."

"Therefore, he's not likely to have finished before noon. Shall I send for them?"

"You wouldn't think me disrespectful? We all enjoy your company."

Jahanara waved Priscilla's weak protest aside. "Of course not. I know how eager you have been to get away from the confines of the harem."

"But—"

"I know because I feel the need to break from these confines as well, even if for the briefest while." She smiled and summoned another messenger. "So, let me do this for you."

Between Taj and Red Fort, Agra

They were just departing Red Fort when the second messenger from Father's harem arrived and delivered a message, this one under Father's personal seal.

Dara quickly read it and hid a satisfied smile.

Finally.

Waving the messenger away, he turned in the saddle to address Salim: "See, I told you this late start on our hunting trip was propitious, Salim! Father wishes to see you as soon as possible at Mother's mausoleum."

"Oh, Shehzada? Care to guess what he wishes of his humble servant?"

Dara smiled, shaking his head. "And risk denying him the pleasure of telling you himself? I think not."

"Very well. I will meet you back upon the road, if the emperor allows it."

"Oh, no, we're going to the Taj as well. It seems my sister is most irritated with me, as we neglected to invite the up-timer lady and her companions to hunt with us."

"What's that, Shehzada?" Rodney asked in passable, if horribly accented, Persian. He and John had been riding, if you could call it that, behind their mihmandar.

"Earlier this afternoon, Begum Sahib informed me, in no uncertain terms, that she is displeased with me. She insists we are missing a lady from our hunting party, namely your wife, Mr. Totman."

"Oh." The senior mission representatives gathered together, speaking in rapid-fire English.

"Have I your permission to ride ahead, Shehzada?" Salim asked.

"Of course. Won't do to keep Father waiting."

Salim bowed from the saddle and sped off.

"We are not upsetting the pear cart by bringing my wife with us, are we?" Rodney asked.

"Pear cart? I do not understand this idiom."

"Apple cart," Bertram corrected the up-timer's Persian. "He means to ask if this hunting with the ladies will cause conservatives at court undue distress, and therefore irritate the Sultan Al'Azam."

Dara smiled. "Oh, no, of course not. Purdah will have to be observed, of course, but it is actually quite common. My mother liked to hunt almost as much as Father. In fact"—he glanced around conspiratorially—"she claimed to be a better shot than he was."

He trailed off as he saw the group of riders approaching at a leisurely pace. "Ah, my youngest half-sister on her way back to the harem, where she is to be prevented from enjoying herself in any way."

"And what, pray tell, merits such punishment for a royal?" Gervais asked, appearing genuinely interested.

Dara smiled, "Jahanara reports she was very bad today—she bit one of her attendants."

Gervais grinned. "Good to see my daughter was not the only one to savage those set to watch her."

"Really?"

"Oh, yes. Nannies and whomever else she could sink those little teeth into."

Everyone chuckled at that, except for Bertram, whose expression seemed an odd mix of disbelief and delight.

Dara suspected that Bertram held some affection for his friend's daughter. He wondered why he hadn't asked for her hand? Surely Gervais would grant his permission?

Taj Mahal

As the gates of the garden had been secured with smooth-cheeked harem guards who watched his passing with suspicion, Salim turned his horse toward the river entrance. A multitude of horses nearly filled the narrow strip of land between tank and the river. Those belonged to all the guards, he supposed.

Salim dismounted and handed his reins to a waiting groom. Making his way around the tower that would, once completed, stand sentinel on the river's edge, he crossed the long, temporary causeway set up to aid in construction.

Recognizing the man in charge, he smiled and addressed the captain: "Peace, Javed."

"Peace, Salim."

He surrendered his weapons with the captain and was allowed entry.

Passing another pair of guards just inside the door, he climbed the stairs two at a time.

Five years ago, if anyone had told Salim he would be on a first name basis with the emperor's personal guard, he'd have laughed and asked the speaker how much opium they'd been smoking.

Then again, achieving a certain height was a necessary prerequisite to any fall, he reflected, walking the gallery to the interior flight of stairs.

He emerged into sunlight again on red sandstone, the white plinth to his right dazzling in the sun.

Eyes requiring a moment to adjust after the shadowed stair, he paused. Few men were visible, slowly removing the brick and wood scaffolding covering the towering white walls of the mausoleum atop the plinth. The site was quieter than he'd expected.

Salim walked around to the front of the plinth.

A group of eunuchs stood guard at the entrance to the garden, opposite the stairs inside the plinth. They watched him approach and turn right, climbing the stairs inside the plinth.

Wishing to avoid interrupting some craftsman's hard work and assuming the emperor would be outside, Salim walked around the far side of the mausoleum. A few more of the scaffold-men came into view but did not appear interested in talking to another of the palace's interlopers.

He came around the building to find Shah Jahan standing along the western edge of the plinth, looking to the west and the temporary gate erected there.

If he recalled correctly, that was the future site of the complex's mosque.

The emperor wore emerald silks that made him stand out like a jewel among the three other men behind him. Not that their clothing did not cost a small fortune—which reminded Salim, he needed to get another set of robes if he was to remain at court.

He examined the men, wondering who they were. Two of them had their turbans tied in the Muslim style, the third in Hindu fashion. The architect and overseers?

He stopped at a respectful distance.

Waiting for the emperor's attention, Salim realized a truth: This is the closest Shah Jahan ever got to being alone. The better part of his court, his servants, even his slaves remained at Red Fort while he paid his respects. No wonder he came here at every opportunity.

Salim did not have to wait long. The emperor rounded on one of the men with him and, in doing so, saw the amir.

Summoning Salim with a wave, Shah Jahan said something to the men with him.

The Hindu shook his head and raised his hands.

Shah Jahan said something more, got what appeared to be another denial in return.

Closing to within a few gaz, Salim made his obeisance.

"Make them stop," said Shah Jahan.

"Your will, Sultan Al'Azam," the overseer replied. The men did not speak to Salim as they crossed his path on their way to the front of the building.

The emperor nodded at Salim. "Amir. Good to see some of my subjects capable of performing their duties without constant supervision."

"I am sorry, Sultan Al'Azam?"

Shah Jahan waved at the backs of the men he'd sent into the building. "Those men were told that I want to review construction without men crawling all over the site, distracting me." He looked up at the monument to his wife. "To better assess how the work progresses, I need to see it without such, you understand."

"Yes, Sultan Al'Azam."

The men disappeared around the corner. A moment later, those working on the scaffolding retreated inside.

"You probably wonder why I summoned you."

"I serve at your pleasure, Sultan Al'Azam."

Shah Jahan turned to face him again, a wry grin twisting his beard. "You strike upon exactly the reason I summoned you. My son has petitioned me for leave to enlist you in his service. If that is your wish, I grant and affirm it."

"Thank you, Sultan Al'Azam. Before giving my answer, may I ask a question?"

Shah Jahan nodded.

"Who will you name as mihmandar to the up-timers after I leave your service?"

The emperor waggled his head. "You will continue to serve me in that office until such time as I grant Dara Shikoh full responsibility for dealing with them, in my name, of course."

Unhappy is the man who serves two masters. Concealing his misgivings, Salim bowed deeply. "Then I thank you for this opportunity to serve your son."

"Serve him as well as you have me, and I have no doubt you will be given rewards commensurate with that—" A strangled cry from the construction site cut across the emperor's speech.

He wheeled around and stalked angrily toward the entrance. "This is precisely why I don't want workers on site while I am here!"

There are to be no workers?

He's alone.

We are alone *up here.*

"Sultan Al'Azam?" Salim said, a few steps behind the angry emperor.

"Is it too much to ask that my orders be obeyed?"

Sudden fear lent Salim's feet wings.

Finding himself beside the emperor, he resisted the urge to grab Shah Jahan's arm and physically restrain him. "Sultan Al'Azam...forgive the question, but am I to understand that it is your standing order that no one but the overseer and architects should be on the site while you are here?"

"Yes! These fools—"

One of the architects emerged from the mausoleum, silks far darker than when he went in.

"Sultan Al'Azam!" Salim grabbed the emperor's arm, hauling him to a stop.

Shah Jahan's response to being touched was instantaneous and showed the man's fine martial training: half-turning toward him, the emperor grabbed the offending hand across the fingers and rolled it up and away, little finger first.

The painful move weakened Salim's grip and freed Shah Jahan's arm. "You dare—?" Shah Jahan began, reaching with his free hand for the dagger at his belt.

The architect staggered, then collapsed not five paces from them, exposing a back carved to bloody meat by cruel sword strokes.

Backing off, Salim raised his hands and pointed at the dead man, shouting: "Assassins, Sultan!"

He wasn't sure if it was his warning or the men boiling from the shadows of the mausoleum, but the emperor slid into a fighting stance and drew blades into both hands.

There were too many to fight, and they were too close to run without risking a blade in the back.

Cursing his lack of weapons and hoping Shah Jahan would use the time to good advantage, Salim bellowed "*assassins!*" as loud as he could and threw himself at the men who would kill his emperor.

He was on the first man in a few strides, ducking a cut meant to cleave his skull and putting his shoulder into the man's belly. They both went down. Rolling in a tangle of limbs, Salim clutched at the other's wrist with one hand while seeking at the man's waist for the dagger he'd seen there.

Dimly aware of the feet of other men running past them at the emperor, Salim strove to finish his opponent as quickly as possible.

White pain flashed as the assassin bit his right shoulder through the silks.

"Dog!" Salim grunted, questing fingers wrapping around the fist the assassin's hand made over the hilt of the dagger.

Heavier, and a bit stronger than his opponent, Salim used his advantages to the fullest: rolling over his opponent, Salim reared back and hammered his shoulder into the man's jaw. The strength in the man's arms went, allowing Salim to snatch the dagger free and shove it into the assassin's gut, sawing upward. Feeling the popping of organ meat as the blade carved innards, Salim sat up and quickly took his bearings.

Shah Jahan must have run several steps before turning to face his attackers, as he was now much closer to the entrance to the harem and backing slowly. A crescent of five swordsmen was trying to bring him down, but the emperor was keeping the assassins at bay with an impressive display of skill.

Others were closing on the emperor, but still more were running past, heading toward the stairs.

"Into the harem. Quickly! Kill him and get to the others!" someone shouted.

"You will not have my children!" Shah Jahan screamed, side-stepping one attack and bringing his sword across in an whistling arc that ended in a spatter of red on the other side of the legs of one of the men trying to run past.

The runner fell in two pieces.

They could not hope to survive this, so they hurried, hoping to swamp the emperor and the harem guards with numbers before dying themselves.

Salim collected the assassin's sword and surged to his feet. Stalking toward the men pressing Shah Jahan, he took one from behind with a crosscut that smoothly separated head from shoulders.

Blood from the corpse shot across the emperor's fine silks. Salim couldn't be sure, but he thought he saw a grim smile pulling Shah Jahan's beard.

Stepping over the corpse, Salim attacked the next man, clearing space to join the emperor in the center of the shrinking ring of blades.

The emperor kept weaving a flickering curtain, blades of Damascus steel the only thing between flesh and the questing blades of his attackers. Salim, knowing he had neither the quality of blades nor the training to equal the emperor, protected his ruler's back with grim resolve.

The failing of fanatics: lacking the greater skill at arms, they could not overcome Shah Jahan and Salim quickly. And so, uncertain they would succeed with a single rush, they delayed.

If they could but hold, the guards would reach them.

It was then he heard the emperor's labored breathing and finally felt the blood from his wound sliding down his arm.

If.

Garden of the Taj

Jahanara sat back, enjoying the cool air as she listened to Monique regale her and several others of the harem with an outrageous tale.

A shout drifted across the garden, the word lost in the distance.

Jahanara looked toward the Taj, saw the eunuchs stationed there turn and step through the partition to deal with the disturbance. She returned her attention to Monique, irritated she'd missed something that had the other women laughing.

"Shehzadi," Atisheh said, jogging up with a smiling Guaharara riding her shoulders, "get the children together. Get ready to move."

"What?"

Distant, discordant sounds reached Jahanara's ears.

Atisheh lifted Guaharara from her seat and pushed the five-year-old into Jahanara's arms, nodding toward the Taj. "Someone has raised the alarm. We sent a number of guards off with Roshanrai, so we do not have our usual complement. Get the children together. Stay calm. Get ready to fight. Trust no one."

"But, where are you going?" she asked, even as her ears identified the sounds: *Fighting? But—*

Oh, no! Father!

"To defend you, of course." Atisheh turned away. She hadn't made it three steps when one of the eunuchs reeled through the jali, bright blood on his face.

"Merciful God!" Jahanara prayed.

Atisheh drew steel and started to trot forward. Two of her tribe joined her, converging from the groups of harem inmates scattered through the garden.

Struggling for calm, Jahanara handed Guaharara off to Smidha. Monique's tale had died with the guard, and everyone was starting to look around. "Ladies, gather your children. Gather here. Quickly."

A band of armed men burst from the opening, bloody swords in hand.

Atisheh and her sisters charged.

Outside the Taj

"So what will we be hunting?" Rodney asked, fidgeting in the saddle.

Dara smiled. "Lion, tiger, blackbuck, anything else we can get."

"Tiger?" John asked.

"Yes."

Dara didn't miss John's pained expression. "What is it, John?"

"Nothing, Shehzada."

"Please, speak freely."

John shrugged and looked across at Angelo and Gervais. Speaking in English and trusting in their greater facility with Persian, he said: "I like hunting as much as the next hillbilly, but *when* we came from, tigers are an endangered species, hunted nearly to extinction."

Dara shook his head. "Really? They are a lethal threat in our lands, killing herdsmen, farmers, and taking their livestock."

Another shrug. "Hunt too much of anything and it will eventually die out, Shehzada."

"I cannot imagine us having such an effect on God's creation."

A nod in the direction of the massive building being erected on the shores of the river was John's only reply.

The entire party looked at the growing building that all of them knew would defy the destructive hand of nature for hundreds of years.

They proceeded in considered silence for some time.

"Where are Father's guards?" Dara asked. "They should be visible, even from here."

Bertram could see a few running along this side of base of the tall walls that rose from the riverside. He looked higher, a flash catching his eye... *steel in sunlight?*

"Shehzada! Someone is fighting up there!"

"I see it! Ride!" Dara put spurs to his horse.

The rest of the party rocked into a canter behind Dara, as his personal guard raced to overtake them.

Chapter 39

Garden of the Taj
January 1636

Two, three, then five, then eight, three more behind them issuing from the archway. The assassins kept coming. There were too many of them, and now they were past the choke point of the stair.

Atisheh drew comfort from her sisters as they pounded toward the foe: They had the advantage of being armored, at least.

"Kill these bitches and find Satan's whore!"

The men spread out before them, trying to get around the armed women and at those unable to defend themselves.

They charged into their midst; she-lions among jackals.

One turned to face her. Expression a hateful mask, he attacked. Atisheh swayed a hair's breadth out of the assassin's reach and countered. Her blade slipped past the man's guard, his defense sending her blade-tip low and between his legs.

He gave a frightened hop to avoid being made a eunuch.

She rolled her wrist to put the edge up. Pushing the tip out and away from her body, Atisheh turned full circle, loading weight on her lead leg to drop beneath another enthusiastic attempt to take her head.

She felt the drag along edge that told her she'd cut across the soft flesh of the man's inner thigh even before he started shrieking louder than Nadira's child.

He clutched at the bloody wound, dropping his guard.

Her left-hand blade took him in the ear, ending the wailing.

Pulling it free, she stepped past the corpse that had yet to fall.

Atisheh found another assassin, met him blade to blade, let the first shock roll through her and into the ground, turning his blade out and away. She moved the left-hand blade in a counter.

Faster, he threw a punch at her face.

Atisheh lowered her chin, taking the blow on her forehead. Stars exploded as she heard knuckles break. She staggered.

Made of sterner stuff than the first assassin, this one ignored his hand and attacked again. Her defense was slow, his blade sliding inside her guard and grating against the mail covering her arm.

She recovered her stance, raised her sword in line with his eyes.

Injured hand curled at his gut, the assassin growled and launched a series of fast attacks which she managed, barely, to keep from finding her again.

"Time to die, woman!" he snarled, slapping her blade aside.

A ululating Gulruhk charged him from the side, blade in both hands, hammering at him.

Together they made short work of the fanatic.

Searching out the next threat, Atisheh glanced around in time to see Umida go down, clutching one assassin to her like a lover, sawing with the dagger she'd lodged in his back while another man hacked at her.

Atisheh looked at Gulruhk.

Panting, her sister nodded.

They charged together.

The River Entrance of the Taj

Another of Father's guards reeled out of the opening, an arrow high in his chest. Pulling his man out of the line of fire and into the shelter beside the door, Javed screamed in angry frustration.

Mastering his temper, the captain of guards set about exhorting his remaining men to make another attempt.

Hoping the man would take notice of him but unwilling to press, Dara pulled at his beard in helpless frustration.

John looked at him, one brow cocked.

Dara gestured at the guard captain, spoke quietly and as

calmly as he could: "He might be forgiven for seeing my presence here as a sign I am the source of this attack."

"Your own father?" John blurted.

The up-timer's loud question attracted Javed's attention. Unwilling to speak, Dara simply nodded in answer.

Javed rushed to his side and bowed anxiously. "Shehzada, they have the top of the stair. We cannot force the passage!"

"Where are the rest of your men?"

"I sent a party around the other side but the harem guards refused them entry. The guard said there were sounds of fighting within, but the eunuchs still refused them entry on the grounds that whatever the conflict, we guardsmen have no right to see the emperor's women."

"And Father is not in the garden, he's . . ." he trailed off.

"Up there. Yes."

Wishing Salim present, Dara looked past the up-timers at his own guard. They would fare no better. "And you can't force your way through?"

Javed's eyes filled with tears of frustration, "God help me, no, Shehzada. At least, not until they run out of arrows. They have set rubble on the floor and erected barricades at the top of the stair." He pointed at the screened-in gallery, midway up the wall of red sandstone that rose from the riverside.

This was even worse than Ramdaspur. How many times must Dara suffer defeats before he learned whatever lesson God would have him apprehend?

"What kind of barricades?" John asked.

Javed cast an irritated glance at the up-timer, opened his mouth to reply.

Dara cut him off: "Answer the question."

The guard captain looked at Dara, back at John. "Bricks from the scaffolds."

"Let me take a look, Shehzada?"

Dara, wondering at the man's aim, waved him to it.

Gervais stepped into the space John departed, waited only a moment before blurting: "My daughter, is she safe?"

The question made Dara's heart freeze. *Nadira! My sisters!*

"Quickly, Javed: were the sounds of fighting coming from the harem enclosure or only up there?"

"I only heard it from up there, Shehzada. I had no report of whether there was fighting inside the harem. I shall send some-one immediately..."

"But they will likely be turned away, just as your earlier effort was."

"Gervais and I will go. They know we're some kind of doc-tors, and can help," Rodney said, a desperate edge to his voice.

"And leave me behind?" Bertram asked, eyes mad with unspo-ken threat.

"I wasn't saying that, Bert."

"Stop shortening my damn name!"

John returned. Praying he would make it quickly, Dara saw the painful decision and the cost to the up-timer's heart of making it.

John spat and turned back to his companions. "Rodney: the boys and I will handle this here. You go see to the ladies with Bertram and Gervais." He turned back to Dara. "With your permission, Shehzada?"

"Permission?"

"To kill those shits up there, and any other that might stand in the way of all of us being certain our families are safe."

Dara smiled, "Permission granted, if you will suffer me to stand with you?"

"Of course." John turned to his fellow up-timers. "Boys, get the guns."

Taj Mahal

Salim sucked in another breath, the shallow cut across his chest burning.

"Die, heretic!" one of the men screeched, lunging.

Too tired to thank God for the man's stupidity in announcing his attack, Salim merely grunted, steel skirling as he turned the blade aside and sent his attacker reeling into the path of another with a hard shove.

"My children!" Shah Jahan rasped.

"I know." Salim flicked a slash at another fellow who looked ready to charge.

"How close"—the emperor was interrupted by the clash of steel on steel, then resumed—"are the stairs?"

Salim looked. They had moved closer during the fight, and

were but ten paces from one of the staircases that pierced the plinth and opened into the garden below.

It might as well be a kos, though, he thought, fending off another attack.

"Ten, maybe twelve, steps."

"Save"—another clash, grunt—"my"—he felt rather than saw the emperor step away as he cut at someone and returned. "—children, Salim."

"I will not leave you to die."

"Already going to."

"*What*?" he said, half-turning.

An assassin made him pay for his distraction, adding another cut to those he'd already taken.

"Gut. First few exchanges."

Salim lashed out, pressing his opponents hard before falling back again. He used the brief respite to look at the emperor: Shah Jahan's fine silks were no longer emerald, but black with blood from hip to ankle.

"The up-timers can —"

"No. Go."

"Your guards. They could—"

"Cannot save them *and* me."

"Sultan . . ."

"*GO!*"

Still Salim hesitated.

Shah Jahan gave him no time to formulate another argument. He stormed forward, taking two of his tormentors down in as many steps. His rush continued, staggering now, sword slowing, but still drawing the killers to him.

Torn between command and conviction, Salim nearly had his sword knocked from his hand.

Fugue broken, he lashed out. The thoughtless blow found its mark, half-severing his opponent's wrist. He ran past while the man dropped his sword to clutch at torn flesh, making the stairs in eight strides.

Corpses littered the stairs, their life-blood slick beneath his feet.

Gunfire erupted. The noise made him flinch, miss a step, and sent him sliding down three stairs in a barely controlled fall.

He stopped at the foot of the stairs.

Too fast for fewer than twenty guns. He grinned, mad hope

seizing him: *The up-timers! With such weight of fire, they may yet reach Shah Jahan.*

Steel on steel and cries in the garden reached his ears.

Would God extend such a hope where none exists?

Reassured that he did the right and proper thing in following Shah Jahan's command, Salim ran off the sandstone court and down into the garden.

Garden of the Taj

Smidha found her among the cypress. The sweating Hindu gave a barely adequate nod before launching into her message: "Nur Jahan, Begum Sahib asks that you join her and the other ladies of the harem until this disorder is ended."

"Am I an antelope, forced to hide in a frightened herd by jackals?"

"No."

"No. I am Nur Jahan, wife to one emperor, mother to another, and I will not hide while danger lurks."

Face twisted in anger, Smidha tossed her head. "As you wish."

"Just as I led the charge to free my husband, so I will not shy from whatever this day brings."

Smidha left, her haste unseemly in one so old.

Beside her, Tara sniffed.

Nur turned to her. "You have them?"

Tara nodded, showing the circlets.

She pointed to a place between two trees to one side. "Wait there. Be ready."

Two men emerged from the trees opposite her, swords clutched in bloody fists.

"I saw an old one come this way. She might be the one the mullah wants dead," one said, peering into the shade. And so, from their lips, the architect of this insanity: *Mohan*. He persisted in using blunt instruments where a fine blade was required.

Knowing he would see her before long and detesting the idea that *she* should hide from the likes of *them*, Nur stepped from the shade and smiled demurely at the assassins.

Because Tara might want certainty to aid in the thing, she addressed the men: "So touching of Mullah Mohan, to think this dried up thing worthy of his rupees."

Startled, both men nearly jumped out of their skins.

Her bitter laughter made them snarl and clutch their blades the tighter.

Come closer, now, this mongoose desires an end to the hissing of snakes. Nur held her arms out at her sides as if in welcome.

Reassured by her lack of weapons, they approached.

Tara's hurled chakram caught the light as it spun across the garden. By luck or skill the steel ring slashed across one man's neck, severing windpipe and arteries.

"Godhhhch!" the man murmured, blood drowning whatever his last words might have been.

The other turned to face the threat. Another of the spinning steel rings struck him high in his inner thigh before sticking in the earth.

He bit back a scream. Using his sword as a cane, he lurched toward Tara.

Spinning her last chakram on her forefingers, Tara launched it at the assassin.

The sharpened steel ring tore his other thigh, bouncing from the bone and away.

He fell, screams an assault on the ear.

She walked the ground between the dead and the dying, and bent to pick up the first man's sword. It required three steps to reach the screaming man, then a slight effort to raise the sword. The blade flashed brightly as she brought it down, bringing mercy to her ears and blood to water the dry earth.

River Entrance of the Taj

"Randy, load slug."

The young man rapidly cycled the action on his Remington, ejecting the buckshot shells. "You bet, John."

"You and Ricky set up on the right side." Left-handed, he would be most comfortable shooting from the right side of the opening. "When Bobby and I start in with the buckshot, you pick your targets and put 'em down."

All the young men nodded as Randy ratcheted six heavy shells into his gun.

"Once I start up, follow me. Watch for ricochets. Don't take any unnecessary risks." He took a deep breath, slowly let it out. "Get going."

A few minutes later they were set up: Dara and the emperor's guard captain at the head of a line of men behind Bobby.

"Ready when you are, John."

John looked around the corner and up. While he couldn't quite ignore the corpses littering the stairs, he still made out two men crouching behind a low barricade of bricks, composite bows in hand.

One of the men at the barricade raised his bow, but John pulled back before he could loose.

John held up two fingers.

Bobby and then Randy nodded.

He took a long step away from the wall before turning around and kneeling.

Bobby, half-facing the wall, slid over to stand in his place.

John brought the shotgun to his shoulder, leaned sideways, covered the target with the bead, and pulled the trigger. The stock punched his shoulder as he sent nine .32 pellets up the stair.

Bobby's shot hammered his ears a moment later.

He pumped, the emptied shell flying, and settled the bead again as Randy's slug thundered.

The man he'd been shooting at reeled back.

John pulled the trigger again, just to be sure.

The man fell out of view.

With a conscious effort, John scanned across for another target.

The other man was slumped face down over the barricade.

Another man appeared behind the first two.

John fired, Bobby and Randy a split second later.

The man's head and upper chest didn't so much explode as dissolve under the impact of the 12-gauge slug and the lion's share of buckshot sent his way.

Three pumps worked in near-unison, spent casings pocking on the flagstones.

John closed his eyes. *Gonna have that shit in my head as long as I live.*

The thunder of Randy and Bobby's guns pried John's eyes open.

A fourth man must have appeared while his comrade fell, because another corpse was sliding down the steps.

Silence settled as the man's slide came to a halt a few steps short of the bottom.

"Cease fire!" John shouted, surging to his feet and mounting the stairs. Slipping twice on things that didn't belong under foot, he made it halfway up before someone got up the nerve to step into view.

John didn't get the shotgun couched in his shoulder before firing. The stock punched him viciously in the collarbone for it even as the redoubled roar created by the close stone walls jabbed needles in his ears. Worse yet, John's haste made for a miss: chips flew from the bricks at the fellow's knees.

The fellow shouted, leaping up.

Ignoring the pain, John seated the gun properly, cycled the pump and fired again.

The man fell back out of view.

A hand grabbed his shoulder, making John start. A sweating Randy stepped past, gun up, *seated properly*, and ready.

Shaking, John continued after, Dara and the rest of the men a flood behind.

It wasn't until he got to the top of the stair and stood among the corpses that he thought to reload. The stair opened in the middle of a corridor, the sun-dappled river visible through the jali.

"Stairs at either end," Dara said.

Deciding on the left-hand stair, John and Randy led the way. As they rounded the corner John was almost skewered by an arrow.

Randy grunted beside him. There was a clatter.

"Shit!" John shouted. Scrambling to safety around the corner, he realized Randy wasn't with him.

John turned.

Randy lay against the wall, an arrow through his chest and shotgun on the floor.

He wasn't moving, not even to breathe.

"Jesus H. Christ!" he screamed, kicking the wall in frustration.

The pain brought him back, made him think through the hurt: "Bobby, Ricky: pull him in while I cover you. Then we'll dig these ticks out."

Tears made aiming difficult, but he managed to cover the boys as they collected Randy.

West, Temporary Gate

Gunshots floated in the air as they left their horses.

A lone eunuch stood in the gateway that would be a mosque once the complex was completed, but was currently being used to bring building materials into the site.

"Hear me! You cannot enter!" the eunuch shouted as they approached.

"No, you listen to me: I'm about ready to tear your fucking arms off and beat you with them," Rodney said. While he used English, his tone and mallet-sized fists certainly carried his meaning across the language barrier, as the eunuch clutched his weapon tight in one fist.

Gervais held up a hand to forestall Rodney carrying out his threat, and said in Persian: "I understand that you are alone, left here while your comrades enter and put down the disturbance, but we must be granted entry. You see, you may have heard that we are up-time doctors, skilled in healing. So you must allow us entry in order to treat the wounded inside. If you do not, imagine the Sultan Al'Azam's wrath when he learns you prevented us aiding his children in their time of need."

More gunplay, followed by a scream, floated in the air.

The eunuch's round shoulders slumped. "Merciful God, do as you must." He stepped aside. "I am surely dead anyway, killed for the failures of others. What's one more thing to take the blame for?"

The party rushed through the gate, following the clash of blades and screams.

They ran along a wide stretch of red sandstone, temporary jalis erected some distance to their right, the tops of trees visible above the screens, and the raised plinth foundation of the Taj directly ahead.

"The stairs up to the top of the plinth are around to the right," Gervais panted, struggling to remember the layout from the mock-up in Shah Jahan's quarters. "The entrance to the harem will be there as well."

"More damn eunuchs?" Rodney grunted.

"We'll at least learn from them whether the women—" Gervais stopped speaking as the wreckage—human and otherwise—came into view at the garden entrance.

"Pris!" Rodney screamed, sprinting now.

Putting his head down, Bertram managed to lose only a little distance on the big up-timer while Gervais lagged behind.

Garden of the Taj

Jahanara, Priscilla, and Ilsa stood between the women and children of the harem and three bloody-handed killers, the only weapons among the ladies a few branches and a knife more suited to carving lamb than combat.

Monique appeared beside her, a brick in hand.

All three of the assassins came to a halt, half-mad eyes drinking in the forbidden sight of another man's women.

Jahanara twitched the silken scarf from her shoulders, revealing more flesh and drawing their eyes to her. She would die before they touched the children. Die before they defiled any of Father's wives.

A rattle of gunfire drove them all from the stillness of the moment.

"We want only the witch, Nur Jahan. Give her to us and the rest of you will not be harmed, I swear it!" the shortest of the men shouted.

Jahanara shook her head in confusion.

He mistook the gesture for denial, stepped forward and made his sword cut the air. "I have no wish to kill women and babes. Give us the witch and the rest of you can go on living."

They have no idea what she looks like.

"She is not here," she said. Truthfully, Smidha having reported Nur's refusal to join them just moments before.

He pointed his sword at her. "Lying bitch! We saw the old woman come this way."

Jahanara drew herself up to her full height, hissed: "I am no liar. I am no bitch. I am Jahanara, daughter of Shah Jahan and Mumtaz Mahal, daughter of emperors reaching back to the mighty Timur, and I am here to pay the proper respects to my mother, you filthy pig!"

"I see her there behind you, lying bitch!" he repeated, sword point moving to point over her left shoulder at Smidha.

A blood-covered Atisheh limped into view some distance behind the men.

She looked away from hope and met the man's eyes. Forcing laughter from a throat made tight with fear, she mocked him: "You name my servant a former empress?"

Trying to keep their attention, she breathed deeply enough to strain her silks and half-turned, presenting her profile. "What think you, Smidha? Should Nur Jahan relinquish her former titles to you, my servant?" she asked, voice heavy with every bit of contempt she could muster.

Smidha sniffed. "I think not, mistress."

Close enough, Atisheh started her charge.

"Nor I."

"Lying, filthy-minded whore!" the man shrieked, advancing.

Chapter 40

Garden of the Taj

"Again with the whore-calling!" Atisheh grunted, bringing her blade down on the short bastard's back just as he started his charge. The powerful, if clumsy, blow severed several ribs where they joined the spine. The man fell face down at her feet, writhing in silent agony.

For her part, Atisheh stumbled to a halt, blood loss and pain drawing the color from the world.

She blinked stupidly, saw his companions turn to face her.

"Good," she mumbled. Raising her blade one more time.

The blonde ferenghi reacted with admirable speed, charging one man from behind, finger-thick branch in hand.

Atisheh staggered toward the other man.

Their blades rang together.

Exhaustion drained her sword arm of strength, made her slow to counter. His second blow cut across her lowered guard and into her chest, shattering mail links and biting flesh beneath.

Dropping her sword, Atisheh closed hands around his wrist.

Yanking him off balance, she bit at him.

Mouth full of beard instead of the flesh she desired, she fell, dragging him with her.

"Bitch!" he grunted, struggling to get his hand free and keep on top of her.

She held on.

The face that appeared over his shoulder made Atisheh smile.

The blood of her enemies spattered her face, a warm and welcome rain.

Garden of the Taj

"Lying, filthy-minded whore!" someone shouted off to Salim's right. He ran in that direction.

A few ragged breaths later Salim broke from cover to see a beauty in silks straddling a man's back. Her left hand was in his hair, pulling his head back. Beneath them both lay the still, bloody form of another.

A few steps away, a blonde woman and another, possibly up-timer woman, were attacking another assassin with sticks.

"Die, filth!" the beauty screamed. Salim looked back in time to see her cut the man's throat.

Legs leaden, he moved to join the assault on the last assassin. He made it all of two steps when someone to his right bellowed: *"Down!"*

Salim threw himself flat.

Chapter 41

The Taj

Dara's men charged past John as they emerged into the sun.

Trying not to think about Ilsa, Randy, or the dead at his feet, John looked around. The stair came up through one corner of a broad expanse of red sandstone. Just to his front right was the corner of the platform that formed the base of the mausoleum.

"Around front. To the stairs!" Dara called, pointing with his sword. His men formed up around their prince and moved out.

"Reload if you haven't already," John said, moving to follow. He heard someone reloading, shaking hands making a chore of it.

They rounded the corner of the plinth without incident and charged toward the stairs.

"Damn them!" Dara cried, coming to a halt near the stairs.

Catching up, John saw the ruins of the jali that protected the garden from prying eyes and the dead men littering the ground.

"They are in the garden with the women, my wife among them!"

John looked at the prince, hoping for an order.

"Die, apostate!" someone shrieked above. An instant later a brick crashed into Dara's head, driving him from view. Those of his guards who carried shields raised them overhead, trying to protect him from any additional missiles.

"Shit!" John yelled again. He was still raising his shotgun when one of the boys fired.

The man who'd thrown the brick fell from the plinth.

Silence descended.

"Dara?" John called.

Dara Shikoh, Prince of Mughals, shoved his men aside and stood. Blood streaming from a cut over his eye and unsteady on his feet, he pointed with his blade: "Kill them! Kill them all!"

Growling, they charged up the stairs en masse. John followed the blood-maddened prince without conscious thought. Together they stampeded through two assassins trying to hold the stairs, hacking them to pieces, then three more at the entrance to the mausoleum, only to come to a staggering halt beneath the half-completed entrance.

Dara's men moaned.

John edged through the bodyguards, came upon Dara Shikoh kneeling before his father.

The Ruler of the World lay among the corpses of four men. His sword arm was missing below the elbow, as if he had flung it up in a last defense of life.

"Father," Dara choked.

Impossibly, Shah Jahan's eyelids fluttered open. "Dara."

"Father?"

His gaze wandered, his words were slow, but Shah Jahan made himself understood: "Let...me...with...her...all time..."

Dara bent, struggled with his father's limp weight.

Tears leaving fresh trails in the blood on his face, Dara Shikoh carried his father into his mother's tomb.

John turned, pushed his way through Dara's guards, "Boys?"

"Here," they chorused.

They met him at the top of the stairs.

"Going to get my wife and avenge Randy, boys."

"Damn straight."

The distinctive, mechanical shick-shack sound of the pump action of a Remington 870 was Ricky's only answer.

A single shot rang from the depths of the garden.

John started running.

Garden of the Taj

Monique threw her brick at the man Priscilla and Ilsa were try-ing to brain, but came up short. She reached down in search of another missile, but Guaharara, her face a study in calm, dropped another brick into her hand.

"Kill the bad men," the little princess commanded.

"Yes, Shehzadi."

"Down!" someone bellowed off to the right.

She needed an instant to translate the word and therefore remained standing while Ilsa and Priscilla threw themselves flat.

A gun barked, shot taking the assassin square in the chest, dropping him in a bloody heap.

"You all right, baby?" Rodney panted, still-smoking weapon up and ready still.

"God, Rodney!"

Bertram burst from cover behind Rodney.

Monique felt such a rush of relief at the sight of him she could barely think.

"You all right, baby?" Rodney asked again.

"Yes, I'm all right. Atisheh's hurt, though!" she said, moving toward the woman.

"There more?" Rodney asked, clearly reluctant to put up his weapon.

"I—I don't think so."

"I doubt any remain in the garden," Salim agreed, slowly standing up.

He reached down and helped Jahanara off the man she'd killed. She overbalanced, came to rest against him, cheek and a delicate hand on his muscled chest. One of his bloody hands automatically found the small of her back, steadying her.

Priscilla shook her head. "Well, if that ain't a cover from one of my lust in the afternoon books, I've never seen one."

The Afghan cocked his head, clearly wondering what the up-timer meant. "Where is Begum Sahib? Is she hurt?"

"I am well, my amir," Jahanara sighed, making no attempt to pull away from him despite his bloody state.

His swallow was audible even from where she stood.

Gervais stumbled up, breathing hard.

Monique ran to him, managing to grab both him and Bertram in a tearful hug.

"Gervais, a little help here!" Rodney shouted, throwing the assassin off Atisheh with one hand. "She's still breathing."

"Save her and you will have your weight of silver," Jahanara declared without removing her head from an increasingly pale Salim's shoulder.

Gervais pulled out of Monique's arms and dropped his bag next to Atisheh. "I'll take his weight of silver, if you don't mind, Shehzadi."

"Both of you, then. Only save her."

"Begum Sahib, I—" Salim swayed, eyes rolling back in his head. He slumped to the ground. Jahanara managed to slow his fall, ended up kneeling on the ground beside him.

Bertram and Monique moved as one, rushing to Salim's side.

"He's lost a lot of blood," Bertram said, inspecting Salim's unconscious form with his hands, as they'd been taught.

"Call out his hurts so Rodney and Priscilla can advise," Gervais said, helping Pris and Rodney remove Atisheh's armor.

Bertram nodded and read out Salim's injuries: "One: shallow cut, not too deep. Chest to shoulder. Two: back of shoulder and down to midriff, shallow. Three: left wrist to elbow, no bone showing, but deep. Nothing else other than . . . abrasions. No obvious broken bones."

"Get sewing."

"Don't we need to clean the wounds first?" Monique asked.

Smidha appeared at her side, a needle threaded with barely visible silk in her hands. She handed the needle to Monique.

"Clean what you can, but stop the bleeding first. We'll worry about infection later. We've got bigger issues here," Priscilla said, hands busy with Atisheh.

"Sewing was never my strong suit," Monique muttered.

Gervais snorted. "No better time than the present to improve your skills."

Garden of the Taj

Nur held still as a group of harem guards pounded past their position, considering her next move. She was sure she'd spied Omid among the guards at the west gate when they entered the garden.

The guards disappeared up the stairs of the plinth.

"We're leaving," Nur said, setting out for the west gate.

"But they wanted you dead, surely the emperor can't blame you," Tara observed, following after.

Nur pointed up at the plinth. "From the wailing up there, the emperor is likely dead. If that is so, I have two reasons for leaving. First: if Mullah Mohan was taken today, or if he *is* taken, the new emperor will spare no effort in making him reveal any confederates. Mohan will almost certainly reveal my previous association with him, if for no other reason than revenge."

"Dara Shikoh will ascend the throne, then?"

"For now, yes."

"Shah Shuja and Aurangzeb will contend with him for the throne, then?"

Nur stopped, turned to look at Tara.

"Sorry, that was a stupid question. Your second reason?"

"Later." Nur resumed walking. "For now, we need to get into Agra, and meet with a particular horse-trader . . ."

"And for that we need to get past the guards," Tara said, gesturing at the gate they had just come into sight of.

"Shouldn't be a problem if, as I suspect, they left Omid behind . . ." Cursing aged eyes, Nur squinted at the lone figure standing in the gateway.

"Who, mistress?"

"A harem guard named Omid. Gargi suborned him some time ago."

"Why should he be left behind when the others moved on?"

"Because I would have it so."

It was Tara's turn to stop. "But how did you know this was going to happen?"

Still unsure if the lone guard was Omid, Nur decided not to admit her frailty and ask, instead walking from cover. As much to calm her own nerves as answer the constant questions, she answered: "I did not, exactly. I merely commanded him to remain at his post if ever there was a disturbance while he was on guard duty and the rest of them left."

"Stop!" the eunuch ordered.

Nur pulled her scarf up and smiled behind it, quickening her pace. "Be silent, Omid, and fetch us mounts."

"Nur Jahan!"

"Be silent, I said! Fetch three horses and be quick about it!"

"Yes, mistress," the eunuch said, cowed.

"So, after we meet your horse-trader, where do we go?" Tara asked, watching Omid leave.

Knowing Tara lacked the training and experience of her predecessor, Nur humored her with an answer: "The Deccan and Aurangzeb's camp. He will want an eye-witness who can justify taking up arms against his siblings."

"But what did you see, aside from the attack on your own person?"

Nur sighed. "Whatever will best support his position, of course."

Tomb of Mumtaz Mahal

"No. No. No," Jahanara could only say the word over and over despite each denial failing to change reality. A fact. Truth. Hard reality like that of the cold marble beneath her knees, outstretched arms, against her tearful cheek.

A workman's lamp guttered, eventually expired, and the increased darkness making her see threats among the shadows. The fear drew Jahanara from her fugue, made her look around for the first time in at least an hour.

Dara was inconsolable. He knelt at Father's side, wracked with silent sobs.

Blinking away her own fresh tears, Jahanara looked over her shoulder at the entrance to the tomb. Guaharara and her nannies were there, as was Nadira, holding a surprisingly quiet Suleiman in her arms.

Only Smidha met her eye. Met her eye and signaled with her hand: *Danger.*

Jahanara stood. Feet tingling with lingering numbness, she approached Smidha.

Her old servant and confidant bowed her head.

"What is it?" The question hard to force from a raw throat.

"Forgive me, Shehzadhi, but we can ill afford this right now."

Jahanara felt her lip curl.

Closing her eyes as if fearful of a blow, Smidha went on in a rush: "Your brother's reign cannot afford this."

"No," Jahanara repeated.

Smidha cast a questioning glance at her.

She sighed. "You are right, it cannot wait. Help me. Clear the room of everyone but Nadira, the babe, and I. I will make

Dara"—she stopped, corrected herself—"the Sultan Al'Azam aware of our need."

Smidha bowed her head. "I am so sorry, my friend, my princess. I would do anything to have changed this day, to not have it so..."

Unable to trust her voice, Jahanara nodded.

After helping Smidha to her feet, Jahanara used the time the older woman spent gathering the others to collect her tattered spirits.

Nadira crossed to her on silent feet. "So hard, this pain."

Jahanara reached out and put her hand alongside Suleiman's head. "This is no place for the babe."

Her brother's wife drew herself to her full height. "We will leave when his father does."

Jahanara let the hand fall to her side. She crossed to the lamp, brought it with her to Dara's side. She put a hand on his arm. "Dara."

He turned his head to look at her, revealing a tearful gash on his brow just above the hairline.

Behind her Nadira sucked in a breath.

Jahanara reached out, stopped short of touching his wound. "Brother, we must have that seen to."

He shook his head, whispered: "No."

She started a different argument: "Father needs tending to."

He didn't look at her. "I attend him."

"And you do him good service, but there are others who can take over from here."

"No."

"Your son is here, as is Nadira. We have concerns that only you may see to."

"Yes, husband, we have need of you."

His gaze drifted to his wife. "Nadira. You are unhurt?"

"Yes, my love."

"Take Suleiman from this place."

"We will only leave with you. That wound needs seeing to."

"I will stay here."

Nadira looked across at Jahanara. Suleiman roused, started crying.

Jahanara tried again: "Dara, you must come out with us. To have your wound treated by the up-timers, to attend to critical matters. Things move without you. We must learn who was behind this attack, whether another is coming. You must decide half a hundred things."

"I will stay here."

"You cannot."

He looked at her then, eyes black with rage: "I. Will. Stay. Here!"

She met his anger with her own, blazed back at him: "And let us all fall to a similar fate as Father? Would you see that?" She pointed a shaking hand at Suleiman. "See your son killed? If you do not apprehend the one behind this, then the person who managed to strike Father down will be free to plot, free to kill your son, your wife. No one will be safe."

He hung his head.

She continued, relentlessly seeking the words that would draw him from his stupor: "Sultan Al'Azam, you must rise and take the reins of power or see the end of all you hold dear."

"I am not he," Dara rasped.

"Yes, you are. Your brothers are not here, and may have been responsible for this regicide, making you Sultan Al'Azam. Save your wife and son, and discover who is behind this vile act. Save us all. Defend us. Lead us."

He closed his eyes, tears flowing again.

"Please, husband," Nadira said, taking his hand. "Please."

At length, Dara Shikoh nodded. He tried to rise, fell back to his knees.

Both women helped him to his feet. Suleiman began crying in earnest, wails echoing from the walls.

One side of Dara's mouth curled in a half-smile. "Take our hungry son to his wet-nurse, Nadira. I will follow shortly."

"Yes, husband." Nadira glanced at Jahanara, who gave an encouraging nod. Sensing movement, the baby quieted as Nadira mounted the stairs.

Dara slowly turned his head to look at his sister. Taking in her bloodied hands, he asked: "Are any of the harem dead?"

"I do not yet know exact numbers, but it was a close-run thing. All the eunuchs stationed between the plinth and the garden as well as five of the warrior women died defending the harem. Atisheh may still perish, and I am told that Salim may succumb to his wounds as well.

"We came across three dead slaves on our way here, as well, and I am told that Father's architects were also slain."

Dara shook his head, wincing. "But none of Father's concubines, no one from the family?"

"Nur is still missing, along with one of her servants and at least one other eunuch. They may be dead beneath some bush, missed in our haste. We hurried here. I wanted to see with my own eyes..." She let the words stop.

They stood in silence for a moment, aware that to look again on Father's still form would keep them here longer than prudence would dictate.

Dara sighed, set out for the stairs. "I will find Father's killer. Find him and end his days, whether he is one of our blood or not."

"Do you suspect Shah Shuja or Aurangzeb?"

Dara waved a hand, the movement sending him into a stagger that fetched him against the wall beside the stair.

Alarmed, Jahanara clutched his arm, straining to keep his greater weight upright.

"What?" he mumbled, blinking in the lamplight from the stair.

Jahanara swallowed a gasp. His left eyelid was closing a heartbeat after his right.

"You need to see the up-timer physicians."

"Not yet. Just now I need to walk up these stairs and reassure the guards and court that I live and am in full control."

"Yes. Good. But then you must see them as soon as possible."

"Send someone to make sure of the garrison at Red Fort."

"I will."

He braced himself, then pushed off for the exit. "Merciful God, I am not ready for this."

She steadied him. "It seems He has decided otherwise."

"My court was already terribly depleted while Aurangzeb and Shah Shuja still have their milk-brothers and trusted allies. Indeed, they both have armies already raised and blooded. What do I have?"

"You have the treasury here, your wife, your son, and me."

That alarming, imperfect smile bent his lips again. "Surely I cannot lose, with God providing me the service of such a mighty host."

"If you were not already injured, I would make you pay for such sarcasm."

"Peace, Sister."

Because they both needed to get used to it: "Peace, Sultan Al'Azam."

River Entrance of the Taj

The men of the mission climbed out of the stairwell, his friends carrying Randy. John emerged last, tired beyond tears. They trudged toward the front of the mausoleum, the droning of a large crowd louder with each weary step.

John squinted up the plinth. The entryway to the tomb was crowded with milling guards, slaves and servants. Their uneasy faces and tense body language were visible even at a distance.

"Just set him down. Looks like we're going to have to wait a while," John said, nodding up at the mausoleum entrance.

Bobby and Ricky eased the makeshift litter to the ground a few yards from the stairs.

"I'll just go check on the ladies?"

John glanced at Gervais, couldn't summon a reason why he shouldn't, and nodded. He walked with the older man, stopped short of the steps. "If you get a chance, let them know we're ready to leave."

"I will, John."

He didn't know where they were going to bury Randy, though. Maybe the Jesuits would let them bury him in their graveyard?

Cradling his shotgun, John put his back to the plinth and slowly slid to the ground.

Looking down at Randy's still form, Rodney muttered, "So far from home."

John nodded, wishing he could look away.

"So far from everything he knew..."

"Are you *trying* to make me feel worse?"

Rodney spread his hands in surrender. "No, John, just saying."

"Good, 'cause I already know I fucked up! He was right in front of me, Rodney."

"Sorry, man."

"For what? Might have been you I let get shot."

"Let, John?"

He nodded, staring at Randy's face. "I should have been paying attention. Should have been out in front."

"You what?" Ricky asked.

"Should have been me out in front, Ricky."

"Bullshit, John."

"What?"

Ricky shook his head. "Sorry, but that's complete bullshit: I was behind both of you. Randy was next to you, not out in front! None of us saw the asshole with the bow till it was too late. It's not your fault. If anything, I was in the way when you tried to back up. Randy didn't even get a chance to move."

Bobby spoke up. "Ricky's right, John. We all knew the dangers before we signed up, and when your number's up, your number is up."

John, realizing he wasn't going to convince them of his guilt, changed the subject. "Where did they get the fucking bows, anyway, and why didn't they use them on the emperor?"

Bertram cleared his throat. "Dead guardsmen down in the gallery. They were posing as workers. That's how they managed to get so close to the guards in the first place."

"Any idea who they were?"

"Well, they weren't particularly skilled with their weapons, they were content to die for their cause, and most of them screamed a lot of 'infidel' and the like, so I assume they were religious fanatics."

"Okay, any idea who would send a bunch of religious fanatics after the emperor?"

"Not yet, but everyone seems eager to get their hands on whoever is behind it."

"That why we're still sitting here, thumbs up our asses?"

Rodney shook his head. "Come on, John, give 'em a break, they just lost their dad."

"And we just lost a friend."

"I doubt they will see the two things equal, John."

Rodney grunted, punched his chin at the entrance. "Looks like someone's finally making a move."

Chapter 42

Red Fort, The Vine Court
January 1636

Jahanara, tired beyond words, was looking forward to a long bath and even longer rest as she entered the harem courtyard. Ilsa and Monique walked slightly ahead of her, looking with some degree of paranoia around the darkened courtyard. At her request the mission women had, after collecting firearms from their men, served to supplement her remaining bodyguard until more of Atisheh's kin could be found for the duty.

Thoughts of Atisheh made her ask: "Ilsa, did Priscilla find time to tell you how Atisheh fares?"

After seeing to the loyalty of his guard and garrison, the new Sultan Al'Azam had finally allowed Rodney and Gervais to see to his injury. Nadira had insisted Priscilla also consult from behind a jali, leaving Atisheh and Salim to the care of inferior physicians.

"She said that so long as they hadn't missed some internal bleeding, she would likely make it."

"Thank you."

She spied Roshanara standing alone beyond the low marble fountain Father had installed. In no mood to speak to her, Jahanara sent a polite nod in her sister's direction.

"Do not look at me so! It's not my fault!" Roshanara wailed, crumpling to the marble flags.

The unsolicited denial brought Jahanara's entire party to a

halt. Jahanara glanced at Smidha, hoping the older woman would catch what her own tired mind missed.

Smidha responded with a tiny nod.

Aware she walked blind along a precipice, Jahanara asked: "Why not?"

"I didn't know he planned this! I had no part in it!"

Jahanara waited for more. When Roshanara merely continued to weep, she decided to risk showing her ignorance. "They claim otherwise."

Roshanara looked at her, fresh tears making her make up run. "He lies! I knew nothing of it, I swear!"

He. "And the other?"

"He said she was the one he wanted punished for betraying him, that no other would be hurt. That's all I did: provide him with where Nur would be, I swear it!"

Nur, whom they already knew to have been one of their targets. Now to determine who "he" was... "You were a fool to trust him."

Roshanara shook her head, fresh tears beginning. "He said he could be my teacher again once he was free from Nur's slander, that Father would thank me for ridding the court of her presence, and that God would look upon me with favor for my help."

Jahanara's eyes narrowed, guessing the author of the plot. "Mullah Mohan solicited information from you concerning Nur's whereabouts and you provided that information to him, knowing he intended to kill her, our kin."

Roshanara did not correct her naming of Mohan, confirming her guess.

"And because Father had her under his protection in the harem, Mohan could easily guess where Father was likely to be, as well, allowing him to place his fanatics at the construction site in advance."

"I swear before God: I had no inkling of the other thing!"

Hot, bitter anger surged in her. Her feet, unbidden, carried her across the space separating them. "That other *thing*, the one you refuse to speak of?" she said, standing over Roshanara with an ugly knot of anger swelling beneath her breastbone. "It is the murder of our Father, our *Father!*"

"I didn't—"

"Be silent!" she hissed. The angry knot ripped loose: Jahanara slapped her sister hard across the cheek. The vicious crack of the blow echoed from the courtyard walls even as Jahanara struck again and again, a blind rage overriding everything else: "Stupid fool! Stupid fool!"

In her fury, she seized Roshanara and forced her head into the water of the fountain pool. It required Smidha and Monique's combined strength to drag Jahanara off her sister.

"How could you? You killed him! You killed Father!" she cried as they pulled her away.

Slowly returning to her senses, Jahanara began to shake. It was all she could do to stand as she watched Ilsa help the nearly drowned Roshanara to the edge of the fountain.

She ordered Roshanara be removed from her sight, commanding Smidha find two reliable eunuchs to guard her until the Sultan Al'Azam could decide her fate.

Hollow inside, Jahanara stood by while her orders were carried out.

As Roshanara's choking whimpers slowly faded, Monique stepped in front of Jahanara.

Resisting the urge to snap, Jahanara managed a half-civil, "Yes?"

"Forgive me, Begum Sahib, but in light of what your sister said, I have some things to tell you."

"Not now. I need a bath and fresh clothes before I can bear any further revelations."

"Of course."

Jahanara Begum Sahib managed to make it halfway to her quarters before the tears began anew.

Red Fort, The Harem

Monique woke to a dry hand on her shoulder. She cracked an eye.

Smidha stood over her, face etched with fatigue.

She groaned and sat up. Dimly recalling the muezzin calling the faithful to morning prayer as she dropped off to sleep, Monique glanced out across the broad balcony. From the light just touching the tower tops, it was scarcely an hour past dawn.

"So sorry to wake you, but Begum Sahib sends for you now, while Dara appears for the masses."

"Yes. All right." Glad she'd taken the time to wash the blood off and change clothes before sleep claimed her, Monique followed Smidha into Jahanara's apartments.

The princess was immaculately attired, hair and make-up complete.

Monique bowed.

Jahanara gave her a tired smile in exchange. She gestured both Monique and Smidha to the cushions beside her. "Would you tell me what you wished to say last night?"

Monique spent a moment organizing tired thoughts. "Due to the delays in construction on the mission caused by the riots, my father and I were discussing the court and recent events. Mullah Mohan, Nur Jahan, and Roshanara were all spoken of at that time."

"Why?"

"In the mullah's case, we spoke of him because we noted the increased religious tensions, and entertained the idea he might be behind them."

Jahanara sniffed. "A safe assumption in light of yesterday's events."

"Yes. From there the conversation moved on to, and forgive me for saying so, it seemed the court was out of touch with the tensions at large in Agra. My father said he would ask Salim when the opportunity presented itself.

"I told him I would discuss the issue with you once an opportunity presented itself. He then remarked that I often spoke of you and Nadira, but rarely of Nur and Roshanara, asking why that was. I told him that Nur did not make any effort to interact with us, and that Roshanara was, to my view, lacking in social graces."

Another tired smile. "Diplomatically put."

"The very next day, the day before New Year's by our reckoning, I asked a few questions of our translator, Sahana. She informed me that Roshanara and Nur had started spending time together after the death of Nur's servant. From last night, I gather Nur Jahan believed she was milking Roshanara for information about the person who killed Gargi, when it was actually Roshanara on the milking stool."

Monique paused, gauging Jahanara's reaction. She found Jahanara's flat, steady gaze somewhat unnerving, especially after witnessing the woman's capacity for sudden-and-final-violence.

Realizing she had delayed overlong, Monique resumed her report: "Believing Roshanara to be in contact with the person who ordered the killing, Nur set her servants to watching Roshanara's."

"That person being Mullah Mohan."

"I believe so."

"But why murder Gargi in the first place?"

"To draw Nur out."

"Yes, but why?"

"What if Mohan believed her the author of his fall from grace at court?"

"But he said nothing of it when Father was stripping him of his titles."

Smidha snorted derision. "The likes of *him*, admit to defeat at the hands of a mere *woman*? Better ask the sky to change color to suit your mood than believe Mullah Mohan would admit such a thing."

"I *told* Father that Nur had somehow arranged for Mohan to fall."

"You did?" Monique asked.

Jahanara nodded. "A suspicion formed when the English had their firman revoked. Mohan appeared to cast happy glances at the jali where Nur and I—"

She stopped, a faint line appearing between fine eyebrows. "Actually, Roshanara was also there." She shook her head, shrugged. "I assumed Mohan was pleased with something Nur had done and reported as much to Father when he learned of the attack on the English. I suppose it could have been Roshanara, but that does not fit the narrative as we know it."

"No, we're missing someone," Monique said.

"Don't you mean some*thing*?" Smidha asked.

Jahanara held up a hand. "No, Monique is right. At some point, someone had to stand between Nur and Mohan, make each think they could rely on the other. Otherwise, how could one enjoy enough trust to betray the other?"

Monique pursed her lips, said thoughtfully, "Surely not Roshanara?"

"However great her acting skills in deceiving Nur, last night's display would argue against her being the spider at the center of a web of such intrigues."

Smidha grinned. "She did fold up like a tent at the least provocation."

Jahanara's flat stare killed the older woman's smile.

"Who, then?" Monique asked.

"Shah Shuja, Aurangzeb, or Wazir Khan, though Nur's brother has never been known to be—" Her eyes went wide. "Aurangzeb! Firoz reported that it was he who petitioned Father to bring Nur here, *and* he was Mohan's student when a child, eating up that man's hate for non-Muslims."

"Surely he didn't order Mohan to kill Shah Jahan?"

Jahanara shrugged. "Some weapons are as dangerous to the hand that wields them as they are to any opponent, religious fanatics among them. Once unleashed, they tend to kill until stopped."

"But when and why did he unleash Mohan in the first place?" Monique asked.

"Salim," said Smidha.

"What?"

"I had reports that someone matching Salim's description was waylaid in Agra just after his return from Grantville. Salim was a student of Mian Mir, as was Mullah Mohan."

"Wait, what?" Monique asked. "I thought Mohan as orthodox as they get."

"He is." Smidha waggled her head as she clarified: "But he was not always so. I remember, Begum Sahib: Mohan was among Mian Mir's entourage when your grandfather Jahangir paid him a visit. You were about five, then. It wasn't until a few years later that Mohan left Mian Mir and joined the Naqshbandi Order."

"And no one hates like the freshly converted."

Jahanara nodded. "Indeed. And then one of Mian Mir's students returns to court from Grantville, rising in royal esteem almost instantly and without apparent effort."

"So Mohan asks Aurangzeb's permission to kill this student of his rival?"

"Yes, though Mohan may see Salim himself as a rival, too."

"Why ask Aurangzeb, though? Why not just do it and keep it secret?" Monique asked.

"In hopes of demonstrating his loyalty and desire to serve, of course."

"But—"

Jahanara stopped her with a raised finger. "You are, I think, a victim of the history of your European dynasties. Because there is no primogeniture among us, once a male of the Mughal Dynasty reaches adulthood he is forever surrounded by those who would either offer support in exchange for favors or seek means by which they may demonstrate their willingness to subject themselves to that prince's authority.

"Through such people, each prince develops a court that he hopes to use to secure the throne for himself. Should he prove successful in vying with his brothers, his court becomes the ruling one, and those who supported it reap great rewards."

"But Dara—"

"Lost most of his court and all of his personal military strength at Ramdaspur."

"Oh."

"Indeed."

Red Fort

Another wave of shouted acclaim reached them from the riverfront. Dara Shikoh was making his first public appearance as Mughal emperor.

As his advisors deemed it best if the ferenghi were absent during the presentation of the new emperor, Dara had asked them to remain out of sight.

Rodney and Gervais were still caring for Salim and Atisheh as well as the other survivors among the harem guards, so John and the rest of the mission men retired to the cool morning shadows of one of the outer courtyards.

Firoz Khan ordered the slaves from the courtyard and departed himself once he was certain they had enough food and drink.

"Where we gonna bury him?" Bobby asked.

Ricky hiked a thumb over his shoulder. "There's a church in Agra."

"I thought I heard bells on New Years," John said.

"Yeah, nice one, too, at least from the outside."

Bertram scrubbed his face with both hands. "Ricky's right. There is a church in the city, and it's got a graveyard, but it also happens to be run by Jesuits."

"Will they allow it?"

"Maybe. I can ask."

John shrugged, shaking his head. "Dara'll probably have a tomb built for Randy if we ask."

"True, though I doubt it would be politically wise for him to go to such lengths for a non-Muslim just now."

"I was half-kidding anyway..." He ground his teeth in frustration, finally mumbled: "What the fuck are we doing here, anyway? Randy got killed because we're a bunch of hillbillies here to make a damn buck, not act like some sort of SEAL team."

"The mission has done good work here, John. Some have earned quite enough to live on comfortably for some time, the ladies especially."

"I know that! It's just... you know as well as I do we haven't even come close to doing the one thing we were sent here to do!"

"We'll get there, John. The man we fought beside and Randy died in front of is now Sultan Al'Azam. I can only think that a firman of trade will be the very least of the recognition the Mughal mission will receive."

"Sure, but then how do we get us and the dope out of here? Not to mention the saltpeter. There are at least two other brothers—both with bigger armies than Dara's, mind you—who will shortly be on their way here, looking to topple Dara. Do you think they'll look kindly on us ferenghi? Let us stroll out with a shipload of opium and saltpeter, let alone come back for more?"

Bertram shrugged. "One problem at a time, John."

John threw up his hands. "Sure! One problem! One problem with twenty thousand and more troops!"

Bertram rounded on him and said calmly: "John, I'm getting a bit tired of your constant anger and bitter sarcasm. We are where we are. We can control a very few things about our situation.

"As our leader you have made good decisions at every turn and, yes, bad things still happened. That's not your fault. It's not mine." He poked a finger into John's chest. "It's just what damn well *is*."

John opened his mouth to respond, but Bobby spoke over him, "Bertram's right, John. You're taking this stuff way too personally. Get a grip. We need you thinking straight and sharp."

"Especially now, John," Bertram said, looking over John's shoulder.

John turned. Dara walked from the portico lining the courtyard, leaving his advisors behind.

The side of his face was purple and swollen, the sewn gash
an angry red eye at the center. He stepped very close to them
before speaking, voice a raspy, exhausted remnant: "I did not
wish to interrupt your important discussions, but pressing business limits the time I might spend with you."

Noting a very slight slur to Dara's speech, John bowed. "Not
a problem, Sheh—" he corrected himself, "—Sultan Al'Azam."

Dara ignored the slip. "You came here seeking a firman of
trade from my father. It shall be my pleasure to grant the United
States of Europe such a firman at this afternoon's durbar. Later
we will discuss the details of what I am certain you will find to
be very favorable terms."

John, feeling Bertram's smug look without needing to see it,
bowed more deeply. "My thanks, Sultan Al'Azam."

"None are necessary. It is I who must thank you. Indeed, it
is I who has yet another favor to ask of you, now that you have
discharged your duty to king and country."

Swallowing the correction that immediately sprang to mind,
John merely nodded.

"Will you help me preserve my family, my rule? My brothers
are sure to resist me. I would enlist your knowledge, your ideas,
in securing for my people a better future, one free from such
fanaticism as that which caused my father's death and plunged
this land into servitude for hundreds of years."

Red Fort

Smidha entered Jahanara's quarters at a carefully controlled pace.

Her caution was warranted. The palace was uneasy: everyone from the basest, low-caste slave to Begum Sahib herself
was consumed with dread for what the future held. Only eight
years had passed since the last emperor had gone to his eternal
reward, and while that emperor's death had not resulted in an
all-out civil strife, the years preceding that event had contained
much of rebellion and war.

Jahanara was on the verandah despite the cool evening.

Smidha thought to fetch a shawl and offer a gentle reminder

about catching a chill, then realized Jahanara had selected the location with an eye to preventing eavesdroppers.

She collected the shawl anyway, approached, and made the proper obeisance.

Jahanara looked up from her correspondence. "You have something to report?"

Smidha nodded, stepped close and presented the shawl, murmuring, "We have him."

The princess waved the shawl away. "By whose hand?"

"Abdul and Iqtadar."

Jahanara stood, "Who?"

"Abdul and Iqtadar, kinsmen of Amir Salim. They were... most enthusiastic in their efforts."

"He yet lives?"

"Yes, Begum Sahib."

"See them rewarded, and warned to keep their silence on it."

"Yes, Begum Sahib."

"Where is he?"

"I had him brought to the Jasmine Tower, Begum Sahib. None but the men involved know of his presence."

"Good. Tell Atisheh. Ask if she wishes to have her litter brought there."

"Yes, Begum Sahib."

"Do not trouble my brother with this report."

Smidha winced. "Yes, Begum Sahib."

"You do not approve."

Smidha waggled her head. "Not exactly: I worry that your brother will not approve, Begum Sahib."

"The Sultan Al'Azam cannot be associated with what I am about to do. If it were known that he had a hand in the killing of"—she nearly spat the next word—"a *respected* mullah such as he, no matter the provocation, it would spark rebellion in many quarters. No, this must be done quickly, and in complete secrecy."

"I do not believe your brother would see it that way, Begum Sahib."

"A good thing he will never learn of it, then."

Smidha shrank from the flat anger in Jahanara's eyes. "Your will, Begum Sahib."

"Yes. My will."

Epilogue

February 1636

Bijapur

Mahabat's horse archers, responsible for covering Aurangzeb's exposed right flank, fell back before a determined charge of Bijapuri heavy cavalry. They fled up the slope and away from the sharp action along the banks of the Bhima. Fired by the possibility of easy victory, the heavy cavalry followed. Both units disappeared over the ridge after a few minutes' hard riding.

Aurangzeb shifted his gaze, watching as a large, well-armored mass of infantry charged his lines. The main Bijapuri advance slowed, then stalled as the Rajputs met them blade to blade, shield to shield along the riverside. After several long minutes of hand-to-hand the Rajput line flexed, consuming the inroads the Bijapuri had won with their charge.

The response was not long in coming. Another unit of Bijapuri footmen swung from behind the swordsmen and worked around outside the flank of their vanguard. Taking up positions along the base of the slope leading up out of the valley, they raised arquebuses and began to fire into the Rajput flank.

Their sustained fire started to take its toll, men dropping.

Hold, just hold, Aurangzeb willed them from his elephant. He didn't like to command from the animals, prone as they were to go berserk when stung, but, stationed some four hundred gaz behind his Rajputs, the massive animals were the perfect bait to draw the infantry onto Rajput arms.

More men died, cut down, shot, it made no difference to the dead.

Hold.

With a thunder of hooves, a mass of cavalry appeared from behind the enemy lines. Sweeping out and up the slope around the arquebusiers, they slowed, forming a wedge. Aurangzeb identified Shahaji near the point. Lines dressed, they galloped forward, heading toward the exposed flank of the infantry forces.

Aurangzeb held his breath.

Shahaji's charge crashed home in the Bijapuri line like a high mountain avalanche meeting the tree line: screaming men rolled under, crushed, shoved aside. Dying on two fronts and unable to retreat into the river, the Bijapuri foot broke and ran to the rear, pursued by Shahaji's men.

Aurangzeb let the stale air in his lungs fly free. It was one thing to buy a man, quite another to rely on him.

He called down to a waiting messenger: "Remshad to bring the camel corps forward after they've mopped up the Bijapuri cavalry that chased Mahabat over the hill."

"Yes, Shehzada!"

"And bring me my horse!"

He was just changing mounts when a rider in stained messenger greens rode up.

Content that the rest of the battle would resolve according to his wishes, Aurangzeb waved the man permission to approach.

The man threw himself on the ground at Aurangzeb's feet.

Bad news.

"Speak."

"Forgive me, Shehzada, I bring terrible tidings." He reached into his messenger case.

"Speak."

He pulled a sealed letter and held it up as if the flimsy paper could shield him from a prince's anger. "Shehzada, I beg your forgiveness, I..."

"Speak, damn you!"

"Forgive me: Shah Jahan is dead!"

Aurangzeb feel the earth shift like sand beneath his feet, stammered, "H-how?"

"Merciful God forgive me, but the Sultan Al'Azam was murdered, Shehzada."

"What?"

"Assassinated."

"Who?"

"No one knew at the time I was dispatched by the newswriter."

"Who?"

The man buried his face in the dirt, mumbling.

"Speak clearly, man!"

"No one knew, Shehzada."

A part of him spoke from the dark vaults of his heart: *This is what you wanted.*

Not this.

Aurangzeb turned away from the man, from the news, from the voice in his head, from everything.

But the voice was cold and unrelenting. *Yes, this. This is what you wanted.*

No.

You lie, even to yourself.

"I must pray," he mumbled.

Be quick, though, said the cold voice. *Shah Shuja and Wazir Asaf Khan will be marching to seize the throne from that weakling Dara.*

Goa

The Compte Linhares, Viceroy del Estado da India and Governor of Goa, handed his practice blade to a waiting page, chest heaving in an effort to catch his breath. Having long since found such exercise an excellent way to clear the mind and keep his martial skills in order, he made a point of engaging in heavy practice in the salle every day.

As a slave approached to begin mopping the rivulets of sweat from his owner's round shoulders, Linhares snatched the towel and began working to dry himself, irritated, not with the slave, but by the fact he had yet to find the right words for the letter he must write the king.

The additional troops required to maintain their possessions in Africa and elsewhere would not be forthcoming if he appeared to have let the opportunity pass him by.

Trying to explain how such adventurism would further drain

their already limited coffers would fall on deaf ears, despite the fact they had to know the governor of Goa didn't have the manpower on hand to garrison the forts, let alone mount a military expedition!

The church bell rang, reminding him of his other great aggravation as viceroy: the Jesuits.

The damn Jesuits. They recruit every soldier that comes off our ships, making brothers of them!

Not that he really blamed the soldiers. Lacking proper pay from the crown and any good prospects, the religious orders made for a tolerably good life and a guarantee of at least two meals a day. The same could hardly be said of service to the king.

But the Jesuits were constantly making their own reports, trying to inflame Philip's crusading spirit and undermining Linhares' reputation at court.

Worse still, lacking knowledge of what they wrote in their reports, he had very little room to maneuver, and none to dissemble.

Linhares covered his scarred torso with a fresh tunic and left the salle.

The Jesuits were as much a headache for him as the Dutch were these days, and far less easily dealt with. A man could rely on the Dutch to fight their battles with blade and shot, as a man should.

At least the English were no longer in a position to contest their dominance here. The Danish, now, they seemed to be in the ascendance after the events in Europe, though Christian's man Crappé knew what he owed Linhares.

And if the king, or more likely, Olivares, orders me to back one or another of the claimants to the Mughal throne and I refuse? At least ten months remain before I must be concerned with direct orders regarding the Mughal succession. Given the reports on the comparative talents of Shah Jahan's sons, I doubt the succession will take that long to be decided.

Linhares smiled.

And that is what I shall write of, to both preserve my reputation and secure the necessary assistance from home...

"Fetch me pen and paper. I will write on the verandah."

Magdeburg, capital of the United States of Europe

"So, all things considered, Michael, it seems as if your negotiations with Gustav Adolf are going well." Rebecca Abrabanel finished her cup of tea and set it down. Across from her at the table in the dining room of their townhouse, Mike Stearns had his hands clasped behind his head and was gazing at their daughter Sepharad. The three-year-old girl was absorbed with a new doll Mike had brought her from Dresden. The doll was just a thing of stuffed linens, not the fancy porcelain figurines for which Dresden would become famous in the next century.

That assumed, of course, that the course of history in this universe would run parallel to that of the one the Americans had come from. As propositions went, that one fell in the category of "dicey."

"Yes, they are," Mike mused.

But his thoughts were still on the doll. "Do you remember that trade mission we sent to India? It's been almost two years now."

"Yes. Has a report come in?"

"Not a word, so far as I know, in almost a year. We know they made it to India, but after that . . . They just seem to have vanished."

"Communications *are* very slow, across that distance," Rebecca pointed out. "And will be until a radio connection can be set up."

"Yeah, I know. I just hope they're okay."

"It is a dangerous world. Here, as much as anywhere."

"Don't remind me. I just got done fighting a battle in the middle of a snowstorm because I figured it was my best shot at beating a general who was a lot more experienced than I was."

"And you proved to be right."

"So I did. That time. We'll see what the future brings."

"What is the worst that could happen to them?" Rebecca asked. "After all, they will be under the protection of one of the world's most powerful dynasties. Shah Jahan's rule has stabilized and he should remain in power for another . . ."

Her brow creased with thought. "I cannot remember the exact history. But at least another twenty years, I am sure."

Mike grunted. "Maybe. But you see that doll?" He nodded in the direction of their daughter.

"Yes. What of it?"

"Well—supposedly—sometime in the next century, Dresden will become famous for its porcelain dolls. But will that actually happen? There's just no way—"

Sepharad chose that moment to accidentally tear off her doll's arm. The thing really wasn't very well made. Immediately, she set up a wail of grief and displeasure.

"I rest my case," Mike concluded. "For all we know, our trade mission triggered off a civil war, Shah Jahan's been assassinated, all hell is breaking lose—they're between a rock and a hard place."

Rebecca rose and went over to calm their daughter. "Michael, please. I really think you are engaging in hyperbole. Surely the situation will not be that tempestuous. They may already be on their way home."

Mike thought about it, for a while. "In other words," he said, "maybe they're now between the Devil and the deep blue sea."

"Michael!"

Cast of Characters

The Mission Principals

John Dexter Ennis: USE TacRail veteran and titular leader of the Mission. Technology specialist for the Mission.

Rodney Totman: NUS Army Medic, former college football player. Medical expert for the Mission.

Priscilla Totman: Paramedic, married to Rodney. Medical expert for the Mission.

Bobby Owen Maddox: Up-timer and USE second lieutenant of TacRail Unit, security specialist for the Mission.

Ricky Wiley: Up-timer and USE second lieutenant of TacRail Unit, security specialist for the Mission.

Randy Baldwin: Up-timer and USE second lieutenant of TacRail Unit, security specialist for the Mission.

Ilsa Ennis: Down-timer, married to John Dexter.

Gervais Vieuxpont: Down-timer and one-time con-man, skilled linguist and father of Monique.

Monique Vieuxpont: Down-timer and one-time con-woman, skilled linguist and daughter of Gervais.

Bertram Weiman: Down-timer, spy for the USE, and distant relation to Don Nasi.

Lønsom Vind crew

Captain Rune Strand: Danish captain with experience at the Dutch trade in the Far East.

Mate Loke: Long-service Danish sailor, Rune's second.

The Mughal Royal Family

Shah Jahan: Emperor of India, Sultan of Sultans.

Asaf Khan: Father-in-law of Shah Jahan, General and Governor in his own right.

Nur Jahan: Wife of Jahangir, Shah Jahan's father.

Jahanara Begum: Eldest daughter of Shah Jahan and Mumtaz Mahal.

Dara Shikoh: Eldest son of Shah Jahan and Mumtaz Mahal.

Shah Shuja: Second son of Shah Jahan and Mumtaz Mahal.

Aurangzeb: Third son of Shah Jahan and Mumtaz Mahal.

Roshanara: Second daughter of Shah Jahan.

Murad: Fourth son of Shah Jahan, child.

Guaharara: Third daughter of Shah Jahan, toddler.

Umara and other Notables of Shah Jahan's Court

Mullah Mohan: Orthodox mullah of renown and repute, one-time student of Mian Mir.

Mukhlis Khan: General and Umara in Dara's princely establishment but imperial employee.

Baram Khan: Noble of Jahangir's court that served Nur against Shah Jahan's bid for the throne.

The Harem

Diwan Garyan: Chief eunuch and manager of Shah Jahan's harem.

Firoz Khan: Eunuch harem manager.

Smidha: Jahanara's eldest and most trusted advisor.

Gargi: Nur Jahan's advisor.

Tara: Gargi's chief lieutenant.

Atisheh: Chief among the female harem guards.

Gulruhk: Female harem guard.

Umida: Female harem guard.

Ratna: Harem astrologer.

Prasad: Eunuch, harem slave entrusted with Jahanara's personal messages.

Sahana: Harem slave purchased by the court from Jadu Das to serve as translator.

Gopal: Jahanara's mahout.

Navin: Stableboy of the royal household.

Dara Shikoh's Princely Household

Nadira Begum: Dara's wife and cousin.

Suleiman: Dara's infant son.

Talawat: Gunsmith, part of Dara Shikoh's princely establishment.

Kwaja Magul: Eunuch advisor employed by the emperor to serve Dara.

Mohammed: Captain of Dara's personal guard, appointed by Shah Jahan.

Suleiman Khan: A captain of Dara's forces and his foster brother.

Aurangzeb's Princely Household

Mahabat Khan: A captain of cavalry troop.

Carvalho: Portuguese artillery captain and mercenary.

Samarjit Khan: Rajput commander and zamindar.

Sikhs

Hargobind Singh: Sixth Guru of the Sikh religion.

Bhidi Chand: Disciple of Sixth Guru.

Others of note

Amir Salim Gadh Visa Yilmaz: Afghan adventurer who returns to India with up-timer histories, student of Mian Mir.

Iqtadar Yilmaz: Afghan cousin of Salim.

Tariq Yilmaz: Afghan kinsman of Salim.

Angelo Gradinego: Venetian con-man, now debt-slave to Surat's Diwan.

Jadu Das: Hindu merchant in Agra, old ally of Salim.

Dhanji Das: Hindu merchant in Surat, sibling of Jadu.

Mian Mir: Sufi Saint, teacher to two generations of Timurid princes and friend to the Sikhs.

Kashif Khan: Eunuch Diwan in charge of Jahanara's affairs in Surat.

Murad Reis: Dutch convert to Islam and pirate.

Zuberi: Swahili trader and resident of Moçambique.

Joao De Melo: Portuguese New Christian kinsman of Bertram and Nasi, trader in Moçambique.

Glossary of Terms

Akbarnama: Book of Akbar, one of the great Mughal Emperors.

Atishbaz: Caste-workers who manufacture firearms and cannon.

Begum: Princess.

Begum Sahib: Princess of princesses.

Betel: A leaf containing stimulants that is consumed in southeast asia, noted for causing staining of the teeth in regular users.

Caravanserai: Way station on a caravan route. Often paid for out of royal coffers.

Chakram: Sharpened throwing rings of thin steel hurled like a frisbee off the fingers.

Dastak: A scepter, specifically a symbol of diplomatic status and protection of the sovereign.

Deccan: Plateau in north-central India.

Diwan: Royally-appointed manager for some specific trade or bureaucratic entity .

Diwan-i-Khas: Hall of public audience.

Diwan-i-Am: Hall of private audience.

Ferenghi: Foreigner, usually European.

Firman: Written permission or order. Necessary for trade.

Qalam: Writing instrument.

Gaz: Distance, much like a cubit or yard.

Howdah: Passenger compartment on an elephant, sometimes enclosed.

Jagir: Income property rights, not usually overseen in person by the holder, a Jagirdir.

Jagirdir: Holder of a jagir.

Jali: Ornate stone or wooden screens to preserve purdah.

Julabmost: Nonalcoholic fruit drink.

Jizya: Muslim tax on non-believers.

Katar: Triangular double-bladed punch dagger often used in the off hand.

Khan-i-Saman: Manager of a harem's dealing with the outside world, usually a eunuch.

Kharkhanas: Craftsmen collected by a royal, the produce of which finance many things.

Kos: Length of distance equivalent to approximately 2.25 miles.

Maghrib: Afternoon prayers for muslims.

Mahout: Elephant handler and trainer.

Mansab: A set of jagirs, often scattered throughout the empire.

Mansabdar: A holder of mansab.

Mihmandar: Person responsible for the upkeep, care, and security of an envoy visiting the Mughal court.

Nizam: Mughal title for foreign princes and sultans—a way to avoid admitting in writing that another could hold the title of sultan.

Nökör: Personal guard of a prince.

Pulu: Polo.

Purdah: Separation of women from men in accordance with cultural and religious norms.

Shehzadi: Princess.

Shehzada: Prince.

Sowar: Cavalry trooper. Also: one of two rankings in the Emperor's court, this one denoting how many actual sowar were paid for out of the rank-granter's treasury. Inspections were common.

Sultan: King.

Sultan Al'Azam: High Sultan, the emperor's honorific.

Umara: Nobles of the court.

Wazir: First advisor, minister.

Zamburak: Camel gun, small cannon like a swivel gun aboard western ships.

Zamburakchi: Camel gunners.

Zamind: Land rights to a settled region.

Zamindar: Recipient of land rights to a region, usually resided in or on and defended by the Zamindar himself.

Zat: Courtly rank, strictly a sign of the emperor's favor, compensated with cash allowances and jagirs, but no troops.